What You Pay For

Also by Claire Askew

All the Hidden Truths

CLAIRE ASKEW

What You Pay For

HODDER &
STOUGHTON

First published in Great Britain in 2019 by Hodder & Stoughton
An Hachette UK company

1

A CIP catalogue record for this title is available from the British Library

Hardback ISBN 978 1 473 67307 6
Trade Paperback ISBN 978 1 473 67308 3
eBook ISBN 978 1 473 67309 0

Typeset in Plantin Light by Hewer Text UK Ltd, Edinburgh
Printed and bound in Great Britain by Clays Ltd, Elcograf S.p.A.

Hodder & Stoughton policy is to use papers that are natural, renewable
and recyclable products and made from wood grown in sustainable
forests. The logging and manufacturing processes are expected to
conform to the environmental regulations of the country of origin.

Hodder & Stoughton Ltd
Carmelite House
50 Victoria Embankment
London EC4Y 0DZ

www.hodder.co.uk

For my little brother, Nick

Monday

Helen Birch watched as the red neon digits on her car's clock clicked over from 0344 to 0345. Their dim light was the only illumination she had as she felt around for the cardboard cup of coffee she'd brought along, stone cold now, its edges worried by toothmarks.

'Fifteen minutes,' she said.

Beside her, DC Amy Kato stirred. They'd come together, Birch picking up a yawning Amy outside the stair door of her Tollcross flat at 3 a.m. The idea was that they'd keep each other company, but they'd mostly sat, fidgeting, in a thick silence.

'Shit,' Birch said. 'Were you asleep?'

'No.' Amy twisted in the passenger seat. Birch heard the stab vest she was wearing creak. 'Um. A little. Sorry, marm.'

Birch smiled. She was amazed DCI McLeod had allowed Amy to come with her in the CID Mondeo: she knew that he frowned on workplace friendships in general, and her friendship with Amy was doubly distasteful to him given their difference in rank. The other DCs and uniforms were packed into riot vans and manning panda cars, stationed in ill-lit backstreets around the set perimeter. Birch imagined them upright, alert, waiting for the go order. DCI McLeod was out there, too: his own dark-coloured, unmarked car parked somewhere on the other side of the harbour.

'Don't sweat it,' she said. 'Just be ready for the go.'

Birch and Amy had been stationed on the breakwater: a desolate spot far from the main road, beyond the high-rises and away from the lights and moorings of the yacht club. On Amy's side of the car, the sea wall rose up like a shoulder. Above it, they could see the red pin-pricks on the struts of the Queensferry Crossing.

In front of them, the vast darkness of the firth. At the end of the breakwater, a dim green light let boat traffic know the point at which the land ended.

The rest of Birch's unit were in a riot van, parked round the corner on Hesperus Crossway. Tucked behind the land's last stack of buildings, those officers couldn't see what Birch and Amy could. Through the strait in front of them, a steady stream of boats trailed towards the harbour, the tops of their masts illuminated by the red and white lights of fishing vessels. Among the convoy, a handful had lit the beams of their stern lights, or cast a greenish glow across the inky water from their flanks. They were trying not to look uniform: to a passing night-bus driver or graveyard shift worker, these were just fishermen bringing home the night's catch. On the eastern harbour wall, fishmongers' vans had lined up. Men would be hanging around there, waiting to offload cargo from the hulls of the little boats.

'God,' she said. Her teeth were set on edge. 'I really hope we're right about this. There's a whole lot riding on Glasgow's informant.'

In the gloom, Amy smirked. 'I know,' she said. 'All looks a bit *fishy* to me.'

Birch made a stifled snort. 'Oh don't. It's too early for the fish jokes. Especially if this all turns out to be a hiding to nothing.'

Amy was still grinning. 'On a scale of one to ten,' she said, 'how bad can it be?'

Birch closed her eyes.

'Get it, marm? *Scale*? Like—'

'Yes, Kato, I get it.'

The clock ticked over to 0350. The thick silence returned, filling the car like invisible smoke. Stop being such a humourless bitch, Helen, Birch thought. Snap out of the foul temper already. Amy was just trying to lighten the mood. What was this, anyway? Rage over the fact she'd been passed over to head this investigation? No: she didn't want it, not really. It was just today. It was what today meant.

'It should've been you.' Amy's voice still had a smile in it, as if she'd read her DI's mind, and wanted her to know it.

Birch shrugged. 'I guess it's worth praying that it *is* all a wild-goose chase,' she replied, trying to ignore what Amy had said. 'Otherwise who knows what time we'll all get home.'

'You don't think we will, then?'

Birch sipped her cold coffee, feeling the cup's sponginess against her teeth. 'Will what?'

'Bring him in.' Amy nodded backward, in the direction of the back-up vans, the perimeter. 'Solomon. Folk seem pretty hopeful.'

'Sure,' Birch said. 'We all want the big prize, right? I do, too, as much as anyone. But I don't think it's likely. This is a guy who's dicked us around for donkey's years. He's always been a step ahead. It looks pretty impossible.'

Birch felt, rather than saw, Amy's raised eyebrow.

'Well okay,' she said, remembering her internal pep talk: enough of the attitude, Helen. 'Nothing's impossible. But it's *borderline*, you know?'

Amy nodded.

'Not that I've been telling anyone that.' Birch jerked her head, the same way Amy had. 'It'd be like telling them there's no Father Christmas.'

They were quiet again. 0353.

'*You'd* do it,' Amy said.

'What?'

'You. If you were in charge of this investigation, you'd bring him in. No question.'

Birch smiled. 'Quit brown-nosing, Kato.'

'Nope.' Amy took a chug of her own cold coffee. 'I mean it. I don't get why you're not heading this up. McLeod's decisions make no sense.'

'DCI McLeod,' Birch said, keeping her voice level, 'is the SO on the scene. And I *was* just up on a disciplinary. You can't possibly have forgotten.'

Amy looked away. Amy knew fine well: she had been asked to give evidence as part of the hearing.

'*That* made no sense either,' she said.

Birch arranged her face into the well-shit-happens expression she'd practised in the mirror. 'Oh, I deserved it,' she began, but the thought was lopped off by a flash of excitement as her phone buzzed: once, twice. Was it McLeod? Was there a development?

As she scrabbled at her hip and grabbed the phone she felt Amy lean in, wondering the same thing. But no: the name that appeared across her unlocked screen was 'Anjan C'. Birch flinched the phone out of Amy's immediate eyeline.

'What's the deal?' Amy said.

Birch glanced at her, then back at the phone as she thumbed in the unlock code. 'False alarm,' she said. 'Non-work text. Stand down, officer.'

She waited until Amy sighed and tipped the coffee cup up over her nose before opening WhatsApp to read the text in full.

Morning. Can't sleep, making tea. Mind if I use the last of your milk? Then, below: *Caught yourselves a mob boss yet?*

Birch tried to prevent herself from blushing. She side-eyed Amy, then typed back: *No word . . . will tell you when. Help yourself to anything.* She looked at the message for a few seconds before adding a reckless *x*, and hitting send.

'You didn't,' Amy was saying.

Birch shoved the phone back into her pocket. 'Hmm?'

'Deserve it,' Amy said. 'The disciplinary. It was bullshit. And besides, you were cleared.'

Birch looked down at the steering wheel. She'd tried the tack that Amy was taking: tried it in her own head, late at night when she couldn't sleep for thinking again and again about the Three Rivers case and what she'd done right, done wrong. She'd really tried for *this is bullshit*, tried to feel hard done by. But it was true: she'd deserved it, because she'd been stupid, and stupid cops are bad cops. She'd broken all her own rules, too: once upon a time she'd have rolled her eyes at police dramas in which the protagonist threw away the rule book and rode off into the crime scene solo. Who did she think she was?

'No,' she said, letting her gaze hang in the middle distance, the steering wheel's Ford logo swimming, refocusing. 'It was what needed to happen.'

Something buzzed. At first, Birch thought it was her phone again, and she smiled, imagining Anjan. Maybe he was climbing out of the shower – her shower! – to text and say how impressed he was with the water pressure. Maybe he'd add a kiss back this time. Maybe he'd tell her he'd had a great evening, and could they do it again soon? He'd wanted to stay over in spite of her early start – well, middle of the night start, really, but—

Birch had to snap out of the daydream. The buzz was her radio, and McLeod.

'Landside units stand by,' he said. 'Five minutes till Operation Citrine is *go*. Marine unit, move to go position. That's five minutes till *go*. Over.'

The coastguard and accompanying police patrol boats were anchored, unlit, on the other side of the sea wall from Birch and Amy's position. As the fishing vessels' radar passed them, they'd have looked like moored, static craft. Now they were chugging – still without lights – across the harbour mouth in formation. If all went to plan, there'd be no escaping the net of police personnel, by land or by sea.

'Ready?' Birch asked.

Amy nodded. 'Ready as I'll ever be, marm.'

'You nervous?'

There was a pause. 'A little.'

Birch gave a short nod. 'Good.' Leaning forward in her seat, she patted herself down to check for kit: clip-on radio, baton, cuffs. The kevlar casing of her vest made a weird, hollow sound. 'Nervous is good. Keeps you on your toes.'

Amy was checking herself over, too. 'McLeod said at the briefing we should expect them to be armed. That they'll have guns.'

Birch could detect a tremor in her colleague's voice. 'Most likely some will,' she said. 'But just stay focused. We outnumber them, and they'll see that pretty fast. We've got an armed response unit on standby. Plus, they've probably all been educated on how stupid an idea it is to shoot a police officer.'

Touch wood, Birch thought. Don't tempt fate. And then, yet again, Stop it, Helen. It's all going to be fine.

'It'll go like a Swiss watch,' she added, as much for herself as for Amy.

Quiet again: an unnerving quiet. Birch pictured her uniformed colleagues sitting stiffly in their hidden vehicles, holding one long, collective breath. Some had come through from Glasgow, wouldn't know the terrain, might not know what name to call if they needed help from a colleague. 0358. Birch imagined she could hear the chug of the marine units, the slap of their wake against the break-water. 0359. Their informant – the person this whole raid was riding on – was in the wind, vanished. They were acting on blind faith in their Glaswegian colleagues, who seemed to know little themselves and had disclosed barely any of that.

Fish, she thought. These boats are going to be full of fish. There's going to be no sign of Solomon. We're all going to be—

The radio crackled.

'All units go,' McLeod shouted, making the speaker fizz. 'This is your go order. Repeat, this is your go order.'

Birch turned the key in the ignition, and the car lit up. The air came alive with sirens. In the harbour mouth, the police boats' prow floodlights flicked on almost in formation. The harbour became a ring of white light.

Birch gunned the engine and peeled right, away from the sea wall. Her job was to command the unit that would block off one possible escape route: a rough-hewn bay area to one side of the harbour, too shallow for moorings but once used as a slipway. If any of the fishing vessels' crew decided to try to swim for it, this would be where they'd wash up. She knew she'd been all but benched: this wasn't exactly the thick of things. But still, adrenalin made her head pound as she drove the short stretch, tyres kicking up grit, Amy bracing one spread palm against the dashboard.

They neared the harbour edge, the boats and, beyond them, the fishmongers' white vans, now surrounded by panda cars with flashing blues. Men had begun to scatter in all directions, jumping overboard or pelting along the slippery harbourside, flinging cargo into the water.

'Guess it's more than just fish after all,' Birch yelled as the car skidded to a halt in the agreed position. But Amy was already half-way out of the door: it seemed she was eager to show that the nerves she'd felt weren't going to stop her pitching in.

Outside the car, a cacophony. Birch's own siren rang in her ears: the many others blaring around the perimeter felt like echoes bouncing back off the buildings and the breakwater. In the prow of his boat, the leader of the marine unit was roaring into a bullhorn. '*Police! You are surrounded!*' Birch could hear Russian voices: everyone was shouting. She decided she might as well join in.

'Right, lads,' she bellowed, as uniforms half jumped, half fell out of the back of the van that had squealed up a few feet away. 'I want a nice orderly line on this slipway, okay? Close to the waterline as you can. Eyes peeled.'

The officers fanned out, a collective *yes marm* passing between them.

'Everyone ready? First one to bring me a bad guy gets a gold star.'

Across the water, Birch could see men being cuffed: pressed against the flanks of vans chest-first while their rights were read. The van drivers were easy, though: on the fishing boats, and in the water around them, there was still chaos.

'Two o'clock!' one of Birch's officers yelled.

'Yep, eyes on him,' shouted another, along the line.

Birch could see it now herself: a thrash of white water nearing the shore. She jogged along the line. 'Let's get some light over here!' she shouted, and almost as she said it, she saw Amy – on the far end of the formation – had swung round her flashlight to oblige.

In the water were two men, kicking strongly, pushing a wooden crate. The uniformed officer who'd got eyes on them had broken from the line and begun to wade in down the stone slope.

'Police!' he yelled, up to his knees in water. More torch-beams swung in his direction. Birch could see the men were white, wearing dark clothing. They were big guys, powerful swimmers. They looked mean.

'Police!' the uniform bawled again. 'Come ashore!'

The men were still in fairly deep, treading water now, sizing up the situation. The uniform moved in further, now up to his waist.

Birch reached for her radio. 'This is CA38, Birch,' she said. 'I'm on the western flank, two suspects and cargo in the water. Requesting marine unit assistance, repeat, requesting marine unit assistance, over.'

The radio crackled.

'If you don't get out here,' the uniform was shouting, 'I'll charge you with resisting arrest.'

The other officers dithered.

'CA38, Birch.' The radio was loud with cross-channel interference. 'Repeat, requesting marine unit—'

'This is McLeod.' He was panting, she could tell even through the static. 'No can do right now, Birch. Either hold them there for now or get in and fish them out, over.'

Birch blinked, and came off the channel.

'Thanks a fucking bunch, sir,' she muttered. Her team were looking round at her, waiting for her order.

'All right,' she said, 'I trust you're all good swimmers?'

A couple of the uniforms glanced at each other.

'Good. Everyone between DC Kato and me, fall back. Keep eyes on the water – where there's one, there may well be more. The rest of you, it's time to get wet. I want a V formation . . .' Birch stretched her arms out to show the vague gist of what she meant, but some of the officers were already wading in. In the torchlight – wavering now, as Amy moved to her new position – the men seemed to have conferred, and were making to swim backward, into the centre of the harbour, dragging their box of tricks with them.

'Oh no you don't!' The uniform already in the water lunged forward, and began swimming towards the pair.

'In *formation*, I said!' Birch yelled, but the other officers were still a fair way behind. Amy was nearest to her now, shining her torch onto the churned water.

'Kato,' Birch barked. 'Who *is* that?'

Amy turned, and the torchlight flicked away. 'I believe it's Malton, marm. PC Jaden Malton.'

Someone in the water yelped, then – a sort of wet, strangled noise. Someone else shouted, '*Light!*'

Amy flicked the torch-beam back up.

PC Malton had reached the two men in the water, but one of them was now wrestling him, holding his face under the surface as the other perp clung on to the box, drifting, a gap opening between them.

'*Shit*,' Birch hissed, and grabbed her radio once again.

'This is CA38, Birch. I've got an officer in difficulty on the western flank, we need that marine unit, sir!'

Nothing. McLeod must have been busy. PC Malton's legs kicked, his head still pushed under, his swimming colleagues closing in on the wet fight.

'Does anyone copy?' Birch cried. 'I repeat, I have an officer in difficulty—'

Finally, another swimmer reached PC Malton. Amy's torch wavered, but Birch watched as the newly arrived officer reared back in the water and kicked the perp square in the face. PC Malton surfaced: Birch could hear his grateful first gasp even over the din of the raid.

'DI Birch,' the radio said. 'This is Marine Unit One. I copy, but we're—'

Birch wasn't listening. She ran past Amy, down onto the loose shale and into the water. She instantly regretted her plain-clothes choice of thick trackpants, which became lead weights around her legs. The V formation she'd ordered had broken up in the water: PC Malton and the perp who'd held him down were now being pulled to shore, while two other uniforms manhandled the wooden crate, its keeper still trying to stay attached to it. Birch waded in to her waist. The water felt thick and stank of boat fuel. She held out both her arms and PC Malton clawed up at them, falling against her so she staggered. His breath sounded like cloth being torn.

'Okay, Jaden,' Birch said. 'You're okay. Can you put your feet down for me? Can you stand?'

A few feet away, Malton's perp was resisting arrest, flailing in five feet of water.

'Fucksake,' Birch muttered. Then, to the officers in the fray, 'Someone get some cuffs on that scumbag, will you, please?'

PC Malton hooked his arms over her shoulders, and steadied himself against her frame. Once he'd found his footing, she realised he was around five feet eleven, the same height as her, but also very young – he could have been twenty-one.

'Okay, Constable,' she said, meeting his eye. 'I suppose that's one way to do things.'

Malton clearly couldn't speak: his chest heaved. Out of the corner of her eye, she saw three of her team finally drag the first perp upright and wrestle his hands behind his back. The second, it seemed, had decided to come quietly: he'd surrendered the crate, which was now being carried ashore.

Birch began to wade backward, keeping a hand on Malton's arm. 'Mind how you go, son,' she said, 'we've got all the time in the world.'

It wasn't true, of course: Birch glanced behind her at the ragged line of officers still on the shore. 'Kato,' she yelled, turning her head away from Malton so as not to deafen him. 'Any more sightings in the water?'

There was a pause.

'Negative, marm,' Amy called back. 'The eastern flank seems to've hoovered them up.'

'Okay. Hold your positions though, eyes open.'

Birch felt first one foot, then the other, splash out of the water.

'Dry land,' she said into Malton's ear. 'You made it.' She let go of the young officer and he folded onto the ground, coughing hard.

'This is CA38, Birch.' She crouched down next to Malton, one hand on his shoulder as he vomited water. 'Requesting a medic to our position, repeat, requesting a medic. Western flank, north of Hesperus Broadway, over.'

'All right, Birch.' McLeod was back, and sounding irritable. 'Medic's on her way. Now do me a favour, would you?'

'Sir?'

'Arrest whatever you've got there and then get your team over here. It would seem we've just nicked Solomon Carradice.'

M ore than anything, I remember my sister.
I suppose that's the way when you're the youngest kid. My sister was nearly five when I was born. She's probably seven or eight in my earliest memories. We got on okay sometimes, but mostly I remember us fighting. Mostly I remember her doing things I wasn't allowed to do yet, because I was small. I remember her getting things I wasn't allowed to have, and hating her for it.

She was always there, though. One day we went to Glasgow. No idea why ... there must have been some important or official reason for Maw to schlep the two of us all the way on the train, and me still in the buggy. I was pretty wee. I remember we were on Gordon Street, because we'd come out of the train station. I'd laid back in my buggy and watched the glass roof of the station portico sliding by overhead, giving way to this tall red stone building across the street, towering up. You don't get that red stone in Edinburgh. Anyway, we stopped there, on Gordon Street, and Maw let go of the buggy for a second. There's a postbox at Central Station, so I always imagine she nipped to post a letter. Or maybe something dropped and she had to pick it up: a toy or a blanket or one of my socks. And my sister was there, of course. She used to walk alongside the buggy with one hand low down on the handle. When we got older Maw would tell people stories about how my sister always wanted to push the buggy: she wanted folk passing by to think that I was *her* baby, that *she* was taking care of me. They were designed to embarrass my sister, but I hated those stories, too. They made me realise that she must have seen me the same way as her baby dolls: something to dress up and carry around. Something make-believe.

But next thing, we were flying down Gordon Street, vaguely downhill, towards God knows what, and people were shouting. Women were shouting. I remember the dizzy feeling, watching those tall red buildings blur past overhead, seeing pigeons rattling up between them. As soon as Maw's back was turned my sister had grabbed both handles of the buggy and run. We went zigzags. We must have crossed two big roads, and she can't have stopped to look for the traffic because I don't remember us slowing. I remember hearing Maw behind us belting out both our names and *stop* and *stop her*, which she must have yelled at other people as we clattered by. I probably loved it at the time. I probably laughed and squealed as little kids do when they're zoomed about in the air by their granda or strapped into the baby swings and swung up high. Maw says we got as far as the Royal Exchange Square before someone tackled my sister to the ground. She always claimed to have no memory: of the day, of the act, of being skelpit raw right there by the Royal Exchange with half of Glasgow stopped to watch. I remember it all. My first real memory of anything.

Nella, I called her. That wasn't her name but it was as close as I could get with my gummy kid-mouth, and it stuck. Maw called her it too. Da was gone before I can remember: long before Glasgow and the buggy and the skelping. Maybe before I ever spoke, so it might be that she was never Nella to him.

Nella the elephant packed her trunk and said goodbye to the cir-cus. That's what Maw and I used to sing to her. When I got a bit older I'd make fart noises as Maw sang the *trumpety-trump* line, and Nella would swat at me or go off in a huff. We fought about everything and nothing. We shared a room. I used to throw stuff at her over the curtain that Maw had rigged up between our beds. She used to hide my toys in her half and then scream at me for going past the curtain to find them. We nicked each other's pocket money, such as it was. We bit and scratched. But she was always there. Whatever we did, we did together.

There was one night when she admitted to remembering the buggy incident, or at least she didn't deny it. We were both at this party and I'd got profoundly stoned and was lying on a sofa – whose sofa? Whose party? It feels like a million years ago. The grass was really good, but I'd overdone it like I always used to. Someone could have come and sawn my legs off and I'm pretty sure I'd have let them. And Nella sat down next to me. She had a coffee mug in her hand, a *Star Trek* mug. I remember that so clearly: it had a bad screenprint of Quark and Odo from DS9 running all the way round. I remember fixating on it as we talked. I remember saying, *NellaNellaNellaNella*, over and over – her name running into itself like a weird circular chant – I remember enjoying how it felt to make the sound. And then I said, 'Why did you try to steal me from Maw that time? In Glasgow?'

They'd made punch at that party. They'd filled the bathtub with as much alcohol as they could find, all mixed together, and then sloshed in carton after carton of orange juice. It was disgusting, strong as rocket fuel. Nella had dipped the coffee mug in and was sipping this bathtub punch with a hard face. I expected her to say, *You're so fucking stoned* or *It's fifteen years ago* or *You know I don't remember that*, but instead her eyes went sort of distant and she was quiet.

'I wanted to take care of you,' she said, after a while. 'I didn't want to hurt you or anything like that. I wanted a shot at taking care of you. That's all.'

I was falling asleep by then, she'd waited so long to say it. But she said it: I remember, I heard. She reached her hand out and put it on my head, and weaved her fingers into my hair. I slipped off into sleep then, fast. Out like a light. Out like a thief in the night.

'DI Birch.'

Birch was dreaming. It was one of those dreams where she *knew* that it was a dream, but she was going along with it anyway. It was night. She was standing on the Portobello promenade, outside the front gate of her own house. She was looking towards the city – looking along the little terrace of houses that, in the daytime, had neat square gardens with bedding plants and friendly cats. Her terrace was a good place, a place she loved, and she'd longed to live there ever since she was a tiny child. But the dream had changed it. The houses were in darkness. Birch knew, somehow, that no one lived in any of them. She was the only one there.

'DI Birch.'

There was a storm. The streetlamps along the prom were dimmed, like old gas-lights, and in the tarry sky above, lightning whip-cracked in giant arcs. She felt herself jostled by a hard wind. She could hear the sea – up close by the prom like it got at high tide – but it sounded violent. Beside her, the salt-crusted bars of her garden gate chattered in their fixings.

'Birch.'

Someone was walking towards her, up the prom. He began as a tiny doll of a figure, and moved slowly, but she knew who he was. As he got closer, she could see the wind yanking his hair around, though his face was indistinct. She realised his coat was tattered, the bottoms of his trousers scuffed, and his feet were bare. He must be cold, she thought. He must be so cold. He was still young: the age he'd been when he'd walked out of her life and vanished, though thirteen years had passed. No, fourteen.

Fourteen years ago today: even in the dream, she corrected herself. At last, he reached her. He stopped about four feet away and they stood there, looking at one another, as the sea hissed beyond the railings and ridiculous Hammer Horror lightning opened up the sky.

She opened her mouth to say *Charlie*, but there was a colossal crash, right beside her head, as though someone behind her had thrown something.

'*Helen!*'

Birch flinched awake. DCI McLeod had brought his palm down hard on the desk, where about half an hour ago she'd put her head down – just for a minute, just to rest her eyes. Now he was standing over her: watching as she jolted upright in her chair, aiming for nonchalance and missing by a country mile.

'Sir.'

It was the first time that night that she'd looked at him properly, and she realised McLeod looked strange. His usual bespoke suit had been replaced by a black turtleneck and dark grey jeans. They looked wrong on him. He'd had his massive stainless-steel watch on throughout the raid though, no doubt a subtle hint as to who the commanding officer was. He just oozed authority, somehow, like background music he hadn't worked out how to switch off. No matter what had gone down, Birch doubted he'd have been willing to dive into the harbour.

'Sweet dreams, DI Birch?'

Birch could feel herself turning red. 'I'm sorry, sir.' She raised one hand to her cheek to check she hadn't drooled, or sat up with a Post-it stuck to her face. 'I just nipped in here, to – um. I mean, I was up at two thirty.'

McLeod made a snort sound. 'We were all up with the lark this morning, Helen.'

Yeah, all right, she thought. Crossed off the shortlist for Cop of the Year once again, I get it.

McLeod raised an eyebrow, and for a hot, panicked second Birch thought she might have actually spoken out loud.

'Not getting much sleep at the moment?'

There was the cruel hint of a smile on his face. Oh God. Did he know about Anjan? No, surely – there was no way he could know.

Birch lifted her chin, began to right herself. 'Nothing out of the ordinary.' She thought for a half-second and then added, 'Congratulations, sir. You ran quite the operation.'

It worked. She saw McLeod let go of his annoyance and push out his chest, just a little.

'Thank you, Helen,' he said. 'There was a fine team at work this morning. I take no credit on a personal level.'

Liar, Birch thought, but she said nothing more. She rolled out what she hoped was a genuine-looking smile.

'Okay.' He'd lost interest in her nap now. She was out of the doghouse. 'Full briefing in fifteen minutes. I suggest you get some coffee in you.'

She watched him stride out of her office, balled her hands into fists, and rubbed her eyes. 'Stick up the arse,' she whispered, blinking away stars from her vision. 'Fucking brilliant, Helen.'

She was in the Ladies, fixing her face at the sink, before she remembered the dream. Her dreams about Charlie were always weird, but that one had been weirder than most. That it had happened on his anniversary was natural: she'd been thinking about him a lot, these past few days. She didn't talk about him much any more: she found that telling people *I have a brother who disappeared one night with only the clothes on his back, hasn't been seen since, and is presumed dead* could be a bit of a mood killer. But she suspected that not talking about him, shelving him in the back of her mind wherever possible, only made the dreams more vivid. The fact that he'd been dressed in rags, and his feet were bare – that spooked her. She didn't like to think what it symbolised.

She patted a bristly paper towel over her face and avoided her own eyes in the mirror. She still didn't understand how someone just disappeared – how even a senior police officer could search for over ten years and fail to find a trace. It was rare, in this day and age: there were digital footprints, bodily fluids, *clues*. Charlie was a smart boy but he wasn't *that* clever. He ought to have left something behind. Dead or alive, she should have found him by now.

She held her hands palms down under the power dryer, watched as the blast of lukewarm air pooled and dented the skin. Against her hip, her phone buzzed, and before she'd really realised what she'd done, she found herself back inside the cubicle, putting down the lid so she could sit and read. She was thinking of Amy earlier, peering over her phone screen – thinking about McLeod asking why she hadn't been sleeping well. No one could know about Anjan yet. She couldn't let anything jinx this.

Just heard, the message read. *Congratulations, Detective Inspector! Make sure you've got something to charge him with – clock's ticking.* Birch rolled her eyes at this – typical lawyer. *Hope it's not feeling like too much on Charlie's anniversary. Go easy on yourself. A x*

Birch looked at the glowing screen in her hand. She looked at it for so long that after a while it faded to black and the phone locked itself. *Go easy on yourself.* Anjan was being kind, but she regretted telling him about Charlie. She'd felt the anniversary of her brother's disappearance drawing closer for weeks now, and she'd been using it as an excuse for things. She'd never have gone for that first drink with Anjan, for example, had she not felt it so keenly. She knew that this – what? Relationship? – was inappropriate. But it's Charlie's anniversary next week, she'd thought, saying, yes. It's just dinner, and I'll be stronger in a few days. I can put a stop to it then. When they'd gone for a drink afterwards, the thought had been, Sure, I don't want to go home yet. And then everything had got hazy, and she'd found she was telling Anjan all about her little brother: the boy who walked out of his uni halls one evening – carrying only a wallet and the clothes he stood up in – and never came home.

'Not a trace, even now,' she'd said, putting her hands on the table in front of him, palms up, a beseeching gesture. 'Fourteen years next week, and not a trace.'

After that, Anjan was kind, and kissed her. And then she was happy to go home, as long as she didn't have to go there alone.

Birch cringed, wanting to stop the flashbacks before they went any further. She thumbed the phone back to life so she could see the time: 8.25 a.m. Anjan would be at work by now, assuming he'd made allowances for the longer commute from her place. He will have, she thought. She and her fellow officers had long ago nicknamed Anjan Chaudhry 'the Brain'. And here she was, feeling – in a slightly uneasy, fluttery way – happy that he'd put an *x* on his text. Ridiculous.

Briefing in five, she wrote back. *Thanks, Anjan. Sorry if I got weepy on you last night.* She didn't remember crying, but she also wouldn't have put it past her last-night self. Unsure of how to sign off, she wrote, *Keep in touch. H x* She hit send, and clattered up and out of the cubicle before she could regret any wording.

Briefing in five. Christ. McLeod would be insufferable. And Anjan was right: if they couldn't find something sharpish to charge Solomon with, he'd be sprung like a hare from a trap. This man had friends everywhere, and decades of favours just waiting to be called in. Whatever they had on him *had* to stick, or Operation Citrine would have been a costly embarrassment, in more ways than she cared to count.

She laid her phone down on the sink's Formica surround. She was appraising the violet bags under her eyes – procrastinating, she knew, in her last moments of freedom before the briefing – when the phone began buzzing against the counter, making her jump. As she reached to swipe 'answer', she felt almost certain that the voice on the other end would be her mother, calling as she always used to on Charlie's anniversary to speak tearfully and in circles while Birch clucked and soothed. Her mother, demanding to know what her daughter had been *doing* all these years – wasn't this why she joined the police force anyway? How could it be taking *this long?*

But no – Birch shook her head. It couldn't be her mother, for the simple reason that she'd died nearly two years ago. She'd gone to her grave still clinging to a bone-deep conviction that Charlie was alive, that he had to be alive – and despairing of the useless daughter she'd entrusted to go out into the world and find him.

The screen told her the number was withheld.

'It's Birch,' she said.

On the other end of the line, there was a sound almost like the start of a laugh, cut off. A strangled noise. Then silence.

'Hello?'

Birch could hear breathing now: not loud, but ragged. The sound of a person laughing, but trying not to be heard. Laughing or crying, she thought, as she listened. It could be crying.

'Who is this?' she demanded, and then realised she sounded like every person in every film and TV show who got a call from someone who sat on the line and refused to speak. She took a long breath, and listened to the distant, odd wheezing.

'Okay,' she said. 'If you're not going to talk to me, I'm going to hang up. Got it?' She waited. 'Okay,' she said again, and lowered the phone, swiping to end the call.

0:21 minutes, the phone informed her. *Call from Number Withheld.*

Birch looked up again, at her reflection. She pulled a smirk, a what's-wrong-with-people-eh? sort of expression. But in the look the mirror threw back, she could see a touch of fear. It had been years since she'd had a crank call, and it had never happened on her work phone. Random people shouldn't have that number. It might have been an accidental dial, she told herself. But something scuttled down her spine like a cold spider. This was already far from her average Monday: the middle-of-the-night start, the dawn raid, then Charlie wandering through her subconscious mind to say, *Remember you still haven't found me.* Now this. She was keen to get to the briefing: keen to be out of this dripping, windowless space and among other people. She switched the phone to silent mode. Without looking back at her own eyes, she ducked out of the bathroom and into the comforting strip-lit glare of the corridor.

McLeod was in his element. Birch had only caught the tail-end of his introduction to the briefing, but had witnessed enough to gather that in spite of his list of thank yous, it was mostly humble-bragging and patting himself on the back. As she'd slipped in, she'd eyed the big-I-am types, the ones shipped in from Glasgow.

A handful of older DIs – too past it for the smash-and-grab of the dawn raid – the men for whom Operation Citrine could be every-thing. Men with long memories of Solomon Carradice. Men who remembered a Glasgow that was really fucking mean: meaner than Edinburgh's streets could ever be. Sure, Birch was stung that she'd been stuck fishing small fry out of the sea, but she could only imagine how these guys felt. She hoped, for their sakes, that Anjan's prediction about charges didn't come true.

'Operation Citrine,' McLeod said, with such a flourish that Birch jumped. She'd been watching one of the Glasgow DIs remove his jacket, his face an anxious pink, his forehead slick. He'd unbuttoned his shirt cuffs and rolled up the sleeves. On his forearm was a dark tattoo, ancient, spread like a beached jellyfish. It looked like a forces tattoo. She'd been trying to make it out.

'An unmitigated success,' McLeod was saying. 'You all did what you had to do, and brought in our man. I'm proud to be able to say he's safely in one of my cells this morning. Now we just need to decide what to do with him.'

Birch wondered how the older Glaswegian DIs felt, watching McLeod fiddle the arithmetic to turn himself into the man of the hour. Were they angry? Or were they ashamed at having spent so long chasing Solomon, only to have him scooped up by some career-fast-tracked smarm-merchant who wouldn't know the harsh realities of the street if they jumped up and bit him?

Birch flinched a little at her inner monologue. Jesus, Helen. She really was in a bad mood today. An anxious mood, she realised, touching her hand to the phone in her hip pocket, and thinking for the five thousandth time about Charlie. She even quite liked DCI McLeod . . . sometimes, and in small doses.

'Solomon Carradice.' McLeod pressed a button on the remote in his hand, and on the screen behind him, Solomon's most recent mugshot appeared. 'Born Alexander Solomon Carruthers in 1942 and still going strong. Various aliases over the years, but most commonly known simply as Solomon.' McLeod paused, and glanced behind him at the mugshot. 'Handsome devil, isn't he? Doesn't look a day over a hundred and one.'

A collective snort unsettled the room's quiet. Birch kept her attention on the screen, that mugshot she'd already spent hours staring at. It was a few years old now, taken the last time Solomon had been brought in. He'd been accused of committing GBH on a lady friend who turned out to be a sex worker, Birch remembered. She'd withdrawn herself from the case and then disappeared. He looked every inch the well-kept, harmless old gent: if you bumped into him in the street, you'd imagine a lifetime of diligent service at the electric board or somewhere, followed by a bungalow and grandkids on weekends. McLeod was right, his face was heavily lined, but there were no old scars, no chips in the facade. He looked like a grandpa. Worse: he looked like a *nice* grandpa.

'Now,' McLeod went on, 'I know this will be familiar to some of you, but this is for the youngsters in the audience.' Birch watched as he made a sweeping glance around the room, noting that for just a moment he paused and looked at Amy. Birch frowned. He'd had a downer on the young DC for too long, and Birch suspected it was due to her friendship with the woman. McLeod didn't seem to see work as a sociable place. It was fifty–fifty every year as to whether he'd even attend the Christmas night out.

'It's important that those of you who are new to this case understand the MO of Solomon and his fraternity,' McLeod said. 'It's likely that, even if you meet only the lowliest of his associates, you'll encounter a very stubborn kind of loyalty. It's going to be hard to get these men to talk, but talk they must if we're going to have any chance whatsoever of making this case stick. I suggest that we approach them with as much knowledge already in place as we can. Forewarned is forearmed, as they say.'

A couple of the younger officers already had their tablets out on their laps, waiting to take notes.

'Solomon,' McLeod went on, 'must have started out well enough, because his first official brush with the law wasn't until age twenty-one.'

Before Birch's eyes, the elderly Solomon on the screen morphed into a hot-eyed, angular young man, sullen in his first ever mugshot, his fistful of curly hair almost as pale as the backdrop of the flecked black and white print. McLeod was still speaking.

'He had a stall down the Barras, selling everything the modern 1960s home might require – most of it procured from the back of a lorry, surprise surprise. He was a keen amateur boxer, and it seems that through his fighting he met enough of Glasgow's criminal underclass to keep a nice little business going. He also cultivated a reputation for being extremely good with his fists, as many of the women in his social circle discovered to their detriment. Yes, young Solomon was a handy hired thug and wife-slash-girlfriend beater, as well as being a very effective fence. He was nicked a time or two but always seemed to be able to show his nose was clean. Didn't help that back then, of course, our predecessors had a tendency to take the line of, *just don't aggravate him next time, Mrs Carradice.* He did well enough with his so-called business that he bought himself a shopfront and set up as a jeweller and gold merchant.' McLeod clicked the button again, and a black and white photo of a shopfront appeared.

'Young Solomon's first property,' McLeod said, his tone almost that of a proud parent. 'The first of many . . .'

A sort of collective giggle had started up in the room. Birch opened her eyes wide, made them focus back on the seated officers in front of her. One of them – someone sitting near the front – had raised a hand. It was a big hand, and the man it belonged to had pointed his index finger straight at the ceiling, like an eager kid in a primary school class. The collective laughter only added to the effect.

McLeod paused. 'DI Robson?' he said. 'You have a question?'

The hand disappeared. Birch realised it belonged to the man whose tattoo she'd been staring at.

'A comment,' the man said.

McLeod straightened a little. 'Go on.'

'Well, with aw due respect, sir, we've only got this bastard in a cell for so long, an' for most of us here, whit you're saying is well-kent history. For the rest of ye, I agree ye ought tae know it, but it's in yer files an' ye can read at yer leisure.'

There was a general sharpening of attention in the room.

'I jist wonder if,' DI Robson went on, 'we couldnae maybe skip to the most recent part, then we can aw get on wi' getting the guy *charged.*'

McLeod paused. He looked nettled. Birch wondered how much time he'd spent putting the briefing together – then she realised he'd probably spent about thirty seconds, which would have consisted of asking someone else to do it for him. She had to admit, she disagreed with DI Robson: the more time she could spend here, listening to the chequered life story of Solomon Carradice, the less time she'd need to spend sitting behind her desk, trying to do work while thinking in circles about Charlie. But she could see McLeod was reading the room, and that she was very much in the minority.

'Okay,' McLeod said, after what felt like a long and somewhat uncomfortable pause. He began to press the clicker in his hand rapidly, and images flashed over the screen. Mugshots in which Solomon got progressively older. A courtroom sketch of him standing in a dock. A map of the Balkans, then one of Russia. Numerous crime scene photos, which flashed by too quickly to really identify, though Birch could see a few of them depicted corpses. Finally, McLeod settled on a slide that read *Operation Citrine*.

'So.' McLeod was annoyed, but trying not to look it. 'Early last month, we began to receive information from a person who identified themselves as an employee of Solomon's. At this point I must thank our Glasgow contingent – many of whom are in this room – for their hard work in liaising with this informant. His stories were found to be credible, and it was largely upon his evidence that Operation Citrine was built. From our informant, we learned that . . .'

Birch frowned. McLeod had flicked to another map slide, one that showed the police positions from that morning's raid. She knew about this – they all did. They'd just *done* it, for goodness' sake. It was like McLeod had skipped a step. Who was the informant? What had he told them? How had he ended up in the wind? It was none of her business, of course – the informant belonged to

Glasgow, and this was, after all, a briefing about Solomon. But it was typical of McLeod to gloss over the informant's disappearance rather than admit there'd been a slip-up or share whatever plan might be in place to sort it out. She spent the rest of McLeod's now rather truncated speech wondering who knew what: was the informant dead, or had he just gone quiet? Was anyone doing anything to find him? And how the hell had he been persuaded to sing in the first place? She knew it was highly unusual for one of Solomon's boys to break ranks: members of his fraternity *never* talked to the police. What had happened here? What was different? She cursed the disciplinary she'd emerged from only weeks earlier. Technically, no one had been given command of the ongoing investigation yet, but Birch was pretty sure that the DI selected was not going to be her. This was need-to-know-basis stuff, so she'd likely never find out about the informant, unless he turned up dead: a distinct possibility. As McLeod finished up, she waited to see if any other officers would raise their hands, as DI Robson had. No one did.

Instead, the room began to blink and stretch. Birch had another sudden memory of primary school: that weird moment right after the teacher switched off the subtitled biology video and flicked all the lights back on. The students, glassy-eyed and rueful. Her colleagues looked like that class.

The older Glasgow contingent were the first to get to their feet. Their movements developed an urgency that Birch recognised from watching perps leave particularly gruelling interviews: they were in desperate need of nicotine. As they began to file past her, Birch realised she'd been leaning in the same position against the room's back wall for too long: one shoulder and the arm that hung from it had begun to prickle and ache. She straightened up and rolled her shoulders like a prizefighter squaring up to an opponent. Really, she thought, the only opponent she cared about was the seemingly endless block of hours still left in this particular working day. As she began to think about yet more coffee (and then, that perhaps she ought to eat something before too long), an unexpected face drew level with her own.

'Aye, hen.' One of the Glasgow DIs had stopped in front of her, and nodded at her limb-loosening exercise. 'That was a long yin for sure. I'll need a few bevvies at the end of *this* day at the office, I'll tell ye.'

Birch smiled. 'You and me both.' She looked down at the tattoo on his arm. Even close up, it was hard to make out. 'DI Robson, right?' she asked. Her questions about the informant were still swirling in her head. Perhaps this man could answer some of them. 'I was about to get a coffee – care for one?'

The man tipped back his head and knocked out a laugh. Birch saw the yellowish tongue of a lifelong smoker, and two neat lines of fillings, the colour of mercury, in his open mouth.

'And jist who're you round here, hen? The secretary?'

Birch blushed, but she also laughed, and extended a hand. 'DI Birch,' she said, 'Helen.'

His hand was like a rough, dry paw.

'Aye, I'm Robson,' he said. 'They call me Big Rab, folk I like.' He smiled at her: a smile she knew he must have deployed to devastating effect as a younger man. 'And I think I like you, DI Birch.'

She let him study her for a second, his hand still clamped around hers. She tried to guess his age and got no further than a vague decade, but wondered if he'd come out of retirement for Solomon. Come out, she thought, or stayed out: an old grudge.

'Tell ye whit, hen,' he said, dropping her hand. 'Bring yersel down to the pub with us lads tonight, aye? I'm keen fer a chat wi' all the senior Edinburgh officers on this case. Youse have no idea whit we're dealing with here, all due respect. I've some stories about Solomon Carradice that'd make yer hair curl, an' I plan tae tell them.'

He gave her a hard look, which she hadn't expected. She blinked.

'I cannae tell ye,' he said, 'how vital it is that we keep this man behind bars, DI Birch.'

For a moment, Birch felt pinned down by his gaze, but then he seemed to relax a little, stop scrutinising her.

'So aye. Come tae the pub tonight. We'll maybe have a wee bit of . . .'

Birch smiled, glad to be free of his stare. 'Talking out of school?'

Robson glanced over his shoulder at McLeod, who was fussing papers into a briefcase. He turned back, that devastating smile on his face once again. 'You,' he said, pointing at Birch with a crackled finger, 'are a smart lassie.'

First book I ever read to the end was *The Lord of the Rings*. It was kind of a brag: I wanted to be seen carrying it around, that muckle doorstop of a book. I guess I was thirteen or so. Thought it'd make me look smart . . . guess it *did* make me look smart. Trouble was, I hadn't done the mental arithmetic far enough to realise that looking smart sometimes gets you your arse kicked. Smart draws attention to itself.

So I should have ditched the book but found I couldn't. I got hooked. And the reason being, I loved Elvish. No joke. I loved the idea that you could go off and write your own language out of nothing, not just enough for people to believe in it in a book but enough that it actually worked on its own, and people could learn it. I learned it – learned to write it anyway. It meant no one could spy on anything I wrote. I wrote lists of my enemies on the front cover of my maths jotter and they all took the piss out of my weird code-writing, having no fucking idea. I kept a sort of fair-weather diary and never needed to hide it from Nella. It was good having a world of my own I could go to, and a way of writing that no one else could understand. Boromir was always my favourite character. I felt a bit like him sometimes: trying to do right but always fucking up, because teenage boys always seem to fuck up. I *got* it. If I'd been in his shoes I'd have tried to steal the ring, too.

So what got me into all this? Elvish. Blame Tolkien.

Because of Tolkien I took all the languages when I got higher up the school. I hated sciences and couldn't wait to drop all that like a hot brick – ditto history. I liked geography but only because we got to draw maps. I took geography, PE, French, German and

Spanish. They didn't even teach Spanish in my school back then – I had to get in a minibus all on my own once a week and get driven to the next town, where they had an academy school.

PE was absolute shite. I'd become the weird *gayboy* who read big books and wrote in Elvish and ditched wood tech to go and do frog-speak in a class full of girls. I'd made the mistake once of saying in front of those knuckleheaded guys that I had a *natural aptitude* for French, and they bollocked me about it for a year or more. I didn't know the phrase until Ms McLean had said it to Maw at parents' night. Those cunts. I wish now I'd asked which they thought was more gay: girls leaning over you every five minutes asking you to conjugate verbs for them? Or cuddling six other sweaty pubescent lads in a scrum before all getting naked together? Maw told me to just ignore them, and I didn't have a da to tell me otherwise, though back then I wished I did. They used to take the piss out of me for that, too – *hey gayboy, when ye were born yer da took one look an' fucked right off.* So yeah, I hated PE, but I was all right at it, and it was easy to pass.

Tolkien got me into big books too: got me a rep for reading them. And once you've got a rep in high school it's easier to make the best of it than try and ugly-duckling your way into something else. I didn't have that many pals. I studied. Fucking cliché, but books kept me company. And I wanted the biggest ones, wanted to fight the biggest, hardest bastards the library could find. Turned out the biggest, hardest bastards were all Russians.

Not that many folk have read *War and Peace* all the way through. Better believe I fucking have. But *The Master and Margarita* was my favourite, angsty little sixteen-year-old me. Folk took the piss but I mean, it's got the devil in it, and a lairy talking cat who drinks vodka and carries a gun. It got *banned* and that made it cool. Bulgakov was my gateway Russian. I was obsessed with that book. First thing I did when I turned eighteen was get a Behemoth tattoo. By that time I'd got As in my three languages and started on *The Brothers Karamazov*. I'd been saving up to go to Russia: I wanted to see the Patriarch's Ponds in Moscow and ride the Trans-Siberian railway. I knew fuck all really, but the one thing I did know was I'd need to learn the language – use that *natural aptitude* of mine. I had this vision of sitting in a big coat and a fur hat outside a Moscow café, middle of winter, smoking a cigarette and reading Tolstoy in his native tongue. In my defence, I was a wanky eighteen-year-old who'd been coddled by his maw and never been anywhere. Small-town kid bags fancy degree in Russian, packs up, leaves and never comes back; is smart enough to go it alone. That was my future as I saw it. I guess, when you think about it, a fair bit of that came true.

'Sir, all I'm asking you to do is confirm your full name for the record.'

Birch stifled a yawn.

The perp sitting across from her noticed, and smirked. 'No comment.'

'Sir.' The man sitting to Birch's left was DS Scott: a tall, lanky member of the Glaswegian cohort who'd been on McLeod's back-up team that morning. God, that seemed like weeks ago. Could this day *really* still be happening? 'Sir, I haven't even begun questioning yet. If you can confirm your full name for the record, we can proceed.'

'No comment.'

Birch sighed. She knew exactly how this was going to go. She'd known before she walked through the interview room door.

'DS Scott.' She said it as gently as she could.

Her new colleague looked at her, and the perp sat back and looked at them both.

McLeod had tried to make this look like a gift: she was going in to interview with a Glaswegian sergeant, an opportunity to mentor and guide. Bullshit, Birch thought. Operation Citrine had gone a little *too* well, in that they'd arrested every man at the scene, and there weren't enough personnel to process them all, even with the Glaswegians around. He was treating her like a constable, just another body to boss around. She was interviewing the boat pilots, the van drivers, the bag men. And DS Scott wasn't exactly feck-less, although at this point it did seem like he needed some help.

'Perhaps we should just move this along,' Birch said. 'We can proceed with questioning, for now, using this gentleman's preferred name.'

DS Scott moved his eyes to the tabletop. Birch sensed him shuffling imaginary paperwork.

'Very well,' he said, looking up again. 'Mr Toad. What is your relationship to—'

'Toad,' the perp said.

Birch watched Scott's eyebrows disappear into his hairline.

'I'm sorry?'

'Toad. It's just Toad. Not *Mr* Toad.'

She looked the guy up and down. She could hazard a guess at the sort of work he did for Solomon: his knuckles were webbed with so much scar tissue that each fist looked frosted, like a cupcake. He was getting on a bit: he had the look of a man who'd once been very muscular, but had gone soft around the middle. He must have been scarier once, but even now Toad was the sort of man that women crossed the street in broad daylight to avoid. On his neck, a tattoo in Cyrillic. He said the word *Toad* like *Toat*.

'Charmed,' she said, holding his gaze, 'I'm sure.'

'What is your relationship to Solomon . . . *Toad*?' DS Scott said the word like *Tood*. His Weegie accent made the stupid hard-man nickname sound practically cute.

'No comment.'

'How long have you worked for Solomon, *Toad*?'

'No comment.'

DS Scott sighed a long, deliberate sigh. 'An easier question, perhaps. When did you come to Scotland?'

Toad's lips thinned. 'No comment.' The threat of a smile seemed to scuttle around his face, never quite landing.

'Any family here?' DS Scott sounded blithe. Birch could tell he wasn't. 'Or did you come here for work?'

'No comment.'

Birch banged her hand down on the table. It hurt, but the room rang with the noise of it, and she watched Toad jump.

'I'm tired of this,' she said. She could feel the day's bad mood boiling inside her, somewhere behind her diaphragm. This was her sixth interview, and she was tired of hearing those two words over and over. 'Is *no comment* the only phrase you know? Lived here a while and that's all you can muster?'

The scuttling smile stopped dead. 'I speak good English,' Toad said. A muscle twitched in his cheek. She'd offended him.

'Yeah?' Birch sat back in her chair. 'Prove it.'

Quiet hung in the room. Birch wanted to rub her sore hand, but instead folded her arms, felt it throb in her armpit. No one was talking: they'd all been well trained. She wondered, again, who the *hell* this mystery informant was, and what had happened to make him talk.

'Let the record reflect that Mr Toad said nothing,' Birch said. 'And therefore I remain unconvinced.'

The perp curled his lip, and showed her his top row of teeth. One, a canine, was missing. Another was a dark, clouded grey.

'Looks like you could use a dentist, Mr Toad,' she said. 'Does Solomon not cover dental work for his employees?'

She could feel DS Scott looking at her. Her irritation was hijacking the interview.

'No comment,' Toad said, folding his lip back down.

Scott put one hand on the table. This was for her benefit, Birch knew – he was telling her he wanted control. Get back in your box, Helen, she thought. A knock sounded on the other side of the door, and while DS Scott turned towards the sound, Birch stayed still to see if Toad would flinch. He did not.

Amy poked her head around the door. 'This gentleman's solicitor has arrived,' she said, and then vanished again.

When Scott turned back, Toad's smile made a proper appearance: it revealed that the bottom row of teeth was every bit as foul as the top.

Scott got to his feet. Fuck, Birch thought. She felt like she might just have been starting to fluster the man. She had no choice but to stand, too.

'We'll give you some alone time,' Scott said, still breezy as anything.

Birch walked over to the voice recorder, but paused to look back at Toad before switching it off. '*Baba s vozu – kobyle legche*,' she said.

DS Scott stopped, framed in the doorway. Beyond him, in her peripheral vision, Birch could see the vague suited shape of the solicitor. Toad, meanwhile, blinked at her. For a split second, she panicked – her pronunciation must be rusty after all these years. But then she saw he had understood.

'Let the record reflect,' she said, her finger held above the pause button, 'that I said *good riddance* . . . and that Mr Toad here is Russian.'

It had been dark a while by the time Birch got out: she'd been at the station for over fourteen hours. Her eyes stung. Her mouth tasted like battery acid: too much coffee. It was cold out, and Edinburgh blew its trademark hard wind between the buildings. It had rained. Birch stood in the door's yellow square of light, and listened to the distant wet hiss of traffic on Crewe Road. The car park's floodlights refracted in puddles, windscreens, the fluoro panels of panda cars.

At the far end, she could see the dim figures of a few men, huddled together with collars turned up. She watched as the lit ends of their cigarettes flared, flared, flared: the long drags of a frazzled day. She was about to cross the tarmac to speak to them, when the door opened behind her and a gaggle of staff stepped out. One of them said her name, and she turned.

'Evening, Amy.'

DC Kato flapped one hand at the gaggle, already disintegrating in various directions into the night.

'See ya, girls,' she called, and then stepped into Birch's square of lobby-thrown light.

'Quite the day, eh, marm?'

Birch hauled a stream of good, cold air into her nose. 'Sure was,' she said. 'What did you get done?'

'Oh.' Birch felt Amy roll her eyes more than she saw it. 'Lawyer liaison. Call them up, see them in, bring them their green tea, see them out. Repeat. All day.'

'Green tea?'

Amy smiled. 'I think word's got around about the coffee in this place.'

On Crewe Road, a siren.

'Some of these solicitors are *mean*,' Amy was saying. 'And it was all big guys, I was surprised. I'd expected at least some of them would be legal aid types.'

'No.' Birch had noted the same thing herself. 'Solomon'll be bankrolling all this. Make sure no one grasses, no one cracks. And he's got them all well trained: I did a dozen interviews today, boat guys and drivers. *No comment* to everything, every single one. Won't give real names, only their ridiculous aliases. It's a real dog and pony show.'

Amy was quiet for a second. 'You were interviewing the *drivers*?'

'Yeah.' Birch looked down. She could feel her cheeks prickling. 'McLeod needed all hands on deck. We're all pitching in.'

Amy frowned. 'I hear DI Crosbie was assigned Solomon. Heading everything up.'

'Yeah.' Birch rolled out the speech she'd been rehearsing for this moment. 'And good luck to him. It's a case and a half to try to pull off. Couple of days to make something stick or we have to let Solomon go. And he'll have some absolute bastard of a lawyer.' She paused for what she hoped was a natural-seeming amount of time, then lied, 'So yeah . . . rather him than me.'

Amy was nodding, looking down the car park at the cigarette ends weaving like fireflies in the damp night.

'There is no lawyer yet,' she said. 'That's one bit of liaison I haven't done.'

Birch turned to face her friend. 'Okay, *that's* a surprise,' she said. 'I'd've thought Solomon's solicitor would be banging on the door before we even walked him into the custody suite.'

'No,' Amy said. 'It's weird, isn't it? Maybe he wants to represent himself?'

'That'd be pretty fucking confident. I heard Robson is sitting in with Crosbie?'

Amy looked back at Birch. 'Robson is the Glasgow DI? Yeah. And DCI McLeod is even sitting in for some of it.'

Birch bit at a scrap of skin on the inside of her lip. She remembered Toad's gappy smile, the match-flare in his eyes at the proverb she'd recited. 'I doubt he's saying much,' she said. 'Not without a lawyer. That's *weird*.'

Amy shrugged. 'Rumour has it,' she said, 'he's a pretty weird guy, our Solomon.'

'Well, here's two fine lassies.'

The door behind them had opened: Big Rab sidled out of it, an unlit cigarette already in his mouth.

'DI Robson,' Amy said. For a second, Birch thought the younger officer might curtsey.

'Big Rab, darlin'.' Rab drew level with them and nudged Amy's elbow with his own.

Amy blushed, which made Birch smile.

'Rab,' she said, 'this is DC Kato. One of Edinburgh's finest, and set to be our chief constable before we all know it.'

As Birch had predicted, Amy blushed deeper.

'Call me Amy,' she said, holding her hand out to Rab. 'Since we're all off duty.'

'Pleasure to meet you, darlin'.' Birch watched Rab fold Amy's hand into his own as though it were the handle of a spoon – the same grip he'd performed on Birch herself, earlier, at the briefing. He nodded down the car park at the smokers, their crow shoulders. 'We out-of-towners are on the hunt for a bevvy or two. Can you recommend us an establishment, either of you?'

Amy looked at Birch as Rab leaned towards her, lowering his voice. 'Preferably,' he said, 'one where the walls dinnae have ears.'

They ended up in Kay's Bar. She knew one of the bartenders: James was also a plumber and had come highly recommended by one of her prom terrace neighbours. He'd done a great job fixing leaks when she'd moved into her crumbling little house. Every time she went in for a drink, she promised him more work once she got better settled: a whole new bathroom, new washing machine, fitting an outside tap. She'd lived there for nearly a year now, and these days he'd just started to laugh.

The snug in the back had a couple of tables occupied, but Birch strode in and sat down. As seven other officers followed her

– most of them large, tattooed Glaswegians – the other drinkers quickly picked up the signal to sup up and move. Rab went to the bar for a round, taking Amy with him 'to carry'. Birch watched as her colleagues settled, squeezing into the cosy little space, their faces wrung out and sleepy. DS Scott frowned down at his phone as an older officer talked at him in rapid firebursts. The voices in the snug were low, and every so often a different face flicked up towards the bar, like the face of a dog who's heard the distant rattle of his bowl. Birch had ordered a tonic water and lime: she knew that any alcohol consumed now would just send her straight to sleep. Plus she needed to drive home, and the idea of even that short journey made her wearier still.

Perhaps it was tiredness that made her do what she did then, or perhaps it was tradition. She did it every anniversary, and every anniversary she told herself that she'd never do it again. She thumbed open her phone, and looked at Charlie's number in her contacts. Fourteen years she'd kept it, transferring it into every new phone she got. She used to know it by heart and now didn't, which bothered her. It might have been disconnected by now. This year she might get a bounce-back. Then she could stop. Then she'd know there was no point.

But now, she pressed *start new message*, and the thread opened up. Thirteen identical texts, all sent exactly one year apart. She never cut-and-pasted, rather she typed the words out in full every year.

Charlie, I miss you. Please come home. x

She'd only made one change. Last year's message also read *I miss you*, but the previous twelve all said *we*. *We miss you*. Then her mother had died, and Birch had wanted to text Charlie and tell him, but the very idea also stung like the press of a brand. So she just changed the *we* to *I*, and thought maybe from that clue alone he'd know, and come back at last from wherever it was he'd gone. Birch hit *send*. Fourteen messages now. And Charlie was dead – he *had* to be dead – and she felt absurd. Next year, she thought, I won't do this. Next year will be the year I stop.

She flicked back to her inbox, and her stomach flipped: a message from Anjan.

I think we need to talk, Helen. Give me a ring. A.

She stared at the message. Talk about what? *Talk about what, Anjan? Oh God.*

A fizzing glass landed on the table in front of her, and she jumped.

'. . . and one fun-free cocktail for the lady with her face in her phone.' Rab made a flourish, then positioned a low stool between his knees and manoeuvred his bulk down onto it. 'You all right, hen? You look a bit green in the gills.'

Birch shoved her phone into her pocket, and pasted on a smile. 'Oh, fine,' she said. 'Just awake too long, like all of us.'

Rab nodded, and lifted his pint. 'But we survived,' he said, 'and that cunt's in a cell right now, where he belongs.'

Birch picked up her glass. It was slithery with condensation. She clinked it off Rab's.

'To surviving,' she said.

'Aye.' Rab raised his voice. 'And to the cell that Solomon sits in!'

A general chorus of *weeeeeey* went up in the snug, and the officers raised their glasses. A silence followed, as each drank deeply. Birch sipped her tonic, and in her fugged mind, prayed to God, the universe, anything: Lord, let Crosbie find something that sticks.

Rab put his pint down on the table with a glassy thud. 'Now,' he said, squaring his forearms on the table's lip and leaning in towards Birch. 'About that briefing this morning.'

Never mind that, she thought. What the hell does Anjan want to talk about? But she put her own elbows on the table and leaned forward too, pushing the thought away.

'What about it?'

Rab sniffed. 'Well,' he said, 'it was the official version, wasn't it? Tidy. All ancient history, wi' the new stuff all *allegedly* and *might be connected to*. You ask any of the boys in this room.' He cocked his head in the direction of the other officers, talking quietly in trios and pairs. 'They'll tell you there's no *allegedly* about it. Put away Solomon and you'll be putting away a fucking plague – one that's been festering in Glasgow for fifty-odd years.'

Birch nodded. 'Trust me, DI Robson,' she said, 'there's not a single officer at Fettes Avenue who doesn't understand how much is riding on a conviction here.'

Rab snorted. 'No disrespect, darlin',' he said, 'but I honestly don't think ye do. There's officers I've worked with had to end their careers because of that bastard. Had to move out of Glasgow, change identities, go and live in safe houses. He's a real old-fashioned scumbag: hates Catholics, hates women, especially hates the polis. He loves tae feed us false evidence, set up blind alleys an' then watch us run intae them. He likes tae keep an eye oan us, likes tae think he kens what we'll dae next before we even ken ourselves. He got in wi' razor gangs as a wean, learned aw that off them. Learned how to beat a man so his ribs go through his lungs but it won't leave a bruise. Yer man mentioned his wife this morning – he should've said *wives*, 'cause Solomon's had plenty, mistresses an aw. He gets older, they never seem tae. They've aw felt the back of his hand, every last wan. Patched a couple of them up mysel', in my time. And as a *businessman*, as yer boss called him, Solomon learned – and I mean learned *fast* – how to make other hard bastards dae his dirty work for him. There's been times that whole streets in Glasgow were fronts for Solomon's boys: money laundering, fencing jewellery, art, fucking car parts – whatever. Drugs, plenty of drugs. When the Berlin Wall came down Solomon got to know some real hard cunts on the Continent: Chechens, Georgians – and Russians obviously.'

Birch raised an eyebrow. 'Of course,' she said, thinking again of Toad.

'For a while he was working with Balkan gangs, smuggling fags into the UK. He made a mint on that. Fucking *cigarettes*. The early nineties was boom-time for the Solomons of this world, fucking hellish for us. It's before your time, darlin', I dare say.'

Birch nodded. It was, but she'd heard tell.

'We could never *get* him,' Rab went on. 'We'd get the guy in the fishing boat whose so-called catch was all unbranded fags from Bulgaria; we'd get the boys he'd paid to drive the fishmongers' vans and deliver them – yeah, this job this morning wis classic, his speciality. But we never got *Solomon* – could never make it stick. No one would grass on him, not *ever*, not even close. They'd go off to the jail like lambs. We'd raid flats we knew were brothels and nick girls who had no papers, no English in their heads, came all the way here from Ukraine in the back of some refrigerated truck; even *they* wouldn't breathe a word. All too scared of the boss man, and rightly so. We're talking about a guy who'll go after anyone, disnae gie a hoot fer status, influence, whatever. He's disappeared bankers, bought politicians all over the Continent.'

Birch's eyes widened.

'Dinnae go thinking this is aw embellishment, hen,' Rab said. 'No one's safe. Even us polis, like I say. It disnae matter who ye are, once Solomon sends his boys tae find ye, that's it. I don't know where the informant is for Citrine, hen, but I hope he's disappeared himself good and proper. Greenland maybe . . . that might be far enough. But Solomon will be looking for him now till he draws his last breath. Unless he's in a cell, a grass like him is as good as dead.'

Birch shivered. She found his informant comment curious, having thought Big Rab would know far more than she did. Perhaps he did, and was testing her. All she knew was no one else was talking: the success of Operation Citrine might hang on this one informant's testimony.

'Okay . . . look, Rab,' she said, 'I should tell you, this investigation feels pretty tightly sealed. When it comes to that informant, the details of how this all came about, all that, I'm pretty much in the dark. I assumed *you'd* be the man with the facts.'

She paused, testing him right back. Big Rab didn't blink.

'You maybe don't know,' she went on, 'but I just recently went through disciplinary proceedings over Three Rivers. I was cleared, but I think I'm still a bit persona non grata at the moment. McLeod's keeping me out of sight of the press, or . . . something.'

She realised she was rambling, trying to convince herself. The face of DI Crosbie – a man she had to admit to never having liked – loomed in her mind's eye.

Rab frowned. 'Three Rivers,' he said. 'That college shooting? Ye gods, that was a shite business. Really got a pasting in the bastard media, didn't we?'

Birch felt her mouth thin into a line. 'We did,' she said. 'And it drove me so nuts I went a little vigilante on a journalist. Hence the disciplinary.'

Rab raised his eyebrows, a *do tell* gesture.

'We had previous.' Birch gave a little shake of the head to indicate he shouldn't pry further. 'And he pushed my buttons. Got me over a barrel. But it could have turned out worse. He's on remand right now.'

'Grant Lockley.'

Birch nodded, and Rab beamed. 'Little weasel, that one. You were the arresting officer?'

She could feel herself blushing, and realised it was with a guilty kind of pride. 'I was.'

'Well, fucksake, Birch!' Big Rab leaned back from the table and smacked his knee with one hammy palm. 'I'm sure I'm not the first to say you did a fine day's work *that* day.'

She tried to swallow a smile.

'And what's more,' Rab added, 'I'm sure your DCI McLeod agrees.'

He did: Birch knew. He'd made no secret of the fact that he'd seen the disciplinary as a formality – he'd circled the wagons, and sure enough, it had all turned out fine. *We only need the smell of due process*, he'd said, *to appease the press some*. Birch hadn't been fully happy about any of it, but she'd gone along with the due process all the same.

She shook herself. 'I'm afraid the fact remains,' she said, 'that you've bought the wrong girl a drink. I'm just doing the grunt work on the Solomon case. DI Crosbie's your man.'

Rab sat up straight. 'DI Crosbie is a fine officer,' he said, in a tone of voice that suggested he thought the exact opposite. 'But

I'm a tight bastard, hen. Ask any one of these lads. I'm very careful about who I buy drinks for.'

Birch frowned. 'Well, I'm flattered,' she said, 'even if I'm not quite sure what you mean.'

Big Rab winked then, and Birch saw Amy – sitting across the room with DS Scott – notice, and raise a teasing eyebrow at her.

'Like I told you before,' he said, 'you're a smart lassie. You'll figure it out.'

Birch forced herself to walk to the car without looking at her phone again. Sitting at traffic lights, waiting to turn left onto Queen Street, she fancied she could feel it vibrating in her handbag, but knew it couldn't be. It was after ten. Anjan wouldn't text at this hour, it wasn't his style. No, she was imagining the phantom of Charlie texting her back: finally replying to say, *I've missed you, too – I'll meet you at Mum's. I'm sorry. I'm coming home.*

Leith Walk was quiet. As she passed, Birch glanced in at the smudged, lit windows of Joseph Pearce's bar, La Favorita, the youth hostel. Buses floated by in their lanes like steamed-up fish tanks. The car felt dark and empty, home still far away. Charlie was fourteen years gone. Anjan wanted to talk. Crosbie wouldn't find anything to stick to Solomon and Operation Citrine would fail. Grant Lockley would walk free. As she rounded the road's chicane by the Seafield water treatment works, Birch felt tempted to close her eyes and let the car drift: to skid straight through the barriers and down into the sea.

Tired, she thought. You're just tired. Everything will seem better with some sleep. To keep herself on the road, she counted the hours she'd been awake: more than twenty. Again: the phantom vibration of her phone. Every traffic light switched to red as she approached.

She'd told herself she'd wait till she was inside before she looked, but found she couldn't. She parked behind her house, next to the Chinese takeaway about ten doors up, then killed the engine and turned on the overhead light. Her throat clenched: those notifications hadn't been imaginary. The phone lit up with missed call after missed call. She counted seven. And one text from Anjan.

Call me any time, it read. *I want to talk to you before tomorrow. Please, Helen. A.*

Birch frowned. The message was almost a relief: that *please, Helen* suggesting a little softness. But there was also an urgency in it. What could Anjan possibly need to say that had to be said at eleven at night?

The calls were not from Anjan, though: they were all from a withheld number, and they'd come at careful fifteen-minute intervals. Seven calls. In her tired brain, Birch thought, Seven times two is fourteen. Fourteen years today he's been gone. It's Charlie: it's Charlie phoning me. The thought hurt. Her eyes stung, too dry for tears.

She heard a noise, somewhere down the street, and her eyes flicked up. In the rear-view mirror, she watched a man hoist himself from behind one of the garden walls along the terrace. Indistinct in streetlight, he balanced at full height atop the eight-foot wall: still, as though listening. Birch fumbled the light off, thumbed the button on her key, and locked herself in. He was a way off, but at the right place in the terrace. The garden he'd come from could be her own.

She watched as the man dropped onto the pavement below, disappearing behind the string of parked cars. She found she was holding her breath. Now he was nearing her: his footsteps close enough to sound on the wet street. A car hissed by. *Stop*, Birch willed it, suddenly not wanting to be alone. As though the driver had heard her, the car did stop, perhaps twenty yards beyond her bonnet, the brake lights casting red streaks on the road. Behind her, the wall-climbing man reappeared: visible in the rear-view, his hood pulled up. Walking in her direction. And the stopped car was reversing.

In her hands, the phone vibrated again, and the screen came to life, flooding the car's interior with light. Birch cursed, flinging it into the footwell. On the screen, that same withheld number: another fifteen minutes had passed.

The car that had stopped was a dark saloon, a Mercedes, she thought. Now it had come up alongside her – crept backward and pulled up cheek to cheek with her door. The windows were tinted. The car had got too close, as though whoever was driving it didn't want her getting out.

Birch felt adrenalin flood her system: her vision glitched, and her hands and feet went cold. She turned to scrabble in the glovebox for her baton, and almost shrieked in surprise. The wall-climbing man was now standing at the passenger door: upright, not bending to look in at her. She could only see his pelvis: black jeans, the glint of a heavy belt buckle. His hands were crossed in front of him, inches from the car window: gloved, but big as rocks. Birch froze. The phone, now face up under the pedals at her feet, vibrated again.

Somehow, she remembered she was a policewoman, and witness to a possible break-and-enter, too. She bent at the waist and ducked her head to squint up at the wall-climbing man. *I'll report this*, she reassured herself, *and I'll need a description for when I do.* She found she'd surprised him: as her face appeared below him, he stepped back, and into a patch of orange streetlight.

Birch had microseconds, but she registered buzzed, dark hair. The man's nose and mouth were covered by a skull bandanna: in the gloom, he was a ghoulish jack o'lantern. But before she could see more, he was gone: she heard rather than saw him skirt round the car, and walk into the road. As she twisted back upright, she heard the back passenger door of the saloon next to her slam closed, and then the engine fired and the car took off into the wet night. She caught half the registration number, but not the useful half: SK65. Or was it 55? *Fuck. What just happened, Helen? Fuck.* The dark folded back in around her. The phone at her feet had fallen quiet.

Her house was halfway down the prom. The walk there from her car – parked by the comforting lit window of the China Express takeaway – felt endless. The ground underfoot was greasy with frost. She refused to look back, and instead fixed her gaze on the streetlight nearest her gate. One hundred steps more, Helen. Now seventy. Now fifty. Her heart clattered in her ribcage like a useless propeller. The tide was a long way out: a creepy whisper on the edge of hearing. Very few windows were lit: most of her neighbours were older, and went to bed early. Nearing her house, she recalled the dream she'd had when she fell asleep on her desk that morning. The houses all dark, derelict, left behind. Her teeth chattered.

Finally, she reached her rickety gate, and allowed herself to look back. There was no one on the prom. No car parked at the end, no one watching. But the beach at her back was a wall of dark: she felt as though it were rising up behind her, like a net waiting to be thrown. She wished she'd left a light on somewhere, anywhere, inside her house. The streetlight shone on its cracked render, and the dark windows stared back at her like the sockets in a skull. Stop it, she commanded herself. After all, he could have been in anyone's garden. But he could also have been in yours, Helen. The fear wouldn't be shaken off. Birch remembered Big Rab's words in the pub: *No one's safe. Even us . . . once Solomon sends his boys tae find ye, that's it.* She didn't want to believe it. Maybe it's just someone you nicked once, trying to give you a fright. But why today, the day they'd arrested Glasgow's most fearsome mob boss? Her head swam. She felt like she'd spent all night listening to ghost stories, and now she'd seen a ghost.

She reached the front door, cracked her baton, and let herself in. She walked through the ground floor of the house, turning on every light. She checked the back door – still locked – and the kitchen windows. She went upstairs and turned on every light there, too: even the bathroom, whose overhead bulb fizzed and irritated her. From the tiny spare room she looked out over the back garden. The shed looked secure, and she could see the glint on the big padlock in the tall gate set into the wall. The hand holding her baton shook a little, but there was nothing.

Birch pulled the curtains closed in every upstairs room, but left the lights on. She padded downstairs and did the same there, swivelling the venetian blinds in the living room closed. She checked and double-checked the locks on the front door, then walked back to the kitchen and poured herself a half-tumbler of whisky. The liquid jostled and slopped as it fell from the bottle held in a shaking hand. The baton sat on the worktop next to the glass. There's nothing, Helen, she told herself. You just got a fright. You can calm down now. But the other side of her brain fought back: Rab said Solomon likes to keep an eye on police. Why wouldn't he have his boys watching senior officers on the case?

She carried her whisky into the living room, let the smell of it singe her nose. She sat down on the couch and laid the baton across her knees, then took a drink, and waited. After a moment or two, the whisky's warmth began to spread through her chest, and she took another long slug from the glass. Good. Her hands were trembling less. There was nothing. There was nothing. It was fine.

Birch took her phone from her pocket, trying to decide what to do. She could call the station, report what she'd seen, and ask a panda car to come out and do a drive-by. But then, she reasoned, she could technically do that herself – you are a police officer, after all. It would make sense for her to walk out of her own back gate, right now, and do a quick patrol along the backs of the houses. She could look for broken locks, signs of forced entry. But the man had *climbed*. She was exhausted, liable to miss things, and very much not keen to go back outside in the dark, baton or not. But . . . what would she report, if she phoned it in? She sat with the tang of whisky in her throat, swithering, and doing nothing.

Her phone was silent. There were no new calls, no new texts. The house was silent, too: every so often, a car swished by out beyond the high garden wall. Somewhere near the window, a seagull called, making her jump. But there was nothing else. Nothing *wrong*. Just that list of missed calls, and Anjan.

Shit: she'd forgotten all about Anjan, and now it was nearing midnight. Well, fuck it – he'd said to call any time. It would help with the brain fog, she decided, to hear a human voice. The whisky was halfway gone now, lighting up her veins like a hot circuit board.

'Helen,' he said, as the call connected.

'Hello, Anjan.' She tried to sound bright. 'Sorry it's late.'

'It's all right,' he said. 'I imagined it might be a long one today. I'm just glad you called.'

Birch waited. The line between them fizzed. She realised she was still listening for noises in the house, in the garden outside.

'You wanted to talk to me,' she said at last.

'Yes . . .' Anjan drew the word out delicately, stalling for time: a courtroom trick. 'There's no easy way to say this, but I wanted you to hear it from me before someone else came to you with it. Helen . . . the firm. We're going to be representing Solomon Carradice.'

She'd held it together this long: through the early start, through the long, grinding workday that was also Charlie's anniversary; through the embarrassment of being sent into interviews with deck-hands and low lives; through the creepy phone calls and the cryptic merriment of Rab in the Kay's Bar snug. Through – what? Whatever that was just now, with the dark Mercedes and the skull-faced man. A break-and-enter she'd interrupted? An attempted car theft? It might not turn out to be either of those: she might never know what it was. She'd kept her head up for twenty-one wakeful hours. But now it fell into her lap: she bent double, over the baton across her knees, pushed her face into her trousers' scratchy fabric, and sputtered out a sob.

'Helen?'

Another sob. Her throat sparked with the whisky.

'I'm sorry. But . . . I think you're overreacting just a bit. I—'

All the day's sadness and bad mood and weirdness rose up in her chest then, provoked, like a dog on a chain.

'Fuck you.' She sat up so fast that her drink splattered onto the couch. '*Fuck* you, Anjan. Overreacting? I've just had the world's *worst* day, have you any *idea*—'

'Please,' he said, 'please. Please, Helen, please.' His voice rose with each repetition.

She stopped.

'I'm sorry.' His voice was level again. 'I'd forgotten – until just now, I'd forgotten about Charlie's anniversary. I'm sorry about that. But I wanted to tell you tonight. I'm trying to do the right thing.'

'When you say *the firm* . . .' Birch gritted her teeth. 'You mean *you*, don't you? *You're* going to be defending Solomon Carradice.'

There was a long pause. Birch imagined Anjan standing in some shiny, spotless kitchen.

'Representing,' he said, his voice a little quieter. 'But . . . yes. Yes, I am.'

Now her ears were ringing. She could see patches on her vision. She was dimly aware that if some skull-masked assailant were to break in now, she'd care less about that than what she was hearing.

'Do the *right thing*?' She was shouting. 'I've never known you defend a guilty man, not *ever*. What's happening here?'

On the other end of the line she felt him snap into business mode.

'Helen,' he said, the consonants sharp. 'Like anyone, Carradice must be *proven* guilty. And frankly, I am not convinced that he can be.' He seemed to wait for a moment, then added, 'I don't think you're convinced, either.'

'I am entirely convinced,' she said, 'that he is guilty. I am entirely convinced that he has been . . .' Birch remembered Rab's words earlier. 'That he has been a plague on our streets for the past fifty years. He's just good at keeping his nose clean is all. And sure, you're right – I'm terrified that we won't make anything stick, that he'll get to go back to his antics, scot-free. But if you represent him, there's no point in the fucking trial. You *know* you'll get him off – you're the best.' She tailed off. When Anjan didn't speak, she continued, 'I don't know how you can do this to us.'

When he spoke again, his voice was stiff. 'Detective Inspector Birch,' he said, 'I have to do my job. The firm has brought some pressure to bear: this will be quite the landmark case. And forgive me, but I fail to see what business it is of yours how I—'

'Are you kidding?' The whisky was talking now, and Birch couldn't stop it. She felt as though she were watching herself from behind glass: mouthing at herself to stop, but the message wasn't getting through. The other self, the one on the near side of the glass, was screeching. 'You made it my business when you *spent the night here* last night! When you decided to ask me out! You know we can't see each other if you're defending the perp I'm trying to put away! So you've basically picked him over me, haven't you? I knew that date was a mistake, I knew it.'

As soon as the words fell from her mouth she wanted to reel them back in, the way a magician who's vomited coloured handkerchiefs can pack them back into his top hat once he's done.

'A mistake,' Anjan said quietly. 'A mistake.'

Birch clamped her mouth closed, and sucked her lips inside her teeth to prevent herself from speaking again. The dry sobs she'd heaved out had now turned into quiet tears. She wanted to take a deep breath, but he'd hear her. He'd know she was crying.

'Very well,' Anjan said at last. 'I may see you, tomorrow, at the station. Until then.'

There was a pause, then her phone beeped: call ended.

Birch sat very still, the fingers of one hand laced around the now empty tumbler. The spilled whisky had grown into a patch and was dampening her thigh. The mantelpiece clock told her it was a quarter past midnight, and a thought occurred to her: Well, at least it's not the anniversary any more. The house was quiet again. She was still shaking, but now it was with anger, not fear. And she'd made a fool of herself: she knew that already, in spite of the rage still pulsing around her head. She'd wrecked everything, and everything was wrecked. Birch stood up, swaying. She couldn't remember the last time she'd eaten. The gloved and skull-faced man outside was all but forgotten. Ahead of her was the hardest task of all: to set aside everything that had just been said, and sleep.

Of course, nothing's ever what you imagine. My *natural apti-tude* got me exactly nowhere once I got to the University of Glasgow. I'd been a huge fish in a tiny wee pond back in high school, but this was the big leagues. And Russian is fucking *hard*. There's a whole other alphabet to learn, for starters. I got put in this shared flat with four other guys. The only one who ever worked as hard as me was Arne, this dude doing law. The other three were doing philosophy or geography or other piss-about subjects and they just hung around toking weed and bunking off lectures. I got to kind of hate them. They got to kind of hate me. I used to wander round the flat at night when I thought they were all asleep, pacing back and forward and speaking Russian to myself. Trying to make phrases stick. Trying to keep hold of my daft laddie dream of smoking outside a Moscow café.

I was pure skint as well. I know all students are, but I felt like it was just me, like I was the poorest kid in the world. I had to buy all these textbooks – it felt like endless textbooks and endless reading and endless negative bank balance. I was fucking rooked, and I was raging about it. The flat was on the Great Western Road, right near Kelvinbridge subway but six crippling floors up. My window looked down over the park there, where all the posh Toryboys used to go and stroll with their girlfriends on a weekend. Sunny days, when I'd be bent over my textbooks, hunched over in the dreich wee world of my room, I got to hate them, too. I got to hate all of it. Maw couldn't afford to help me out – I occasionally begged some money off Nella but she wasn't exactly flush. It turned out uni was an absolute bastard and after the first six months it was only some warped sense of pride that was keeping me there.

And I had to make money. I worked in the Blockbuster Video on Byres Road and it was a class job: I'd jump on the subway, get there for six at night, finish late, rent a DVD out for free and wander the twenty minutes home with all the drunks. Me and the other lads working there used to drop the big slab chocolate bars on the floor through the back, accidentally-on-purpose, so they were no good for sale and we got to eat them. I liked it there. Got a crush on a lassie with green hair and a nose ring who used to come in. But it was minimum wage and fuck-all hours, like two nights a week. It wasn't enough.

There was this guy used to show up. Big hulking guy, built like a bear. He liked horror movies, the real sick ones: female hitch-hikers getting locked in cabins and mutilated, that sort of thing. He came most nights I was in, always got three discs and a two-litre Coke. The other lads used to joke he was in the Russian mafia, and yeah, he had this thick accent that I'd clocked was Russian the first time he walked in.

One night he comes up to the counter and I'm nineteen and gallus, so I speak to him in Russian. Probably shit Russian, look-ing back, but he got it. He sort of looked at me for a minute and then spoke back. And after that we'd speak Russian to each other: him going slow so I could understand, giving me time to formu-late my replies. I told him about my degree and all that. Even told him about the Moscow idea and all my plans for trips and Tolstoy and blah blah blah. Embarrassing, in hindsight, but he listened and was cool with it. I told myself he was some tragic exile or something, and he never got to speak his mother tongue and he appreciated me like I was a kindred spirit or some naïve teenage shit like that. We'd been chatting like this maybe a couple of months. Then he comes in one night and asks me if I'd take a bit of extra work on the side. *I know you have your studies*, he says, *but I need someone I can trust. A hard worker. This job is for a friend.* Translation, he says. Translate some documents, Russian to English, cash in hand, *boom*. He said what the money was and I could have kissed him. *It's sensitive. Sensitive documents.* Then he leaned in close over the counter – I remember – and spoke into my ear, and in English, to make sure I'd understood. *You cannot tell anyone about this job. Do you hear what I am saying? Anyone*. I shook his hand, clueless as anything. I didn't give a fuck. He had me at the word *bablo*: loot. Money. Green.

Tuesday

Birch was in her mother's house. Her mother's bedroom looked the way it had at the end: the hospital bed that had to be carried upstairs folded, like some enormous, terrifying mousetrap; the IV stand with its bladders of saccharine liquid. Big brown tubs of pills on the windowsill: she'd always shuddered at the little wraiths of powder-dust that rose up under their lids. But the bed was stripped, empty, and the house was quiet. She was too late: her mother had already died.

Beside the bed was a door Birch hadn't noticed before. She knew this building, its thin walls: the door could lead to nothing more than a shallow press. The bars were bolted up around the bed, as they had been at the end to stop her mother from rolling out, and Birch skimmed a hand along the topmost rung as she moved to the door. The bar was freezing cold, in spite of the strong sun at the window bouncing off the plastic mattress, the plastic jars. She flinched her hand away as though burned, and with the same hand flattened, put her weight against the mystery door.

Oh, Birch thought, as the door swung open. It's a dream. She felt a surge of relief.

Beyond the door was a wooden staircase. The wood was dark and the steps were thick wedges set into a massive newel post. They turned a corner, slanting up into a gloom that buzzed like TV white noise when Birch tried to look. She stepped into the stairwell and turned back, her mother's grim little bedroom caught in the doorframe's sickly lozenge of brightness. Then the mystery door swung shut, and a series of clicks said an unseen hand had locked it from the other side. Her mother, something told her. Her mother's vengeful ghost had banished her to some attic room, some place she'd kept hidden all these years.

Birch's curiosity gave way to panic. She turned and battered the door with her open palms, crying for help. On the other side, her mother's voice, the way it had been at the end: rattling in her throat like a crow trapped in a flue. She was only feet away beyond this door. Birch made fists and hammered till the skin on her hands was raw. She called her mother's name, and the voice that she heard come out of herself was a girl voice, the sound of her eight-year-old self. Petulant. Inaudible beyond the wall, which seemed to grow thicker – the sound of her mother beginning to fade away. Birch ran the pads of her fingers across the door, searching for the edges, for some way to claw it back open, so she could be heard. But the surface before her was smooth now: plastered over and sticky with damp. She'd been walled in, and beyond the wall she caught the edge of her mother's laugh.

At first, Birch heard the alarm as a sound in that space beside her: the panicked beep of a smoke alarm, perhaps, telling her to get out when she knew she could not. Coming around was a shock. She opened her eyes and looked directly into the hot glare of her bedroom's overhead light, dappling her retina with after-images. *Of course.* The bulbs had burned all night in this room, and in every other – her little house awake all night in the long black strip of the prom.

It was still dark out: she knocked off the alarm as the digits on her phone clicked over to 05:01. She'd last checked at 03:24. Birch felt relieved that she'd dropped off, but also dreadful: the grogginess of ninety minutes' sleep far worse than the glassy calm of no sleep at all.

Somehow, she levered her legs over the side of the bed, and stood. She'd laid the open baton by her side on the mattress, and now she saw that she'd rolled over on to it: its impression a deep red welt on her thigh. Birch tugged down her oversized T-shirt and shuffled to the bedroom door – baton in one hand, mobile in the other – to listen.

This was ridiculous, she knew. If someone had wanted to get into this house and hurt her, they'd have done it in the dead of night, not waited till now, when the early pre-work runners and dog walkers would surely already be out. Straining for sounds of a phantom intruder, she could hear the city waking up: the distant swish of traffic. Sirens. Out front of the house, a cyclist's comforting bell. Slowly, the events of the night before returned to her, bizarre and dreamlike after that short stretch of sleep.

Still, she found herself creeping the length of the landing, baton raised, to check out every room. She poked the weapon in behind doors, and opened the spare room wardrobe though she knew it was packed from top to bottom with her own disorganised crap. This is ludicrous, she thought, descending the stairs at a snail's pace, trying in vain to avoid the creaky spots. The living room was empty, the kitchen too. The back door remained untampered with. Birch unlocked it and stepped out baton-first into her little yard with its rain-peeled IKEA coffee table, birdbath, crumbling shed. The orange heads of streetlights bobbed beyond the wall like shiny daffs. There were deep, black shadows, but the lamplight bounced off the fat padlock on the shed: intact. The slabs under Birch's bare feet were crispy with frost. She hopped back inside, onto the lino.

'Yeah, hide in the shadows,' she said aloud, to a garden she knew was empty. 'See if I care. Just stay the fuck out of my house.'

She slammed the back door and locked it again, her cheeks burning.

Scoffing at herself, she wondered if she ought to check the under-stairs cupboard. Although it was also stuffed with tat – much of it brought from her mother's house and not yet sorted – she couldn't be sure that some slim-built assailant hadn't folded himself away among the boxes, waiting to spring.

As she passed back through the living room, she smelled the spilled whisky. The phone call with Anjan came back to her all at once, like she'd tripped and suddenly her whole frame was splayed over concrete. *Shit.* The memory halted her, her arm bent into a lopsided V, the half-lifted baton frozen in the 5 a.m. air. She felt suddenly, uncomfortably awake. Afraid she might be sick, she sank onto the sofa, the potential under-stairs murderer forgotten.

Birch sat and listened to the distant tick of the kitchen clock. She began counting the ticks: *twenty-seven, twenty-eight, twenty-nine*. As she counted, she replayed everything she could remember from the phone call: her crying, him stiffening up into strictly professional mode. When she reached seventy ticks of the clock, she stabbed the baton closed against her palm. It hurt. She threw it down onto the sofa beside her, and felt it ricochet onto the floor.

'Oh *fuck* you, Anjan.'

He'd come into the station today and she'd have to see him. She'd have to act the same as everyone else, and pretend that she and Anjan hadn't been flirting for months, hadn't gone out for drinks, hadn't slept together, that she hadn't raged at him over the phone. She'd have to fake the same cold seething that her colleagues would reserve for him – she'd have to pretend she hated him, too. And then he'd be his usual brilliant self for Solomon, and Solomon would walk free. Solomon would *get away with it*. She imagined Big Rab's face shuttering up as he heard the news: not guilty. She imagined having to be the one to tell him. *Rab, I'm sorry, I'm so sorry*. She remembered the cheer that had gone up last night in the snug when he'd spoken of Solomon locked in a cell. And the night before that: she remembered watching Anjan's deft fingers as he unbuttoned his shirt and thinking, This could be the start of something. Birch put her head in her hands.

'Stupid, Helen,' she said. 'You're so fucking stupid.'

Beside her on the couch, her phone rang, and she jumped. Number withheld: it was 5.15 a.m.

He gave me a bunch of emails to translate. They were to do with money, mostly: I had to learn a bunch of financial jargon in Russian really fucking quickly. I didn't understand much of the content. *Units*, these emails talked about, but units of what? I was never really sure and, frankly, I didn't care. I liked the challenge of trying to decode them, but only because they were full of text speak, shorthand, idioms; it was amazing for my Russian to be honest. As well as the finance stuff I was learning a fair bit. And I never really questioned the *why* of it all: he'd told me he did business with guys from all over, and not all of them had Russian, but everyone had at least a bit of English. That was enough explanation for me. I just said, *Sure pal, whatever*, and took the cash.

Obviously now I realise it was a test. He wanted to see how biddable I was, how much of a blind eye I'd turn if he crossed my palm with silver. He upped the stakes bit by bit, giving me more stuff to work on, bigger documents, and references to dodgy activity started to appear. An email giving directions to some *vstrecha*, some meeting place, say. I got to learning some drug slang. He wanted things turned around faster: after a few months he started calling me up and dictating to me in Russian while I typed stuff out for him in English. He'd put wodges of cash in the DVD cases when he brought the discs back. He had my number all right. I was some naïve little *žlob* who'd say, *How high?* when asked to jump. I didn't even question it, really: embarrassing, when I look back on it now. But to cut a long story short I basically stopped doing my uni coursework and spent most of my time working for him. I was learning more fucking Russian that way anyway – including conversational because he and I talked so much. Toad, I called him. All these years and I still don't know his real name. We don't have real names, any of us. We don't have real lives. We're invisible, we walk through walls, we shapeshift. We're the ghosts of the people we used to be.

Sort of appealing, isn't it, that idea? Back then – or before I met Toad – when I was skint and fucked off, I used to have this daydream. I'd be able to freeze time, just for, like, five minutes every so often. Not enough to make me age way faster than the rest of society or cause a space-time rift or any shit like that. But imagine: enough time to whip round a shop, everyone around you frozen, just pick up whatever you wanted, and walk out. Enough time to unclip a guy's Rolex while he's standing there with his phone up to his ear and stock-still, no idea . . . in fact you'd take the phone, too, right? Five minutes is enough time to browse, even: pick what you want before you stick it in your pocket and walk away. I used to daydream about that. And I'm jesting – it wasn't Rolexes really, or anything like that. Just . . . a nice bottle of wine on a Friday night, or, I don't fucking know . . . organic orange juice. It was shit like that which felt like a luxury, but such a tiny pissing luxury that it was like a slap in the face not to be able to afford it. Toad – that cash he threw my way was my five minutes. Thanks to Toad, I drank the orange juice. Then I bought the vodka to go with it. And that's the thing. We're never fucking happy with anything, any of us – we're always asking, *Right, what's next?* That was me. I downed it all and then I slammed my glass back on the bar for another. Always more. You can't blame me. It's the human fucking condition.

B irch was later than she'd wanted to be, in spite of the 5 a.m. start. Getting off that couch had been hard; making herself get dressed for a likely audience with Anjan after last night's palaver had been even harder. She'd stared into her wardrobe for a long time, unsure quite what she was looking for. It was only after she'd got dressed and gulped a half-cup of scalding coffee that she realised: she was looking for the outfit that would make her most invisible.

She stalked through the bullpen, hyper-aware of her puffy face, last night's lack of sleep draped around her like an itchy scarf. She'd hoped to get into her office and shut herself in without being noticed, but before she was even halfway across she heard Amy's voice.

'Marm.' The younger officer had stood, and was striding towards her between the desks.

'Morning.' Birch pasted on the best smile she could muster. Amy looked great as always. Of course she does, Birch thought. She's twenty-eight.

'I've been trying to reach you this morning.'

Birch winced. The phone had rung at 5.30 a.m., at 5.45 a.m., and each time she'd picked up to hear that same weird, hoarse breathing. The crank calls were pissing her off. She wanted them to stop, not least because then she could file away the nagging idea that they were somehow connected to her weird encounter with the skull-masked man.

She couldn't tell Amy any of this, of course. She hadn't reported the encounter yet, though it was second on her day's to-do list – right after *hiding from Anjan*.

'Oh yeah,' she said, 'sorry, I put it on silent last night, and then forgot I'd done it.' It was bad bullshitting, she knew.

Amy eyed her for a second, before continuing. 'I just wanted to let you know,' she said, 'I've heard who Solomon's lawyer is.'

Birch pulled her mouth into a straight line, and tried to make her eyes go blank. She couldn't know before Amy, without having to explain how she knew before Amy. Fuck, she thought, this would have been so much easier over the phone, too.

'Tell me.'

Amy opened her eyes wider, and for a fleeting second Birch wondered if this was for dramatic effect: that Amy knew everything, that perhaps Anjan had told her in some bizarre outburst. But no.

'Marm, it's Anjan.' She paused for a moment. 'You know – Chaudhry. Anjan the Brain. I couldn't believe my ears when I heard.'

Birch could feel her mouth opening and closing, like a fish. She was too tired for play-acting, but she found that her anger from last night was still there. 'Well, fuck,' she said. They stood in silence for a few seconds, and she added, 'Fuck that guy.'

'Yeah.' Amy was looking at the floor now, shaking her head. 'I don't like our chances quite so much now.'

Birch looked down at the same spot Amy was fixating on. She let her eyes blur, and watched the shimmery negative shape the blue marl carpet made between the four pointed toes of their shoes.

'Okay,' she said, after what felt like a long time. 'Okay.'

Amy shook herself, and glanced at her watch. 'I dare say he'll be in first thing,' she said.

Birch dragged her gaze back up from the carpet, and zeroed in on Amy. 'Listen,' she said, 'just keep these worries to yourself, okay? The Glasgow guys might not know Anjan's rep quite so well – let's not unsettle them needlessly just yet.'

Amy was nodding.

'As far as you're concerned, Anjan is just another lawyer.' Birch realised she was saying the words for herself, too. 'And . . . let's stay positive, shall we? Maybe he only wins so much because he usually defends the good guys.'

The effort required for this show of optimism was almost too much: Birch could feel herself sagging. But it worked: Amy smiled.

'Fingers crossed,' she said, 'you're right. And I'll keep it on the downlow.'

Birch smiled back: it was half-arsed, but genuine. 'Good girl.' She turned towards her office door. Just a few paces: she could make it in there, hole herself up and—

'Oh, marm?' Amy was twisted on one heel, ready to walk away, but sporting a grin Birch didn't understand. 'Who's the lucky guy?'

At this, a couple of heads nearest to Amy flicked up from the glow of their computer screens.

Birch frowned. 'Lucky guy?'

Amy nodded towards the office door. 'You've got a suitor,' she said, in a put-on schoolgirl tone that Birch found grating. 'There's no hiding it now.'

She felt blood draining from her face, pulled by the sudden, frenzied drumbeat of her own pulse. What? Did they know? Had Anjan – *what the fuck?*

Birch turned on her heel and beelined for her office door. It was ajar. Behind her, Amy was giggling, following her. No, Birch thought. Just go away, Amy, please . . .

Her desk was a paperwork landslide, the way she always left it. However, someone had levelled a little clearing amid the mess, and sitting on that square of desk was the most extravagant bouquet that she had ever seen. She felt her heartbeat speed up. White lilies: their blooms as big as hands held open, their peppery stamens daubing the air with scent. Fourteen of them.

'They're stunning, aren't they?'

Birch could find no words. Inside, the tide turned: the blood rushed back to her face, and her head began to pound. She elbowed Amy backward and loped away, ignoring her colleague's splutter of confusion. When had Anjan done this? He must have arranged the delivery yesterday, before they'd fallen out, perhaps to cheer her up on Charlie's anniversary. But they'd talked about this – they'd *agreed*. Take things slow. No going public. Now he'd had flowers delivered to her office? What had come over him? As she covered the bullpen's gap once more, Birch dug her phone from her pocket and thumbed it into life. Five missed calls.

'Oh, fuck off,' she hissed.

She scrolled her recent calls and speed-dialled Anjan. Three rings. Four. Five.

'Anjan Chaudhry speaking.'

His voice made Birch want to spit.

'Are you in the building yet?'

She felt his bafflement on the line.

'Good morning, Helen,' he said. 'I've just parked. I'm on my way in as we speak.'

His voice was like acid. Good, she thought. She could feel her adrenalin building, spoiling for the second round of the fight he'd conceded the night before.

'I'll meet you in reception,' she said, and hung up.

As she rode the lift down, her phone buzzed in her hand. Another fifteen minutes had passed. Her fear melted by rage, she picked up the call.

'Hello again, fuckface,' she said.

Silence on the line. Or not quite silence. The sound of a person listening.

'Is this really your life?' she asked. 'Is this literally the best hobby you can come up with, scumbag? Sitting by a clock counting down the minutes till you can phone me again? I pity you, to be honest. You hear me? It's pitiful.'

She waited. The sound on the line didn't change.

'Okay then,' she said, as the lift doors slid open. 'You have a great fucking day.'

Even as she hung up, she could feel doubt sliding over her like cold rain. I shouldn't have said that, she thought, let them get to me, whoever they are. But that particular anxiety could wait in line. Anjan was standing at the reception desk, pinning a pass on his suit lapel – presumably waiting for Amy to come down and do her lawyer liaison bit. His made-to-measure camel-hair coat was arranged in the crook of his arm, his cashmere scarf spilled over it like a splash of paint. Birch's insides felt like boiling stew as she crossed to him.

'What, precisely,' she said, 'are you playing at?'

Birch tried to keep her voice low. She hooked him by the coat-slung elbow and steered him out of the receptionist's earshot. Before she could move him as far as she'd have liked, he shook himself free.

'Helen,' he said, his voice a thin line. 'I'd like you to calm down, please, and tell me what is happening.'

Birch huffed air out through her nose, then regretted it: she sounded like a bratty teenager. 'You tell me,' she said. 'What on earth is with this flower stunt? I mean ... we talked about this! What were you *thinking*?'

Anjan's tone was quieter now. 'I'll ask you again,' he said. 'Please explain what is happening.'

Birch blinked. He'd spoken as though she were a skittish horse he wanted to calm.

'The flowers,' she said, that doubt beginning to settle upon her again. 'The delivery of flowers, just now ...'

Anjan said nothing. He watched her, one eyebrow slightly raised.

'Wait,' she said. 'It ... wasn't you?'

He shifted his stance, squaring up to her. 'Helen, I don't know what you're going through right now, but I really think you need to ...'

Too late. She was already running: past the lift this time, and through the double swing doors into the stairwell. It was instinct: she had to put as much distance between herself and Anjan as she possibly could. Her face burned with embarrassment, and questions had begun to course through her head. *If not Anjan, who? Why? Has someone died? Have I forgotten something?* She barrelled upwards, two stairs at a time, nearly colliding with DS Scott but swerving and carrying on.

'Sorry, Scott!' She heard her own shout echo into the stairwell, but she was out onto the landing of her floor before she could catch any reply he made. Back across the bullpen she went, this time at a clip and breathing hard, paying no attention to the raised eyes of her colleagues as she passed. Her office doorframe stopped her as she clattered against it, and yes – there they still were, the stinking lilies, dropping their smeary red pollen all over her files. In her head she heard her mother's voice: *They're funeral flowers. I wouldn't give them houseroom, myself.*

Birch swallowed hard. Her lungs were burning from the sprint. She edged into the room, placing her feet carefully as if the flowers might rear up and lunge at any sudden move. Her breath came ragged as she skirted the desk, the stench of the waxy white blooms almost solid in the air. She saw it now: behind the gathered greenish bulb of the vase, tucked half out of sight in the paper morass. A plain white card, embossed with the florist's chic logo. With a twitchy hand she flinched it up from beneath the bouquet's canopy and opened it. As she read the hand-penned message, she let out a short, involuntary sob.

For Helen. May Charlie rest in peace.

Birch's hearing stuttered in and out. She flipped the card in her hand: no name, no initials, nothing on the back beyond the florist's Instagram handle in a neat, serif font. She reached forward with one hand and scrabbled on the desk around the bouquet's base, shoving papers aside. She knew there'd be no further clue, but oh how she wanted one. Just something else, she thought, looking back at the card in a kind of mad desperation. She was being targeted now, she was almost sure: this wasn't just what Rab had warned her about, that Solomon liked to keep an eye on the police. This was about *her*, specifically. But why? She fumbled papers onto the floor. This makes no sense. There has to be something else.

In her pocket, the phone rang. She fumbled it up to her ear. 'Yes?'

That silence again. That thick, listening silence. Into it, Birch breathed back, rasping.

At last, a voice. 'You like that better, DI Birch?'

A man's voice, with an accent. Birch sputtered for air, but no – the line had gone dead. *What the hell? What the actual, living hell?* Her head swam. Something was going on here, and she couldn't fathom it out. She was tired, and confused, and scared. What was somebody playing at? And how dare they – *how dare they* – bring her brother into it?

'Well, isn't *this* a bag ae washin'?'

Birch's pulse made a scissor-kick. Standing in the office's open door was Big Rab, a worried-looking Amy at his side. He glanced back at her, and added, 'That was wan o' my granny's wee expressions.'

Birch's mouth was open: she could feel it, but she couldn't seem to pull it shut. Between her fingers, the florist's card had bent in her grip.

'Now then, lassie.' Big Rab crossed the room, passing the sinister blooms as though they weren't even there. He laid one big bear-paw of a hand on her jittering shoulder. 'Now then, lassie,' he said again, 'now then.'

The fatherly gesture made Birch want to cry. She looked up, stricken, at his moonish red-white face.

'I reckon,' he said, with a hint of a smile, 'that there's some things you'd like to tell me, darlin'.'

For a moment, Birch felt pinned under his gaze. She found she couldn't speak, but she nodded: yes. The skull-masked man. The phone calls. I was going to report it, she thought. Yes.

'Magic,' he said, stepping back for her to stand. 'Coffee and a bun it is, hen.'

He glanced up then, and Birch saw him wink at Amy.

'I'm buying,' he added, 'natch.'

I'm not saying I didn't know the kind of guys Toad was working with. I'm not going to tell you that I didn't know he was into some serious shit. But I kept telling myself that it had nothing to do with me. I was helping some guy whose English wasn't great to sort out his emails, and getting a bit of pocket money for it. Where was the crime in that? Loads of students did translation work or proofreading for money. At worst, I thought I was probably doing some tax evasion – okay, I *was* doing some tax evasion – but fuck-sake, I was strapped and it was cash in hand. No one declares cash in hand income, right? It's like a law of the universe. This was the bullshit I fed myself.

The guys at work thought Toad was my drug dealer, and I just kinda let them. I started bumming around in the flat like the stoner philosophy students. My classmates couldn't understand how I was still passing, because I barely showed up any more – but of course, I was getting all this practice in with Toad, and in the verbals I was chucking in a bunch of niche slang and idiom I'd learned and getting brownie points. I thought I had it all worked out.

Then one night Toad rocked up at Blockbuster.

'*Privet, Schenok!*' – this was his standard greeting. *Schenok* is basically *pup*, and for some reason he found it hilarious to call me that. I guess it just sort of stuck.

I assumed he'd been drinking. He had this usual walk, that . . . well, he *sidled* everywhere, you know, walked like a man who doesn't want to be noticed. But he was such a huge bear of a guy that it looked weird, drew more attention to him if anything. But that night he didn't sidle in. He came over to the counter in big loping strides, shouting, '*Schenok!*'

'Hey, *zhabka*.' I was in a bad mood, so felt like snarking him off, and because he seemed to be in a *good* mood I thought I could get away with it. You see, *zhaba* is *toad*, and it's a gross, mealy sort of a word in the mouth – I often wondered if that was why he picked it, to make him sound creepy and tough. That's if he picked it at all ... maybe it was foisted on him, the way he foisted my name on me. But yeah – *zhabka* is different. It means *little toad*. It's like, aww, look at the cute ickle baby toad; it's a fluffy sort of nickname. Emasculating. I'd been wanting to try it out on him for weeks.

He looked at me for a second, then he said, '*Davaite soobrazim na troikh!*'

This was a new idiom on me. He must have been able to see I was struggling; something about three guys? Russian is fucking weird. Anyway, he basically laughed in my face and then eventually translated himself.

'*Schenok*, your shift is finished in an hour! Let's go drinking, I said.'

Now, a couple of things. First: when a guy who looks like Toad asks you to go drinking, you hesitate. I mean I knew he'd be able to drink me not only under the table but under the entire fucking bar, and probably still wake up fresh as a daisy next morning whereas I'd likely be in A&E having everything pumped out. And second: he's a fucking *Russian*. This was a Monday night, I think. I sort of stood there opening my mouth without sound coming out. I'd never seen him laugh so much.

'*Vinograd*,' he said. 'One hour.' The Grapes: a die-hard Rangers bar out by Kinning Park, six subway stops away. I knew that was where Toad drank, he'd mentioned it to me before. It was a cash-only place, no doubt a bit rowdy. But cheap – I reasoned it had that going for it.

Anyway, I get finished and I daunder over there. I'd no idea what he wanted, but in spite of the fact that he was clearly into some stuff – and almost certainly pure fucking mental into the bargain – I'd never been frightened of him. I liked him, in fact – kind of the way you like your oddball uncle. I guess I assumed he was just passing, fancied a few bevvies, whatever. I know, I was green as fuck. And that was about to change.

I got over to the Grapes and you know, it was a Monday. So it was all their regular guys: been there since eleven in the morning, staring down into their pint glasses and occasionally staggering out to the pavement for a wee smoke. Basically dead to the world; at least, not a single one batted an eye when yours truly walked in, not even the barman. And I cast around for Toad and I saw him in the furthest corner, his back turned to me; and across the table from him was sitting the hardest cunt of a man I think I've ever seen in my entire life, then or since.

I walked over and this guy looked up at me as if I'd killed his entire family. Knowing what I know now, I should have been shitting myself, but at the time I was actually just annoyed – if you can believe it – that Toad hadn't told me it really *would* be three guys out drinking, like the idiom said. They weren't talking, just sitting there. I got to the table and Toad sort of leapt out of his seat and for a second there, I thought he was going to hug me.

'*Schenok!*' he said.

I stood and looked at him, and then at the other guy.

'This is Tsezar,' Toad said.

I think I nodded to him. He just carried on looking at me, like I'd mortally offended him.

Anyway, Toad shuffled round and offered me his seat. I didn't desperately want to be sitting opposite Tsezar and his dead eyes, but when a guy the size of a grizzly bear has already got out of his seat for you, you take up the offer. Then Toad did the strangest thing – so I thought at the time, anyway. He walked up to the bar, smacked his hand down on the drip-mat, right in front of the barman, and yelled, 'I am buying drinks for everyone in this bar!'

Obviously I was baffled, but a cheer went up, and the regulars all started shambling over to get their free booze like they were worried Toad was going to change his mind. It's a cheap place, and there weren't that many in, so I guess the damage wasn't crippling . . . but it wasn't till later that I realised why he did it. He wanted everyone in that pub to forget they'd ever seen him. If the polis walked in the next day and asked, *Did anyone see the unmistakable giant Russian dude, a man we consider armed and dangerous?*, he wanted to make sure that the reply would be, *Dunno what you're talking about, officer. I was just here drinking with my pals like usual.*

It wasn't until I saw Toad in action that I realised how smart he could be.

Anyway, he brought me a pint and I sat there and sipped it while he and Tsezar chucked their double vodkas back. I really wasn't the brightest kid. I had no idea the shit that was about to go down.

Rab had steered her back out through the bullpen, one hand hovering behind her shoulder, not quite touching, but somehow propelling her forward nevertheless.

'You just go and clean yersel' up, hen,' he'd said, his voice softer now. 'Take your time, I'll be here.'

Birch had stood for a while, looking at her own face in the mirror. She couldn't quite believe how bad she looked: her eyes sunken by lack of sleep, her skin pink and blotchy. The mascara she'd ham-fisted on that morning was now redistributed in streaks across her face. She'd wadded up a paper towel and soaked it, then done her best to erase the evidence of her own emotional detonation.

It wasn't the first time she'd had messages 'from Charlie'. In the wake of the disappearance, when Grant Lockley had made it his personal mission to fill the papers with the murkiest speculations he could find, it had happened a fair bit. Well-meaning bystanders with impossible so-called sightings: Charlie getting on a city bus at the same time every morning, as if to commute. Charlie drinking in the Gunner in Muirhouse. Charlie on a beach in Spain, even. Cranks writing intricate letters insisting they knew the truth. The odd cruel arsehole who'd claimed to *be* Charlie: usually abroad and in need of money in vast sums. Chancers. Fantasists. But none for many a year now . . . and never anything like this.

It was hard to run away from what this might be, now: it most likely wasn't someone she'd booked once having a laugh at her expense, and it definitely wasn't some lonely random-dial weirdo. This person was invested: those flowers weren't a cheap Interflora job. The phone stranger, the skull-masked man, his friends in the dark grey Mercedes: were they connected? And if they were, what did they *want*? For the life of her, she had no idea.

Now, she sat opposite Rab in one of the canteen's bucket-like plastic chairs, a cup of milky tea on the table between them. Rab was watching her drink it: he'd loaded it with sugar the way her granny used to whenever anyone took a fainting fit. He'd helped himself to a sad-looking Danish pastry with implausible yellow custard at the centre of its swirl. His hands shook, just slightly, and Birch wondered if this was a permanent affliction, or if it was just a while since Rab's last smoke.

'With all due respect,' she said, after they'd sat quietly for a while, 'shouldn't you be somewhere right now?'

Rab grinned. 'Probably,' he said. 'But I like tae prioritise.'

Birch sipped her saccharine tea.

'So,' Rab said, lifting the entire Danish between his thumb and two indelicate fingertips, 'now you're going to tell me what's been going on, darlin'.'

She took a deep breath and, stalling for time, blew the non-existent steam off the surface of her tea.

'Okay,' she said at last. 'I have a little brother. Or I did have.'

Rab nodded. 'Charlie Birch,' he said.

Birch found herself smiling, the way she sometimes did when someone recognised her brother's name. It was funny, him being a little bit famous – except it wasn't at all, because he was also probably dead.

'You know,' she said.

'Aye. You think I came up the Clyde on a banana boat, hen?' Rab laughed. 'Excuse me, another o' my granny's. It wis a big case for a while there. I mind yer man Lockley writing up a storm in the papers.'

Birch rolled her eyes. 'You and everyone else,' she said. 'But you know my feelings about that.'

Rab waited, so she went on.

'Okay, so ... if yesterday I seemed a little, I don't know – *off*, that's because it was Charlie's anniversary. The anniversary of his disappearance, I mean. Fourteen years.'

Rab waggled his eyebrows at her. 'That long?' he said. 'Holy Mary Mother of God, does the time no' fly, hen? But anyway . . . go on.' He opened his mouth and bit off about one-third of the Danish: a sign that he didn't plan to speak again for a while.

'It's hard every year,' she said. 'But this year it felt worse, with Operation Citrine and everything, you know? And maybe something about just having got back out there, after the disciplinary. For a while I couldn't keep busy . . . I had too much time to think about him.'

Rab was chewing, and nodding.

'But also,' Birch went on, 'something happened yesterday. Well, a few things happened actually. And I don't know what the hell's going on, but I don't think it was an accident that it all kicked off on the anniversary. Someone knows about Charlie.'

Rab swallowed. 'Someone?'

Birch closed her eyes. 'Sorry,' she said. 'These . . . I'm getting funny phone calls. Like . . . silence on the line. Someone listening to me. A man. The first one, yesterday, there was breathing – but not like a heavy-breather sort of call, more like laughing. Like a creepy, husky laugh. Then the rest, just silent. Or they have been. Until today.'

Rab took another giant mouthful.

'Yeah,' she said, feeling her face begin to prickle. 'Today I kind of lost it, and . . . I spoke. I said some stuff to them. Or him. Whatever. I showed he was getting to me.'

Rab chewed, watching her.

'Maybe I brought it on myself,' she said, 'not taking him seriously, ignoring the calls. Now he's upped his game.'

She tossed the florist's card across the tabletop to Rab. She watched him enact a calmer version of her own reaction: he read the message, frowned, then flipped the card to look at the back. No further clues.

'You think they're one and the same?'

Birch nodded. 'He was on the phone,' she said, 'as you walked in. He mentioned the flowers. Or seemed to, anyway. But there's something else, too.'

'Aye, go on.'

She closed her eyes, trying to see again what she'd seen the previous night, trying to conjure it.

'There was a man,' she said. 'In my back garden – or I think he was. When I got home last night, he climbed out over the wall and walked up to my car. It was right after I'd parked, like he'd been waiting for me.'

Opening her eyes again, she saw a switch flip somewhere in Rab, and he went into interview mode.

'Description?' he said.

'Medium height,' she replied, 'maybe five ten, five eleven. Lean guy – he had no trouble scaling an eight-foot wall. Dressed in black jeans with a belt, a big belt buckle, and a plain hoodie. Very short dark hair, like a buzz cut. Caucasian, I think, but it was dark, and he was wearing this skull mask.' She corrected herself. 'Well . . . a bandanna with a skull face on it.'

She could see Rab taking mental notes.

'And he approached the car?'

She nodded. 'Came right up to the passenger window and just stood there,' she said. 'Hands folded in front of him. And then . . . Rab, it was so weird. This car pulled up on my driver's side, cheek-by-jowl, close enough to touch, nearly. In fact, it drove past me, but then stopped and reversed back. And this guy walked around the back of my Mondeo and got in the other car – the back seat, driver's side. A dark-coloured Merc, before you ask. Black, or maybe dark grey.'

'You didnae get the reg?'

Birch flushed. 'SK65,' she said, 'but that's all – and I'm not positive.'

Rab posted the last chunk of Danish into his mouth, looked down into Birch's half-empty tea cup, and chewed.

'That,' he said, after a long time, 'is an uncanny thing, agreed.'

'I'm sorry,' Birch found herself saying. 'I'm kicking myself for not getting the number plate. My phone was ringing too, this same withheld number guy, and . . . it all happened fast. I was . . .'

'You were terrified, lassie, and no shame in being so,' Rab said. 'Dinnae go fretting. The only way ye went wrong was not phoning up here and making a report on the spot. And ye ken *that* fine well.'

Birch sighed. 'I know. I just . . . when I got in, the house was still all locked up. Nothing gone from the garden.' She remembered the call with Anjan. 'I was tired and . . . got distracted. But nothing else happened all night. I mean, was there even a crime?'

Rab rolled his eyes, a thing she wouldn't expect a man of his age and bearing to do. She almost laughed.

'Was the garden secure?' he asked. 'Locked?'

'Yes.'

'Grounds for trespassing, then. Threatening behaviour too, for sure – come oan. Ye'd take it seriously if some elderly wifey phoned that in.'

Birch grimaced.

'Aye.' Rab put his forearms onto the table, and leaned towards her. 'So what's good enough for a wifey is good enough for you, all right? Enough secrets. Promise me.'

Birch nodded, though she felt queasy. I don't want secrets, as such, she thought. But I do want privacy . . .

Rab was patting at his various pockets. At length, he produced a biro, and a scuffed-looking business card: yellow and black, not his own card, but one for a Glasgow-based taxi firm. He turned it over, and wrote a mobile phone number on the card's plain back, *BIG RAB* in all caps next to it.

'That's me,' he said, 'out of hours. Anything else happens, I want you to call me.' He held the card out to Birch.

She looked at it.

'Come *oan*, lassie,' he said, flapping the card at her. 'It's no' like calling the cavalry. It's just if something else happens that you cannae put yer finger on, and ye want a chat about it. All right?' He flapped the card again. 'Take it, there's a good girl.'

Birch sighed, but there was a smile under her exasperation. She dropped the card into the breast pocket of her blouse.

'Now,' Rab said. 'The big stuff. If ye had tae make a guess, who is it that's phoning ye?'

Birch frowned.

'Wild guess,' he said.

She looked down into the beige tea, half gone now, its surface turning oily. 'I'm sorry,' she said. 'I've been racking my brains trying to think: who have I wronged, who have I nicked in the past who might be recently out and wanting to wind me up? I mean, there are probably some old perps out there who'd like to have a go, but how many of them have my work number? Or are this persistent? Who'd link it to Charlie? I can't get it straight in my head. I can't make it add up.'

'Lockley?'

Birch paused, then shook her head. 'I don't think so,' she said. 'I've wondered about that, but it's not his style, to be anonymous. There's nothing he's more fond of than saying his own name. No way he'd send those flowers and not sign the card. And he wouldn't be making the calls – he's on remand for hacking phones and the Police National Computer. If he had to explain how he got my number it wouldn't bode well for his case.'

Rab was nodding again, wearing a look that Birch couldn't read, but didn't like.

'Someone close to Lockley?' He didn't seem to want to let the Lockley idea go – as if he didn't believe it but wanted it to be true.

'I can't think who. Or why, really. His fans are a whole lot less rabid now he's up on criminal charges.' Birch snorted. 'Funny that.' She turned her eyes downward again, but in the margin of her vision saw Big Rab pass a hand over his eyes.

'Well, lassie,' he said. 'I'm no' a fan o' this theory, but it looks pretty likely from where I'm sitting that aw this is linked tae the Solomon case. Operation Citrine, day one: these phone calls start. And intimidating the polis is a Solomon speciality.'

Birch glanced back up at Rab. He looked tired. The shaking in his hands had increased.

'I guess,' she said. 'But I'm not a big fish in this operation. Surely it's Crosbie they want. Or DCI McLeod, or you.'

Rab shrugged. 'Aye, but . . . without sounding auld-fashioned, we're *men*. It's no' Solomon himself, thanks to the bars he's behind – it'd be his boys. If they'd been told tae intimidate wan of us, they might well start wi' a woman, it's their speciality. An' they're no' the brightest sparks. Blunt instruments, shall we say. Although – the flowers. That isnae just some thug that's done *that*.'

Birch put her elbows on the table, and made a bowl for her head with her laced hands. Her neck ached. She was feeling every second of her sleepless night, all at once.

'You see?' She could tell her own voice was muffled behind her hands and arms and hair. 'It's maddening.'

Birch held her head that way for a long time. She knew she was in danger of dropping off to sleep, in spite of the buzzy overhead lights, the hard plastic table under her elbows and Rab right across from her, waiting for her to speak. She shifted slightly, pressing the heels of her hands into her eye sockets and watching the neon-green fractals her retinas made. She did this for so long that she half expected Rab would have stood and left by the time she sat up again. But no, there he was: leaning back in his chair, his arms folded, his loose gaze fixed on nothing in particular.

'Of course,' he said, when he saw she'd recovered. 'I have tae ask . . .'

Birch blinked. The fractals still swam in her vision. 'Ask what?'

Rab's expression sharpened, and he eyeballed her. 'Charlie,' he said. 'Is there any chance that Charlie really *does* send his love?'

Birch flinched hard, like she'd been slapped. 'I don't know what you mean,' she said, though she did.

'Where *is* Charlie?' Rab kept his arms folded, but pitched forward to rest them on the table. Birch blinked. 'Do you know?'

She felt oddly stung by the question, wondered why he was asking it. Her head fizzed. 'No,' she said. 'There hasn't been a proper lead in fourteen years. A couple of blind alleys, but – no.'

Rab held his hands up, as if she were pointing a gun at him. 'Now, I'm talking just tae talk for a second,' he said. 'But if there's been no evidence . . .'

Birch scraped her chair back, hard, shocking him into silence. She stood. 'No, Rab. Please don't. Please don't speculate like that.'

He looked up at her. His mouth was open, but he didn't look stung. Not exactly.

'It's been fourteen years,' she said. 'If you think I haven't heard every conspiracy theory going, then you're dead wrong. If you think every time I get a cryptic spam email or a mis-sent letter I don't immediately think, It's Charlie, then you're not as smart as I think you are. It's never Charlie. It never has been Charlie. And it's not Charlie now. I'm certain. And the reason I'm certain, is Charlie is dead. He *has* to be dead. There's just no way he could still be alive and me not know about it. It's not him, I'm sure. I'm totally, totally sure.'

She wanted to say more but she didn't really know what. She found her breathing was a little hard.

Rab gave her a look. 'Ye ken, darlin',' he said, 'I find, wi' the benefit of my advancing years, that actually ye cannae be *totally sure* about much.'

Birch closed her eyes. In her head, she was counting. *Eight. Nine. Ten.* 'I know you mean well,' she said. 'But that isn't really very comforting.'

His look turned a little frosty then, but his tone stayed warm. 'It wasn't necessarily meant tae be,' he said. He pushed his own chair back a little, but didn't drop his gaze. 'I'm just tryin' tae get a handle on what's been happening.'

Birch said nothing, though her mind was running: Surely not, she thought. Surely my missing brother wouldn't make himself known by sending me fourteen white lilies? No, she decided. It had been a long time, but she knew Charlie. It just wasn't a Charlie thing to do.

'I'll log this,' Rab was saying. 'It'll go in the Operation Citrine file. I'm sorry tae say it, but there's reason tae think it's maybe connected with Solomon. Senior officer from the raid team starts getting funny phone calls later that same day? An' then a dodgy visit after dark? Sounds like intimidation tactics tae me, hen.'

Birch looked hard at Rab. 'You know way more about Solomon than I do,' she said. 'You've seen how he operates. If this is Solomon, or Solomon's boys, how worried should I be?'

Rab gave a shrug, as though he were shouldering on an invisible coat. 'I'll ask around,' he said, 'see if anyone else oan the team's had calls, or anything else they cannae explain. It might no' just be you. But darlin', I'll be honest wi' ye. Solomon's one radge bastard, a violent, woman-hating bastard, too. I hope for everyone's sake that is aw a coincidence an' nothing tae dae wi' him.'

Birch shivered.

'We'll get ye set up wi' a panic button,' Rab said. 'An' that number I've given ye, my number? That's twenty-four-seven, okay? If ye think the panic button's overkill, I'm there, whatever time. I'm back-up, right?'

She felt sick. She needed to eat something, and to sleep, and to find the elusive missing piece of this weird *why me?* jigsaw she suddenly seemed to be living in. Rab was looking at his watch, preparing to stand. He'd said his piece.

'But if I'm right,' he added, 'ye're due to start interviewing shortly. So you get back up in that office now. I've had they lilies put in the prayer room for ye. DS Scott took the liberty of taking a few photos first, for evidence.'

In spite of herself, Birch managed a smile. 'Thanks, Rab.'

He shrugged, and began to pat himself down for the packet of cigarettes she knew he must have been thinking about all this time, the same way she'd been thinking about checking her phone.

'Nae worries,' he said. 'And ken the phone calls?'

She nodded, slightly rattled by his apparent mind-reading.

'You're right, ignore them,' he said. 'Phone on silent, that's my advice. If it is some nutter calling, dinnae give him the satisfaction. An' if it's Solomon's boys, they'll soon try something else if they cannae get ye that way. Let's see if we can get them tae show their hand, eh?'

Great, Birch thought. Suddenly I'm bait for gangsters. 'Sure,' she said, with forced cheeriness. 'I mean, why not?'

It took them a while, but eventually they started to talk. I've learned now that it's the way of hard cunts – I mean the truly, truly hard bastards of this world – to knock back a few bevvies before they get down to business. One thing a real hard man will never do is look eager. And there's definitely a macho thing about not being the first to speak.

It surprised me that Tsezar broke the silence first. He'd been so quiet and reacted so little to any of his surroundings that I'd started to wonder if he was deaf.

'I don't know why you brought me here,' he said. Then, after a beat, he nodded at me and said, 'And I don't know who this is.'

Tsezar was Ukrainian, I could tell as soon as he began to speak. He spoke a kind of pidgin Russo-Ukrainian: a nearly-but-not-quite Russian that I had to think hard while listening to. Toad seemed unbothered.

'You lost something,' Toad said, 'that belongs to Solomon.'

That was the first time I heard his name. At the time, I hadn't a scooby who Toad was referring to. But something clicked: he'd been calling me lately, dictating to me in Russian while I typed in English, something about a missing *unit*. Those units again.

'It wasn't me,' Tsezar said. 'I'm not there every hour of every day. Someone else was asleep on the job, not me.'

Toad ran one fingertip around the rim of his glass, making a grating hum. 'Where the cloth is thin,' he said, 'that is where it tears.'

I remember making a mental note of the idiom.

'Then speak to Vyshnya.' Tsezar sort of squirmed in his chair, still looking mad as hell but maybe also a little scared. 'She is the *priemnaya mat*.'

It took me a minute, but: *foster mother*.

'I am not going to go dealing with the *nasedka*,' Toad said. 'With the *brothel keeper*. Solomon entrusted you, Tsezar. A man takes responsibility for his women.' He leaned forward then, making the shot glasses clink. 'Always,' he said.

Now I could tell Tsezar was actively trying not to look rattled. I wasn't trying at all. I was confused as all hell, and though I didn't know why I was there I knew it couldn't be good. I wanted to go buy some beers and walk home through the park and get in my shit single bed and close my eyes and sleep.

Toad had other ideas. He ploughed a conspiratorial elbow into my ribs. '*Schenok*,' he said. 'Do you know the saying, *It is a bad workman who has a bad saw?*'

I just nodded, mute.

'And you believe it is true?'

Tsezar looked at me. He wanted me to be on his side, but surely also knew that however stupid I looked (and fuck me, I must have looked stupid), I knew better than to disagree with Toad.

'Sure,' I said.

'And what do you think to this man, who blames his *devushka* for his own failings?'

They both looked at me. I had to say something. As if it might be less committal, I switched to English.

'I reckon that's pretty shady, Toad.'

Tsezar frowned. He hadn't understood.

'He says you are . . .' Toad translated in Russian, and then said a slang word that must have been both unique to Ukrainian and pretty fucking offensive, because suddenly Tsezar was lunging at me across the table, and the old boys with their free Toad beers were looking up, hungry for the fight.

Toad had choreographed this, I could tell. He swung one big arm round Tsezar's bent neck in a way that looked almost affectionate, while I leapt out of my chair and assumed the classic Scottish-man-about-to-fight pose: taking three steps back and balling my fists like a kid in the playground. The shot glasses clattered on the table as Toad wrestled Tsezar towards the door.

'Too much to drink,' he bellowed at the barman as they struggled past. 'I'll take him now.'

He bundled Tsezar, who was now howling obscenities, out through the swing doors. With all the drinkers staring at me, I felt like I had no choice but to follow.

Outside on the pavement, Tsezar had gone quiet and limp. His head was still under Toad's arm, but his struggling had ceased. I saw why: Toad had produced, from somewhere, the first real-life handgun I'd ever seen. He was holding it at waist-height, millimetres from Tsezar's face, half hidden in the folds of his coat. He looked up, making sure I'd seen it too. Holy fuck, had I seen it. I was mesmerised by it. It was entirely black: black barrel, black grip, black slide. It seemed light as air, the way Toad held it, but it also looked like it ought to be heavy as cast iron. It was like a plastic toy, but was also very definitely *not* a plastic toy. My head was mince, looking at it. I had this really fucking disturbing urge to hold it.

'A little walk, now,' Toad said. He disappeared the gun into his coat, and Tsezar straightened up. His eyes looked wet.

'Don't fuck with me, brother,' he said.

Toad just laughed and gave him a shove out into the road, in a long gap between lit night buses. We began to walk, in single file, like ducks: Tsezar in front, glancing back every thirty seconds at Toad. I trailed them, feeling hungry and tired, wanting to peel off and run, but not daring to. Also, I wanted to see what the gun was for. I admit, I wanted to see where this was going.

At that point I didn't know the bit round Kinning Park all that well, but part of me was praying we'd pass a polis station, still open, that I could run into. But to say what? *I've just seen a guy show a gun to another guy?* This was Glasgow for fuck's sake. And for all the bullshit I'd told myself, I knew that by being in with Toad I was in with some fucking headcases. I wanted to run for it. I just didn't quite know how.

So instead we walked into this car park, mostly empty, not lit except for one streetlight right at the front. Big high wall on one side, and all the racket and tangle of the M8 flyover up above.

Shitty flats up at one end, little square windows with tacky coloured blinds. It wasn't tarmacked really, more like potholes and gravel. Long whitewash lines up the walls to show where the spaces divided. I tripped a couple of times. Toad walked us on, right up the middle. At the far end there were a few vans: trade vans, parked for the night.

'Look, Toad.' As we got to the far end, to the darkest bit, Tsezar turned round. He kept walking, only backward, so he could look at Toad while he talked. 'You haven't even given me chance to fix this. I can fix this. I can find her.'

I was following Toad's dark expanse of back. He didn't speak.

'I'll find the bitch,' Tsezar said, 'and I'll cut her fucking legs off. The merchandise would still work, right?'

You know that expression, *my stomach turned*? I'd never known what that meant until right then. Somehow I'd failed to realise that they were talking about a woman. And it all came home to me: the *units* Toad and his pals talked about in their emails? The units were women. And I knew from those emails that the units got transported in shipping containers. I knew where they came from and where they went. I knew that some units were 'kept for personal use', or deemed to be 'below standard'. When Toad said Tsezar had lost a unit, he meant that a woman had gone AWOL.

Toad said nothing. He walked us as far as a battered, dark blue Transit van, parked nose-out against that high wall. It had once had decals that had been peeled or scrubbed. I could make out the words *stove fitters*, where the paintwork had faded around the lettering. Leaning against the inside of the windscreen was one of those stupid personalised number plates that lorry drivers have. 'VIC', it said. The M8 roared in my ears. I found myself wondering who the fuck Vic had been – whether he was a dodgy stove fitter who hung out with guys like Toad, or whether he'd just flogged his old van for cash to some friendly Russian gent who looked rather like a bear. More likely it was nicked. But I half expected that, when Toad led us round to the back of the van, he'd open up the double doors and the shell would be full of flues and firebacks.

But no: it was full of dark. I couldn't see a fucking thing in there at first, but my eyes grew slowly accustomed. Toad sort of cuffed Tsezar up into the van and for a minute, he got swallowed in that darkness, skiting on his arse along the aluminium floor. Then I could see him again, the only thing in the back of the empty van, except for tarps: tarps on the floor, pinned up and lining the walls.

Toad ushered me in, and I ended up standing with him in the box that the two van doors made around us, the big high wall inches off our backs. I realised that, even if someone in those shite flats opposite had looked out with binoculars then, they'd have seen fuck all.

Tsezar's face seemed to glow in the dark, incandescent with terror, and he held his white hands up like pale stars. What little light there was bounced off his wet eyes. I'd never seen proper fear till then – I mean proper fucking primal, animal fear. He was saying something I couldn't pick up, perhaps because it was Ukrainian or perhaps because my brain was flooded with such overwhelming *what the actual fuck* that my old faithful 'natural aptitude' just fell away. Toad took the gun out of his coat again. I didn't dare look at it, but I knew from the way he'd shifted his stance that he'd done it: his feet planted, wider apart, in the weedy gravel.

'I'll tell Vyshnya,' he said, 'that *Schenok* here is in charge now,' and then the sound of the gun going off nearly knocked me over. My ears rang, so I didn't hear the sound of Tsezar's body hitting the back wall of the van's cab. I watched as his legs convulsed, both feet battering against the tarps. I could see a sheen of dark wetness dripping down the van's insides. I waited for Tzesar to scream, or even to rear back up and laugh and tell me it was a joke. But what I heard instead was a sort of terrible, gurgling rattle. Then, quiet. Tzesar's legs went still. His blood spread in a pool underneath him. It was close range, and I guess Toad was a good shot, even in the dark.

I remember saying *fuck*, over and over again – my own voice sounding muffled under the buzzing in my ears – and Toad laughing at me. I just watched a guy die, I thought, and then I couldn't dislodge the thought and it looped round and round in my brain.

Toad reached round, close to me – too close, the proximity made me feel crowded, sick, jumpy. He took hold of the van door on my side and smoothed it shut, letting it click into its fixings with barely a sound. With that done, he pocketed the gun, and used all his weight to slam the other door home. The clang it made didn't sound much like the gunshot to me, but I guess from inside a double-glazed flat two hundred yards away, you could tell yourself you'd heard the two back doors of a Transit van slam shut, and think nothing of it. That night was my first lesson in the fact that people – your average Joes on the street – they *like* to think nothing of it. They like to assume that it's all okay and they can go on living in their not-bad area, as areas go, police station not far away, no, crimes don't happen *here*, not in my street, all that shit. I didn't know about that kind of wilful oblivion . . . not until that night.

And then Toad strolled out from round the back of the van, gallus as anything. I followed him, as best I could. I felt like every thought my brain was capable of having was in my head at that moment: all of them, all at once. I thought he was going to shoot me too. I thought he was going to burst out laughing, open the cab of the van and Tsezar would be sitting there, laughing too, and it had all been some massive inexplicable prank, a hazing for a club I didn't know I'd joined. I thought I might wake up any second, maybe on the floor of my room with an empty Tennent's can in my hand and curse myself for overdoing it, scaring the shit out of myself. But also I was just fucking tired and starving and confused and wanting my bed. I stood at the passenger side of the van's cab and waited for a siren that never came. In the shit flats, not one single blind was pulled up. Not one single curtain seemed to have twitched.

'We have more work for you,' Toad said. He walked round the van's snub nose and opened the passenger door, then held it, like I was the fucking queen.

It was the first time he'd ever said *we*, not *I*, about the work, and that one word, *we*, turned my whole body cold. I remember my hands prickling like the blood had gone out of them.

'But it's full time, *Schenok*,' he said, 'and you start now.'

Birch spent the rest of the day interviewing, her phone set to silent as Rab had instructed. The calls were less frequent now. They were hourly, on the half-hour, instead. Somehow, this was even more disconcerting, like whoever was calling her had moved on to some new set of rules she hadn't yet learned. Beyond the interview room door, the news about Anjan broke in the bullpen. Any time Birch stepped out, she could hear McLeod stomping around, taking his annoyance out on whomever was closest. She was fleetingly grateful, then, that she hadn't been assigned to lead this case. McLeod had never liked Anjan but knew that Birch did – her remark to Amy about DI Crosbie had begun to feel truer. *Rather him than me.*

With the perps, Birch changed tactic. Most were scheduled for release that day unless they could be charged, and in most cases, they couldn't be charged unless they talked. After her meeting with Rab, she'd sifted back through the briefing file on Solomon, and pulled out the most heinous crime scene photos she could find. Grainy, black and white photos of teenage boys with slashed throats, jumped by Solomon's old razor gang. A grisly close-up of a body police had found floating in the Clyde, blue-fleshed and swollen from days submerged in the water. There were many photos of women, too: alive, but sporting injuries inflicted by Solomon himself, or those close to him. Former girlfriends with both eyes so blackened that they'd sealed closed; women with teeth missing, lips burst, cheekbones dislodged. So much purpled flesh, so much ooze and congeal. Birch's stomach turned every time she flipped them over and slapped them on the table between herself and a perp.

'This is who you work for,' she'd say. 'This is the man you're protecting.'

It achieved very little. The interviewees barely raised an eyebrow: they already knew of their boss's long career, what he was capable of. If anything, today they were bolder: their solicitors sat beside them, their mandatory release time ticking ever closer.

One man – a younger guy, perhaps twenty-five or so – did flinch away at the sight of the photos.

'Disturbing, isn't it?' DS Scott cut in.

'Aye,' the man said. He was almost laughing. 'Why d'ye think I'm no' saying a word, pal? Think I want tae end up like that?'

At lunchtime, Amy dropped by to see her: Birch knew it was her from the thud-thud, thud-thud of her high heels, then the pause outside the door before she knocked.

'Come in, Amy,' she called, and Amy elbowed in through the door with a coffee cup in each hand and a pair of clingfilmed baguettes tucked under one arm.

'Peace offering,' she said, wobbling the coffee down into Birch's hand, and letting the sandwiches roll onto the desk. 'I'm so sorry, marm. About the whole *you've got a suitor* line. I had no idea.'

Birch smiled, and studied the baguettes: cheese ploughman's, coronation chicken.

'It's okay,' she said. 'You weren't to know.'

Amy pointed at the sandwiches. 'Your pick,' she said. 'I've no preference.'

When Birch went for the cheese, she saw from Amy's face that she'd chosen correctly.

'So what's going on,' she asked, picking at the clingfilm, 'on your side of the fence? Any logistical movement?'

Amy sighed. 'Only the slowest kind,' she said. 'I mean, I came in to tell you the one piece of good news: we got the extension. Ninety-six hours we can hold Solomon without charge.'

Birch raised her coffee cup in a *cheers* gesture. 'Wahey,' she said, 'that's a relief.'

'Yeah. But the first twenty-four are already up. All the low-level guys are being released as we speak.'

Birch balled up her peeled clingfilm and threw it, overarm, in the direction of her wastepaper bin. It missed.

'I had a feeling,' she said. 'My interviews were like talking to a brick wall. But nothing stuck to *any* of them?'

'Well,' Amy said. 'Obviously there were so many arrested. We've only got Solomon's crew at this station, the ones picked up along-side him on the eastern harbourside. Drylaw and St Leonard's got some of the others, Gayfield got the ones off the boats, who didn't seem to speak English. I don't know what's going on with them other than hearsay, but it sounds like at least some will be charged. The raid brought in a huge haul of . . . whatever you call it.'

Birch raised her eyebrows. 'Flakka,' she said. 'We think.'

'Right,' Amy said. 'But it's all still with the lab. There are bets on round the office that it's heroin, or crack. Whatever it is, some of the guys were arrested literally *carrying* it, so it's likely there'll be some possession with intent to supply, smuggling charges, etcet-era. The other stations are dealing with that. But I'd be willing to bet it's the same as here, and no one's talking.'

Birch gave a low whistle. It was just like Rab had said, last night in the pub: *They'll go off to the jail like lambs.*

'But no charges here?' Birch asked. 'Nothing for Solomon's entourage?'

Amy shook her head. 'I mean, not much from what I hear. One had marijuana on him so he's up for possession; a couple had falsified documents, credit cards and stuff. They're claiming they had no idea, the usual, so I think we're hosting *them* for a little longer.' She stopped speaking for a moment, to shrug. 'But other-wise, they're all headed to the pub right about now.'

Birch snorted. 'Yeah, them and their lawyers. I couldn't get through to a single one. It's a real bitch.'

Amy was nodding. 'It was always a long shot,' she said, 'that any of them might testify against Solomon, right?'

'Hmm.' Birch was thinking about Rab: their conversation in Kay's Bar, then in the canteen. His kindness. Why was he being so nice to her? She tried to snap back in. 'I mean, yeah; from the sounds of things, Solomon and his higher-ups don't look kindly on those who grass.'

'Honour among thieves.'

'Yeah,' Birch said. 'The worst kind of honour. Was it Shakespeare said that?'

Amy smiled. 'Common misattribution – Shakespeare said thieves had *no* honour. It was actually Walter Scott.'

Birch narrowed her eyes. 'I'm not sure whether to call bullshit,' she said, 'or bagsy you for the next team-building pub quiz.'

'I'd probably disappoint, I'm useless under pressure.' Amy grinned, but quiet fell between them.

'What I can't get over,' Birch said, speaking into it, 'is this informant. *Someone* obviously thought it was worth their while to talk.'

Amy was nodding. 'Yeah . . . and look what happened to *him*. Cautionary tale, I guess.'

Birch flinched. 'Wait,' she said, 'what do you know that I don't? Has the informant turned up dead?'

'Oh. No, sorry. Just speculation on my part. But it's what every-one's saying. Bit convenient, no, that he's disappeared without trace? My theory is Solomon knows he talked, found him, and shut him up.'

Birch realised she had to agree. 'Makes sense,' she said. 'Solomon has form for disappearing canaries – it's in the file. It's just a real bitch for us. It would all have been open and shut if the guy could have testified. I don't know who in Glasgow he was talking to, but I suspect their head will roll for letting him run, right on the eve of the operation.'

Amy was looking at her, and Birch reddened. As a senior officer, she probably ought not to speculate on the conduct of her colleagues, especially when she'd recently had her own wrists slapped.

'So,' Amy said, after a moment. 'What does an underappreci-ated woman work on when her case is wasting away under a less qualified DI, anyway?'

Birch flushed. 'All right, keep your voice down. Door's open.'

Amy only grinned wider. 'Everyone thinks it, marm,' she said. 'Even DCI McLeod is regretting his life choices, I think.'

Birch pulled a face. 'All he's missing is the chance to tell me he was always right not to trust Anjan,' she said, 'and lawyers are all the same and can't be trusted, blah blah blah. Bet DI Crosbie's just loving that little speech.'

'Oh trust me,' Amy said, jerking her head backward in the direction of the bullpen, 'we're all of us basking in the glow of his current Zen state.'

'Jeez, I'm sorry.'

Amy shrugged. 'It's all right. The place wouldn't feel like home otherwise.'

Amy rewrapped the two-thirds of coronation chicken sandwich she hadn't eaten. Birch had put what was left of her cheese ploughman's – not more than a couple of bites at the snub end of the baguette – down on the desk. She sometimes forgot how dainty Amy's manners were.

'No all-nighters, that's the main thing.' Amy stood, the sandwich in one hand, her untouched coffee in the other. Birch wondered if this was a comment on her bloodshot eyes. 'I'll leave you to it, marm.'

'Give 'em hell, Kato,' she said, as Amy juggled her unfinished lunch to pull the door closed.

Quiet settled on the office then. Birch looked down at the Lockley file in front of her, and the words swam into moving, furry lines. Why *was* Rab being so kind to her? she found herself thinking again. If she concentrated, she could feel the scribbled business card in her blouse pocket. It was comforting to have someone to call. Right, Helen? Comforting. Yes, it was.

Back home, she wedged Rab's business card on the mantelpiece, in the corner of the brass frame that held a photo of her mother. It sat there almost like a caption in an art gallery – like the woman in the photo had been named BIG RAB – and had it not been the photo it was, Birch imagined she might have been amused. Instead, she was trying in vain to relax. It was a wild night outside: the weather forecast said gusts of up to 70 mph were due, but above the roof of her little terraced house it seemed as though they'd already arrived. She'd parked her car elsewhere: a few blocks up in a crescent-shaped residential street, nearer to Portobello's main drag. She'd then walked those few blocks along the prom, in spite of the squall of weather that seemed to be blowing in straight off the sea. Had she walked up the road, any dark-coloured Merc driving by could have spotted her, but the prom was largely deserted. A couple of hardy joggers pounded past, and she saw a few cyclists weaving back and forth in the wind, their helmet-mounted strobe-lights guttering. She'd let herself into the house in the dark, and before locking the front door made a full patrol of every room, the same as she had this morning. The wardrobe, the under-stairs cupboard, the garden with its uncut grass blustering wildly. She'd done this without putting lights on: instead, she'd used the pin-point torch on her mobile phone, feeling like Dana Scully in *The X-Files*. In one hand, the torch, and in the other, her baton: a poor substitute for Scully's Walther PPK.

With her search complete, Birch locked both doors, then traversed the house once more in the dark, closing curtains and blinds. No lights on this time: as far as the rest of the world was concerned, she was out. No car outside, no windows lit. Nobody home.

She'd allowed herself a few tealights, dotted about the lounge. In this room, the curtains were thick and the blinds were closed behind them. One flame burned beside her mother's photo, making the picture seem to move in small jerks like the slow frames of a silent movie. BIG RAB, read the caption. On the walls, the candle shadows danced in time with the building wind.

'This is ridiculous,' she said to herself, startling at the sound of her own voice. 'You don't know the calls and the flowers are connected. Not for sure. You don't know if *anything's* connected.' But she couldn't shake Rab's words: *Let's see if we can get them to show their hand.* She hadn't seen him again that day: he and DI Crosbie had been locked in one endless interview with Solomon, still ongoing as she left the station. She didn't know if Rab had managed to ask whether anyone else on Operation Citrine had been phoned, or experienced unusual behaviour. It might not just be her. But anyway, staying in the dark felt safer.

She'd made toast: the only thing she didn't need light for. She hadn't even needed to open the fridge. She'd made four slices, spread two with peanut butter and the other two with chocolate spread. A two-course meal, she thought, as she crunched through the first slice, enjoying the salt slick on the roof of her mouth. Tea of champions. Eating like a queen.

She was trying to keep her spirits up, wartime bomb-shelter style. But it wasn't working: really, she was listening, coiled tight as a mantrap. Clenched between her knees, a cup of tea was turning cold. She'd tried playing a podcast, the volume kept low, but it spooked her, those alien voices in her house. Now she just listened to the wind, the way it rattled the windows. The way it sounded like feet on her chapped upstairs floors; like big men wrestling through the garden hedge to press themselves up to the windows, scrabble at the door. Through her teeth, she cursed it. On her phone screen, a new missed call flashed up, marking the half-hour exactly. She picked up the panic button Rab had requisitioned for her, but she couldn't call for back-up just because she felt a little spooked.

In the kitchen, the infernal ticking of the clock.

Birch shuddered awake as though she'd been kicked. I'm on the couch, she thought. Why am I on the couch? Then she remembered.

Around her, the tealights had burned out. At some point she must have lain down: her head was on the padded sofa arm with a cushion wedged under her neck. The position was painful. She'd pulled a throw halfway over herself, but the room felt cold. She needed to pee. That must have been what woke her. Birch lay there a while, her body a stiff Z, marvelling at the fact she'd slept at all. I was tired, she remembered, I was so tired. Then she kicked herself: but Helen, you were meant to be listening.

And yes, wait – there was a noise. A small, deliberate noise: not the banging about of the weather outside, but a hand-made noise, like the plucking of a harp-string without the note. Behind her, beyond the sofa-back, the hallway door was ajar. And on the other side, at the front door, a series of delicate clicks. She froze. *This* was what had woken her. Outside, somebody was picking the lock.

She felt her body kick up through its gears, towards fight or flight. Okay, Helen, she thought, trying to keep herself level. Okay. You have a few seconds. Let's think about what to do.

Birch had played these kinds of *what if?* games with friends and colleagues many a time over the years. *There's a zombie apocalypse, what do you do? Your house is on fire, what one thing do you save?* Now there was someone breaking into her house: where did she want to be? Top of the stairs, she thought, armed. Best defensive position. But she didn't fancy her chances of getting up there before the front door opened: she definitely didn't want to come face to face with whoever was on the other side, or, worse, be caught retreating with her back turned. Can you get out through the kitchen? She glanced past her feet at the back door. Yes: but she remembered the dark-coloured Merc. These guys didn't work alone. The garden wall was eight feet high and she wasn't the climber that the skull bloke was. She'd be cornered. She *was* cornered. Oh fuck, Helen, she thought. Oh fuck, oh fuck, oh fuck . . .

The final click was louder than the rest, and then there was a more familiar noise: the lock sliding back and the door leaning inward on its hinges. The wind whipped in through the gap: above her, the lampshade swung on its flex. Her phone was out of reach on the mantelpiece: she'd have needed to stand up in order to reach it. The panic button was somewhere near it, though in the dim light she couldn't make it out. But her baton was on the floor beside the couch. She dipped a silent hand from under the blanket, and gripped it, imagining the best way to swing the weapon, depending on how an assailant might approach. They don't know you're here, she told herself. They don't know you're here . . .

The lock-picker stepped into the hallway: Birch felt the air in the house change as he – she assumed – pushed the front door slowly, slowly closed. He was alone, she was almost sure: only one set of feet had padded in over the spiky hall mat. Only one. Okay, good. The lock clicked back into its groove. Now they were alone together.

Go upstairs, she willed him. On the table, that tantalising distance away, her phone display read 02:47. It's three in the morning. Assume I'm asleep, and go upstairs. But as though he'd heard her command, she felt him lean on the living room door, and slink his way inside.

Oh Jesus. Now the man was walking past the sofa: she felt him run his hand along its padded back, just inches above her. In the dark, she'd be a greyish mass – a pile of cushions, the detritus of any living room. I'm just cushions, she shouted in her head, as if she could will herself to disappear. Don't look any closer.

She could hear his breathing: yes, this was a man. He sounded winded, as if he'd been running. She could feel him trying to still himself, could see the dark shape of him as he stood at the far corner of the couch, his back turned to her. Had she been better positioned, she could have reared up then and felled him, or at the very least made a break for the door. But she was still in that same weird Z shape, her legs half tangled in the blanket, her neck pulled into a searing twist so she could watch him move around. He calmed himself, then listened, his head cocked. She held her breath, imagined he could hear her heart, as loud in her ears as a gunning motorbike. Somehow, through the noise of her panic she heard her mother's voice then, soothing as it ever got: *Fear makes the wolf look bigger.* It was a saying she'd used only rarely, but one that Birch had liked and stored away. Now, it made her focus. This is a crime scene. Get a description.

Okay. This wasn't a tall man – he'd be five eight or so, she guessed – but he was big. Broad in the shoulders. She could see his neck was thick, even in the dark. She'd be no match for him, even though she had height on her side. Fuck . . .

He'd stopped listening. As she watched, he padded away from her, into the doorway of the kitchen. He paused there again, and then – to her horror – he flicked on the torch on his phone, and swept it around the kitchen. She registered a dark red jacket, Harrington style, with tartan at the neck. Mousy hair, longish on top, with a trendy fade on the back and sides. Tattoos: on the back of the neck, on the backs of the ears, perhaps on the face. Black jeans. A textbook thug. In her head, she began to pray to something, anything at all. For a moment, the phone torch had thrown an oblong of light back across the couch, illuminating her pale, scared face, the useless baton shaking in her hand. *Don't let him turn around, don't let him turn around, don't let him . . .*

Something heard her. Instead of turning, the tattooed man stepped sideways, disappearing into the long leg of her galley kitchen's L. He must have propped up his phone somewhere, because the light became still. She heard him open a cupboard – the one with the mugs in, the one that creaked – and hiss out a curse.

This was it. Her one chance. Fight or flight, what's it to be? She allowed herself the briefest half-second fantasy of vaulting the couch and nipping out through the front door, phone in hand, without him even noticing: she could pelt along the prom to the car, mash the panic button and call the boys in, or even just bang on a neighbour's front door and fall on their mercy. But no. It was risky: if these guys were smart, they'd have another of their number stationed at the gate. They might be armed. They might have found the car. No. Okay, Helen. Fight it is.

She kicked the blanket off her legs and it shushed to the floor. The tattooed man was rattling around now – carefully, but making a little noise. Looking for something, opening drawers. She unfolded herself off the couch, thanking herself for apparently kicking her shoes off before she'd lain down. She picked up her phone, and felt better to be holding it, but still, she didn't want to illuminate the screen and risk catching his attention. She swept a hand across the mantelpiece, and almost cursed aloud as she felt the panic button drop to the floor. She bit her lip. *Idiot, idiot, idiot.* It was now somewhere in the dark well between the fireplace and the coffee table. She ran a hand around in front of her feet, but could feel only carpet. Okay, stupid, she thought. What's Plan B?

Her first move was to zigzag out of the man's line of sight. The shadows thrown by his phone's white light were a thin comfort, but she padded through them to the threshold of the kitchen door. Remember to breathe, Helen. But she couldn't. The tattooed man was feet away: a stud wall all that stood between her and whatever he'd come here to do.

She could hear him still rooting about, trying to be quiet but growing annoyed, she could tell. What was he *looking* for? A weapon? Something to hurt her with? The knives were in their block by the sink, clearly visible. Wait – was this a random break-and-enter, not Solomon's goons out to get her at all? She almost laughed. Was this man just looking for her valuables? If she stood here quietly enough, might he just nick the telly and then disappear?

Just as she was forming the thought, the tattooed man fucked up. He opened the low-level cupboard at the kitchen's far end, the one she threw her baking trays and cooling racks into and never tidied out. Every time, that cupboard avalanched a clatter of tins and lids out onto the floor, and every time she'd think, Fucking bastard swining thing, and promise herself that one day soon she'd clean it out and keep it all better in future. But now she thanked the lucky star of her own domestic sluttery, as the cupboard performed its party trick and she heard the tattooed man drop to his knees to try to stop the cascade. She stepped into the kitchen, vision twinging at the edges, her hearing cutting in and out with terror. Don't you dare fucking faint, she thought, as she closed the three-pace gap between her baton-end and the back of his vulnerable neck. He was scrabbling on hands and knees, bent almost foetal, trying to stuff the noise he'd made back into the unit and close the door. As she flicked on the kitchen light, Birch registered tattoos on the backs of his hands, and lettering on his knuckles: B-A-B-Y G-I-R-L. Birch looked at the baton and realised it wasn't enough. She tucked her phone under her arm, lunged for the knives and pulled the largest she could reach from the block: its serrated blade flashed under the ceiling light.

'Police!' Birch yelled, summoning as much ferocity as her terrified body could muster. 'I am armed and I am pissed off and you are in my fucking house.' She heard her voice cracking at the edges: fear and rage. 'So I highly recommend you do not move, not one *fucking inch*, do you hear me?'

She stiffened, waiting for him to whip round and lunge at her. But instead, the tattooed man obliged. He let his arms go limp, and as he did, the cupboard swung back open, the baking trays all slithering out around his knees. After the noise subsided, there was a moment of calm: outside, the wind seemed to have died. Behind her on the wall, the clock ticked. Oh shit, Birch thought. What do I do now? Her phone was wedged in her armpit, her hands full of weapons.

The tattooed man shifted his weight.

'Fucking stay still, I said!' Birch heard her own voice reverberate off the tiles.

Then, without moving, the man spoke. 'I'm not going to hurt you,' he said. 'I'm not armed. But will you just keep your voice down, please?'

After that, things happened one by one. Birch lost her grip on the big knife and it hit the flagged floor, ricocheting under the dishwasher and out of reach. She felt something give inside her, like someone had clipped an invisible drawstring. She blinked hard to right herself, and saw that the tattooed man was uncurling out of his crouch. The arm she'd been holding the baton with went slack. The stick's thin end hit the floor and then it, too, fell from between her fingers. As the man turned round to face her, she fell to her knees on the cold floor. I said don't you dare faint, she thought, but knew it was too late now. He stood over her, one hand held out as though he might place it on her head, a blessing.

'Hello, Nella,' he said.

Birch went blind. The high wind had started up again, only now it was inside her head, it was all she could hear.

'Charlie,' she heard herself say, and then everything was gone.

Wednesday

Birch sat up. She'd been lying on her kitchen floor. She didn't know why. The light was on above her, scalding white: it reminded her of the banks of lights in the hospital where she'd had to take her mother all those times. So bright. All the lights in the house were on, in fact. It was dark outside. And out there in the dark, something was looking for her. Something wanted to get in.

Someone was in the room with her. Birch looked up. Her mother was sitting on top of one of the kitchen cabinets, swinging her legs. She looked healthy, strong, younger than Birch herself. The cabinets were impossibly high: they made Birch feel small, like Alice in Wonderland in the court of the Queen of Hearts. Her mother looked at her.

'Why are you lying on the floor?' She was laughing.

Birch remembered, but only as she said it. 'I fainted,' she said. 'Because I thought Charlie was here. There was a man here, and he had Charlie's voice. When he turned round he had Charlie's face, too. Didn't you see him?'

Her mother's smile disappeared. 'Don't be ridiculous,' she said, but the voice that came out of her mouth was Birch's own. 'Haven't you always told me that Charlie's dead? Charlie's dead. Charlie's dead.'

It became a taunt, her mother's voice shrinking to that of a petty schoolgirl, singsong in its mocking.

'Charlie's dead! Charlie's dead! *You* always told me Charlie was dead!'

'Maybe I was wrong, Mum.' Birch had to raise her voice above her mother's chant, which looped back and forth like an old record with a scratch. 'I might have been wrong. I'm sorry. I'm sorry, Mum. I'm sorry.'

'Helen?'

Someone else was speaking now. Her mother was still chanting, swinging her legs, battering her heels against the coated MDF doors of the cupboards. But the new voice was louder.

'Helen. Helen.'

Birch put her hands over her ears.

'Nella. Please.'

Birch sat up. She'd been lying on her kitchen floor. She didn't know why. Then she turned her head, and saw a terrible, frightening man. A man who looked so like her little brother that she couldn't look at him for long. A man with tattoos all over his hands. A man who looked like he might be able to bodily lift her and, if he wanted to, break her in two. A man who had her biggest carving knife in his hand, pulled out from under the dishwasher. And now that man had the audacity to speak to her in her brother's voice.

'Nella. Oh fuck. Thank God.'

He was kneeling about three feet away – far enough that he didn't have to touch her. His face was a mask of pain: he pitied her, she could see that, but it was as though he were behind glass, forbidden to come any closer. He looked abject, such a big man folded down onto his knees, squashed into the narrow gap of the galley kitchen. Such a big man. Birch's mind refused to wrap around the sheer bulk of him. This man who was trying so hard to look like Charlie. But Charlie was never this . . . *macho*.

'Jesus,' she said.

'Yeah.' The man who was and was not Charlie looked away then, and lifted a hand to rub at the back of his huge neck. 'Um. You passed out. I'm sorry, Nella. I didn't mean to freak you out that much.'

'Fuck,' she said. She put her hands on the lino and slithered up onto her knees, then stood. Her head buzzed. She set one hip against the worktop, and teetered there.

The man who was in her kitchen, the tattooed man who looked like Charlie, unfolded himself as she did. He held his free hand towards her, palm up, as though trying to stop traffic. If she fell, he'd catch her, the gesture said. But she managed to stand, and not fall.

'Just take it easy,' he said.

Birch felt the blood sloshing back into her head, returning to its nooks and alleyways. The fuzz at the edges of her vision began to subside. She could hear him as he said again, 'Take it easy.' His palm still outstretched.

Birch looked at him. Her brother. Charlie. Her dead brother. In her kitchen, in Portobello, after fourteen years. Fourteen awful, miserable years.

'Take it easy,' she echoed. 'Take it, fucking, *easy*? Are you *fucking kidding me?*'

Charlie closed his eyes. 'Nella,' he said, and she watched as bright seams of tears formed under his lashes. 'I'm sorry. I'm so, so sorry.'

She flew at him then. She didn't know why, exactly: the fuzz on her vision turned the colour of blood, just like people said. She saw red. She lunged for the kitchen knife.

Charlie was quicker: she must still have been sluggish from coming round. He tossed the knife into the stainless-steel sink. When her body hit his, she had nothing to attack with but her own fists. He allowed her one decent right hook to his cheek before easily neutralising her, in spite of their difference in height, each of her wrists locked inside his big hands, and pulled down so her elbows were pinned at her sides. Birch writhed in his grip: he was strong, but she was self-defence trained and had sparred with bigger men than him on the gym mat. For around a minute they grappled in the weird little aisle of the kitchen, battering this way and that against the cabinets, her socks making her feet skid on the flags.

The whole time, he chanted at her: 'Nella, I'm sorry, please. I'm so sorry. I'm so, so sorry. Nella, stop. Please. I'm sorry.'

She knew she couldn't keep it up. She was weakened from fainting, from lack of sleep, from the adrenalin spike he'd given her breaking in – a high from which she was now plummeting.

He could feel the rage in her subsiding, she knew. His grip on her wrists became looser. Then all at once he let go entirely, and wrapped both those huge arms around her shoulders. She let Charlie hold her up, the muscles in his arms like mooring ropes as she bent to press her face in under his chin. He pulled her body in close and crushed her there, his breath ragged in his chest. Charlie was crying.

'You were dead,' she said, and when her voice came out bubbled and spitty she realised she was crying too. 'You were dead, we all thought you were dead, Charlie . . .'

She could smell him, now, too. Charlie, she thought. Yes, this is Charlie. You can imitate someone's voice, you can bear a striking resemblance . . . but there's no faking someone's smell. And the smell brought an onrush of old memories so vivid she wasn't sure she could bear them. Charlie aged six, climbing into her bed to tell her, *Nella, there's a thunderstorm, and I'm not frightened but I thought you might be frightened so I've come to take care of you*. Charlie, aged thirteen, spraying aftershave on for the first time in front of the hall mirror, and her teasing him mercilessly. Charlie, aged eighteen, blind drunk on his birthday and leaning on her as she half led, half carried him *somewhere* – where, she didn't know. The memory had fractured. But she remembered that smell: his skin, warm and familiar, wrapped around her like a scarf.

'I'm sorry, Nella,' he said into her hair. 'I'm so sorry for what I've put you through.'

She had to pull away then. The memories – coursing through her, filling her with a strange, resentful warmth – were too much.

'Okay,' she said. 'Okay.'

Charlie's arms opened, but he placed one hand on each of her shoulders, as though he still wasn't quite sure that she wouldn't fall down. She found herself stooping the three inches or so to match her brother's height: it was muscle-memory, a thing she always used to do. She looked him in the face, refusing to flinch her gaze away, though every nerve in her brain seemed to be telling her to.

She pulled a long stream of air in through her nose, in an attempt to stop crying. 'I'm going to need you to tell me,' she said – and she heard her own voice come out strangled and cold – 'where the fuck you've been.'

Just for a split second, Charlie smiled, but when he spoke again his voice was stony, too. 'I will, Nella. I'll tell you everything, I promise.' He was still holding her shoulders, and now he gave her a little shake. 'I absolutely promise. But . . .'

Birch followed his gaze as he looked up at the kitchen clock: 3.20 a.m.

'It might take a while,' he said.

She shrugged out of his loose grip, and tilted her chin up. She was exhausted, she realised, but the thought of *waiting* to hear what Charlie had to say was utterly unbearable.

'Then it'll take a while,' she said. 'I want all of it. Every single fucking minute. Fourteen years. You're going to tell me the *whole thing*.'

Charlie cast his eyes down, then. 'Okay,' he said. 'But before I do, and you maybe hate me, I just want to say . . . it's so good to see you. I missed you.'

He smiled, for the first time. Birch wanted to hit him and hug him all at once. She'd missed it so much, that dirty joke of a smile. It rendered her speechless.

'You still look kinda . . . green, though,' Charlie went on. 'Go sit down, and I'll make you a cuppa. Okay?'

Birch raised an eyebrow. 'I'd prefer a whisky right now,' she said.

Her brother flushed. 'That's what I was looking for,' he said. 'In the cupboards. I was going to sit down here, wait for you to get up in the morning. I just wanted a wee nip.'

She smiled. She couldn't help herself. As a student, Charlie had developed a rep for this: at house parties, if no one had opened the booze he'd brought along, he'd take it away again. He'd rifle through other people's cupboards to find the good stuff, the hard liquor, and help himself. Looking at him was exceptionally hard: he was so much someone else, so much a stranger. But yes, as well as that, he was still Charlie.

'It's in the living room. On the floor at the end of the sofa. I needed a bevvy last night.' She remembered the time and corrected herself. 'Monday night. I'd had a *day*.'

It occurred to Charlie: she saw it happen.

'The anniversary,' he said, 'of the night I left.'

'Yeah.' She had no other words for him right then.

For a few moments they stood and looked at each other, the clock clicking its tongue. She could feel herself swaying slightly, the blood that had rushed out of her head still trickling back.

'Okay,' Birch said at last. 'Glasses are in the top cupboard. First one you looked in, the one that creaks.'

He grinned at her, and she had to turn away. Somehow, she made it to the kitchen door, but then turned.

'Charles Arthur Birch,' she said. 'Don't you fucking dare go anywhere, you hear me?'

Charlie didn't reply, but he lifted one big hand to his temple, and – with a solemn look on his face – gave a salute. She heard him flick on the kettle as she lit new tealights on the fireplace. Behind her, he turned off the kitchen light and the house became half lit, eerie once again.

'What's with the dark?' she called back. He was still messing with crockery in there, and she knew she'd made him jump: she heard a teaspoon rattle on the counter.

'Keeping a low profile,' he said, watching her as he manoeuvred into the room. He nodded at the mug he was carrying. 'I thought maybe coffee? Better for staying up late.'

Birch stepped away from the fireplace, took the mug from him. She wanted to cry. He'd remembered how she took her coffee, after all these years.

'Wee dram as well,' he said, pointing to the whisky, and setting down two glasses. 'Like you asked.'

Birch wasn't sure what to do with herself as he settled: she didn't want to sit on the sofa next to him, though she wasn't quite sure why. Knowing it was weird to be standing there over him, she moved past the coffee table and put herself in the uncomfortable rocking chair she never used. It was beside the fire: diagonally across from him now, she could see the moving shadows those fake flames cast on his face.

Charlie was holding his own whisky between both hands. He'd poured himself at least a quadruple measure.

'Talisker,' he said, nodding down at the tumbler. 'Nice.'

'Charlie.' His name was like a soor ploom in her mouth: she wanted to turn it over and over, as though trying to outrun its sourness. 'You said . . . why are you keeping a low profile?'

He turned away from the whisky and looked at her. It hit her then that he carried no bag, was wearing nothing more than a light coat over his hoodie. He looked tired, and as though he might not have washed. Why had he come in the middle of the night – why hadn't he rung the doorbell at 8 a.m. when she'd got up, or phoned the office?

'You're in trouble.' It wasn't a question. Looking at him then, she knew it.

Charlie pinched the bridge of his nose, hard, between thumb and forefinger. This was a grown-up mannerism, one she didn't recognise.

'You could say that,' he said. 'You could say I'm in some deep shit, Nella.'

He squeezed his eyes closed, then released his grip. 'It's basically the same deep shit,' he said, 'that's had me AWOL for fourteen years. Or at least . . . it's a variation on the deep shit theme, you know?'

Birch felt her face harden. 'No, I don't know,' she said. 'Tell me.'

Her brother took a deep breath. She watched his shoulders swell and then subside, like a wave.

'All right,' he said.

She waited.

'About this time two days ago you and your lot ran a dawn raid, codenamed Operation Citrine. An informant told you that Glasgow gangland bastard extraordinaire Solomon Carradice was bringing a small flotilla of unauthorised craft into the harbour at Granton. Boats small enough to get into that wee, tidal, out-of-the-way harbour with its long dark walkways and its weekend pleasure boats. You guys have suspected for a while that Solomon's been using alternative entry points to bring shit into this country without detection. Glasgow's a pain in the arse these days, too many hoops to jump, regulations, officialdom – not to mention undercover polis hanging about. So you reckoned he'd been using smaller ports. Oban, Eyemouth. Fucking *Ullapool*. But Granton's Edinburgh, near the action. Bring a crab-boat full of smack in there and you can have some kid in Muirhouse peddling it before the morning's out. And Solomon's getting old. He's not really one for patience these days.'

Birch realised she was holding her breath. Charlie had information on Operation Citrine that even she wasn't party to.

'So anyway,' he went on. 'Your informant tells you that this is the test run, this is the first crack at a Granton landing, so Solomon's got his biggest boys out there making sure it goes smoothly. He's out there himself, even, which is rare: he's standing out in the cold with a walkie and binoculars. He's waiting for the all-clear. The whole gang is there. Drivers with vans waiting to unload the gear. Foreign associates with skin in the game. Dealers with scales in their back pockets wanting first dibs. This shipment's mainly flakka: you know? *Bath salts*, it also gets called. Sometimes *gravel*. It's massive in Russia, and basically unchecked. There's even an idiom.'

Charlie said something in Russian. Birch blinked. One of her mother's theories had been that he must have gone to Russia, like he always wanted to. Birch never allowed her mother to believe that he'd just up and go, never contact them, and never come back . . . but hearing his fluent tongue now, she wondered if, in fact, Mum had been right.

'It translates,' he was saying, 'to *there is as much salt in Siberia as there is snow. Salt* meaning bath salts. The country is awash with it – it's bigger there than heroin. Of course that's right up Solomon's street, and he wants a piece of it.'

Birch held up her hands, overwhelmed. 'Charlie, wait,' she said. 'How the *hell* do you know about Operation Citrine?'

His eyebrows knitted. Under his left eye, a scar she couldn't bear to look at twitched like an insect. He was looking at her as though she were stupid.

'I'm the informant, Nella,' he said. 'I *am* Operation Citrine.'

I found out later that Toad had been cutting corners with me. He wasn't supposed to need the help of a translator – he was supposed to do the shit he did himself. But he'd got out of his depth. His English wasn't good enough and he didn't want them to know. So he'd been outsourcing his written communication to me and hoping no one would catch on.

Turns out, even a thug can spot the difference when a middle-aged Russian dude whose phrases usually sound ever-so-slightly lost in translation starts writing English like a native, overnight. Toad's a sly bastard, and a hard bastard, and weirdly he's also what the Glaswegians might call a *pure sound cunt* . . . but in many ways, he's not the sharpest tool in the box. He's been in the game a long time, since the days before email and smartphones and cryptocurrencies. Toad can remember when it was all about driving a nicked car with the boot full of contraband cigarettes across some rural European border crossing. The kind of guy who still gets his porn from magazines. And that was essentially what fucked up my whole life.

One of the higher-ups caught wind that Toad was getting help with his homework. He had to fess up he'd been paying me – from his own pocket, mind, he wasn't stupid – to help him with sensitive correspondence relating to just about every nefarious racket that Solomon and his boys had running. But Toad was from the *vory v zakone*, the top tier of Russian ex-cons, and commanded an impressive network of *bandity* across the Russian Federation and Eastern Europe. He was a trusted guy whose name opened doors. Lucky for him – and me – or we'd likely have found ourselves at the bottom of some deep, rarely visited stretch of the good old

Clyde. They couldn't lose him. But something had to be done about this twenty-year-old kid who was running around with no real loyalty to anyone and a laptop full of damning evidence.

When I say Toad's a sound cunt, I know it's messed up, given everything he's done. But to be fair he did also save my life. They were all ready to disappear me, turn over my flat, get hold of the laptop and anything else incendiary that I might have lying around. Wipe it out. Wipe *me* out. For a few days there, I was blithely walking around while somewhere in a darkened room (I always imagined a darkened room, maybe with a poker table and ciga-rette smoke, like the movies) a bunch of hard bastards thought about how they'd get rid of me. But Toad got shirty, thank fuck. Turns out I hadn't been imagining the weird brand of fatherly pseudo-friendship he'd developed. Toad was fond of me. Toad wanted to keep me around. And eventually, he got his way. I never forgot that I owed him.

After we'd dispatched Tsezar, Toad drove us up onto the flyover and through the sickly orange streetlights of Glasgow. I let him. I sat in the passenger seat of Vic's old van and tried not to throw up. When we turned a particularly big sweep of a corner, I felt Tsezar's body roll across the floor of the van and hit the partition, right behind my seat. I really hoped he was fully dead. Like, *really* hoped.

Somehow, I fell asleep on that drive. I was already tired and hungry and I guess the adrenalin that came from watching a radge Ukrainian guy get shot right in front of me ran out faster than you'd think, and I had nothing left. When I woke up, the engine was quiet and Toad was gone from the driver's seat. I had no bear-ings at all. It was dark. I couldn't find my phone – turned out Toad had lifted it while I was asleep, and I never saw it again. Like a fucking useless idiot I just sat there: cold and tired and terrified out of my wits.

Eventually Toad came back, opened the passenger door, and hauled me out. I walked round the back of the van and saw that the doors were open and the inside was empty. Whatever was left of Tsezar had disappeared.

From that yard we walked through a wee ginnel and then in through a door that had a push-button code and swivel handle like they put on the toilet doors in city centre coffee shops. I could smell the Clyde – boat fuel and salt – somewhere nearby. Toad led me through this maze of a building, past a lot more push-button locks, a lot of unseen voices. I don't remember much else, other than following the moving mountain of Toad's back, thinking about how I'd become an accessory to murder, and wondering how the fuck I was ever going to get myself out of this.

'What is this place?' I asked.

Toad half turned as he walked.

'The Gym,' he said. 'The ground floor? It is a gym complex owned by the boss. You can use it for free, if you are a gym person. I am not.'

That went without saying.

'Up here? Other things. I will show you.'

We got to a door that was different to the rest, in that Toad stopped outside it, fumbled with the little stainless-steel numbered lock, punched in the code. There were voices inside – not loud enough for me to make out words, just a low hum. At the sound of the keypad's *ka-dunk, ka-dunk*, they stopped.

I don't know what I was expecting in there, but it wasn't padded armchairs and a big TV. In one corner of the room was a kitchen of sorts, with a sink and kettle and a few cupboards. There was a fridge, and a dartboard on the wall. A PlayStation console had been chucked down on one of the chairs. It smelled like weed. It reminded me of every student flat I'd ever been in.

There were two guys in the room. One was holding a second console and keeping half an eye on a game of *Call of Duty*. I remember noticing he was camping: he'd found himself a nice defensive position and was sitting there, picking off his opponents with the occasional blast of sniper fire. I wanted to tell him he was cheating, but I wasn't quite that stupid.

The other guy was wearing a really fucking nice suit, and under the room's ambient weed smell I caught the sharp edge of his cologne. He was standing, leaning against the wall the TV was mounted on. I could see he'd taken up his post there because it was the only chance he stood of having the first guy look at him while he was talking. The first guy was wearing a hoodie and jeans, and had a sort of football hooligan look about him. The second guy looked so groomed he could have been a hairdresser and, in the context of that room, was immediately far more frightening.

'*Schenok*,' Toad said, elbowing me inside and closing the door.

The PlayStation guy rattled off a round of semi-automatic gunfire in the game, and I jumped about a foot in the air.

The guy in the suit took a long time looking me up and down. I don't often call other men beautiful, but this guy was: his skin was the colour of polished mahogany and he had long, elegant hands. He was clearly not at all impressed by me.

'You know why you're here?' he asked me. He had a mild Scottish accent, which surprised me.

'Um . . .'

There was a simulated yelp, and the PlayStation guy got picked off. He brandished the console in the air as the screen turned red-tinged, then grey.

'Ya fucking bas! They cunts gang up on me every time.'

I couldn't help myself. 'They will do,' I said. 'It's 'cause you're camping.'

The PlayStation guy set the console down beside him, and turned to look at me. He was older than I'd thought, and for some reason *that* made me wish I hadn't said anything.

He looked at Toad. 'This yer friend, Toady?'

'*Schenok*,' Toad said again. 'Yes.'

The PlayStation guy stood up and stretched. Then he walked round the bank of chairs and advanced towards me. I braced myself, assuming I'd be punched. He moved his face near to mine. It was him, I realised, who smelled of weed.

'You're fair cheeky for someone who's got himsel' in deep shit.'

I realised I was nodding. 'Sorry,' I said. It came out like a squeak, and both the guys laughed.

'Oh fuck, Toad,' PlayStation guy said. 'The fuck've you brought us, pal?' He looked hard at me, cocked his head like a bird. 'Ye got any mad skills, *Schenok*? What's that? Puppy boy? What d'you plan tae bring to this eh . . . wee brotherhood?'

I had nothing. I could feel my knees trembling.

'See, Izz back there' – the guy slung his head backward to indicate the suited gent, still leaning against the wall – 'he's meet-and-greet. The schmoozer. Smooth-talker. Brings in the big fancy clients, makes us all look reputable to the general public and what-not. Whereas me?'

He made a fist and jerked it towards my abdomen as if to punch me. I crumpled in response, folding myself almost in half to avoid the blow, and the guy cackled. He'd stopped an inch short of contact.

'I'm just muscle,' he said.

As I straightened up, he nodded at Toad. 'Toady here's our UK ambassador to the good auld Russian Federation, aren't you, son?'

Toad shrugged. I could tell he didn't think much of this guy.

'An' you can call me Fenton,' he said.

I tried to stand up straight. 'Charlie,' I said.

At the edge of my vision, I saw Toad shake his head.

'*Schenok*,' he corrected me.

Great. So I was just *Pup*, now, was I?

'So,' Fenton said. He began to walk around me in a tight circle, looking me up and down. 'What're *you* bringin' tae this merry band, eh? What skills've ye got? Tech, mebbe? Ye look like wan o' they geek types.' He came back round to stand in front of me.

'I'm a translator,' I said. 'Russian.' My voice was piss-weak.

I expected him to laugh, but instead he cocked his head again, magpie-like. 'Oh, aye?' He glanced at Toad. 'Well that's no' a bad start.'

He looked me up and down again, then ruffled my hair with one huge hand. 'We'll lose that bird's nest ye've got goin' on,' he said. 'Get ye liftin' some weights too, eh? Teach ye a few moves. Make sure ye can multi-task.'

I nodded.

He leaned in closer. 'The more useful ye are,' he said, 'the more ye get paid.'

Something clicked for me, then. It was like I finally realised what was going on. I'd seen too much. I knew about the units and the money. I'd just watched a Ukrainian pimp get killed. My old life – life as an impoverished, slacker student kid who worked evenings in Blockbuster and was miserable – had just ended. This wasn't an invitation. It was an induction. I didn't know it then, but I'd just become one of Solomon's boys.

Birch felt like she'd been slapped. She remembered her conversation with Rab, about the informant, in the Kay's Bar snug: *I hope he's in Greenland.* And then something about *as good as dead.* She'd agreed, at the time, and thought, Yeah. Poor guy. That poor informant, daring to grass on Solomon – even Amy, the eternal optimist, had assumed he was dead by now. They'd all seen the file. When it came to a fish as big and ruthless as Solomon, informants disappeared. Everyone knows what happens to a grass, sooner or later. *Snowball in hell's chance.* That's what her mother would have said.

But this wasn't just any informant. This was Charlie.

'I . . .' She had so many questions, but no words for them. 'I mean . . . why? What did you . . . ?'

Charlie had looked away from her again, back into the hissing gas fire. He was wincing. 'I've been . . . working with this guy for a month or so. Polis in Glasgow. I'd got to the point where I wanted out from under Solomon; I just can't keep doing it, you know? A couple of weeks ago, he made me . . . I did something. A thing I never wanted to do, and didn't mean to do . . .'

'Solomon?' He wasn't finished speaking, but she didn't care. 'Solomon himself?'

Charlie blinked. 'I'm afraid so,' he said. 'This . . . thing. It fucked me up, Nella, it really did. I can't sleep. I have these – what do you call them? Night terrors? And flashbacks. I can't concentrate. I can't sit fucking still.'

Charlie lifted the tumbler to his lips, and took a long slug of whisky. She thought she could see his hand shaking, ever so slightly, now he'd mentioned it.

'And it's like . . . it's almost like, that's *fine*, you know, that's what I *should* be feeling because I'm a fucked-up scumbag who's done fucked-up shit and I know that.'

He looked at her, and his eyes were damp once again. 'But what scares me is . . . what if that goes, that feeling? What if I get to the point where I'm just like, dandy with it all? Proper emotionless, you know? I could see it starting to happen, like . . . coping mechanisms and all that. Anger. Wanting to lash out. I can't let myself get like that. You'll think I'm a hypocrite because I've been doing fucked-up criminal shit for fourteen whole years, but like . . . nothing like this. This one time.'

'Charlie.' She spoke quietly, as though to a startled animal. 'What did you do?'

He looked away.

'Tell me,' she said. 'Please. If you don't, my imagination's just going to run riot.'

Her brother was staring into the fire again, shaking his head. 'I can't.'

Birch bit her lip. 'Because of . . .' She realised they hadn't discussed what she did for a living, yet he seemed to know. 'Because of my job?'

He was still fighting tears, but she saw a smile pass across his face, and he snorted. 'No, doll,' he said. 'I mean, it's not the most convenient thing in the world that you're the fucking polis, but . . .'

'Hey.' She said it more sharply than she meant to. 'I joined *the fucking polis* because of you, Charlie. Because I wanted to find you. They were sucking at it, Lothian and Borders, and I thought I could do better.' She dropped her eyes. 'Goes to show what I knew. When *I* couldn't find you either, I just assumed it was because you must be dead.'

He was nodding. 'I did have that choice,' he said, after a pause, 'at one point. Dead, or work for Solomon. I mean, I could have run, and grassed right from the start, but . . . I was smart enough at least to know that that still meant picking the *dead* option, just in a more roundabout way. Plus, these are real gangsters we're talking about. I had to think about you and Maw.'

Birch cocked her head to one side. 'They threatened to come after us?'

Charlie shrugged. 'They didn't have to,' he said. 'Not specifically. Instead they just told me stories of what happened to deserters, grasses, guys who cut and run or tried to go into business for themselves. I learned pretty fast that Solomon doesn't just take out your knees. He takes out the knees of anyone you've ever cared about.'

He looked at her again, and she could see he'd pulled the emotion back into himself, tamped it down like a low fire, the way men do.

'I never talked about you or Maw,' he said. 'I had this naïve idea that they might not know about you, and if I didn't get in contact I could stop them finding out. I was fucking twenty, remember. I was shit scared. But I was thinking about you both all the time. Thinking that you'd be safe. And that you'd probably want me to live, even if I never saw you again. Even if I couldn't get in touch.'

The urge to slap him came over Birch once more. She tasted acid in the back of her throat. 'I don't believe this,' she said. 'How did you *get* yourself there, Charlie? How the fuck did you get in with Solomon in the first place? What were you doing, was it drugs? I mean—'

'Nella.' He cut her off. 'Give me some fucking credit.'

'Oh, what – like you never smoked weed. You were into that stuff, and guess what? Some of those deadbeats you used to hang out with, I've since put away. You remember Richard? That jerk you lived with, the philosophy guy?'

Charlie nodded.

'He went away for possession with intent to supply, after several slaps on the wrist which went ignored.'

Charlie chuckled. 'Wow . . . Richard. What a naughty boy.'

Now Birch snorted. 'Oh, like you're so much smarter? Look where *you're* at right now. How did those life choices work out for you?' She was enjoying this. He'd put her through so much anguish: she realised she was enjoying making him squirm.

'Look, Nella,' he said. 'It wasn't drugs, okay? It wasn't any stupid shit like that. I mean, I was stupid, but . . . it was Russian. I got in with this Russian guy who used to come to Blockbuster, and I didn't realise he was a fucking gangster, and then it was too late. All right? I was a translator, for fuck's sake. I was just trying to make some money on the side.'

Birch paused. She repeated what he'd just said back to herself, in her head. 'You're telling me,' she said, after a moment, 'that you got caught up in organised crime . . . by working at Blockbuster Video?'

Charlie gave his head a fast, dismissive shake. 'Shut up, Nella.'

But she'd begun to laugh. Not because it was funny – it wasn't funny, her little brother had been missing for fourteen years because he'd apparently become a hardened criminal – but because it was hysterical. *She* was hysterical. She'd had maybe five hours' sleep that whole week so far and she was feeling it. It was four in the morning, and she was laughing so hard that she could feel tears beginning to streak her face. She had to hug herself, just to drag in enough breath to keep laughing.

'Well that explains . . .' The words came out choked. 'How you were so invisible. Organised crime. Wow.'

'It's serious,' Charlie said.

Birch let out a low hum, trying to rein the laughter back in. 'I know it is,' she said, in something not unlike a sob. 'It's bloody awful.'

He'd begun to rock back and forth now: the laughing had got to him. 'If I *had* a choice then,' he said, 'I didn't know it. I was what? Fucking *twenty*, and this Russian dude . . . he shot a guy in front of me. He did it like it was no big thing. Like he was showing me, *I do this every day, arsehole*. If I had a choice that wasn't die or get on board, I swear to God I didn't know it.'

Birch could feel herself quietening now. She was still laughing, but it was petering out.

'Until . . . the other week.' Charlie's voice had softened. 'And then I thought I could see a way out. Maybe. Or at least I felt like . . . fuck it, I can't carry on with this. I can't do something like that again, I just . . . don't have the strength.'

With the back of her hand, Birch smeared the tears off her cheekbones. 'Charlie,' she said. 'You have to tell me what you did.'

He was still rocking, making the whisky in the glass between his palms slosh, as though he were on a boat. He was staring down at it, rapt. 'I can't,' he said. 'I really, really can't. Not because you're polis. But because you're my fucking sister, okay?'

Him saying the word shocked her so much that she gasped. It was as though she thought maybe he'd forgotten, after all these years, that that was who she was.

'You'd never forgive me,' he said. 'You'd never speak to me again. And I know it's my fault, it's one hundred and one per cent my entire fault, but . . . we've gone too long without speaking. I missed you.'

He surprised her then. He shifted the weight of the whisky into his left hand, and reached out with his right, leaned over the coffee table, and put one hand onto her wrist. She jumped, and coffee splashed over both of them.

'Fucksake.'

'Shit.' Birch brought the back of her own hand to her mouth, and sucked at the patch the coffee had scalded. It wasn't that bad, she realised: just a shock.

'I'm sorry,' she said.

He shrugged. 'Anyway. You'd never speak to me again.' He said it as though the moment with the hands and the coffee hadn't happened. 'And you'd certainly not want to fucking help me, if you knew.' He looked into her face then. 'And I really, really need your help, Nella.'

They put me in Tsezar's old job. They decided I was essentially going to be the silent heavy in one of Solomon's saunas. Vyshnya, Tsezar's Ukrainian ex, didn't seem too troubled by his passing: the first time I met her she looked me up and down and laughed, without smiling. Vyshnya got her name – a Ukrainian cherry – for her hair, which was bottle-dyed a sort of pinkish burgundy. She was in her late forties but dressed like Lolita, and wore platform boots so high that she usually stood taller than me. She laughed at my scrawniness, how ill-equipped I was to be the strong arm she needed.

'Johns are supposed to be scared of this?' she asked, her eyes kind of frozen mid-roll. Her lipstick matched her hair exactly. She had mirror-image tattoos of two cherries on stalks, one on each collarbone. I didn't know why her place needed a bouncer. I wouldn't have fucked with her in a month of Sundays.

We met in the nightclub downstairs from the sauna. It was around sevenish, so the place was closed, and I remember how fucking dingy and miserable it looked without its disco ball and strobes going. Vyshnya told me she'd give me a tour of the place, as if I were a john. That way I'd know exactly what I was taking care of.

Back then, before I knew better, I just didn't *get* men who went to prostitutes. No . . . sex workers. I'd hear Nella's voice in my head saying, *You mean sex workers*, every time, giving me a scolding. It made me miss her. But yeah, I didn't get it, I was already pretty sure I wasn't cut out for the job.

The door at the bottom of the covered stair was tucked back slightly from the street, a kind of alcove: no sign, no nothing, just a stainless-steel panel with one buzzer in it. If you didn't know better, you could have mistaken the door for a regular old tenement stairwell. I watched Vyshnya press the buzzer on the alcove wall with one long, synthetic nail. No voice came over the intercom: just a fizz of static, and the door clicked open.

The stairwell was fairly nondescript, too: narrow, white-painted, strip-lit. I found myself standing in the crosshairs of two CCTV cameras, which freaked me the fuck out, but Vyshnya was already halfway up.

At the top of the stairs was this dim, windowless room. There were table lamps scattered about – some with red bulbs screwed into them like a proper cliché, others with scarves draped over their shades – and two wall-mounted TVs showing the football on mute. The only other light came from the bright square of a kitchen-style hatch set into the wall: I stood there and watched as Vyshnya disappeared through a side door and then appeared in that square.

'So,' she said. 'The john comes in. You greet him. You say, *Evening, pal*, whatever.' She'd tried for a Scottish accent and fallen way short, but I didn't dare laugh. 'Then you ask, *How long for you tonight?*'

I think I just blinked.

'I will explain,' Vyshnya said, flapping one long-nailed hand to bring my gaze back round. 'Now I show you the place.'

I followed her out of the pink room, and into a much lighter space with yellow tiled walls and a wetroom floor. There were lockers – dark grey metal ones like the ones from school – along one wall. Along the other were three shower cubicles, one of them clearly out of service and filled almost to the ceiling with rolled-up hotel towels.

'First, take a shower,' Vyshnya said, and for a second I got a little hot and bothered, thinking she meant me, right there and then. But she meant the john, of course.

'They put all clothes in here.' She slapped one palm against a locker door, and the room reverberated with its clang. I strung along behind her to the far end of the showers, where she opened another door. Behind it was a cupboard full of bathrobes.

'They are shy, maybe, like some people,' she said. 'They can wear this. But most? They just wear the towel till they go home.'

I was still confused as fuck, but Vyshnya was already heading back to the dark TV room.

'After the shower,' she said, 'the men come back here. They sit down, relax. If they want to drink, I bring them anything. I look after them while they wait. If they see a girl here they like, they pick her. If they don't see a girl, they wait here until one they like comes out.'

There were two women sitting watching the TV. Both were blonde. The man in the towel lounging on the sofa clearly hadn't picked them. They looked happy enough about that.

'Now most importantly, they pay for the time.' Vyshnya crossed to the reception door and folded herself back in behind the hatch.

I almost laughed.

'You want an hour?' She addressed me as though I were the john, play-acting. 'You pay me thirty-five. Forty-five minutes is less, a half-hour is less.'

I nodded.

'The man decides how long,' Vyshnya said, 'you take the right money.'

I just nodded, over and over, like one of those dogs you used to get on the parcel shelves of cars. Okay, I thought, so I take the money. The job kind of reminded me of Blockbuster. Guy comes in, psyches himself up, picks what he fancies for his hour's entertainment, and I take his money. Except the entertainment here was . . . well, I was trying not to think about it.

'Simple, no?' Vyshnya said.

I had to admit that it was. She frowned at me then.

'But also,' she said, 'very important. You help me look after these girls, understand? Most men who come here, they are very good, respectful. They pay the right money. But some men are not good, they hurt my girls, or they try to . . . how do you say in English? Bargain with me. We do not bargain here. And for these men, I need . . .'

She was looking me up and down again, with some distaste.

'You need a bouncer,' I said. 'You want me to kick the bastards out on their arses.'

I saw Vyshnya smile for the first time, then, though there was no warmth in it. 'You understand,' she said.

I looked down at myself. I was wearing the clothes I'd been standing up in when Toad drove me away from that car park. I'd been wearing them for three days. Three days among these men and women and I was already ashamed that I'd ever considered combat trousers a good idea. I wasn't bouncer material. Or I wasn't *yet*.

'Better get down the gym, then,' I said, but Vyshnya's smile had faded.

'Some of my girls,' she said, 'have come a long way from their home. They have been tricked, they have been treated bad. Your *Solomon*' – she spat the word out like it tasted bad in her mouth – 'he has told lies to them. Had his men use them badly, with no pay. It is wrong.'

I couldn't help but nod. After all, I agreed with her.

'I look after them.' Vyshnya was still speaking. 'Try to make this home for them. You are part of this too. This is your job, too. Look after my girls.'

I thought about Tsezar, what had happened to him. 'I promise I will,' I said. I glanced down at my sorry self once again. 'I mean . . . I'll get there.'

Birch yawned. She couldn't help herself: it was after four. She had no desire to sleep, she only wanted to stay up and hear what Charlie had to say, but her body was beginning to rebel. Her thoughts were in a fractious knot, and a thin thread of fear was beginning to pull the knot tighter: Charlie was in serious trouble. In fact, Charlie *was* serious trouble. In less than an hour she was supposed to get up and get ready to go to work. What was she meant to *do* with him?

'Can I ask you something?' she said.

'Sure.'

'I want you to answer me completely honestly.'

He looked her in the face, and didn't blink. 'Scout's honour,' he said. When she frowned at him, he changed his answer. 'Okay. Thieves' honour.'

She winced, remembering her conversation with Amy. It felt like weeks ago now. 'I was going to ask,' she said, 'if I knew everything that you'd done in the past fourteen years . . . would I have grounds for arresting you?'

Charlie smiled, then folded the smile away again when she didn't return it. 'I'm afraid,' he said, 'you definitely would.'

Birch put her palms over her eyes, let her neck slacken. She weighed her own head in her hands. 'I thought so.'

'Nella.' Charlie pulled her gaze back up to meet his. It was earnest, almost pleading. 'I'm afraid that's what I need your help with,' he said. 'I'm sorry.'

Birch thought of her mother then. Towards the end, every visit had involved sitting in the padded lady-chair beside her mother's clanking hospital bed, listening to her talk. They'd talked about a lot of things, but often the conversation had meandered back to her mother's primary preoccupation: Charlie. Her missing boy.

'One day,' she'd said to Birch, only a couple of weeks before she died, 'one day you'll find him, Helen. I know you will. He'll come back to us.' The *us* made Birch's heart hurt, as though someone had closed a fist around it.

'When he does,' her mother had said, 'we'll forgive him, do you hear me? I already forgive him.' She'd lain back and closed her eyes, clacked her dry throat against nothing. 'You have to, as well. You have to promise me you will.'

'I will, Mum,' Birch had said, with the conviction of someone who thinks the thing they're promising will never come to pass.

Now, she looked at her brother. 'Tell me what you need,' she said.

'Okay . . .' Charlie took in a lungful of air, and she watched his shoulders rise and fall.

'The guy I was . . . working with,' he said, 'the Glaswegian polis. He offered me immunity. In return for grassing on Solomon and the boys, he said whatever I'd been up to while . . . well, while I've been away. That would all be wiped. A blind eye turned.'

Birch screwed up her face. Yep, she thought. Bingo.

'He said he'd get me out,' Charlie was saying. 'Said they'd spring me and put me in – whatever, I don't know. Witness protection. A safe house, all that jazz. I thought I'd get a whole new identity, a clean slate. Another chance to be a person, you know?'

She realised she was shaking her head. 'Wow,' was all she could manage.

'Anyway.' Charlie hadn't caught the snark in her voice. 'He kept promising, like, *Yeah yeah, just a bit more info, pal, just give us this and then I'll be in touch.* My arse. I realised that I'd put myself between a rock and a hard place. Polis were starting to sniff around. The guys were all whispering about a mole. They knew someone was grassing and I figured it wouldn't take long for one bright spark to figure out that it might be me. And *might be* would be enough.'

Birch was nodding. 'So you ran,' she said.

'Yeah. This Operation Citrine – I knew it was coming. I figured it would be big, anyone on the scene would be arrested, and hopefully some would be charged. If I went then I'd have a couple of days before they realised I wasn't just in custody with the rest. And I thought a couple of days would give me time to ... get some assurances, you know?'

Jesus, Birch thought. Did fourteen years as a gangster really leave someone *this* naïve? 'So you ditched out, what? Sunday night? Monday morning?'

'Early hours Monday,' he said. 'Went AWOL. I was meant to be down there to translate for the boat captains coming in ... as well as extra muscle.' He looked down at himself, and his face was apologetic – his first acknowledgement of the fact that he was almost unrecognisable, physically. 'But I figured when the shit's going down, no one misses the translator.'

'So ... you went to see your contact?'

'The polis? Kind of. I stayed in Glasgow instead of heading over here with the crew. Then I texted him. He wanted to meet in the fucking Buchanan Street Bus Station.' Charlie scoffed at himself.

Okay, good. He'd maybe realised his mistakes, then.

'Anyway, I texted him I'm out – look, pal, here I am, that's me out. Take me to the safe house, whatever. And there was just something about the way he replied. I realised I'd been had: if I waited at the bus station he was going to come and arrest me.'

Birch nodded. 'Yep,' she said. 'How did I guess?'

'All right, all right,' Charlie said, not looking at her. 'No need to rub it in. Anyway, this was Monday, first thing in the morning. Broad fucking daylight. I'd nothing with me – you've seen I've nothing with me. I didn't have time. I thought if I didn't show up to meet him, he'd be there at my door with the battering ram. I just ran. Got on the first train to Edinburgh – from Central, so I didn't go too near Buchanan Street. And now here I am. Fucksake – yeah, I know I've been had.'

Birch was quiet for a moment. She kneaded her temples with her forefingers: she had a sleep-deprivation headache, and it was developing like fog over water.

'He was always going to arrest you, Charlie,' she said, at last. 'Whatever deal he was going to make would only ever have been done with you in custody.'

Charlie didn't look at her. He knew he'd been naïve.

'But, for what it's worth,' she went on, 'I'm proud of you for informing. You finally started to do the right thing.'

Charlie laughed a cold laugh. 'Fuck,' he said. 'Every inch the policewoman, eh? Proud of me. For being a fucking *grass*.'

'Yes.' There was heat in her voice. 'Look what you've put on the line. I mean, you were stupid, Charlie, you don't need me to tell you that. But you chose right. You put yourself at risk, and chose to do the good thing. You need to keep doing that now.'

'You know' – Charlie got to his feet, making Birch jump – 'I don't *love* that you're a fucking police inspector. I mean, what the fuck? Do you know how scared I was, coming here? I thought you might just arrest me on the spot, soon as you found out where I'd been all this time, who I've been running with. I'm *still* sitting here afraid that you're going to whip out the handcuffs and take me in. I mean . . .' Charlie flailed one long arm, and Birch saw the power in it. The power, and the anger. 'Yeah, I'm not as smart as you. I believed that guy when he said I'd get immunity, and now I'm running from the Glasgow polis, *and* running from the cunts I've grassed on, and I've sat here and asked you, straight up, for help. I've basically *begged* you. My own sister. And you're just sat there like some hard-faced bitch telling me I've been stupid.'

At that, Birch was on her feet, too. 'Listen, sunshine.' She pulled herself to her full height, squaring up to him. 'You abandoned me – abandoned *us* – for fourteen fucking years. Fourteen *years*, and not one word from you. Not one clue. I searched for you, Charlie. The reason I am a *fucking police inspector* is because I wanted to find you. I went out of my wits, for years, trying to find you. I looked *everywhere*. And you were in Glasgow, the whole time. I could have walked past you on the Byres Road and never known it. I mean . . . you left me all alone, with Mum.' She could feel tears forming now, unwanted. 'You *left* me, and I had to look after her, all the way through . . .' It was no good. Her face crumpled.

'Yeah,' Charlie hissed. 'That's another thing! I've been in this house what? An hour and a fucking half, and you're only just now informing me that my mother is dead. What kind of cold-hearted . . .' He flung his arm out again, and gulped in air. 'You're a fine fit for the fucking polis, Nella, let's just say that.'

Birch's knees gave way. She sank back into her chair.

'Better that,' she said, 'than a fine fit for the Glasgow gangland. Better that than some rent-a-thug who just happens to have a second language.'

Charlie looked down at her, his jaw working. 'Now you listen—'

That red mist again. Birch thumped the arm of the chair with one fist. It hurt. Then she was back on her feet. 'No, *you* listen,' she said. 'Okay? You're in my house, you're asking for my help, you sit down on that couch and *you* listen.' Birch heard her screeching voice ring in the chimney.

'I tried to tell you about Mum. I put it in the paper, on Facebook, everywhere. I don't overshare, but I did then. I thought, If by some slim chance he's still out there, I need him to know. I tried, okay?'

Charlie held up his hands: don't shoot. 'All right,' he spat. 'All right. I admit, I knew before I got here. Just keep your fucking voice down.'

She pointed at the spot on the couch where his muscled bulk had left a dent. 'Sit down,' she spat.

Charlie obliged, scowling. As he settled himself again, she felt a pang of recognition. He looked just like his child-self, sulking after a telling-off from their mother.

'It was awful,' she said, 'okay? It was bloody slow and bloody painful. And right to the end she was asking for you. Right to the end she was watching the door like you might walk in. The last day, I was with her. And *this* is how convinced I was that you were dead, okay? We got to the last hour or so, and she was basically passed out – I knew she was slipping away from me. And I said to her – I *actually said to her* – Mum, it's okay, you're going to go and be with Charlie now. And then . . . she hadn't smiled in weeks. She'd barely opened her eyes in days. But then, when I said that, she smiled. She smiled big. And she looked actually peaceful, for the first time in ages. Like she believed it was true. And to think, the whole time you were stoating around the fucking Gorbals or something, alive and well. Do you get that? Do you *get* how mad I am with you right now?'

Her brother's face was wet. She could see the gas fire's light shining on his cheeks.

'Yeah,' he said, all the fight gone from his voice. 'I do, Nella. I'm sorry.'

He raised one hand, then, slower this time. And this time she let him reach over and put it on top of her own. His palm was hot and dry. Touching him felt like brushing up against a stove: she felt a strange warmth radiate through her.

'I mean.' With her free hand, she daubed the tears off her face. 'It's . . . it's not *okay*, but . . . it's okay. It happened. And no matter what, I'm glad you're back.'

Charlie smiled a sad, shy smile. He squeezed her hand, and she squeezed back. In her head, she heard her mother's voice: *Good girl.*

From that first shift at the sauna, I guess I was officially a criminal. With the translation stuff, I might have had some sort of *out* – I didn't know what I was looking at, I was coerced, whatever. But as soon as I was on Solomon's payroll, that was it. Of course, that's not how you think about it as it's going on. Seems weird to think about it that way now, like, *Oh, I was just this good, God-fearing boy, officer*; and then suddenly, *boom*: gangster. Technically that's what happened, but it wasn't how it felt.

I did know I couldn't go back, though, and I knew folk were looking for me. It started with Nella's posters, popping up around Glasgow. It was making the lads twitchy, so I had to disappear. First thing I did was shave my head. You know how cold it is being suddenly bald in the middle of a Glaswegian winter? Yeah. Izz gave me these dark glasses and I wore them everywhere. Toad sorted me out with fake IDs, passport, the works. *Nick Smith*, he christened me: as plain a name as you can get. And of course I had to get built. There was a pull-up bar in the booth behind the hatch at the sauna and I was just at it, all the time. That, or press-ups on the floor. There wasn't a lot else to do, and Vyshnya nagged me if I sat around too much.

I saw there was shit in the papers. The missing straight-A kid wasn't all he seemed, he hung with a bad crowd, yadda yadda. That Lockley cunt dug up some dirt on me that Nella and Maw wouldn't have known. I was big into weed, in the years BC: before criminality. I wasn't dealing as such, but for a lot of people I was *the guy* in their *I know a guy*. I'd run up against the law a couple of times, spent the odd night in the drunk tank, got a caution for being disorderly outside a pub in Ibrox. I mean, *Ibrox*. Couldn't quite believe that one. But anyway, I didn't think any of it was major. The problem was Maw's public appeal.

Maw was a single mother, right? Always had been: my entire life anyway. I didn't know much about my da except his name was Jimmy and it was short for Jameson, like the whisky. That, and he beat Maw up. So bad she lost a baby, or at least so Nella said. A baby that would have come between Nella and me. Nella had this early, early memory of being like three years old, toddling out of her room late at night and seeing Maw in the bathroom floor on her knees. Towels covered in blood. The sound of my da smashing plates in the kitchen. And Maw had to get up off that floor, being in the state she was, and put Nella back into bed. I tried not to believe it because I didn't want it to be true, and because it made me so angry that when I thought about it, my vision blacked out. It scared me. I'd never met the guy. So I tried to imagine he'd never existed, Nella and I were just some sort of divine conception, and our maw was a fucking superhero.

The point is she was on her own. We never had money. We never cared. But when I went to uni things got really hard for her. She'd sent Nella, and that was hard enough, but then she had to send me too, right after. I got a maintenance grant, but she still gave me money every month. I think she felt like she had to. Me and my *woe is Charlie* act . . . I thought I was rooked? Maw was stone-cold broke.

So after I went, and they were looking for me, she launched this appeal. Trying to raise some money. She wanted to hire a PI to try to find me, I guess, and I think it was probably just meant for family and friends to donate to. But that Lockley scumbag got a hold of it and then was like, *This woman is asking for money to find her son who's a low-life drug dealer, isn't that unacceptable?* And yeah, plenty of the tabloid-inhaling arseholes of this world found it most unacceptable indeed. And Maw was hauled over the coals, while every single less-than-angelic thing I'd ever done was paraded for all to read.

Fenton used to ask me if I'd like to murder Lockley. We used to talk about it, over a bevvy sometimes: how we'd do it. He'd be easy enough to find and back then no one would have missed him. He didn't have his fan club then. Fenton was dead serious, but I never followed through. I got to be a lot of things, but I was never a murderer. As the years went by that became like the last ragged flag of decency I still had waving. I'd never killed anyone. And I swore to myself I absolutely never would.

They'd reconvened to the kitchen: it was 5.10 a.m., and Birch needed another coffee. It was safe to have lights on now – this was the hour she'd be up and about anyway, and the dog walkers and early morning delivery drivers had already emerged. She liked to think such people acted as preventative witnesses – guardians of the streets before the streets fully woke – though they didn't know it. They were so often the alarm-sounders, too. It was always a jogger or a dog walker who witnessed the opportunistic dawn break-in; or stumbled across a body still warm, still just within the reach of rescue.

She made the coffee strong, and piled in the sugar. One of her eyes had begun to flicker at the edge, a nerve dancing under her eyelashes. Her brother had hoisted himself onto the worktop, and sat there with his legs spread, his elbows resting on his knees. His head lolled.

'I'm sorry, Charlie,' she said, breaking a silence that had settled on the room like snow. 'I can't help you unless I arrest you.'

He looked at her, and in the bright kitchen light she noticed the bags under his eyes for the first time.

'You want to be in a safe house,' she said. 'That's where I want you to be, too. Where no one can touch you. So let me take you in. Operation Citrine needs you back. If you testify against Solomon, we can charge him. We can put him away. But I've got to tell you, without our informant, the case isn't looking all that secure.'

Charlie's head lolled again. She waited, but he didn't say anything. Birch couldn't stand the quiet.

'No one's talking,' she said. 'He's trained them all too well. We can only hold him till Friday unless we find something to charge him with.'

Charlie yawned. 'Didn't you arrest him, like, right next to a boat full of bath salts?'

Birch closed her eyes in exasperation. It was like he was only hearing about every third word. 'Yes,' she said, 'and I'm not in on his interviews, but he'll be claiming he was just *in the area*. Just out looking at the sea view at 4 a.m., no idea what was in those boats coming in. Nothing to do with him, yadda yadda. Doesn't matter if it's obviously bullshit – we've only got two days left to prove him wrong, and the burden's on us. We need more. We need our informant back.'

Charlie shrugged. 'I already grassed,' he said. 'I already told your Glasgow pal everything I know about that job.'

Birch wanted to hit him. She knew he was tired, and frightened, and he didn't understand police procedure. But his responses felt obtuse.

'But you know *more*,' she said. 'About other things. You could testify on everything you've seen and' – she paused, but then pressed ahead – 'done, over the past fourteen years. You could give us all sorts of charges to pin on him. Don't you see? You're the *only one* who'll talk.'

Charlie covered his eyes with his hands, another childlike gesture. She just wanted him on the same page.

'Here's how I see it,' she said. 'You let me arrest you, I put you in a safe house, and you testify. Solomon goes down and you're safe. You'll do some time, sure. But the other option is, you run. The case collapses. Solomon goes free. Then not only are you in danger, but he's also free to terrorise whoever he fancies, whenever he fancies, business as usual. You running will have been for *nothing*, Charlie.'

Charlie dropped his hands, and looked at her with a sudden clarity. 'I know you're not Mother Teresa here,' he said, his voice sharp-edged. 'I get the two options, and they're both pretty shitty for me. But not for *you*, right? If you arrest me, you're all set up. Saved the day, didn't you? But if I run, you're fucked. If they find out I was here and you let me go, your career's finished.'

Birch felt her face redden.

'Isn't it, Nella?'

She set her teeth. 'Pretty much,' she said. 'Which is why I really ought to just arrest you, no more talk.'

Charlie snorted, and held out his wrists. It was a mime that said, *cuff me*, but there was something about it that looked pious, too, like Charlie was reaching out for the Communion wafer. *Forgive me, sister, for I have sinned.*

'Why don't you just do it, then?' he snarled.

Birch dropped her gaze. The clock ticked. 'Because you're my fucking *brother*, okay?' she said. 'Because they'd take you away from me again.'

The kitchen filled with a silence in which Birch could feel Charlie's combative mood fading, replaced once again with the thick mist of their shared anguish: sleep deprivation. Confusion. Grief.

'Where did you sleep last night?' she asked, then corrected herself. 'Monday night, I mean.'

He lifted his head again, and blinked. 'Hmm?'

'I asked ... well, you said you got the train through from Glasgow on Monday, right? Early in the morning. So where did you sleep that night?'

Charlie blew on his coffee – though it must, she thought, be cool by now – then slurped a mouthful. Birch smiled: another old habit she'd forgotten about.

'I didn't,' he said. 'I just kind of ... wandered around. I was trying to figure out what to do.'

She nodded. Then something occurred to her. 'Charlie. You weren't ... *here* on Monday night, were you? I mean, at this house? Hanging around?'

Her brother frowned. 'Hanging around?'

She gave her head a little shake. *Okay – it wasn't him then.* Charlie wasn't the skull-masked man. 'Never mind,' she said. 'I just ... I saw someone in my garden on Monday night. Out the back. Climbing over the wall. I just suddenly thought it might have been you. But of course it wasn't. Just ignore me.' Her voice was stiff and shiny as foil.

'It wasn't me,' Charlie said, sliding off the worktop and advancing towards her. 'But ... there was someone here?'

She looked down. 'Maybe.'

Charlie jerked his head towards the curtained window. 'Out there?' he asked.

'Yes,' she said, still not looking at him. 'I mean, I saw a guy climb over the wall. From outside, I mean, on the street. Down the Joppa end. I was far away. It might not have been this garden at all.' Fuck, Helen – you're a bad liar.

Charlie was right next to her now. 'Nella,' he said, almost in her ear, 'you'd better tell me the whole thing because, I swear to God, you trying to make me think it was no big deal is spectacularly not working.'

Dammit. She'd forgotten that, in spite of his long absence, Charlie knew her. Maybe better than anyone, now Mum was gone.

She rattled off the story of the skull-faced man, the dark Mercedes. It helped that she'd done it once already, with Rab.

'Fucksake,' Charlie said. His tone had changed from exasperation at her sugar-coating to what sounded like genuine fear. 'Fucksake, they know I'm here.'

Birch crinkled her forehead. 'Not necessarily,' she said. 'That was before you got here. Monday night. While you were out walking around. If they *were* Solomon's employees—'

Charlie waved a dismissive hand. 'They were,' he said.

'Okay . . . if they were, then it just means two things. They'd figured out you were gone, and they know that I'm your sister.'

He was quiet. Birch counted a full sixty ticks of the clock.

'I guess,' he said, 'they were casing the place. Realised I wasn't here. Saw you arrive and came to look in the car, see if I was in it with you. They've seen that I wasn't. That's something.'

Birch nodded along as he spoke.

'There's been something else,' she said, 'phone calls. They started on Monday evening.'

She watched her brother's face whiten. 'Fuck,' he said. 'If they've got your number then they must have gone through my stuff.'

'What?'

Charlie made a sheepish face. 'Okay, look,' he said. 'I know I never got in touch, and I'm sorry; but that doesn't mean I haven't kept an eye on you, okay?'

She blinked. 'Kept an eye . . . ?'

'Yeah. I had my Weegie polis pal look you up. Got your work number off the staff intranet. I told him you were my sister. I already knew you were polis 'cause, you know, you're all over Google. Especially lately, with the Three Rivers shit, and all that. So I had your work number in among my . . . my Nella stuff.'

Birch stared at him. 'Nella stuff?'

He was blushing. He looked down at his feet. 'I had a . . . wee notebook thing. If something was in the paper about you, I would cut it out and tape it in there. Like around that Three Rivers shooting, there were some bits. An article about how you'd been put in charge of the case and stuff. Some quotes you'd said at press conferences. Things like that. And you know, when Maw died there were some bits in the paper, some wee bits. I cut out the – what do you call it? – the death announcement you did. And there were a couple of little articles written by bastards who remembered that once upon a time Maw was a bit famous for having an arsehole son who went AWOL. Like *Cash con appeal woman dies, son remains missing.* That sort of bollocks. I hated it, but I cut it out and put it in there. Like a fucked-up family album, I guess.'

Birch pressed one hand over her eyes. 'That explains that, then. How they got my number.'

Charlie was still looking at the floor. 'Yeah.'

'And it explains why they'd come here,' she said. 'I guess they figured this might be a place you'd run to.'

He looked up again, and yes: he was scared. She could see it now: terror sitting over his face like a caul.

'I have to go,' he said. 'If they know about you, and they've already been here . . . *fuck.* I thought I'd have more time than this.'

She could feel his agitation rising: it was a white-noise fizz in the room's still air. He took a step forward, and she had the fleeting image of him sprinting from the front door, out into the morning's darkness and away. He'd be gone again. This time for ever, maybe. She realised she couldn't bear the thought, and stepped out into his path.

'Charlie, wait. Let's just be calm for a minute.'

He put his hands around her shoulders again: not to move her, she could tell, but to prepare to move her should he need to.

'I might not have a minute,' he said. 'I wish you'd told me all that.'

Birch laughed, right in his face. 'Oh yeah,' she said. 'Hey, brother I haven't seen for fourteen entire years! There was a dodgy guy in my back garden the other day!'

He rolled his eyes.

'Sorry, it wasn't exactly my first priority,' she added.

His fingers curled around her shoulders, and he tried nudging her, just slightly, to see if she'd yield.

'Come *on*,' he said, when she didn't. 'You want me to get kneecapped?'

Birch struggled free. 'No, honey,' she said. 'I want you to take a breath, and let me talk for a second, okay? There might be more to this.'

He dropped his hands, swinging them down in exasperation so they slapped against his thighs. '*Fine*,' he said. 'Convince me. But do it quick.'

Birch pointed one finger at his face. 'Stay there,' she commanded, and skidded out of the kitchen and into the living room. She returned carrying her phone.

'All the calls,' she said. 'They're still going on. It's on silent, but they're still phoning. It's hourly now, but other than that nothing's changed. Don't you think if they knew you were here they'd stop with this bullshit? Wouldn't they just come?'

Charlie grimaced. He wasn't convinced.

'I spoke to them yesterday,' she said. 'Yesterday morning. I had no idea who was calling me, what it was about' – she remembered the flowers, and decided not to mention them – 'but it was really starting to piss me off. I got in a foul mood, and . . . well, the next time they called, I picked up.'

He narrowed his eyes. 'And said?'

'The truth,' Birch replied. 'I told them I had no fucking idea why they were calling me, and said it was pathetic and pitiful.'

Charlie reeled away, back into his half of the kitchen. 'Jesus, Nella! You really know how to endear yourself to people, don't you?'

She snorted. 'Well *sorry*. Funnily enough I didn't realise that the arsehole who was phoning me was some bloodthirsty gangster who wanted to come and break the legs of the little brother I thought was already dead.'

The kitchen echoed. As silence returned, Birch watched Charlie's face crumple. He began to laugh: the kind of desperate, weird laughter that Birch herself had been overtaken by an hour or so before. This time, it was infectious: as Charlie's laughter grew, it seemed to fuel her own. Charlie half collapsed against the worktop and then slid down the cupboard-front to the floor. She joined him there, the two of them side by side, backs against the hard MDF as the laughter began to ebb. She quietened before Charlie did, and it felt like surfacing out of deep water. Then they sat there, staring straight ahead at the cupboard doors in front. Charlie, seemingly without thinking, raised his arm and slung it around his sister's shoulders. Birch flinched, but let it happen, then found she liked it there. Her brother's arm: knotted with muscle, warm and alive. She leaned in and rested the top of her head against his chin.

'You mustn't go again,' she said. 'You mustn't run. I couldn't stand it. I'd want to die.' She hadn't realised it before she said it, but once she'd said it, she knew it was true. She would.

Charlie let out a long sigh. She felt it gather in him, his ribcage expanding, then contracting again.

'It's not safe,' he said. 'You're saying you can't protect me, so if I don't run, I die.'

She flinched, and he felt it.

'It sounds melodramatic,' he said. 'But I know these guys. You think this sort of stuff doesn't happen in Scotland, but it does.'

Birch scoffed. 'You remember what I do for a living?' she said. 'I *know* it does. I've seen Solomon's file, I know the deep shit you'd be in if you ran and he came after you. But I *can* put you in a safe house. Like I said: you'd just have to be under arrest.'

When I look back, I realise how many bad things I've done. It's a long list. At the top of it is my da.

It was three years in or so. I was still doing shifts at the sauna, but not as many. I was doing more translation work, but also a whole load of driving. Moving gear, moving the crew, taxiing the girls around. A bit of intimidation driving: sitting outside people's houses, following them around the city, shit like that. It was stuff that didn't *feel* criminal. I know that sounds ridiculous but that's how it was. Vyshnya's girls were happy enough, for the most part. Saunas are *safe*. If you're in that line of work, a sauna's where you want to be. In your own space, setting your own rules, among your pals, and protected by a witch like Vyshnya and a hard bastard like I'd become. Those girls had a problem? One of us would sort it out. They got into drugs? We'd help get them clean again. They had a bastard boyfriend who knocked them about? He'd soon fucking stop once I paid a visit. And the equivalent is working some kerb somewhere and fucksake, we all know how dangerous *that* is. Get in the wrong car and the next thing, you're in a bin bag in bits. In a sauna, the most dangerous thing is getting caught in a raid from the polis. Getting arrested 'cause your last john left a half-smoked joint in your room or some other idiotic crap. Solomon had brought some of those girls to Scotland under false pretences – yet another reason to hate his stinking guts. But while they were with Vyshnya and me, they were safe. We made sure of it.

Anyway. My da.

I'd got comfy. I was doing my thing. I was working for Solomon, sure, but I wasn't hurting anyone. Or at least, not anyone who didn't deserve it. I'd got myself a flat, and I was seeing Hanna, one of the girls. I was earning a good bit of cash. Unlike Fenton and some of the others I didn't really like the bevvy so much, and I'd sorted out my weed problem – 'cause of the raid issue, but also because it made me slow. I was living pretty clean and saving up. It was all good.

Except I couldn't go home. I had Hanna, but I wasn't like some of the guys, who saw their mammies and their aunties on the weekends, who had wee baby nieces and nephews, who helped their auld grannies with their shopping. It's a stereotype that gangsters love their families, but I discovered it's a true one. I was unusual, in that outside our weird fraternity I had no one.

I wanted to get back in touch with Nella more than I could say. I wanted Maw to know I was alive. But they'd made such a racket about me. The posters, the public appeals – it dragged on for years. I'd been in the papers too much when I'd disappeared, thanks to that bastard Lockley. He'd even speculated that I'd fallen in with organised crime. I dunno where he got that from – if someone who knew me talked to someone else who talked to someone else, and Lockley caught wind. Or perhaps he just guessed, and happened to get it right. But either way, I was a flight risk. And Nella had to go and become a bloody policewoman, didn't she? After that there was no way I could get back in touch. If any of the boys knew I'd been in contact with a police officer? That would have been it, for her as well as me. She didn't know it, but her new job made any contact between us even more impossible. I had to disappear, like Toad had – he was pretty much alone in the world, too. We'd developed a sort of honorary father–son relationship, and thinking about me and Toad made me realise . . . there *was* a family member I could maybe reach out to. One who'd never known me, so wouldn't have twigged I was missing. One I wouldn't mind coming face to face with, maybe settling some scores. Long story short, I got an itch to find my da.

I'd come to realise that Solomon knew hard cunts everywhere, and when you're connected to hard cunts everywhere, you can find just about anyone. I talked to Fenton about it. He's a mad, toothless bastard but he's pretty sharp all the same. All the information I could give him was that my da's name was Jimmy, short for Jameson, *yeah, like the whisky*. That, and he was basically the worst sort of man.

'And your sister's name's Helen, right?' he says.

And I say yeah. And off he goes.

I thought nothing might come of it, or that I might have to wait years. I often wondered if my da was dead. I sort of did and didn't hope he was. Bastards like that have a habit of dying young – some altercation or another – but I knew there'd be no satisfaction in it, if I discovered he was gone.

Next thing Fenton's knocking on the door of my flat and showing me a bad photocopy of my own birth certificate.

In news that would shock no one: my da was still an absolute bastard. He'd become something of a washed-up absolute bastard, but he was still kicking.

'I ken where tae find him,' Fenton said. 'Have a wee think. But you jist say the word, and we're there.'

Toad tried to talk me out of it. Poor old Toad. Turned out he'd grown up Russian Orthodox, and although I've never known him set foot in a church . . . well, what you grow up with is what you are.

'Honour thy father,' he said to me, 'even if thy father is a murdering pig.'

'Yeah?' I said. 'What about avenge thy mother?'

He didn't get it. In Russia, criticising someone's parents is a pretty insulting thing to do, and maybe especially their father. Toad reckoned I ought to extend this to myself, too.

'He gave you life,' he said.

I could see he was trying to help, but it just pissed me off. 'My maw gave me life,' I said. 'He gave me nothing. Literally. And the only thing he ever gave my maw was grief.'

He left it at that, but I could see I'd upset him. For the next few days, while I thought about it like Fenton had said, I could see it was bothering Toad. I saw him a couple of times, and as we talked he'd be frowning at me, like he wanted to say something. I realise now that maybe he was worried: he was in charge of me, weirdly fatherly with it, and perhaps he thought me finding my da would ruin that relationship we'd built. But I'm speculating there. I guess he knew it was delicate, that the scales of my decision were teetering. He didn't want to add the final straw.

Of course, it was like a scab. You can try your best, but in the end you've got to pick it. I'd always been mad at my da, ever since Nella had told me that story about Maw and the blood. I'd always daydreamed about what I'd say or do if I ever met him, how I'd get revenge on Maw's behalf. Now I'd fucked up my life, and I couldn't see or talk to my maw any more; but this one thing, I could still do. I was a hard bastard now, after all. Blockbuster Video Charlie couldn't have squared up to his old man. Gangster Charlie could put the fear of God up him.

'That's ma boy,' Fenton said, when I told him I wanted to do it. He's got his own version of justice, Fenton, and this was exactly it.

'So, you have decided, *Schenok?*' Toad asked me. I knew that Fenton had already told him. 'What is it that you are going to do?'

I thought about it for a moment before I answered him. I'd spent that last handful of days fantasising over a fair few scenarios. I remembered one of Maw's expressions, one that I hadn't heard her say in years.

'I'm going to punch his ticket,' I said.

'Okay. If this all goes right, you'll stay? One day, Charlie, that's all I ask.'

Her brother was back on the sofa, nestled into that same dent he'd made. Birch was interested to note that the spot he'd picked was the very place she also liked to sit: opposite her mother's photograph, and now the card, with Rab's spidery handwriting.

'Today,' he said. 'Just today. I'm sorry – I can't promise more than that.'

Birch shrugged. 'I guess that's as good as I'll get,' she said.

They sat and looked at the phone screen. They'd wrangled back and forth for an hour now, and it was nearly 6.30 a.m. Time for the next call: every hour, on the half-hour.

'Just our fucking luck,' Charlie said, looking down at the phone on the coffee table between them, 'if this is the call they decide not to make. Or you pick up and it's like, *hello, we're in the front garden.*'

It was a joke, albeit a grim one: she could see it on his face. But in spite of herself she did glance up at the closed curtains, the slightest hint of grey light beginning to occur to the window beyond.

'They'll call,' she said.

They looked at the phone screen. 06:29.

'Three, two, one . . .' Birch's count was almost spot on. It rang.

Charlie looked at her, his face a strange blank.

'Good morning, scumbag,' Birch said. For a terrible second, she imagined it might be DCI McLeod on the other end of the line, calling her early. It'd be a rarity, but not a first.

But no: on the line, that familiar not-quite silence.

'I've got an update for you,' she said. 'I got sick of you pissing about in my garden, and calling me all hours of the night. I don't think I need to tell you, but I'm a policewoman, remember? I've filed a report with my colleagues.'

She looked at Charlie as she reamed off the next part. 'I have no idea why you're harassing me,' she said, 'but you're now being monitored. I've been supplied with a panic button. So if I see that tacky blacked-out saloon within a mile of my house again, I'll have the cavalry down on top of it and you won't know what's hit you. See also: wankers in Halloween masks climbing into my garden. I have permission to use the full force of the law, and trust me, scumbag, it would be my absolute pleasure to do so.'

The line really was silent now, as though the listener were hold-ing his breath.

'What's more,' she said, 'if you think tracing a withheld number is beyond our capability, then you're even more stupid than you seem. The more times you call, the more likely it is that we'll find you. And with every call that is logged, the case for harassment and threatening behaviour grows. So this is my advice to you on this fine Wednesday morning: last warning. Fuck off.'

Birch flipped the phone from her ear to her palm, and swiped to hang up. The stream of invective had left her heart racing.

'Wow,' Charlie said. 'Nella. I mean . . . *respect.*'

She looked down at the phone screen, which had auto-locked and so only reflected her own tired face back at her.

'We'll find out in an hour,' she said, 'if that's worked. Now for the less fun part.' She swiped the phone open again, and dialled.

It was early still. She got a telephonist whose voice she didn't recognise.

'Morning,' Birch said, pushing her voice down low in her throat to try to sound rough. The sleep deprivation helped. 'It's DI Helen Birch here, can I leave a message for DCI McLeod, please?'

'I can try his extension for you?' The girl's voice was hopeful and bouncy.

Birch almost laughed. You must be new, she thought. 'No, no,' Birch said, 'I know he won't be in yet. I just want to leave a message and then follow up later.'

'I'll put you through,' the girl said again. 'If he's not there, you can leave a message on his voicemail.'

If he's not there, Birch thought. She rolled her eyes at Charlie, who of course wasn't in on the joke. The dawn raid two days ago was the first time she'd seen her boss outwith the hours of daylight in months.

McLeod's voice came on the line and, in spite of herself, Birch sat up a little straighter: ... *after the tone. Alternatively you may contact* ... The message felt endless. Birch flapped her hand at Charlie, the universal sign for using forty words when four would do.

Finally, a beep.

'Good morning, sir,' Birch said, trying not to sound in any way perky. 'It's Helen Birch here. Just calling to say I'm feeling pretty dreadful, and won't be in today. If you have any work you'd like me to do remotely, I'll be checking my email as normal.'

She paused. What else?

'I know we're up against the clock with the Solomon case,' she said, 'but I figured I should take a day and try to fight this off, so I can get back on it sooner.'

Charlie was watching her, one eyebrow raised.

'I'll follow this up with an email shortly,' she said. 'And I'll be by my phone.'

She dithered for a moment, unsure how to sign off. Charlie drew one finger across his throat, a gesture that made her shiver. She hung up without saying anything more.

'Okay,' she said. 'Now you and I can talk.'

She'd sent Charlie off to take a shower, and then to get a couple of hours' sleep.

'I'm not sure,' he'd said. 'I want to be on the lookout.'

'I'll be on the lookout. If anything happens I'll scream the place down. But it'll be light soon, and the prom's always busy. I reckon we're fine for the rest of the day. Don't be paranoid.'

Charlie had peered out through the living room curtains. Outside, dog walkers. Cyclists with their blinking headlamps losing ground against the dawn. The tide, a long way out again, and the sand a wet mirror reflecting a weak morning moon. Traffic on the road outside making surf-sounds all of its own.

'Okay,' he'd said. 'I'm pretty beat.'

She'd shifted all the crap off her bed. A few work papers; a thick novel she regretted starting; a coffee cup with a spoon sugar-glued to the inside. It felt wrong to put Charlie in the spare room with its hard little single divan.

'There might be toast crumbs,' she'd said, shaking out the duvet. A dreadful flashback, then: Oh God. Anjan must have noticed the toast crumbs, too. She'd flushed. 'Sorry.'

Charlie had just grinned, and ducked into the bathroom, a towel slung around his thick, implausible neck.

Downstairs, Birch pulled open the living room curtains, and cracked the blinds. The grey light was pinkish now, the sky streaked with red. *Shepherd's warning.* Through a gap in her unkempt garden hedge she watched a happy Labrador zip off towards the low tideline after a flung stalk of kelp. She shuffled to the kitchen, gathering the empty coffee cups and whisky glasses from the table to dump into the sink. She zipped the blind up, half expecting to see a skull face on the other side of the glass: *surprise.* But the garden looked the way it always did: grass beginning to need a cut, the shed leaning slightly with the pull of the sea winds. She checked the back door, then meandered through the living room and into the hall to check the other. She felt like a big cat in a too-small enclosure, pacing. Waiting for some sort of attack that might never come.

For a couple of minutes, Birch stood on the hall's four-foot square of carpet, listening to the sounds of her brother, just existing inside her house. She rubbed her eyes, terrified she might wake up and find it was all a long, elaborate dream. But no: Charlie was up there with the water blasting, assuming she couldn't hear him singing to himself. She didn't recognise the tune, and when she strained to try to hear the words she realised he was singing in Russian. The bits that he'd taught her years ago were half remembered, largely useless now. When she heard him stop the water, she slipped back through to the kitchen and stood under the window, watching the kettle fog the glass with an empty speech-bubble of steam.

She glanced at the clock: 7.20 a.m.

'Well, Helen,' she said, under the noise of the kettle and her brother knocking around upstairs. 'This is it. You're harbouring a known criminal. You are officially committing a crime.'

Four and a half hours Charlie had been in the house. During that time he'd confessed to a shopping-list of criminal actions, named associates she knew by reputation from other cases, confirmed he was on Solomon's payroll, and disclosed his status as a compromised informant. She should have cuffed him a good two or three hours ago, gone and got the car and driven him to the nearest custody suite herself. She should have read him his Miranda rights and barricaded him in. She should have hit the panic button, called the cavalry and had him taken in on the grounds of breaking and entering, to have the rest extracted from him via interview. She'd have picked from these options with anyone else: any other perp in the world.

But this was Charlie.

'I'm still going to do it,' she said to herself quietly. 'He thinks he's going to walk out of that door later, but he isn't. I *am* going to do it. I'm going to save this case.'

In the back of her mind she could feel some childlike version of herself curling up to cry at the very idea of watching Charlie walk out of her front door, almost as soon as he'd broken in.

It's just a day, she thought. No one needs to know. I'll do it. I just want a few more hours with him.

Upstairs, she heard the stripped pine bedframe creak as Charlie folded his heavy, tattooed bulk into it. She watched the digits on her phone screen tick over: 07:28; 07:29; 07:30. And she held her breath.

No call came.

My da drank in the Gunner off Pennywell Road: Fenton had it on good authority. This was years before they tore it down. He and I got on the train at Queen Street like we were headed on a day trip. To be honest that north Edinburgh part of town always did make me think of the sea: Maw taking us out to the beach at Silverknowes, buying us those syrupy ice pole things that turned your tongue bright blue. I'd become a Glaswegian, and three or so years was long enough that I felt nostalgic, heading back into Edinburgh on the train, past the airport tower and the big Jenners warehouse. I was struggling to stay focused and think about my da at all: I was wondering if I'd run into Nella, or anyone I knew. Not that it would matter, transformed as I was. It's amazing what a tattoo on the throat will do to make people look anywhere but at you.

We got on the 37 bus towards Granton. The fares had gone up. I wanted to sit on the top deck, look out at Edinburgh, but didn't dare ask Fenton. He stoated off to the back of the downstairs, perched himself on the long bench seat. A woman with a fancy handbag moved elsewhere when I joined him.

'We arenae in Glasgow any more, Toto,' he said to me.

It was all the same as I remembered, really. It was summer, and up on the castle esplanade they were building the big metal frames for the seating at the Military Tattoo. There were posters for the jazz festival: I thought about watching the Mardi Gras parade in the Grassmarket, fittingly stoned, and then later watching a beautiful ruby-skinned woman in a tight black dress sing under red Chinese lanterns in a big striped tent. When *was* that? Edinburgh, I thought to myself, I miss you, hen. I felt stupid of course, but the feeling was there like a warm sort of pain. Fenton was looking at his phone. I kept quiet and watched the city go past at intervals, between stops.

I remember it was a bright day, but on the turn. Even Pennywell Road looked smart in the sunshine. But out over the green-rusted skeleton of the gasometer, dark clouds were stacking up, coming in off the Forth.

The Gunner was a badly cladded concrete box – I'd never been there before. It looked like a dead tooth that had turned black. The *E* had dropped off the wall but you could still see the rawl plugs, and the ghost of the letter where the wall had stayed clean behind the sign.

Fenton made me walk by a couple of times, casing the place. He lit a Marlboro Red, took a long drag, then passed it to me. In spite of the weed, I never did smoke straights, and Reds especially felt lethal. But Fenton had done this before: he was psyching me up, getting the adrenalin spike built before we stepped inside.

'I don't know what he looks like,' I realised.

Fenton squinted at me, sun in his eyes. 'I'll daunder in first,' he said. 'You jist follow me, all right?'

For a second, I wondered if this was all a big ruse: Fenton had been dispatched to come and kick seven shades out of some random *anyway*, so decided to pretend it was my da. Maybe he was sick of me getting maudlin over a bevvy and going on with all my *should I/ shouldn't I* crap. But the thought had come too late: I was here now, and Fenton was already crossing the street towards the Gunner's double doors. I didn't have much choice now but to pull up my hood, ditch the fag end, haul myself up straight and follow him.

Fuck, but it was grim. Middle of the day, so only the real pro drinkers in. I registered fast it was a Hibs bar: team photos. Signed shirts in frames. Hibs pin on the barmaid's neckline as Fenton ambled over in his Rangers-blue trackies and ordered us a pint of Tennent's each, with a double Famous Grouse chaser. Two of Scotland's shitest exports. I hadn't been imagining I'd drink . . . thought I'd have a clear head for what came next. But Fenton knew best, and I found as I picked up the whisky my hands were shaking. I tapped it on the bar and then sank it in one. Fenton winked at me.

He propped the bar up with one elbow and I did the same, following his gaze. He took about a quarter off the top of his Tennent's in one long suck. Then he gestured with the drippy glass across the room, and said, 'Yon's yer da.'

I don't know what I'd expected, but it wasn't him.

This guy Fenton was pointing at looked about seventy years old. I'd never known what age he was, how much older than Maw he might have been, any of that; she never wanted to talk about him and beyond a couple of tantrums as a child, I'd never pushed her to tell me. I knew that this man had been powerful, had been violent, but looking at him now I found it hard to believe. He'd clearly been shrunk by years of the drink. His skin was a sort of dirty yellow-grey, and he was thin as a beanpole. Not thin like I'd been before I met Toad and Fenton, and got built. Not wiry. Just thin. The flesh on his face hung loose from his cheekbones, and under each of his eyes was a deep pulled *V* of bagged skin.

Seeing him was almost enough: seeing how abject he was. Gangsters don't really believe in karma – or maybe we believe that we *are* karma, in human form, in action – but if this really was my da, then karma had whipped round and bitten him good and hard. I looked at Fenton, and it must all have shown on my face, because he laughed.

'Yeah, sorry, Puppy boy,' he said. 'I'm afraid ye are indeed related.' He took his elbow off the bar to nudge me. 'Will we go an' introduce ourselves?' he said.

I think I hesitated, but not for long. I remembered Nella, aged maybe twenty, telling my teenage self what she'd seen that night in the bathroom. Then I was over to that table almost before Fenton was.

'All right, Jimmy,' Fenton said. He parked himself in the chair next to my da, slapped his pint down. He'd said it like they were mates of old, like they sat in the Gunner together every day.

I'd seen as I got closer that my da was watching a TV, bolted to the wall in an alcove across from him, and showing some horse race with the subtitles on. Flat racing, no jumps. When Fenton spoke to him he turned. He looked confused, and I could see him doing the mental arithmetic of figuring out where he might have seen this man before. He never had, of course, but my da was a drunk. That sort of thing probably happened to him a lot.

I was able to ease into the seat opposite him without him really clocking me.

Fenton was talking. 'Jimmy Jamieson, Jimmy my man.' Empty patter: giving me time to assess the situation. 'How's it going on the ponies the day, son? How're ye keeping?'

I could see now that next to my da's glass, tucked under one corner of the beer mat, there was a betting slip. I remember thinking he'd been given bad tips.

'Aye, all right, pal,' my da said. He couldn't place Fenton, and his voice was just ever so wary. He had the watery voice of a day-drinker, and the quiver in his throat of a man turning elderly too soon.

He must have felt me studying him, because he looked me full in the face then. Nothing: a blank. No recognition of seeing a resemblance in me, though I've always been told I'm the absolute spit of Maw. He, meanwhile, looked like Nella – or rather, I saw Nella in him. It wasn't like, *wow, my sister is a chip off the old block*; but there was something there. Something around the eyes.

'Fuck,' I said, still looking at his face but speaking to Fenton. 'He *is* my da. This is actually my fucking da.'

He sort of squinted at me then, in a way that made me wonder if he had other kids by other women, if this had happened to him before. Maybe.

He nudged Fenton as if they were lifelong pals. As though Fenton would take his side in what he clearly didn't realise was to come.

'Who's this cunt, then?' he said, gesturing at me.

Fenton laughed, and made as though to answer. But I was on my feet, knuckles curled and pressed into the table: I'd leaned over so close to him that I couldn't focus on his eyes any more, and the details swam.

'My name's Charlie Birch, fuckface.' I said it as quiet as I could, a sort of hiss in the teeth. Not to be menacing, though I guess it had that effect too. But I was aware that folk might still remember. I'd been gone a while, but memories are long – especially in pubs like the Gunner.

It turned out my da's memory was long, too, in spite of the decades of drink. He flinched backward a little, and I watched him give me a cursory look up and down. I saw him take in the bulk of me, the scar tissue patches where my knuckles had scabbed. Tattoos on my neck, on the backs of my hands. I saw him panic.

'Oh Jesus,' he said. 'Oh Jesus, oh Mary Mother of . . .'

He made to stand up, but Fenton was quick. It looked effortless: he grabbed my da's arm and I watched his fingers lock on and whiten. That alone, I knew, would leave a bruise. Fenton dragged him back into his seat, spilling my da's pint. It cascaded over the table edge onto the old man's legs.

'Oh Jesus,' my da was saying. 'Oh Jesus, oh Jesus, oh Jesus.'

'Fucking spare me.' I sat back down then, eyeballed him across the sticky table. Fenton was still gripping the old man's arm. 'Quit the God-bothering, yeah? It's too late. You're going to hell, Jimmy, and if you don't play nice and do as I say, it'll be me who fucking sends you there.'

Her brother was lying on his side, facing her, the duvet pulled tightly around him on all sides, and his feet tucked into the bottom. Birch stood on the landing, watching through the half-closed bedroom door as Charlie breathed his long, deep-sleep breaths. He'd always slept like that: rolled like a burrito in the bedding. The fact that he still did – now he was such a big hillside of a man – made her want to cry for all the ways she no longer knew him.

Phone it in, Helen, she thought. You only need know that a suspect ought to be questioned, at the very least. And you know a lot more than that. Birch closed her eyes. This voice – her own voice, yes, unmistakably her own – was right. Charlie had told her barely anything, but still, she could only guess at the potential depth and breadth of the criminal activity he'd been involved in. To knowingly keep him in her house could be tantamount to becoming an accessory to those crimes herself. And yet ... she wanted *time*. She wanted to find out more. Where had he been, what had he done, and why had he never come home? That was her right, wasn't it, to know those things? After fourteen years: yes, she thought, I have a right. But how to do it? How to keep hold of Charlie, and keep hold of the job? Not just the job, she thought. My whole life.

Slowly, his eyes opened. They looked gummy, screwed up. Birch watched as he came to, not knowing where he was, and then remembered.

'Nope,' she said from the doorway, as he focused in on her. 'It wasn't a nightmare. You're still stuck here with me.'

Charlie levered himself up onto one elbow, and rubbed his face.

'How long was I asleep?' His voice was thick, dehydrated.

'A few hours,' she said. 'It's around two.'

Charlie huffed out air. 'Jesus.' He moved into a sitting position, and the bed creaked. 'I told you to wake me.'

She rolled her eyes. She could feel them falling back into their old sibling patterns, in spite of themselves.

'I just did,' she said, though she'd done nothing but stand, watching him. 'And you needed the rest, don't lie.'

Charlie rolled his eyes at her. 'Yeah, resting me up for my eventual arrest, interrogation and trial.'

His words nettled. There had been that sort of thinking behind it: my bed's a lot more comfy than the hard shelves in the custody suite.

'Eventual, yeah.' It was the only barb she could muster.

Downstairs, she ran him a large glass of water. While he'd slept, she'd opened her laptop and stared at, rather than read, her emails. A terse one from McLeod, acknowledging her phone message. Later, a well-intentioned one from Amy: *Get well soon – goodness knows we need you here!* The email made her feel guilty, but also gave her a stab of hope: had there been some development on the case? *Keep me updated on anything that comes up,* she wrote back. *Anything at all. I want to stay briefed.* She'd refreshed the screen a few times, hoping Amy might reply immediately, then when she didn't, Birch forced herself to move away from the laptop. She'd attempted to clean the kitchen. She'd put the clothes Charlie had arrived in into the washing machine, and the machine's noises had kept her company for a while. She'd felt anger at her brother pulsing around inside her, ebbing away at times, then returning.

'You hungry?' she shouted through to him now. He'd found his place on the sofa once again, dressed in an oversized T-shirt she usually used as a nightie, and a pair of her yoga pants. The shirt had a motif of a black cat with yellow eyes under a CND symbol, and the text along the bottom read *Cats Against The Bomb!*: a throwback to her student days.

'Sure,' he called back.

She was, she realised, ravenous: she couldn't remember the last time she'd eaten. She fished out from the fridge some garlic, sweaty mushrooms, half an aubergine whose cut, dappled end she sliced away and binned. Some vine tomatoes in a tray, whose skins had begun to wrinkle. Charlie padded into the kitchen and snorted at her as the knife slithered around on the chopping board in her tired hands.

'Still a vegetarian, then?' he smirked.

'Yes, and while you're in this house, you will be, too.'

She expected him to stay and talk, but he shrugged off back to the living room. A moment later, she heard him turn on the TV, thumbing the volume down low so that, from the next room, all she could hear was a general white noise of voices.

Birch made pasta: plenty of it, because she remembered what Charlie's appetite was like. She chucked into her boring tomato sauce the last of the red wine she and Anjan had failed to finish that weekend. She fancied she caught a drift of Anjan's smell – his warm, aniseed cologne – as she lifted the bottle. But she knew this was ridiculous. And besides, she was trying not to think about Anjan.

Charlie had managed to find a can of lager somewhere in the back of Birch's fridge. She was impressed, having had no idea it was there. After he ate what seemed like his own bodyweight in pasta-with-grilled-aubergine, he pulled the tab on the lager can and sat back on the sofa, stretching his limbs out every which way. He reminded Birch of a tomcat, in that moment.

'So,' he said, 'you still winching that guy Dale?'

Birch was eating – munching slowly, and thinking – and she found herself near choking on her mouthful.

'Dale *Meadows*?' She couldn't help but laugh. 'Jesus, Charlie.'

Her brother shrugged. 'What? He was the guy you were dating when I saw you last.'

Birch cast her eyes downward, smiling. 'God,' she said. 'I haven't thought about Dale Meadows in *years*. I wonder what he's up to these days.'

'Probably joined the criminal fraternity.' Charlie waggled his eyebrows at her, and took a sip of his beer. 'I hear that's what all the cool kids are doing now.'

Birch rolled her eyes. 'Dale Meadows was *not* a cool kid,' she said. 'I mean, what was I even thinking?'

Out of the corner of her eye, she saw Charlie make a face.

'*What?*'

He grinned at her. 'Oh come on. You liked him 'cause he wrote sappy love poems about you, and got you that bouquet of roses that time.'

Birch's mouth dropped open. 'God, yes he *did* – Valentine's Day one year, he did. How do you even *remember* that?'

Charlie smirked again. 'Keeping an eye on him, wasn't I? That's a brother's job. I didn't like the look of that fucker. Didn't trust him not to break my sister's heart.'

Birch felt something inside her warm, then, and expand. 'Oh, Charlie,' she said.

'All right, Nella – don't get all soft.'

Charlie took another sip of his beer. Birch ate her last few bites of pasta, and set the fork in the bowl on the coffee table between them. The companionable silence settled again.

'He didn't break my heart,' Birch said into it. 'I broke his, in the end.'

Charlie snorted. 'Good,' he said.

For just a moment, it was like everything had gone away. Charlie had never gone missing, their mother hadn't died, there were no crimes committed, no moral dilemma, no secrets, no fear. Charlie had nipped round for some late lunch and a beer. They were just siblings, and that was it . . . just for a moment. But then the moment was gone.

'I need to ask you some things, Charlie.'

She was going to take him in. She *was*. But once she did, he'd be out of her grasp. The potential conflict of interest would be huge: she wouldn't be allowed near him. She wouldn't be allowed to sit in on his interviews, wouldn't know what he was being asked or what was being said. They might have no contact for a good while. She couldn't do it without knowing some more.

Charlie sighed. 'Yeah,' he said, 'I had a feeling.'

She watched him settle down a look of defiance crossing his face, just for a second. He was prepared to push back at her, she could see, if he didn't like her questions.

'How did you make money,' she began, 'all that time? What work did you do, for Solomon?'

Charlie shrugged. 'All sorts,' he said. 'I was a bit of a dogsbody, really. Translation, of course. And I drove vans. Drove stuff around. Followed guys we needed to keep an eye on. Moved . . . people around the place.'

Birch crinkled her nose. 'You were just a chauffeur? I don't buy it.'

Her brother looked down at his hands. 'Okay,' he said. 'Other stuff, too. I beat some guys up sometimes. Guys who deserved it, Nella, I swear it. Guys who *really* deserved it.'

She closed her eyes for a moment. 'GBH,' she said. 'Assault. Aggravated assault. Great.'

'Yeah, yeah,' Charlie said, 'pile up the charges, why don't you?'

'Were you armed?'

She knew the answer.

'Sometimes. Yeah, I was.'

'So, assault with a deadly weapon.'

Charlie flinched, held up one hand like he wanted to stop traffic. 'Quit it. Just ask me what you want to know.'

'Okay. What else did you do for money? For Solomon.'

Charlie looked down at his hands. 'My main job,' he said, 'was running one of his saunas.'

Birch blinked, then sat quietly.

'I know what you're thinking. You're thinking *brothel*. But it wasn't a brothel, it was a sauna. Saunas are licensed premises. We had all our paperwork and everything.'

'Solomon,' she said, her breath catching in her throat. 'You're telling me *Solomon* had legit paperwork.'

He shook his head. 'Not really. Not him, I mean. We did. Me and . . .' Charlie's voice took on a tremor. 'Vyshnya. The woman I worked with. The . . . mother hen, she called herself. We looked after the girls. Solomon has a huge business empire, Nella. It's not like he's there doing spot checks. Vyshnya's name was on the licence, the punters paid in cash. We all took our cut, Solomon got the rest.'

Birch frowned. 'The women there, were they—'

Charlie held his hands up, anticipating her question. 'I don't know where they were all from. Vyshnya told me that some had been brought there by Solomon. That they'd come a long way, had a hard time.'

'They were trafficked.'

His hands were still in the air. '*Maybe*,' he said. 'But not all of them. Hanna, the girl I went out with – she was putting herself through uni. There was a girl there, Karen, she was Scottish. She'd been a cam girl before. It was—'

'But some of them were,' Birch interrupted. 'Or might have been.'

Charlie dropped his hands. Once again, he looked down. When he spoke, his voice was small. 'Yeah,' he said. 'I mean, I know that was something Solomon did. Something he does.'

Birch bit her lip. 'Trafficking in persons,' she said. 'Making you an accessory to trafficking in persons.'

Charlie looked up, his eyes sharp. 'Nella, I said *stop it*.'

But Birch stiffened. She'd heard the creaky rattle of her front gate, and on the path outside, footsteps.

'Upstairs,' she hissed.

For a moment, Charlie looked confused. Then, the rattle of the brass knocker.

'Fast,' Birch added, 'but *quietly*.'

Charlie frowned at her. 'Ignore it?' he mouthed.

But it was too late. Birch was on her feet.

'Upstairs,' she insisted again, and then watched from the hall-way as Charlie tried – with only limited success – to ascend the stairs softly, on the balls of his feet.

Another knock came: knuckles directly on the wood this time. On the other side of the door, a throat was cleared.

'Helen?'

Birch's heart leapt. It was Anjan.

Nobody batted an eyelid as we dragged my da outside, though he fairly hollered. It was that sort of place. Jimmy was that sort of guy. If they hadn't seen it before with him, they'd have seen it before with a thousand others. Only the barmaid looked concerned as Fenton and I half carried him out, each of us gripping an elbow, his weak legs kicking at the floor.

'He's my da,' I said to her. I tried to sound apologetic. 'He's had too much.'

She nodded. 'Aye,' she said. 'He's *always* had too much.'

Jimmy was squirming in our grip, yelling, *Fuck youse fuck youse*, as we hassled him out into the white shock of the street.

We ended up round the back of the Gunner, where the keg hatches and glass bins were. A gaggle of kids was back there, spray-painting crap tags onto the render. Fenton let go of my da, who listed over like a cannoned ship. I shifted my weight, keeping one hand around his arm, and grabbing the back of his collar with the other.

'Quiet down, Jimmy,' I hissed.

Fenton was advancing on the teenagers, waving at them as though to frighten off crows.

'Go an' fuck off,' he yelled.

The biggest of the lads took a step towards him, his hood up same as ours, his hands black and oily with paint. 'Fuckin' make us, Grandad,' he said.

Beside me, Jimmy laughed. I closed my eyes: *Back off, kid. You're messing with the wrong radge.*

'What'd you say tae me?' Fenton stopped, and planted his feet.

A showdown with some feral children. Great.

All the boys had paused in their work now. There were five, total: the biggest one maybe fifteen. I wanted to tell them they ought to be in school; then I remembered what school was actually *like*.

'I said . . .' The biggest boy drew himself up, and mirrored Fenton's stance. In the pocket of his Adidas top, I could see the fingers of one hand working at something. 'Fuckin' make us.'

Three of the other kids shuffled into a sort of formation behind their leader. Only the smallest one, who I realised might be just ten or so, hung back. He was watching Jimmy and me.

'*Gran*dad,' the big kid spat. His fingers closed on what he was looking for, and he drew out a snub folding knife – cheap, I could tell, the kind you bought in camping stores – and flicked it open.

The theatrical flourish made me want to laugh, too, but I knew better. I knew how close this kid was to the sort of beating that would leave him without ribs.

At my side, Jimmy sagged, apparently sick of standing. The moment stretched and hummed, like a taut piano wire.

Fenton made a rattling sound in his throat. At first I thought he might actually be *growling* at the kid: the sound was low and animal, like the kind a Rottweiler makes as it pushes up its hackles. But then the sound changed, and I realised he was laughing. A guttural, cold sort of laugh. I felt it send up the hairs on the back of Jimmy's neck.

'Are ye takin' the piss, kid?' Fenton said, with what sounded like genuine mirth in his voice. 'Are ye *actually* yaffing me?'

The big boy tilted his chin up, defiant as anything, but behind him, his goons eyed one another. I watched as the littlest one quietly laid down his spray can, and began to shuffle backward out of the yard.

'This is my patch, Grandad,' he said. His voice was a little less certain now, but he was trying not to show it. 'Go and take your junkie friend somewhere else.'

For a second, the whole gang glanced over at Jimmy.

I glared back at them.

Fenton was still laughing, but the laughter was ebbing away. He reached behind him and I saw it for a split second, just shoved there in his waistband, right against the skin, like this was *Die Hard* or something. Then he flipped it over with something like grace, and pointed the business end at the big kid.

Beside me, Jimmy let out a sigh that sounded like a mower shutting down. I felt the fight go out of him.

The fight went out of the big kid, too, though it took him a minute of looking down the barrel of Fenton's matte black Glock. The little one didn't need telling: he turned tail and pelted out onto the tarmacked street. All seven of us stood and listened to the *smack smack smack* of his tiny trainers as he ran.

'All right,' the big kid said. He raised his free hand slightly, and with the other he palmed the small blade back into its casing. 'Nae need, pal. We didnae realise, okay?'

The goons had fallen away, and were gathering up their spray cans in the deliberate manner of young men who are frantic, but don't want to show it.

Fenton let go the safety. I saw the gorge rise in the biggest boy's throat. Now both his hands were up, the folded knife pinned onto his right palm by his thumb. He was looking at the gun.

'Hey, where'd you get that, man?' In spite of his fear, I could see his eyes glittering with desire, thinking of the power he could wield.

'Never you mind, sunshine.' Fenton angled the barrel in the direction of the street. The goons were already halfway there, backing out as fast as they dared. 'Dae me a favour, will ye?'

I waited to see what Fenton would say. I expected some smart-mouth comment.

'Dinnae go looking for wan o' these,' he said, nodding at the Glock. 'Stay in the school, dae yer homework, make yer mammie proud, okay? I'm speaking tae all of ye.'

I think my mouth must have fallen open. Beside me, I heard Jimmy whisper, 'Yes.'

The boy snorted. 'Ma mammie's deid,' he said. 'I'm already fucked.'

As though shaken from the spell the gun had put him under, he ducked out from its path and hooked up the can of black paint into his hand. Taking this as their high sign, the goons ran for it, but their leader turned his back on the barrel of the Glock and sauntered to the edge of the yard with his chest out, casual. I almost whistled in awe of his swagger.

'But thanks for the advice, Grandad.'

He rounded the corner, and only then did I hear the same *smack smack smack* of his unlaced Nikes on the tarmac.

Fenton turned then, letting the Glock drop and hang loose in his fingers. 'Some kid, eh?' he said. He was grinning.

Beside me, Jimmy was staring at the gun. I realised I was, too. I wanted Fenton to put it away. This wasn't the deal.

Instead, Fenton took one long step towards Jimmy, raised his hand and with it, the muzzle of the Glock. I heard it clunk against the flat plate of Jimmy's skull. In my grip, I felt him go dead still, stiff as a door.

'Any last words,' Fenton said, 'for your boy?'

Jimmy flinched, but he couldn't move the gun, pressed as it was into the centre of his forehead. I remember thinking, If he shoots this cunt now, I'll end up wearing his brains. I had a light-coloured hoodie on. That was stupid, I thought.

'Fenton,' I said, hissing through my teeth as though somehow I thought my da wouldn't hear. 'This wasn't the deal.'

Fenton raised one eyebrow at me, and laughed again: not the Rottweiler laugh, but his usual short, sharp cough of a laugh.

He pulled the trigger.

Anjan was standing on the doorstep, a brown paper carrier bag in his arms.

'Hello, Helen,' he said.

Birch had opened the door less than a foot. She'd put her face into the gap, and now looked steadily at the bag he was holding, so she wouldn't have to look at his face. Her jaw hung loose: she couldn't think what to say, yet she knew she ought to say *something*, make some sort of noise, so Anjan couldn't hear Charlie making it to the landing and looking for a place to hide.

'What are you doing here?' It was the only thing in her head, right then.

Anjan looked disappointed by her welcome, then glanced backward, towards the prom. 'Could I . . . would you mind if I came inside?'

Birch blinked at him, and he seemed to draw himself up a little taller, as though summoning some extra reserve of patience.

'It's just . . . with the case ongoing I know that I shouldn't really be seeing you.' He smiled, trying to appeal to her. 'I really wanted to check in with you, but . . . I ought to keep a low profile here.'

It made her shiver, hearing him say the words Charlie had said to her, just the night before. He wasn't a man to be put off, she knew that. She had no choice but to open the door, step to one side, and admit him. As soon as he was fully in the hall, she reached past and locked the door in his wake.

'Sorry, Anjan,' she said, trying to find the manners her mother had taught her. 'Come in.'

Too late, she remembered the pasta dishes. They sat on the coffee table: two plates, two forks. They stopped Anjan in his tracks, and he turned to her.

'You have company,' he said.

She didn't like the way it was phrased: an observation, not a question. 'No,' she said. She could feel her face reddening with the lie. 'Just last night's dishes. I'm just not being very houseproud right now, I'm afraid.'

Birch scrambled past him and clattered the plates one onto the other. Anjan reached down to take them, his hand brushing her forearm.

'Let me,' he said, and juggled the dishes out of her hands and into his own. His skin was warm. Birch wanted to take one of those hands and hold it, hold on to Anjan's steady presence.

Charlie had placed his empty lager can on the floor under the sofa arm. She stepped past it, hoping Anjan wouldn't see, and led the way into the kitchen. On the drainer: two dirty coffee cups. Before he could follow her in, she dumped them down into the sink, along with the empty wine bottle.

Anjan set down the plates and cutlery on the worktop, his quiet breath and warm smell at her shoulder.

'You can go through,' Birch said, 'and sit down if you want. I'll make some tea?'

But of course, he was taking none of her orders. 'Don't be silly,' he said. He smiled, a small teasing smile. 'I don't want you to treat me like a guest.'

Birch smiled back. She was trying not to think of her brother, squirrelled away upstairs, listening.

'Lots of milk, no sugar, right?' she said.

Anjan's smile grew. 'You remembered.'

Birch blushed. 'Of course.' She turned away and opened the cupboard with the creaking door, fished out two clean mugs.

'I heard you weren't well,' Anjan said.

When she turned back to begin making the tea, she saw he'd put down the bag he'd been carrying and leaned against the worktop in front of it. She liked the look of him there, more relaxed than she usually saw him. She liked having him in her space, filling it with the good energy that he seemed to radiate naturally.

'And I didn't like the way we left things yesterday.'

Birch ceased her hasty movements. Her hands went limp, and she looked over at the drainer with its scatter of teaspoons, crumbs, the plates' smears of pasta sauce. 'Yes,' she said, 'that was my fault. I misunderstood, and I behaved badly. I owe you an apology.'

She heard the brown paper wrinkle as he stood upright again, brushing against the bag's side. Then, he crossed the small space between them and his hand alighted on her shoulder. She flinched, surprised, but glad of his touch. She realised she'd missed it.

'Don't worry about it,' he said, his mouth close to her ear. 'But . . . are you all right? I mean, I know you're off work. But are you . . . *all right?*'

Birch paused. She felt held there by him, not unpleasantly: his right hip lined up with her left, his right hand on her left shoulder. She liked it: it felt safe. Anjan was smart: a small, childlike part of her wanted to ask him to stay, ask him to just sort everything out. Make it all go away, Anjan. If anyone can, it's you.

Then she remembered. *Except . . . you work for the enemy now.*

'What do you mean,' she asked, 'all right? Do you mean mentally?'

She wasn't looking at his face, but she knew he was frowning.

'I didn't mean it like that,' he said. His hand squeezed her shoulder, but then, ever afraid of telling a lie, he added, 'not quite.'

She shrugged the hand away, and slid sideways, running her fingers along the drainer.

'This is a bloody hard case,' she said, 'for everyone. You made it about fifty times harder. So yeah, I'm not having the best week of my life.' She paused: Understatement of the century, Helen. 'But that doesn't mean I've gone mad,' she added.

She'd shuffled into the nook of the galley kitchen now, as far as she could go. She turned, at last, and faced Anjan fully. He'd been at the station, she could see it on him somehow. He was wearing his camel-hair coat, and the bag he'd brought in matched it in colour almost exactly.

'I'm sorry,' he said. 'That was thoughtless of me. I was just told that you were unwell, but . . . well, you always look so good, Helen.'

She blushed again, before she could stop herself. 'Yes, well.' The bag was stamped *Valvona & Crolla* in green ink. 'I'm not over here having a mental breakdown, I promise.'

Finally, she looked at his face again. She was being combative, mainly because of Charlie, and, for a brief second, she wished her brother hadn't shown up. Everything in her was telling her to forgive Anjan, to decide the hell with this case, walk over and comfort him. He looked tired, too, she saw. He might be as tired as she was. And she'd hurt him.

'I'm sorry,' he said. 'I'm so sorry that our' – he paused, then went on – 'our relationship has rather taken a turn. I was so enjoying being with you. Enjoying . . . seeing where it might go.'

She had to keep her guard up. You have to. 'I don't think I need to remind you,' she said, 'that you deciding to defend Solomon Carradice rather did for our relationship.'

'Represent,' he said, without a blink. 'Not defend.'

Yeah yeah, she thought. So you keep saying.

'You just said yourself,' she went on, ignoring him. 'You shouldn't even be here. I'm likely to be a witness for the prosecution.'

Anjan's eyes hardened again. She knew what he was going to say before he said it, so she cut him off.

'Yes, I know,' she said. 'Only if the case goes to trial.'

Anjan looked away. He nudged the bag a little, steadying it against the drainer. It nudged the red-smeared plates, and the pile of dishes shifted towards the sink. Birch saw him notice the two coffee cups.

'I'm very sorry,' he said again. Birch noted that he really did sound it. 'Sorry that you're struggling to build a case. But I'm doing my *job*. The firm—'

She felt her stomach twist. 'Let's not talk about it,' she said, her voice spilling out so suddenly that it shocked her. 'We shouldn't be, anyway. And I can't handle it. Not today.'

He gave a quick nod, and then dropped his gaze. He seemed to be looking at her feet on the tiled kitchen floor. Birch realised it was after four o'clock, and she was still in pyjamas. She couldn't remember if she'd washed off yesterday's make-up. She dreaded to think what her hair looked like.

'Sorry, I'm not a pretty sight—' she began, but Anjan had begun to speak, too. He looked up at her, awkward under his long, dark lashes.

'Sorry,' she said. 'Go on.'

His voice was quiet. 'You look just fine,' he said. 'You always do. But I was saying, I ... brought you a few things. Provisions. I know how hard it is being unwell. Stuck in the house.' He gestured towards the brown paper bag.

'Valvona and Crolla,' Birch said. 'Very nice. I appreciate that, you really shouldn't have.'

She thought that perhaps Anjan Chaudhry might be blushing, just a little.

'It was my pleasure,' he said, still speaking softly. 'You deserve some TLC.'

In the tense silence that followed, Birch was overwhelmed once again with the desire to stumble back across the kitchen and into Anjan's arms. She wanted to be held, and stilled. A weaker, smaller part of her also wanted to throw something at him: the big frying pan, perhaps, or a plate. Something that would make a loud noise, smash into a thousand shards, take some of the anxiety from her body and spirit it away. I must look wild, she thought. Wild-eyed. She realised he was giving her a look she couldn't read.

'Is there anything you'd like to tell me?'

He seemed to blurt it: the little darkening room reverberated his words, made them strangely sharp. Above them, Birch imagined she'd heard a footstep, the creak of a floorboard. Charlie shifting his weight, listening.

'Yes,' she heard herself say. 'There's *everything* I'd like to tell you. There's so much.' She felt the starchy pasta turn in her stomach. The blood in her feet ran cold, the skin prickling. 'I'm in a bind and I don't know what to do.'

Don't, Helen, she thought. Don't. He's the defence. Don't throw yourself to the sharks.

Anjan was waiting. Around her, the whole house held its breath.

Don't.

'But I can't,' she said, and saying the words felt like taking the first breath after struggling in deep water. 'I can't say any more. The case. Like you said . . . you shouldn't even be here.'

For a moment, neither of them spoke, or moved. Then Anjan took a long inward breath, and straightened his coat.

'You're quite right,' he said. 'I shouldn't. But I'm glad I got to see you, and I hope you feel better.'

He was already heading for the kitchen door. Birch trailed after him, her feet still cold, all the blood in her body racing around in her chest, in her pink face.

You almost told him, Helen. You idiot.

Moving towards the door, Anjan looked down at the lager can on the carpet beside the sofa. The fluid line of his exit wavered, but he didn't turn. At the door, Birch stood back and let him fiddle the lock open. He glanced back at her, his hand on the latch.

'I'm here,' he said. 'If ever you do want to . . . talk. About anything at all.'

She still wanted to throw something, smash something. But she also wanted to cry.

'Thank you,' she said, her voice little more than a whisper. 'Take care.'

He opened the door. 'See you . . . tomorrow?'

Oh God. She had been trying not to think that far ahead. She tilted her chin up and tried for a smile. 'Tomorrow,' she said, and then Anjan was gone.

Birch stood with her ear to the door, waiting until his smart shoes had crunched away down the path. When she heard the gate slot closed, she pushed down the snib on the Yale lock and then turned the key in the mortice. When she turned, Charlie was standing at the top of the stairs, looming down at her.

'Who in the name of hell,' he said, 'was *that?*'

I'll never forget the sound Jimmy made as Fenton pulled the trigger on that gun. I still hear it sometimes, when I have nightmares. Sometimes he's there, my da, and it's him making it; other times I open my mouth in the dream, and I make that noise myself. It was the sound of pure, distilled terror – a sort of howl, the last of Jimmy's rotten soul giving out. I let go of his arm and he hit the ground like a sack of wet soil.

Fenton stood over him, laughing. He levelled the gun above Jimmy's head and pulled the trigger again, then again. Each time, the same loud, hollow click. On the sticky tarmac, I watched my da gibber and cry, spit-bubbles blistering on his lips.

'Are ye frightened, Jimmy?' Fenton said.

My da couldn't speak, but he pressed his palms together as though in frantic prayer. He nodded.

'Good,' Fenton said. 'While ye're down there, I want ye thinking back. I ken ye're addled wi' the drink these days, and it's a while back. But when this kid's sister was a wee lassie' – Fenton nodded towards me – 'his mammie got pregnant again. Wanted a new wean to add to the family. Didn't she, Jimmy?'

My da's eyes were pink as a rabbit's. I could see the blood vessels in them, broken by fear and booze. He smelled pretty rank.

'*Didn't she?*' Fenton yelled.

I jumped, and my da squirmed and wailed. 'It wisnae,' he said. 'I didnae . . .'

Fenton drew his foot back then, and drove it into my da's side, sending all the air out of him. This was it. Time for me to step up. Mimicking Fenton's movement, I did the same, planting my foot slightly higher in the side of Jimmy's body. I heard the wet snap as his ribs caved. He howled again, higher pitched this time.

'What ye did, Jimmy' – Fenton was still shouting, and I was kicking and kicking methodically now, punctuating his rant – 'was *beat* that baby oot. Was *kill* this laddie's brother or sister. And ye ken that fine well.'

I looked down at my da, spasming on the ground in fear, in pain, in the dirt. I realised he was nodding. He admitted it.

'But . . . the drink,' he coughed. 'It wis . . . the drink.'

I booted him again, in the same spot as I had at first. No snap this time, just a dreadful, sloshing sort of thud. Jimmy folded in half, his face a mask of pain. Fenton circled him, lining himself up to cave in the other side.

'Okay,' I said.

Fenton glanced up at me.

'Okay,' I said again. 'That'll do. That's enough.'

I saw Fenton frown. I got the feeling he thought we were just getting started. But for a second, I held his gaze, and saw him get it. This was *my* da. I'd got what I wanted.

In truth, I felt sick. The old man *made* me feel sick – making excuses, even now, as he snivelled down there among the trodden fag butts and stale piss. But I also felt sick at myself. I'd never had a father. I'd known he was out there, somewhere in the world, and deep down, I'd always wanted him back. There was a part of me didn't care what he'd done, I just wanted him – there, alive, near me. And now, here he was. Hadn't I got my wish? And wasn't I just showing myself to be every bit as bad as the old man: a hard-nosed arsehole who hurt people and didn't care? Hadn't I also abandoned my sister and my maw? Who was I to dole out justice? I wanted to throw up.

Above us, the clouds that the Forth had pushed in were break-ing: fat drops of rain began to detonate on the tarmac.

I bent down over my da's jack-knifed body. I wanted to speak, but I couldn't think of a single word to say.

'Charlie,' my da croaked – softly enough, but it made me swivel upright again and cast my eyes around like a trapped cat. I hated him, and I wanted to comfort him, and I wished I had never gone to Fenton with any of it. Like so many things, I wished I could get out and start it all over again. *Don't remember me.*

'Charles,' he whispered. It was so quiet that I almost didn't hear. Above us something gave, and the rain opened out like a sail.

I stood over the old man, upright now. Out of the corner of my eye, I saw Fenton hitch his hoodie up and tuck the Glock away, out of the weather. He tugged his hood up round his face. Time to go.

'Look at yourself, Jimmy,' I said. I reached out one foot and toed the old man's body, as though he were roadkill, but in the corners of my eyes I could feel the sting of tears. 'Just fucking look at yourself.'

He was keening now, his arms wrapped around his smashed ribcage. I spat. I saw the white star of it land on the side of his neck.

'That's for my maw,' I said, and then followed Fenton out of the yard and into the rain.

Birch had retreated to the kitchen. She didn't know quite how to answer her brother, so she'd simply walked away. She filled the kettle and let it boil. Charlie had gone into the bathroom: she heard him bang the door of the cabinet. She couldn't seem to focus on anything other than berating herself: she really had been about to tell Anjan everything. She'd been about to hand Charlie over to the defence counsel, and potentially end her career in the same breath. Did Anjan care about her enough to become accessory to a crime, too? Of course not. How could she have been so stupid, as to nearly tell him that the Operation Citrine informant was upstairs in her bedroom?

She poured out two cups of tea, and the water wavered with her shaking hands and slopped across the worktop. Upstairs, Charlie was quiet. She'd expected him to schlep down the stairs and follow her: she had no idea what he was doing up there.

At last, his tread on the stairs. He did away with the stealthy dance that she had started: his feet landed on every loose board, every creak and squeal. The house seemed to be groaning under his weight. Birch wrung the tea-mopped cloth and leaned back against the sink.

'What,' Charlie said, appearing in the kitchen doorway, 'the actual, *actual* fuck?'

Birch had to try not to laugh: she'd forgotten about the yoga pants and shirt. Over the top, he'd thrown on a waterfall cardigan she'd kept in the wardrobe for years and never worn. It was mustard yellow. He pulled it across his chest now, and folded his arms.

'What are you *smiling* at?'

Birch bit her lip, and gestured at his outfit. 'I'm sorry,' she said. 'It's the costume.'

Charlie placed his hand on the worktop beside him. Birch was struck by how similar his gestures were to her own, when frustrated. Sibling mannerisms.

'Yeah.' Her brother was scowling. 'Whatever. Now tell me who the hell that was and why you just nearly shopped me to him.'

Birch blinked.

'Yes,' he said. 'I was on the stairs. I heard. This ain't a big house.'

'Listen,' she said, 'I'm sorry, but—'

Charlie flailed an arm. The cardigan billowed in its wake. 'You know what,' he said, 'I don't actually care. Where are my real clothes?'

'They're here, in the washer. But they're wet, honey.'

Charlie bent, opened the washing machine and began hauling his clothes out, slopping them onto the tiles. The kitchen filled with the purplish smell of laundry detergent.

'Look. I'm sorry, I lost it a bit for a second, there. But I didn't say anything, did I? I sent him away.'

Charlie ignored her. He picked out the boxer shorts from the pile of damp clothes and, straightening up, flicked the fabric against the front of the washer. It made a wet cracking sound. Birch felt a spray of droplets settle on her forearms.

'That was a pal of yours, though, wasn't it?' Charlie said. 'You polis. Wouldn't be surprised if you gave him the high sign to come back in fifteen minutes, pick me up.' Charlie turned his back on her, rolled off the leggings, and began to wriggle himself into the still-wet boxers. He huffed as they dragged against his skin, as the baggy T-shirt twisted itself around him.

'Anjan isn't a policeman,' she said. 'He's a lawyer.'

She knew as soon as she'd said it that she shouldn't have. Charlie twisted his head over one shoulder to look at her.

'Whose lawyer?'

Birch had opened her mouth to speak, but no sound came out. She watched Charlie un-knot his jeans from the pile of fabric on the floor. When she did speak, her voice was miserable, tiny.

'He's working on the case.' She didn't have the strength for a lie. 'He's . . . Solomon's lawyer.'

Charlie's eyes boggled. 'Nella.' He snapped the jeans out to straighten them, and in spite of herself, she jumped. 'Tell me you're not serious.'

'He's also a *friend*,' she said, trying to rally. 'He came over to see if I was okay. And I didn't *say* anything. He's gone.'

Charlie was wrestling the jeans on now, shaking his head. 'Gone for now,' he said. 'But you can't tell me he wasn't suspicious.'

Birch passed a hand over her eyes. 'I'm sorry,' she said. She really was. *Idiot*, she thought, *idiot, idiot, idiot*. 'But I think it's going to be okay, honestly. Anjan's a good guy.' And defending a fiend, she reminded herself. That too.

'Yeah, yeah,' Charlie said. 'Why don't you run after him? He could help you arrest me, like you've been saying you ought to.'

'That's not fair.' Anger was bleeding into her voice now. 'I've been saying I want to help you.'

But her brother was contorting, the wet jeans halfway up his thighs. 'You polis are all the same,' he said. 'Wouldn't know how to actually help someone if they drew you a fucking diagram.'

Birch threw up her hands. 'What help do you *want?*'

He rounded on her. 'I want what I was fucking promised! Why do you think I came here? I thought you could make them give me what they promised!'

Quiet fell between them. After a moment, Charlie began pulling up the jeans again, but less frantically. They slid over his skin and Birch watched as he fumbled with the fly, the buttons greasy with detergent.

'You're still talking about immunity,' she said.

'Yeah.' Charlie straightened up and glared at her. It was the first time he'd met her eyes since he'd come downstairs.

'Charlie,' she said, 'I've told you, it's not going to happen without you going into custody. You're in *dreamland*.'

Her brother snorted. 'See? All the same.' He broke his gaze and reached down for his crumpled T-shirt.

Birch spluttered. There were a thousand things she wanted to say, and they seemed to swirl around her like leaves in a high wind. 'I can help you,' she said. 'I *can* help you. But I'm not a fucking miracle worker. No judge on earth would let you off with every-thing you've done. But if you agree to testify—'

Charlie shot upright again, the T-shirt balled in his fist. 'Exactly!' He was shouting now. 'If I agree to testify – against the biggest scum-bag you or I have ever fucking known – I get nothing? I get chucked in jail with the same guys I just grassed on? What sort of justice is that? If I help put away that cunt I should get a fucking community service medal.' He flapped open the T-shirt. It sounded like a wet sail.

'So wait.' Birch was furious now. Her head was thumping. 'What you're saying to me is, where's my reward? You want to be *rewarded?*'

'Yeah. I do.' Charlie shrugged her cat T-shirt to the floor and dumped his own over his head. 'Is it too much to ask that I get to walk away after, and have a life?'

Birch reached up and pressed one hand to her forehead. 'That's just not how the world works! You committed fourteen years' worth of criminal acts. It was your choice to do that. I mean sure, there are deals to be made, but—'

Her brother took a step towards her. For the first time since she'd come out of her fainting fit on the kitchen floor, Birch felt afraid of him.

'Did you say it was my *choice?*'

The feeling in her ribcage was familiar. She'd felt it as she lay on the couch, listening to him break in.

'Yeah.' She squared up to her brother, showing him the extra inches in height she had on her side. 'Yeah, I think it was.'

For a moment, they eyeballed each other. Birch realised every muscle in her body was tensed, waiting for the next spat line, or even for a blow. But then, Charlie seemed to shrink back.

'Then you don't know shit, Helen,' he said. 'It was a mistake even coming here.'

His eyes dropped to the floor. He tugged the T-shirt down over his stomach, then reached for the hoodie. The floor between them was slick and shiny. Charlie's clothes stuck to him at odd angles. Though she could tell he was still angry, he looked beaten. He'd obviously really thought she could give him what he wanted. He'd thought she could make it all go away.

'Listen,' she said, watching him drag the hoodie onto his shoulders. His garments' wet fabric gave off a slimy sound that made her want to cringe. 'There are things we could do. If you confess to everything you've done, if you testify—'

'No, Nella, I—'

'If you *testify*.' Birch was realising this was her last chance before – something. Before Charlie did something decisive. 'If you agree to cross-examination. That, with a guilty plea – there could be a deal.' She tried to meet his eye. 'There could be a *good* deal.'

He looked at her again, like she'd wanted. She wished she hadn't made him: his face was shuttered up now, and icy.

'You don't know what I've done,' he said. 'You don't know what I'd have to deal my way down from.'

Birch wanted to hit him then. She wanted to run at him, hammer on his chest with her fists. Did he think she was stupid?

'You killed people,' she said. 'Is that it? Is that the great mystery? You killed people . . . and yet you want a hero's medal and to be able to walk away.'

Charlie stared at her, as though he couldn't believe she'd said what she'd said. His mouth was slightly open. On his arms, the hairs that had been slicked down as he rolled up the damp sleeves of the hoodie were beginning to spring back, little by little.

'Yeah,' he said, after a pause that seemed endless. 'But I'll settle for one out of the two.'

He turned then, and walked out of the kitchen. The damp clothes squelched.

'No.' Birch followed him. 'No, Charlie, you can't just run out on me.'

He wheeled round. 'Why not? You can just go back to assuming I'm dead – that seemed to work out pretty well for you.'

Birch spluttered. A hot lump was growing in her chest. Its name was panic. 'How can you *say* that? How can you – after what you put us through, me and Mum—'

Charlie snorted, and turned back to his course through the living room. 'Don't start,' he said.

Birch trailed in her brother's damp footprints. 'Okay,' she said, 'fine. Screw me, and screw the fact that you helped send Mum to her fucking grave, screw the last fourteen years, *whatever*. But Charlie – Solomon is going to walk free at nine o' clock on Friday morning, unless you do something. Unless you step up to the fucking plate.'

Charlie ignored her. He'd made it to the hallway, found his shoes, and was bent double, puffing, trying to get them onto his slick, bare feet.

'For goodness' *sake!*' Birch realised she was screaming, but her brother was inches from the door now. Her baby brother, who she'd tried to find for over a decade. Her baby brother, about to walk out into a night that was filled with knives. 'Are you really such a coward? Are you really going to let him get away with it? With everything he's done – because you don't want to face the consequences of your actions?'

Charlie unfolded himself so quickly that he almost head-butted her. She took a step back.

'Yeah,' he said. 'Of course I'm a coward. Of *course* I am. I've seen what this man can do. I am *terrified* of him. Have been for years. You're not going to lecture me on this shit, because I hate, loathe and detest the guy with every fucking sinew in my entire fucking being. Do you get that? Do you understand?'

A fleck of his spit landed on her cheek. She didn't dare reach up to wipe it away.

'No,' he went on. 'Of course you don't. You don't know fuck all about what this man is capable of, not really. And yet you're asking me to grass on him, and grass on his boys, and then go and sit in the same fucking jail as them all. And I'm supposed to see *that* as *help?*'

Birch was shaking. Her fingers and feet prickled as the blood ran out of them, rerouting to her hammering heart.

She could only stand and look at her brother. The damp clothes clung to him in patches, and the shoes he'd wrenched onto his feet were still undone, laces snaking over each other.

'Don't go,' Birch said quietly. 'Stay and face it.'

He looked at her, and she could see that all the anger had gone, and been replaced by sadness.

'I should never have come back, I'm sorry. I should just have stayed dead.'

As her brother turned, and began to reach for the door handle, she lurched towards him, fingers clawing at the fabric of his clothes.

'Don't go, honey, please. *Please*. It might just be a year or two, if you get a deal, then you could—'

'Nella.' He put a hand on her arm, stilled her. 'I wouldn't live a year or two. It's better this way. This way I stand a chance.'

Birch couldn't help it. She threw her arms around him, and tried to cling on. 'Please, Charlie. Please don't. Please don't leave me alone again.'

Charlie hooked his arms out from her grip, and took hold of her shoulders. Without hurting her, he tensed the powerful muscles he'd built and gently manoeuvred her off him.

'It's a cliché,' he said, 'but you're better off without me, Nella.'

He let her go, then turned and opened the front door. The garden outside was dark now, and pushed its cold breath into the space with them.

'I love you,' Charlie said. Closing the door on her stricken face, he became Charlie Birch: Missing Person all over again.

Years, I worked for Solomon without ever meeting him, speaking to him, or even really seeing much evidence of his existence. He got talked about a lot. He got talked about the way I assume fundamentalist Christians talk about God, or how kids talk about Father Christmas. It was like, *Solomon is watching you. He knows if you've been good or not, so be good for goodness' sake.* I didn't even know much about him, just that he was a notorious fucking radge, and everyone was frightened of him. He was also about a hundred years old by all accounts, so I wondered how scary he could really be. I found out the hard way.

I'd been going with Hanna about two years or so by then. I saw the guys, the johns. I understood that there was no chance of her falling for any of those cunts, and getting stolen away from me. But even if she had been . . . you know, it was casual. I'd have been sore over it, but it would have been fine. And whenever any of them got heavy with her – or with any of the girls – I was the guy who got to straighten that scumbag out. Like Vyshnya said, it didn't happen all that often, but when it did, I'll admit, I got that wee bit extra thrill out of it, knowing I was defending my girl's honour. Some sort of fucked-up chivalry, I dunno. And Hanna was a good girl, with . . . protection, and that. She was careful. We did all right.

So there was this one night that I wasn't there, at the sauna. I was out doing a driving job for Toad. In the HR structure, as it were, Toad was sort of my line manager slash mentor. I did the stuff he asked me to do – translating, driving, kicking crap out of someone, standing quietly in the background and watching someone else kick crap out of someone. Then he'd hand me an envelope of cash, or sometimes I'd get promised something in kind – nice watch, good shoes, the thousand-pound briefcase of the guy I'd just beaten up. Very occasionally, I'd get a favour. But mostly, cash. As far as I was concerned, I worked for Toad, and Toad was an all right guy. I didn't ask where the jobs had come from, I didn't ask *who* or *why*. I just did it . . . whatever *it* was.

That night was a wash-out. One of those *I'll owe you one* rarities. It was a weeknight, a Wednesday. Quiet at the sauna, so Vyshnya was waiting out the place on her own. She had me on speed dial. I wasn't far away.

I'd been told to sit in the van – Vic's old van – and watch this flat. Eventually, Toad said, some guy would come out and I'd follow him to wherever he went and give him a message. Not the knuckleduster kind: Toad had given me an envelope that I was supposed to literally put into this guy's hand.

'This is a good message?' I'd asked in Russian. 'He's going to like what he reads?'

Toad laughed. 'Very much no,' he'd said. 'Deliver without words.'

I'd been sitting there fucking *hours*. It must have been winter, because I got there as everyone was heading home from work, and it was already dark. I saw the guy go in, and texted Toad to say so.

Just wait, he texted back. *Then follow. You're a good friend.*

Hours went by. I watched the lights come on and go off in different rooms in the flat. I watched the guy's silhouette move around behind the blinds. At one point he came out in the close to smoke.

He's outside smoking, I texted. *Can I deliver?*

Toad seemed annoyed. *Follow instructions*, he wrote back. *Wait till he goes.*

I obeyed, but I was bored shitless. The van's radio was broken, and I had to keep my phone usage down to save the battery for later, when I'd need to check in that the job was done. I had to watch, too, of course. But there was sweet fuck all to watch.

The phone buzzed. It was around nine. I picked it up, hoping Toad had texted back to let me off the job. But it was Hanna.

Solomon's here. You need to come.

I remember feeling a little shiver of something: electricity, fear, guilt. But also a weird nervy excitement. *It finally happens. I finally get to meet the infamous Solomon.*

Babygirl, I texted back. *I'm on a job for Toad.*

She was online, wrote back straight away. *You have to come. He's mad.*

I dithered, but not for long. I wasn't sad to be ditching out on this fucking boring job that Toad wasn't paying me for anyway. I turned the key, and Vic's old engine coughed awake.

You okay?

It took her a minute to reply, and I sat there looking at the phone screen, and listening to the engine.

I'm scared, she wrote back. *Drive fast.*

Thursday

Birch woke coughing, a dry cough that felt like it might never stop. Her heart beat its fists against the closed door of her chest. She felt as if she had something inside her that she needed to get out, but as she coughed and coughed, she realised there was nothing. She pushed herself back into the pillows, and forced herself to lie still.

It was fine. It was all fine. You're at home, in your bed, and everything is fine. Birch squinted at the bedside clock: it was just after five. She'd slept okay, considering. Considering what?

Oh yes, she remembered. Everything is not fine.

Today was the last day. Twenty-four hours, and then they'd have to let Solomon go. She'd have to walk back into the station, which would – unless some miracle had happened while she'd been away – be a hive of panicked, last-ditch activity. She'd have to look her colleagues in the eye, knowing that she'd bungled their case. She'd found the missing informant in the biggest organised crime bust her force had ever known ... and then she'd let him run. She'd told no one. She *could* tell no one, unless she wanted to lose her job. Besides, even if she called for a manhunt and sent the boys out to look for Charlie, she'd only succeed in letting Solomon and his gang know, once and for all, that Charlie was indeed their man. Gangsters didn't follow due process. They'd find him first, and this time he really would be dead.

She'd spooled through this train of thought over and over in her head as she lay in bed staring at the ceiling – aloud. Okay: say nothing, you keep your job. Charlie might get away clean. It might all be fine. But then, the terrible flip-side: How will you live with yourself, Helen? You should have cuffed him as soon as you saw him. You've shattered this case into bits. You. The worst thought had come as the bedside clock read 00:00. Suddenly: Every one of Solomon's victims after this moment is on your conscience. Anyone he hurts, anyone who dies. Your fault.

Birch was glad to make it to Elcho Terrace, where she'd parked the car. She hadn't quite realised until she began walking how tired she was of the four walls of her house, how cage-like they felt. In a fit of what she knew was extreme paranoia, she patrolled around the car, checking the tyres, wheel-arches, bending double to peer underneath. Remembering a spy movie she'd seen once, she walked as far away from the car as she thought the signal would reach before hitting the button on the key and unlocking the doors. When nothing happened she felt sheepish, but, nevertheless, she opened the driver's door to check the footwell, and patted down the underside of the steering console with a shaky hand. She peered into the back seats, and opened the boot. Finally, glancing around to see if anyone was watching, she popped the bonnet and poked around underneath – not knowing what she was looking for, but looking all the same. There was nothing. The car appeared untouched.

It's all fine, she thought. Still, as she turned the key in the ignition, she held her breath.

Well, that was ridiculous, wasn't it? She sat at the traffic lights on the corner of Brighton Place, letting her pulse settle.

Once she got onto the wide stretch of Seafield Road East, Birch pushed the hands-free phone button on her steering wheel, and used her formal interview voice on the empty car.

'Dial,' she said, 'Amy Kato, mobile.'

Dialling Amy Kato, mobile, the car's robotic phone lady replied. She said *cat-oh,* not *Kato.*

'Morning, marm!' Amy sounded as cheery as ever, though it was before eight. 'Wasn't expecting to hear from you today!'

Birch smiled. It felt like a long time since she'd heard her friend's voice. 'Morning,' she said. 'McLeod been spreading the word that I'm a plague victim?'

Amy laughed. 'Not DCI McLeod,' she said. 'DI Robson.'

Birch raised an eyebrow. 'Big Rab?'

There was a pause.

'Well. You didn't look too great after . . . the flowers incident.'

Birch eased her speed down to make the sharp bend by the Seafield sewage plant. In the early light, the seagulls hung over the outlet pipes like flakes in a big, ugly snowglobe.

'I'm all right,' she said. 'Mainly just been pacing around my house, going nuts.' It was true, but it sounded weird, so she added, 'You know I hate being sick.'

'Oh,' Amy replied, 'I'm the same.'

Birch almost snorted. She couldn't remember a time Amy had had even so much as a bad hair day, let alone taken time off sick.

'Listen,' she said, 'I'm glad I got you. I know you won't be in yet, so it's good of you to answer.'

Amy laughed. 'If you think that, then with the greatest of respect, you're mad. I've been in nearly an hour.'

Of course. The last day left to make something stick. Tomorrow morning, Solomon walked free. *Because of you.*

'Oh God, yes,' she said. 'Time flies when you're having no fun at all. Sorry.'

On the other end, Amy just laughed.

'I was actually calling,' Birch said, 'to get an update on that. Solomon. Any movement happen while I was gone yesterday?'

She pulled up at the lights beside the industrial estate. The flags on the Fiat garage pattered in the wind. She could smell the grease and singe of the McDonald's Drive-Thru. Her mouth watered. She prayed Amy would say something good.

'It's getting desperate, marm.' Amy's voice had turned grave. 'I mean, I'm not being told everything, but it's like Crosbie's made no headway at all. They've been in the interview room pretty much solidly with Solomon . . . and Anjan of course.'

Of course, Birch thought. That elastic-band pull in her chest again.

'And nothing. Between you and me, DCI McLeod is about up to ninety.'

I bet he is. Birch almost said it aloud, but then thought better of it.

'We've got twenty-four hours left,' Amy said. 'And it's not looking good. If we only had a witness – that's what Crosbie keeps saying. If only someone would talk, anyone. It would be a start, at least.'

'The informant,' she said, a little too sharply, and before she could help herself.

Amy didn't seem to notice. 'Yeah,' she said. 'But they're looking all over. Crosbie's had the team out shaking up any known associates they can find. They've been in Low Moss and Barlinnie and Shotts, even the Young Offenders at Polmont, trying to get some perps on board, to tell them something. Like I say, it's getting desperate.'

Birch was cringing. 'And no one will sing.'

'Nope,' Amy said. 'A wall of silence. Solomon's got them all well trained.'

'Or shit scared,' Birch replied, 'which I guess is about the same thing, when it comes down to it.'

She slid past the Polish supermarket, the tyre garage, the scrapyard. The car's brakes squeaked as she misjudged the amber light outside the Pond pub and had to come up short. Amy was quiet.

'We need the informant,' she said at last. 'That's what I can't stop thinking. That informant must know *everything*, because otherwise . . .'

'Otherwise how could Operation Citrine have gone ahead.'

'Yeah,' Amy said. 'I know it's way above my pay grade, but how did we lose him? If DI Crosbie knows, he's playing his cards close to his chest. DCI McLeod, too.'

Birch felt struck dumb. But underneath the endless chant of blame, another thought struck her. She hadn't been the first person to let Charlie run. Amy had a point.

'What about Big Rab?' she asked. 'DI Robson, I mean. How does he seem?'

She listened while Amy thought for a moment.

'Calm,' she said. 'Now you mention it.'

Something prickled on the back of Birch's neck. She remembered Big Rab's kindness – his interest in her. The business card on her mantelpiece with his personal mobile number scrawled on the back.

'The informant came to us via Glasgow,' she said, musing aloud. 'Via Big Rab's team. So *that's* why McLeod doesn't know anything. But if Rab knows more, then . . . why isn't he letting on?'

'Your guess is as good as mine,' Amy said.

'I'm on my way in. I assume DI Robson is around?'

'Of course,' Amy said. 'You need to talk to him?'

'Yeah,' Birch said. 'I think I do.'

Birch hit her left-hand indicator. She'd right her course at the lights.

'That's funny . . .' Amy said.

There was quiet on the line.

Birch shuddered. 'Amy?' She could practically hear her colleague's mental gears whirring.

'It's just . . . DI Robson,' Amy said. 'I mean, it's just a funny coincidence, but he mentioned he wants to talk to you, too.'

Birch shuddered again, and this time it reached her arms, twitching the car slightly in its path. A strange new unease settled in her already uneasy mind. 'Did he say why?'

Amy's voice brightened. 'Not to me,' she said. 'But don't worry, I don't think you're in trouble.'

You have no idea, Birch thought, how much trouble I am in. 'Thanks, Kato,' she said, and hung up.

Big Rab's face hung in her mind: sitting across from her in the Kay's Bar snug.

Your fault, said the voice in her head. You let him run.

I drove about as fast as Vic's van would allow: not fast enough. It felt like I got stuck behind every Glasgow city bus out that night. At one point I got stuck behind a fucking gritter. I didn't bother trying to park: I dumped the van on the pavement outside the sauna's front door, passenger-side wheels up on the kerb. I stuck the hazards on, locked up and ran inside.

At the top of the stairs, Izz was standing, keeping guard.

'You came with Solomon?' I didn't bother with niceties.

Izz shook his head. 'He called me,' he said.

I looked around the lounge – Vyshnya's fancy word for the waiting space. No one there: not one single punter. Not unusual, for a Wednesday night, but there were no girls there either. The TV – the TV that I'd *never* seen not switched on – had been turned off. No sign of Vyshnya. The lounge was deserted.

'I've been instructed,' Izz said, 'to turn guys away. Solomon wants the run of the place tonight.'

I sensed an irritation in his voice that wasn't aimed at me. When I looked at Izz, I saw that he wasn't in his usual finery. He still looked sharper than a goon like me could ever hope for, but he was in jeans, a dark-coloured shirt with a subtle pattern. Loafers and no socks. I realised he had been off duty.

'Why'd he call you, man?' I asked.

Izz gestured at the hatch, behind which I usually sat. 'You weren't here. I was nearby.' He raised one well-groomed eyebrow. 'In the *pub*.' When I said nothing, he added, 'And he just loves to bring someone running. I'm amazed he's never done it to you.'

This didn't really compute, but I didn't want to get off topic. 'Okay, okay. Can you tell me what happened?'

Izz shrugged. 'I got here. Solomon was there –' He gestured at the long, low sofa on one side of the lounge. 'He's got four guys with him. Malkie, Abdul and a couple I don't know. They were kicking a couple punters out when I arrived. Telling them the shop was closed for tonight. Solomon wasn't best pleased that there was no muscle here.'

I closed my eyes. I remembered what had happened to Tsezar.

'Fucksake,' I said. 'I mean.'

Izz studied his nails. 'It wasn't like Vyshnya couldn't handle shit. It was pretty quiet from what I could see. She was on it.'

'She said that?'

'Yeah.'

Izz came by sometimes, used the place. He knew what was up.

'I don't think it was a good idea,' he said.

'What?'

'For Vyshnya to talk back to Solomon. She wasn't exactly polite.'

'Izz,' I said. 'Solomon got Toad to disappear the last guy that worked here.'

He blinked. 'And?'

'That guy was her boyfriend. I can see why she'd be less than friendly.'

'That was years ago.' Izz shrugged. 'And whatever . . . it doesn't take a rocket scientist to know that you don't get insolent with the big man. Vyshnya's been round the block. She knows better.'

I cast around the room again. I was shitting myself, to be honest. Yeah, it was years ago, but I couldn't stop thinking about that night with Tsezar. Seeing him in the back of Vic's van, his hands held up like white flags.

'What did she say?'

Izz looked me up and down, and sniffed. 'She defended you, Puppy boy,' he said. 'He asked where the muscle was and she said she'd given you the night off. He wasn't happy with you, like, at all. But she insisted it was her decision, she didn't need you tonight. She told him to keep his nose out of her business.'

I shuddered. '*Her* business?'

'Yeah,' Izz said. 'I think that was what did it.'

For a minute, we were quiet. I could tell Izz wasn't as chill about the situation as he was pretending to be.

'So . . . where the fuck is everyone?'

His face clouded. 'Solomon . . . he told the guys to all pick a girl.'

I felt a bit sick. I didn't know why tonight was different, but it was. 'Hanna,' I said.

'Yeah.' Izz looked down at his shoes. 'Sorry, man. She went in with one of the guys I don't know.'

Okay, I thought. This is just a punt, like any other. He's just a punter, like any other. I knew it wasn't true, but I told it to myself anyway.

'It's fine,' I said, though my voice betrayed that it wasn't. 'But where the fuck is Vyshnya?'

Izz shook his head. He was wearing an expression that might have been disgust. 'There were four girls in,' he said.

I looked at him blankly. I knew that. I'd been in last night, seen the rota.

'So when they'd all picked . . .' Izz waited.

'*What*, Izz?'

'Only Vyshnya was left.'

I looked at him. Then the penny dropped. 'Solomon picked Vyshnya,' I said. 'He wanted to punish her.'

Izz nodded.

'And they . . . ?'

'Yeah.'

The sick feeling was growing. 'But . . . Vyshnya doesn't *do* that.'

Izz shrugged. 'Looks like she does tonight.'

In the car park, Birch passed Anjan's big saloon, its cream interior matte and butter-soft, vague under the mix of streetlight and early morning gloom. As she approached, the station looked like it always did: a lumpen cube of a thing, the lit windows on each floor striping it dark-light-dark. But as soon as the lobby doors swung shut behind her, she could feel the crackle of collective anxiety. Twenty-four hours left, and no leads.

Heads were down in the bullpen: Birch reached her office door without anyone so much as raising their eyes to look at her. She stood over the desk, shouldering off her coat, and flicked on the computer. In her inbox, fresh interview transcripts from Solomon's Tuesday and Wednesday conversations with Big Rab and DI Crosbie. She sat down to skim through them, beginning to feel a caffeine itch. It turned out Solomon wasn't a brick wall like he'd trained his associates to be: his replies to Crosbie and Rab were short, but practically jovial in places. He was whip-smart, arrogant and confident that he'd walk free: it was all there in his answers. They were empty statements, wide-eyed and calculating. *Who me? I'm just a sweet old man,* they seemed to say, like the wolf dressed up as Red Riding Hood's granny. Anjan's name appeared at the top of each transcript: he'd been in the room, but barely passed comment. He didn't need to. It was clear to Birch, from even a cursory read, that Solomon was running the show.

'Morning, hen.'

Rab had managed to materialise in the doorway without her noticing: clearly she'd been more engrossed in the transcripts than she'd thought, as stealth was not a skill Rab really possessed. She jumped.

'Glad tae see you're a wee bit better,' he said.

Birch blinked. Oh yes. You were 'sick', Helen, remember. 'Lots better,' she said, 'thanks.' God, you're a dreadful liar.

'DC Kato said ye were hoping fer a chat,' Rab said.

Birch raised an eyebrow. 'Likewise,' she said.

Rab looked down at his feet, then back at her. Amy had said she wasn't in trouble, but . . . something was most definitely wrong. She felt her heart rate tick up. What did Rab know? She'd been wondering that for days now.

He rifled in his trouser pocket and held up a single key on one of the station lanyards. 'Interview room seven's free,' he said, lowering his voice. 'Might be best if we talk privately.'

Oh shit, Birch thought. I *am* in trouble. But in spite of herself she smiled, pushed back her chair, and stood. 'Detour for coffee?'

Rab paused, then nodded. 'Aye, why not.'

Interview room seven had aggressive fluorescent lighting, and no windows. Birch squinted as she walked through the door that Rab pushed open and held for her. She wondered how many times she'd been in this room, eyeing a perp – sometimes a solicitor, too – across the plain table. She and whichever officer was sitting in would always take the chairs with their backs to the wall. The table was not in the middle of the room: interviewees sat with a short stretch of empty space behind them, so they couldn't lean back and get too comfortable. Because she'd walked in first, Birch took her usual seat. Big Rab eyed the perp's side of the table and, after a pause, laid his coffee down there. Before he sat, he reached over and pulled out a plug from the wall.

'Can't be too careful,' he said, trying to make light of the action. The plug powered the room's recording equipment.

Birch tried to keep her expression even as Rab settled into his chair. The endless undertow of blame still swirled in her mind, but quieter now, muted by her curiosity over what he might say to her. This conversation wasn't suitable for the refectory or even her office: he must have decided that up front. As he took a long drink, she realised she was holding her breath.

'Well, lassie,' Rab said at last. 'I'm afraid I've no' always been totally honest wi' ye.'

Birch felt her eyes widen.

'But it's getting serious now,' he went on. 'Time's short. You and me need to be on the same page.'

If only, she thought, but she stayed quiet.

'So.' Rab seemed to be struggling to get started. 'Ye ken that oor informant for Citrine came out of Glasgow?'

Birch nodded. 'Yeah.'

'And ye ken that oor informant for Citrine has been . . . misplaced.'

She tried not to shiver. 'Yes.'

Rab looked at her so sharply then that she almost jumped.

'So . . . dae ye ken who that informant is, DI Birch?'

Oh shit.

Birch had no idea what her face was doing. She hoped it didn't look guilty, or scared, which was what she felt in that moment. She screwed up her nose, aiming for confusion.

'Do I know . . . where the informant is?' It was a dodge, and an obvious one. 'No, I don't.' That, she thought, is the truth, at least.

'No.' Rab spoke patiently. 'I said *who*. Dae ye know who it is?'

Birch's hearing did something weird: for a moment, all she could hear was the blood of her own pulse, up to ninety, in her ears.

Oh God, she realised. I am about to lie. To a fellow officer. About a live case. A high-stakes case. She blinked. 'No,' she said, and felt her voice tremble. 'I have absolutely no idea.'

You do not have to say anything, she thought, but it may harm your defence if you do not mention when questioned—

'I do,' Rab said.

Birch looked at him. She couldn't believe she hadn't thought of it before. 'That means it was you. The informant came to *you*.'

Rab nodded. 'Aye.' Then, after a pause. 'We were talking fair regular for a few weeks, there.'

The Glasgow polis, that was all Charlie had said. Her mind was a storm of panic, of questions, an indistinguishable rolling tangle.

She fought to get on top of it. 'Then . . . that means it was also you' – she formed the words slowly, so nothing unwanted would slip out with them – 'who lost him in the first place.'

Rab looked down at the table. Amy was right. He did seem calm. But not confident. The room was full of a sort of dead calm, the calm of a man who's realised he's beaten.

'It was,' he said.

'Do Crosbie and McLeod know that?' The question just happened to fall from the tangle first.

For the first time since they'd sat down, Rab seemed a little shamefaced. 'No,' he said. 'I told them my team were investigating – which they will, when aw this is done. An' said that I wouldnae name the officer in question. Not yet.' He looked up at Birch again. 'They think I'm protecting wan o' my guys,' he said. 'They just dinnae ken it's me.'

She tried to keep her expression steady.

'I'll come clean soon enough,' he said. 'Face up tae whatever I get. But this is *my* investigation. I've been efter that bastard Solomon my hale career. I set this up, an' I brought it in. I willnae be shoved on the sidelines fer a single mistake.'

Birch found she was nodding. That, she understood. Hadn't she, herself, felt a sting of resentment when she'd been sent to the Granton breakwater, away from the main thrust of the Operation Citrine raid? Hadn't she lied to Amy – and to herself – about how she felt over Crosbie being given the case? What Rab was saying made sense to her: it would make sense to most police personnel, she guessed, especially those of Rab's generation. You don't get to DI level without a competitive streak. She'd been right: Solomon was an old score Rab had been waiting to settle. Of course he wasn't going to sit this out.

'But how?' She felt breathless from computing all that Rab had said. 'How could you let him get away from you, when you knew how much was riding on all this?'

You could have held him, she was thinking. You could have made it so he couldn't run away again.

Rab wasn't looking at her.

'He's a smarter lad than I gave him credit for,' he said. 'Saw the writing on the wall. But I thought I could fix it. I thought I knew exactly where he'd go.'

To me, Birch realised. You thought he'd come to me. Everything made sense now: Rab's interest in her, the questions he'd asked. The business card with his private mobile number, his instruction that she call him first, before anyone else.

'Where?' she asked. It didn't sound remotely convincing to her, but she'd lied now, and she needed to keep up the fiction.

'Your house, lassie,' Rab said.

Birch stared at him, waiting for the revelation she knew was coming.

'It's yer brother, Helen.' He was speaking quietly now. 'The Citrine informant is yer own wee Charlie Birch.'

There it was. Someone else knew, and had said it to her, out loud. She tried to look shocked.

'Charlie is missing,' she said. That wasn't a lie. 'Charlie has been missing for fourteen years.'

Rab folded his arms, and leaned over the table. 'Aye,' he said. 'He once wis lost . . . then briefly, he decided tae be found.'

How would I react, she wondered, if I were hearing this for the first time?

'You're sure it was Charlie?' She paused, then added, 'Over the years, there have been some people trying to pretend to be him. They used to contact my mum.'

Rab's expression didn't change. 'It wis him, lassie.'

Birch closed her eyes. She could feel her eyelids pulsing with the tension in her head. Her jaw was clenched. Could she tell him? Could she admit that her brother had been in her house only twelve hours ago? No, she thought. Of course I can't. Rab's revelation didn't change anything, not really, especially now she'd decided to lie. It's just you now, Helen, she thought. You made this bed, and now you're going to have to lie in it.

It seemed to take for ever. Izz and I stopped talking: he went and sat on the couch, looking around him and, every so often, sighing. I got in behind the hatch where I always sat. I watched Izz from the corner of my eye, and tried not to think about what Solomon might be asking of Vyshnya. Tried not to think about Hanna. We'd drifted a little, lately, and I'd been toying with the idea of jacking it in. I knew it would make work awkward for a while, that was what had stopped me. But when she'd texted me *I'm scared*, I'd felt a protective anger so strong it had shocked me. I resolved to try harder for her, if I made it through the night.

Izz had been called away from something he cared about. He wasn't sighing out of boredom alone.

'Were you on a date, man?' I asked.

He looked hard at me. 'Oh, fuck off,' he said, which meant *yes*.

I was buzzing with adrenalin, couldn't sit still. I did fifty push-ups, then lay on my stomach with the smell of carpet tiles in my nose, arms singing from the effort. I rolled on my back and tried to count the filaments inside the ceiling light's fluorescent tubes. It was so quiet I could hear my watch ticking, but I was trying not to listen too closely. The rooms were soundproofed, I knew that. But I still didn't want to risk hearing anything.

The sound that alerted me to something happening – at last – was Izz clearing his throat, a *heads-up* noise that sent me scrambling to look through the hatch. One of the guys – Abdul, I knew him a little – had emerged from the corridor. I saw Izz get to his feet as Abdul approached, and the two men clapped one another on the back: that weird, aggressive man-hug thing.

'You good?' Izz asked him.

'Yeah, cool, cool,' Abdul said. He looked over and nodded at me. 'All right?'

I skirted sheepishly out into the room. 'Yeah,' I said.

Abdul produced an overlarge vape, dragged on it, then sent a mushroom cloud of flavoured smoke up through the air. I watched Izz crinkle his nose.

'The fuck,' he said pointedly.

Abdul laughed. 'Banoffee pie, man,' he said, 'fucking delicious.'

Izz took a long step backward. 'Whatever. I guess if you want to smell like a teenage girl.'

'So, um.' I sounded like a fucking idiot, but my heart felt like a time bomb in my chest. 'What's the deal?'

Abdul looked at me. He was soft in the face, jolly even, and he was wide as he was tall. I knew Izz rated him. He seemed sound.

'Okay, listen,' Abdul said, lowering his voice. 'Best thing you can do right now is downplay, right? Show deference. You were out for ten minutes getting . . . fuck, I dunno, condoms or something. You were doing your job and you left Vyshnya to it. She'll back you up, man. Just kiss the old man's arse, yeah?'

Izz was nodding.

'Okay.' I pushed out a long breath. 'Hey, thanks.'

'No worries,' Abdul said. 'Just don't make him mad, okay? She ought to've known better.'

He meant Vyshnya.

Izz clicked the fingers of his right hand, once, low down by his hip. A signal. Solomon was on his way.

I couldn't quite believe the look of him when he stoated out of that corridor and into the room. I could see how he'd look dwarfed next to Abdul, big guy as he was. But Izz is built like a fucking ballet dancer, and Solomon still looked wiry next to him. Thin and hard, like he was made out of rope. I'd been told his age before, but I realised I hadn't expected him to be quite so bloody *ancient*.

'Gentlemen,' he said. Abdul shifted out of the way so the old man could fold himself down onto the sofa.

He looked like someone's grandfather. White hair, aviator-style glasses with the brass wire frames. Sure, he was dressed natty: but like a pensioner going to a tea dance.

This? I remember thinking. This is the hard cunt we're all fucking terrified of?

'Boss,' Abdul said, nodding at me, 'this is Vyshnya's muscle guy.'

I watched his eyes adjust: I was standing some distance away and I guess his vision wasn't what it used to be. Then he zeroed in on me and I felt cold. His eyes were the palest blue I'd ever seen: eyes like a white cat.

'They call you *Schenok*,' he said.

I nodded, trying to stand up straight, like I was back in school and I'd been called into the headmaster's office. 'Sometimes,' I said, 'yeah.'

His lips were very thin. I watched something that could have been a smile play around them.

'Our mutual friend Toad,' he said, 'is rather a fan of yours.'

I said nothing. I wanted to look at Izz, but I didn't dare break Solomon's gaze.

'You're his protégé, yes?'

He was well spoken, or . . . oddly spoken. He talked slow and sort of affected, trying to flatten out his Weegie *r* and *u* sounds. His *you're* sounded almost like *yore*.

'I suppose I am,' I said, trying to sound calm.

'Charlie Birch,' he said.

My real name didn't get used, not any more. Sometimes *Schenok*, or Fenton would call me *pup*, or *the wean*, which I hated but went along with. Most times I went by the name on my fake IDs: Nick Smith, Smith for short, like the guy from *The Matrix*. Sometimes I worried it was so plain I'd get rumbled, going through passport control or even just handing my driving licence over. My birth name was gone, out of necessity, out of safety. Hearing it from this man's mouth felt like a threat.

'The wanted man,' Solomon said.

I tried to shrug it off. 'Not these days.' I even tried to muster a smile. 'Case is stone cold.'

'Ah.' Solomon looked up at Abdul then, and I watched the big man avoid his gaze. 'Cold. A dead man, then, perhaps?'

I shivered, and ground my back teeth together to stop it from showing. 'Charlie Birch is,' I said, 'sure. Good riddance.'

All I could think about was Tsezar. Toad slamming the back door of Vic's van on the silent dark in the wake of his gunshot.

'But Charlie Birch,' Solomon said, 'has a sister.'

He crossed one knee over the other. I heard the fabric of his slate-grey trousers *swick* with static.

'Yes.' I had to say it. He knew anyway.

'A policewoman.' He was looking right at me. There was something about him that made me think of a lizard. He didn't blink as often as he ought to.

'I believe so,' I said. I couldn't stand myself then, honestly.

There was a silence. Though I couldn't look at him directly, I could see in the murky corner of my vision that Izz was looking down at his shoes. He and I both jumped at a noise from the corridor: the other guys had begun to emerge. Doors opened and closed. I heard male laughter.

'All very interesting.' Solomon held my gaze a few seconds longer, then turned to the three other goons as they came into view. The waiting room suddenly felt very full, and full of pungent male skin, muscle, sinew. I longed to get back in behind my hatch. Leaning against the wall in there was an iron bar and right then my palms itched to wrap around it, lift it, feel its wicked heft.

'The boy known as *Schenok*.' Solomon waved a long-nailed hand in my direction.

The three guys turned to look me up and down. None of them was familiar to me.

I steeled myself to be ambushed, bent backward, bundled down the stairs. Or perhaps they'd punch me out and drag me, oblivious, elsewhere. I wondered if I could make it into the hatch space before they got across the room. I wondered if I could barricade myself in there. I wondered whose side Izz would be on if I did.

But Solomon clapped his hands together, once, twice, and their collective attention zeroed in on the old man.

'Well, boys,' he said. 'A good time was had?'

The goons made appreciative noises.

'Excellent,' he said.

We all watched him stand. He did it elegantly, but moved slow. He wasn't the man he'd been, I could see – but I knew now that if I got out of this room unscathed, I'd never breathe easy in his presence. There was something deeply unsettling about him. Something *wrong*.

He moved towards Izz and extended his hand. The left, I noticed.

'Sir,' he said, as he and Izz shook. 'Thank you. Your services, though excellent, are no longer required.'

Izz gave a deep nod that was ever-so-nearly a bow.

'I do apologise,' Solomon added, 'for having disturbed your evening.'

'Happy to help,' Izz said, but he began backing away as soon as his hand came free of Solomon's grip. As he passed me, he shot me a look that said, *See you on the other side.* I knew better than to acknowledge it.

Solomon waited until he could no longer hear Izz's feet on the carpeted stairs.

'Surprisingly good man,' he said, to no one in particular, 'for a black.'

I actually bit my tongue then: I felt a wedge of it between my back teeth. Behind Solomon, Abdul shifted his weight, seeming to shrink ever so slightly.

Then the old man advanced towards me, his four companions falling into a sort of formation behind him. I knew it was too late for the hatch, the bar, the barricade. I made myself stand still, and not recoil. It took every single nerve in my body.

When he came level with me, I realised we were almost the same height. That meant Solomon had been tall once, because I could see his frame was condensed with age, twisted down like metal left out in the elements. His face was close to mine, and I was confronted once again with those milky blue eyes.

'I trust,' he said, 'that after this evening, I will not hear of you working additional jobs again?'

Fuck. He knew that I'd been out doing favours for Toad. 'Yes,' I said. My voice was hoarse.

'I'll ensure your mentor understands, too,' Solomon said, 'that you have certain priorities.'

I nodded.

'You're lucky,' Solomon said, 'to have Toad.'

I wondered how many times Toad had had his card marked now, and how many times he had left. This was the second time he'd apparently saved my arse. Though they were still here. They could still hurt me.

Solomon looked me up and down, then. Apparently approving of what he saw, he stepped back, and smiled a grisly smile. 'You,' he said, 'are a promising young man.'

I ought to have felt relief, but none came.

'A fine translator, too,' he was saying.

I swilled around in my throat for what was left of my voice. 'Thank you,' I said.

'I'm glad,' Solomon said, cocking his head and looking, again, somehow lizard-like, 'I have your loyalty.'

I nodded. I nodded and I couldn't stop. But it didn't matter. Solomon swept past me, and Abdul and his friends fell into step behind him. None of them met my eye as they filed past, out of the white-painted door with its fire exit sign glowing overhead. I listened as the five of them creaked and shuddered down the stairs, and I waited for the sound of the stair door banging and the electric bolt clacking home.

'But . . .' Birch said. She was stalling for time, so she could think. 'Perps recycle identities all the time. Charlie's presumed dead. What's to stop one of Solomon's guys using him as an alias?'

Rab tipped his head, as though considering it.

I could tell him, she thought. He fucked up, too. He lost the informant. Maybe he'd understand.

'I see yer thinking,' Rab was saying. 'But he didnae use the name Charlie Birch. He wis Nick Smith when he came tae me. Obviously *that* wis an alias.'

Birch tried to listen as her thoughts raced. No: what Rab did isn't the same. Charlie did exactly what he expected him to. Rab tipped Charlie off, but that was an accident. Really his only mistake was hoping I'd do the right thing.

'So I decided I'd run some checks,' Rab went on. 'First I bought him a coffee, got a partial fingerprint. Yer brother was previously fingerprinted in 2002.'

'Yeah,' Birch said. She must have looked at Charlie's profile hundreds of times since she'd become a policewoman. She knew it by heart. 'Drunk and disorderly in an Ibrox pub.'

Rab nodded. 'That wis it,' he said.

Rab did everything right, she thought. He expected you to fall into step. And you didn't. He followed a hunch, but *you* committed a crime. No, she realised. She couldn't tell him. The realisation hurt, and the hurt was unexpected. It would have felt so, so good to be able to come clean.

He was still speaking.

'I ran the partial print and he wis a match, but I still couldnae be sure. I needed more. He tried tae be careful, but I managed tae meet him, just one time, where he'd be caught on CCTV. The photos matched, too. He's grown up some, yer kid brother, but it wis him all right.'

Quiet fell.

'Charlie,' Birch said. Her brother's name in her mouth made her want to cry. Fuck it, she thought, it helps with the lie. She let the tears come. 'Charlie, working for Solomon.'

Rab had been keeping his face neutral, she could tell. But now, as she cried, he broke. His expression changed to one of sympathy, and he extended a hand across the table to take hers. She'd convinced him: the lie had worked. And with crying, of all things, she thought. The oldest perp trick in the book.

'I'm sorry, lassie,' he said. 'I honestly thought he'd come tae you. I thought ye'd get him tae tell ye more. Tell ye something we could use. I thought I'd got the measure o' the guy. I didnae think he'd just *run*.'

Birch felt sick. She'd broken the law. She'd lied about it. She'd wrecked Rab's plan to bring Charlie in – a plan that had worked like clockwork, up until the point where *she* needed to step up. She'd wrecked the case. And now her brother really *had* run. Solomon's boys might have found him already.

A new thought struck her. 'Why didn't you *tell* me?' Her voice was feeble. 'On Monday, in the pub. Or . . . whenever. Why didn't you *say* to me, your brother's about to turn up on your doorstep?'

Whatever, Helen, she thought. As if you'd have been any more likely to arrest him if you'd known he was coming. But then, she thought, I might have. I really might have been able to do it, if I'd prepared myself.

'Because,' Rab said, 'I thought if he was going to arrive wi' you, I wanted him tae get there and feel safe. Feel like he really had caught ye by surprise. I wanted him to settle somewhere, jist for a few hours. I wanted him tae *talk*, an' feel like his every word wisnae being recorded for legal purposes. If ye'd been ready, waiting wi' a wire on ye or half the force in yer front garden, that could have been it. I wisnae sure if he'd just shut up like a clam if we spooked him, like aw Solomon's other guys. I lost him, but I really thought I'd find him again, and I didnae want to jeopardise any chance to keep him talking.'

Birch couldn't help it. She let her face fall into her hands, so Rab couldn't see it. Your plan went like a Swiss watch, she wanted to say. I just spectacularly fucked up.

'But,' Rab said, 'it wisnae a bad thing I had cause tae hand ye a panic button. I'd even considered putting surveillance on ye, if I'm honest, but it would have raised questions about why, and I'd have needed tae fess up that it wis me that lost him. Like I say, I'm no' ready for that jist yet.'

'Surveillance?'

Rab nodded. 'I didnae ken if he might be violent.'

Her head snapped up again then, and she eyeballed him. 'Why would Charlie be violent? To me? I'm his *sister* . . .'

Rab blinked. Tone it down.

But when he replied, his voice was gentle. 'Because he's been working fer Solomon, hen. I'm sorry tae tell ye this. But I doubt he's the same wee Charlie Birch ye remember. He's done a lot of bad things. He's hurt a lot o' folk in his time.'

Birch remembered hearing her own voice, only a day or so ago, reciting all the charges she reckoned she could level at her brother. *GBH. Aggravated assault. Assault with a deadly weapon.* Something else wormed deep inside her, too, adding to the general nausea she felt. The more she thought about it – and she couldn't help but think about it – the more she suspected Charlie was guilty of murder.

And yet, you let him run.

Rab had levered himself upright. He walked round the table to stand next to her, bending to place one meaty arm around her shoulders. The gesture brought his face close. In another context, it might have been stifling, but Birch found it comforting. Fatherly, almost, though she wouldn't know.

'I'm so sorry, lassie,' he said. 'I've royally cocked up this hale case.'

You're sorry? she thought. You have no idea.

'But,' Rab was saying. 'Yer brother's alive. He's been alive, these fourteen years. I mean, being a violent wee shite, I'm afraid tae say. But alive.'

Birch felt able to tell another truth. 'You don't know that,' she said. It sounded like she'd spat at him. 'Not now. Not now he's gone again.'

Rab straightened up. She'd wounded him. But there was no way to help it, unless she confessed, and then the tide would turn and rush in to drown her. Rab would be disciplined, no doubt, for *his* supposed mistake. But if *hers* were to surface, it wouldn't just be the job she'd lose. She'd be up on criminal charges. She wouldn't be able to afford the legal bills. It would be splashed all over the press in the most humiliating terms: the special terms reserved for police officers who broke the law. She imagined Lockley rejoicing in his prison cell, and a cold wave of revulsion passed through her. Social media would crucify her. Anjan would have nothing to do with her, ever again. And underneath it all, Charlie would still be gone – for ever this time, whether dead or run to some far corner of the known world to hide. No matter what, she'd lost him.

So yes, she thought, her head frighteningly clear now. Yes, I will let Rab take the fall. It's a much smaller fall, one he'll come back from. My brother is the only one who knows what I did, and he's gone. I will keep up the lie. An internal voice – more her own than the first – replied, Who the fuck have you become?

'Helen?'

She realised she'd been staring dead ahead, looking at the white-painted breezeblock wall on the other side of the room. Rab had his hand on the door handle, ready to let her go free.

'Ye should take some time tae think, lassie,' he said. 'Process, ken?'

Birch looked up at him. Because nodding was called for, she nodded.

'It's a long shot, now,' he went on, 'but if ye can think of anywhere – I mean *anywhere* – that Charlie might have run . . . will ye tell me right away? Time's against us.'

Again, she nodded. 'I will,' she said. 'I'll think on it, Rab.'

She stood, a little too fast. Her head buzzed. You did it. You fucked up and you lied and you might just get away with it.

She walked over to Rab, who twisted the handle and opened the door. He stepped back to let her through, ever the gentleman.

What sort of person are you?

As she passed him, Birch looked into his face. 'I'm sorry,' she said, and at that exact moment the same words came out of his mouth, too.

For what seemed like a long time, nothing happened, except she could feel DI Robson scrutinising her, still harbouring, she knew, a seed of doubt about something. She shook herself a little, and broke free, stumbling out into the corridor beyond. Immediately, she cannoned into someone.

'Helen.'

Two hands wrapped around her upper arms, and steadied her. The face she looked into now was Anjan's. His smell coiled round her like a warm scarf.

'Are you all right?'

As he loosened his grip, Birch raised a hand to her face. Her fingertips came away smeared with mascara, and her face felt hot and puffy.

'Shit,' she said. 'I'm a mess.'

'Are you back at work too soon?' Anjan asked. His face was full of concern.

She hauled in air. She was aware that Rab was still only feet away, locking the interview room door, listening.

'No,' she said. 'I'm fine. Forgive me. I just . . . had a moment.'

She pushed her shoulders back and tried to straighten her spine. Anjan's expression didn't change. I must look like absolute crap, she thought.

Anjan reached out his hand again and took her arm, this time near the elbow. The touch surprised her, but she allowed him to gently steer her up the corridor and away from Rab.

His voice dropped to a near-whisper. 'I'm sorry, Helen,' he said, still pulling her along. 'But I'm worried about you, and I want to talk. Properly, not here.'

Birch shook her head. 'Like I said last night, we shouldn't. Not with the case.' The words were bitter in her mouth. 'I'm fine, really.'

Anjan glanced backward. Rab had begun to walk away in the other direction, having taken the hint.

Birch wondered what he must think: he was still a little suspicious of her. Now she was whispering with the defence lawyer. If this were a TV show, she thought, suddenly, I'd be the bent cop. Then, quick on the heels of that realisation, another came. You *are* a bent cop, Helen.

But Anjan was still talking. 'I know that, I do. And *you* know I'm a stickler, ordinarily. So surely you realise how important this is to me, that I'm bending my own rules? Please?'

Birch sagged. She felt exhausted. Everything was wrong and there was nothing she could do to make it right. The path of least resistance was open before her, and it would be so easy to take it. But from somewhere, she summoned a final shred of energy. 'I'm sorry,' she said. 'I really can't.'

She stepped through Anjan's warm cloud of scent, and walked away.

It was a while before any of the girls ventured out of their rooms. Out on the street I could hear the distant whooping of drunk lads, headed to the nearby strip clubs. In an hour or so some of those same blokes might be in this very room, waiting for the next available girl. I knew I had to get my head together. I was at work, after all.

One of the doors opened: Karen's, at the furthest end of the corridor. She must have unlatched it pretty gingerly, because I didn't realise she was there until she screamed, and scared the living shit out of me.

'Vyshnya! Oh fuck.'

She clattered towards me down the corridor, as fast as her skyscraper heels would allow. I jolted upright, and she skidded to an uneasy halt beside the couch.

'Oh Jesus,' she said, throwing her hands up. 'I thought you were fucking *dead*, pal. I thought they'd offed you.'

I tried to play it cool. 'Nope,' I said. 'Just loafing about like usual.'

Karen rolled her eyes, and swivelled on one hip back towards the corridor. A couple of the other girls had poked their heads around their own doors.

'False alarm.' Karen flapped her hand at them. 'Sorry, chicks.'

Chicks was Vyshnya's name for the girls: not in the derogatory English idiom sense, but in the sense that they were her flock, each one her own personal *ptashenya*. I felt as though something had tightened around my throat.

One of the pale faces hanging in the gloom of the corridor was Hanna's.

'Babygirl,' I said, in a voice still cracked with fear. 'It's okay. They're gone.'

I watched Hanna slide out into the corridor, one hand on her throat, pulling her dressing gown up tight at the neck.

Karen squared up to me. 'You sure? They're not coming back?'

I glanced over at the exit door. 'I fucking hope not,' I replied.

Hanna arrived at my side. It seemed melodramatic to pull her into my arms, though that was what I really wanted to do. Instead, side-on, I put one arm around her shoulders and squeezed. She didn't let go of the dressing gown collar.

'Where were you?' she said. Her voice was very quiet.

'Yeah,' Karen chimed in. 'Enquiring minds want to know.'

My throat was dry. 'Baby . . . you know I was working for Toad tonight. It was a shitshow of a job to be honest. I was basically on my way here, and—'

'Yeah,' Karen spat. 'Fuck that, actually.'

I tried for a glare, but couldn't muster it. She was right, after all. 'Vyshnya said she could handle it.'

Karen snorted.

'Wait.' Hanna's voice was still small, fluttery. 'Where *is* Vyshnya?'

I felt a stab of panic. It was as though my mind couldn't handle what Solomon had asked of Vyshnya, and had let the knowledge slide out of view.

All the girls who'd signed up to work that night were now in the lounge, or dithering in the corridor, listening to us talk. Only one door was still closed.

I let go of Hanna, dodged Karen and strode down the corridor. I felt the girls press in around me as I pushed against the door knob. It turned, but the door wouldn't give.

I banged on it with an open palm. 'Vyshnya?' I said, and bent to put my ear close to the wood. Nothing.

This time I yelled. 'Vyshnya!' I tried the door again, putting my back into it this time. It gave a little, and I knew from the handle turning that it wasn't locked, but somehow *stuck*.

'Vee?'

Karen was now beside me, banging on the door too. *Vee* was the nickname the girls used: I'd never been allowed.

'If you're in there,' I yelled, 'stand back, I'm going to kick down the door.'

From the other side, a sort of softened bang – a weak fist whacked against the inside of that same door. I felt it reverberate through my palm, still resting on the wood.

'Vee?' Karen said.

There was a collective holding of breath, and on the other side of the door, a sort of low, animal moan.

'Fuck!' Karen smacked me, hard, on the arm. It stung. 'She's hurt in there. She's behind the fucking door and he's *hurt her.*'

Behind me, the girls began to whisper and fuss. I tried to stay calm, crouching low. If Vyshnya *was* lying behind the door, she'd hear me better there.

'Okay,' I said. 'Vyshnya, if you're down there and you can, I need you to move away from the door. We need to get in and help you, okay?'

No answer.

'Okay, Vyshnya?'

I straightened up and tried the handle again. It gave, and the door shifted open a few inches. It was dark inside, but putting my face into the gap, I could see that there was indeed a dark mass on the floor behind the door. Vyshnya was breathing hard, making small weak movements.

I swallowed, and tasted acid in my throat.

'You're doing great,' I said through the gap. I tried to keep myself pressed up to the jamb, so none of the girls could see in around my body. 'Just a little further and I'll squeeze in. Keep going.'

Behind me, I could hear Hanna praying in Russian, and Karen hissing, *Oh fuck, oh fuck* over and over.

It seemed to take an eternity, but eventually Vyshnya was able to shuffle across the floor far enough that I could get one arm and shoulder in through the gap – then a leg, which enabled me to hook the bulk of myself in. The room was almost black-dark, and smelled like bad things: blood and fear.

Halfway inside, I twisted back round and looked Karen in the eye. Her mouth was inches from mine: she was ready to follow right behind.

'Stay the *fuck* outside,' I whispered.

She eyeballed me for a half-second, then stepped back.

I softened my voice in gratitude, and added, 'I'll get you in here when I need you, okay?'

I saw her nod. As I turned back, I heard her say, 'Okay, girls. Let's get sorted . . .'

I wrestled my way through the gap and closed the door behind me. 'Vyshnya,' I said. The carpet underneath me was spongy with damp. I fumbled behind me and turned on the light.

Vyshnya was at my feet. I looked down at her, and threw up, clamping my lips closed so I wouldn't vomit onto her. I had to leap over her bundled body and run to the corner of the room, with its long mirrors and small white sink. I spat up the contents of my mouth. They were a vivid yellow. I coughed, strings of phlegm sticking to the front of my shirt. I didn't have time to clean up. The stink of my vomit added to the general stench of the room.

From the corner, I could see the whole scene. Vyshnya was lying between the door and the bed. She was naked, tangled in a sheet that had once been white, but was now mostly purpled with blood. I could see that after Solomon had left she'd either fallen or crawled from the bed, and made it over to the door: there were bloodied finger-streaks around the handle. Her face, pointed up at the ceiling, was so bruised that her eyes were hidden, squeezed closed. She looked like she ought to be dead.

I spat into the sink a final time, tensed every nerve, and walked over. The carpet was wet with blood: I saw that my shoes were covered in it. I couldn't see where it was coming from – in spite of the beating she'd taken to the face, she had no open head wounds. Both her arms looked broken, and perhaps her legs too, though it was hard to tell with the sheet twisted around them. I realised I'd need to examine her.

'Vyshnya,' I said, as softly as I could. 'It's me. It's Charlie.' It was my real name that came to me in that moment, as though I wanted to offer her some small vulnerability of my own. As though that would make anything better. 'I'm going to have a look at you, okay? You're going to be okay, but I need to see where you're hurt.'

I put one hand up to her swollen face, to touch her jaw. She began uttering an urgent stream of curse words in spitty Ukrainian. It seemed that somehow her jaw was fine, but now she was moving her mouth, I could see teeth were missing.

'Okay,' I said. 'I know your arms are hurt. I won't touch them. But I need to see your legs.'

Vyshnya groaned, and made to clutch at the sheet, but her hands seemed almost useless.

'I'm sorry,' I said, in Russian, and then bent to peel the sheet from around her feet, as gently as I could manage.

She made a sort of seething sound. Without even moving the sheet all that much, I could see her lower legs were broken, too. I found myself having to swallow down bile again.

'Cunt,' I spat. 'Absolute fucking *cunt.*'

I dropped the sheet back onto her legs, and she seemed to relax just the slightest bit.

'I'm sorry,' I said. 'I'm so sorry.'

I put one hand on her stomach. Her bruised eyes were leaking tears. I ran that hand up one side of her ribcage, and then down the other, trying to ignore the fact that by doing so, I had to touch her breasts. Their flesh was bruised. On one, there were teeth marks.

'*Scumbag,*' I hissed.

I sat back and took an inventory. Solomon had beaten Vyshnya around the face, knocking out teeth, making her almost unrecognisable. He'd broken both her arms and, it seemed, both her legs. My cursory check of her torso suggested her ribs were intact – I was thankful, because even with my limited medical knowledge, I knew that broken ribs could puncture organs, and kill you from the inside out. She was bitten and bruised all over, but it seemed there was only one place the blood could be coming from. I closed my eyes, and for the first time in my adult life, I prayed.

Vyshnya let out a long, rattling sigh.

'It's okay,' I said. I realised I was angry, that the anger was spark-
ing through me, revving my body's engine into overdrive. 'You are
not going to die in this room, okay, Vee? That *scumbag* is not getting
away with it.'

I got to my feet and cracked the door ajar. The other girls had
disappeared somewhere, but Karen was right there, her ear
pressed close to listen.

'What's he done to her?' she said.

'Fucking *everything*,' I said 'I need sheets. Towels. Whatever you
can find. Get as many as you can and shove them through this
gap. Then get in here. Don't let the others in.'

'Okay.' Karen turned.

'Wait,' I said, and her face flicked back. In her eyes, I could see
steely tears. 'Just . . . be ready, when you come in, okay? It's bad.'

She said nothing, and was gone.

I sat down next to Vyshnya's ruined legs, and waited.

'I'm so sorry,' I said. 'I am *so* sorry I wasn't here. Fuck. Vyshnya,
I'm going to make this okay. I promise. I promise you're going to
be okay.'

A tumble of white fabric came through the gap in the door, and
then on the other side I heard Karen say, 'No. Just me.'

She squeezed one leg through the gap, then her torso. She'd
taken her high heels off, and her make-up had run down her face.
For a fleeting moment, I wanted to stand up and hug her – a thing
that I don't think she'd ever have allowed. But then she looked
down at Vyshnya, and took in the carnage of the room, and it was
too late.

'Right,' she said. Her face went grey, and I could see her legs
shaking, but she stood still for a moment, then closed the door
behind her. 'Right, where do you need me?'

I gestured to the sheets, and she bundled them over to me.

'Come down here,' I said, 'and let her know you're there.'

Karen dropped to her knees beside Vyshnya's shoulder. 'Hi,
Vee,' she said. Her voice trembled, but I watched her set her jaw.
'It's Karen. We're going to fix you up, okay?'

Vyshnya's head stirred: a nod.

'Okay,' I said. 'She's bleeding. I think from her . . . from . . .' I couldn't say it.

'He raped her.' Karen's voice was so matter-of-fact that it startled me. 'Mother*fucker.*'

I looked into her face, and saw her rage was even larger, more all-consuming, than my own.

'What do we *do*?' I said.

She stood, walked around me, and then knelt down again beside Vyshnya's legs. I could see that her knees and shins were streaked with the blood from the carpet.

'*You*,' she said, 'have to call an ambulance. *I* am going to stop some of this bleeding.'

I paused. My head buzzed with shock, confusion, anger.

Karen balled up a new white sheet, and pulled the bloodied one fully away from Vyshnya. Yes, that's where the blood was coming from. I had to resist the urge to throw up again.

'You're doing so great, Vee,' Karen said, as she eased the wounded woman's legs apart and pushed the fabric up between her thighs. 'I'm going to press on this and try to slow things down, okay? It's going to hurt, my love, I'm sorry.'

But Vyshnya nodded. I couldn't imagine the agony she was in.

Karen flicked another sheet in my direction. 'Cover her up, for fuck's sake,' she said, 'she doesn't want to be seen like this. And call the *fucking ambulance.*'

I did as I was told, and draped another of the clean sheets over Vyshnya's torso and hips. Again, she seemed to relax just a little, though it might have been me trying to make myself feel better. I balled up the bloodied sheet and carried it over to the sink, dumping it in on top of the last streaks of my own sick.

'If I call an ambulance,' I said to Karen, 'we'll all be arrested.'

She looked up at me. Her hands were covered in blood. It looked somehow *wetter* than I'd ever imagined blood could be: it shone on everything. 'No,' she said. 'Just me.'

I blinked. 'What do you mean?'

Karen stared at me, her face screwed up with contempt for the useless, wretched man I was. The man who'd got them all into this shit.

'Yeah,' she said, 'they'll see it as a chance to run a raid. You're right. They'll bring cops with them. I wasn't born yesterday, I fucking know *that*. But you can't arrest someone if they're not fucking *here*, can you? They'll only get me, and . . . well, *whatever*. I've been in the nick before, I can take it.'

I think my mouth fell open.

'Go and get the girls,' Karen said. 'Tell them to get everything out of their rooms that belongs to them. Anything that identifies them. You get them and you get all *your* shit and you put everyone in the van and you get them out of here. Do it fast, you'll be out before the ambulance gets here. I'll stay here with Vyshnya and deal with . . . well, whatever comes through that door. You can tell that bastard Solomon that you ran, with the girls, and I wouldn't go. I called the ambulance. If he comes near me I'll fucking castrate him.'

I couldn't quite believe what she was saying. My head spun.

'Do me a favour, though?' Karen grimaced. Her hands were still pressed into the reddening sheet. 'Get the condoms and shit out of all the rooms. Get all the money out. No need to leave them evidence, yeah?'

Vyshnya coughed then, and through her wrecked teeth hissed, 'Yes.'

Karen smiled at me. Tears were running down her face, but I could see she was resolute.

'See?' she said. 'The boss lady says so. Now go call the ambulance and get the fuck out of Dodge.'

I stood there for a couple of seconds more, looking at Karen. She was maybe five foot three, fine-boned, twenty-four or so. But something inside her was made out of steel. I was awed.

'Thank you,' I whispered. Then I ran for the door.

By the time evening came, Birch had switched to autopilot. She spent her afternoon rereading interview transcripts, looking for even the tiniest crack that further examination might lever open. These were desperate measures on the part of McLeod and Crosbie, she knew, and she could turn up nothing for them anyway, so impenetrable was the wall of *no comment*. Darkness fell outside but the DCs remained at their desks in the bullpen, reviewing evidence again and again in a sort of desperate loop. Solomon would be up late, she guessed, being grilled for as long as Rab and Crosbie could stand it. McLeod was on call. Fifteen hours remained before they'd have to let Solomon go.

Birch followed the tail-lights of a cab along Raeburn Place, past the shuttered cafés and the Mexican craft store with its twinkling coloured lights. On Dundas Street a number 23 bus pulled out into her path, and she suddenly realised she wasn't driving home. But the route she was taking was familiar: she still hadn't kicked up out of that autopilot headspace. By the time she'd trailed the bus to the foot of the Mound, Birch realised: she was going to visit her mother.

She parked in Castle Terrace car park, not trusting she'd find a space any closer. From there she walked up Johnston Terrace as quickly as the hill allowed. Above her, the hewn castle loomed. A bright moon rose above the esplanade, broken perfectly in half like a smashed plate. A coin toss, she thought, light or dark. Somehow, she'd already lost.

Her mother's little flat – the last place she'd ever lived – was on the top floor of Thomson's Court. The windows looked out over a close that cut between Johnston Terrace and the Grassmarket.

Though it was a slightly longer walk, Birch would always approach from the back. At this time of year, when the dark was still coming in early, she'd liked to cut down the steps and see her mother, framed in the lit window, waiting for her daughter's approach. Birch had moved the armchair to that window herself, the one in the living room with the bird feeder propped on the ledge. Her mother would wave to her from it, then Birch would watch her lever herself up, and begin the slow teeter from there to the front door. The timing worked perfectly: the time it took her mother to cross that short stretch of floor was the same time it took for Birch to get down the close, onto the Grassmarket, and up into the porch to ring on the buzzer.

Now, she stood looking at that same window, the one her mother no longer spent her days at. The bird feeder was gone, and the flat's new inhabitant had hung heavy curtains, already drawn against the dark and cold. Around their edges, Birch could see a thin seam of light, but it wasn't the cosy yellow glow of her mother's shaded table lamps. The flat held none of its old warmth any more, none of the warm feeling Birch realised she had come looking for. She felt so foolish that she found herself glancing around, to see if anyone was watching her.

The cobbles on the road were greasy, and the air was sharp under that white half-moon. It was a little after seven: across the misty valley of the city, somewhere in Tollcross perhaps, a church spire clock shone like a coin. She'd been thinking of Charlie all day, looking at the time, counting how many hours he'd been gone. How long had he been awake? How far had he got? Was he still hidden, still safe? Now, as she dropped her gaze from her mother's window and began to walk, Birch wondered about how he'd eat, whether he'd be hungry. He might be cold, too: she found herself hugging her jacket more tightly around her. The warm, steamed windows of the tartan shops and restaurants made her feel colder still, and alone. She was only a few yards away from the Thai Orchid: Birch inhaled its cloud of hot, welcoming scent and found herself thinking, I wish things could just be normal. For a split second, she imagined an alternative world in which she could have taken out her phone, texted her brother and said, *Hey, I just went to Mum's old place and now I'm lonely. Fancy coming out with me for Thai food tonight?* It was a thing she'd literally never done. Would she ever get to? No: things hadn't been 'normal' when it came to Charlie for a very, very long time.

A few steps into the close, something made Birch stop, and look up. She felt minuscule under the huge shoulder of the castle, its black bulk against that peachy light-polluted sky. Along the walled esplanade, tourists were still poking their smartphones over the battlements: Birch could see the tiny supernovas of flash as they tried to capture the Old Town's sprawl, the spires and domes of Tollcross, the art school, the university. She realised she'd come here for another reason: because a part of her thought that Charlie might have done the same. He was running, and as far as she knew he had nowhere safe to go. Neither did she, so she'd come looking for her mother. Might her little brother have had the same thought?

It was ludicrous, but she decided she ought to check: the building's porch would be open, and she could ask a neighbour to buzz her into the stairwell. She wondered how it would feel, climbing those stairs to her mother's floor and standing outside the white UPVC front door once again. She'd stood there so many times, listening to her mother's hard breathing as she fumbled with the locks. Charlie had never done that. Charlie didn't know.

Castle Wynd South, the close's sign said. Steep steps that chicaned between the high walls of tenements. This close was unusually wide, Birch thought, and well lit. The iron handrails had been polished by many palms over the years, and gleamed under the streetlights' orange glow. Below her, Birch could hear the distant shush of traffic on the wet road of the Grassmarket.

But about a third of the way down, she stiffened. Someone was descending the steps behind her. It's fine, she thought, as she felt her pulse rise in her ears, people must cut through here all the time. The tread was heavy, softened by the soles of trainers or perhaps hiking boots, and the stride was big: a man's. He was gaining on her, too.

The close zigzagged, halfway down: Birch was coming up to a brick wall that would force her to turn right, then left, before the steps plunged down again in a straight line to the street. As she reached the wall – graffiti tags, peeling Fringe posters – she used the change in direction as an excuse to glance back. Again, her pulse quickened. The man was tall and broad, dressed in a dark sweater with the hood pulled up. His face was in shadow. This part of the close was invisible to the Thomson's Court flats above.

Just make it round the turn, Birch thought, taking the right as fast as she could, and upping her pace towards the left. Just make it to the second corner. Then the bright lights of the Grassmarket would appear before her: she'd be able to see a rectangle of road and cars and windows. If she had to scream, someone would hear her. Someone would look up.

But she didn't make it to the turn. The man was upon her, one hand closing on the back of her jacket collar, hauling her backward into the bottleneck of the close. She made to scream, but he brought his other hand down hard over her mouth. He smelled like dirt and rolling tobacco.

Birch flailed. All four of her limbs were still free, so she windmilled her arms backward, striking downwards at the man's hips, stomach, groin, trying to land a blow. She tried to plant her legs and resist him dragging her back against the wall, where the shadows fell between the streetlamps and any witness glancing out of their window would have to squint to see anything. As she did this, she tried to assess his strength: the arm that braced his hand over her face didn't budge, but this man wasn't muscled like Charlie was. His hands were rough, and he was already breathing hard as they scuffled on the wet paving. He was an older man, she decided, and she matched him, roughly, for height.

'Fucking Jesus Mary mother of Christ,' he hissed, flecking her ear with spit. 'Dinnae make this worse than it's got tae be.'

Glaswegian, Birch thought. White. Fifties.

With one elbow, she managed to strike him hard in the solar plexus, and she felt him give a little in the middle.

'Bitch,' he spat, and the hand that had been on her collar disappeared. Birch brought both her hands up to wrestle his other arm from her mouth: she bent and contorted, trying to squeeze from his grip. But then . . .

'Fucking *stop it*,' the man whispered. He pushed something cold and round against Birch's temple.

Her first thought was annoyance: she'd almost been free, goddammit. But her second thought was gun. And then that was her only thought: *gun, gun, gun*, like a chant in time with her pounding heart. She went limp.

'Jesus,' the man said again. She'd tired him, she could tell. Now they stood in a strange, frozen pose: her hunched against his body, and him bent around her with one hand still over her mouth, and the other holding the weapon to her head. Birch listened for any sound of assistance: a footstep on the steps above or below them, a noise in one of the tenements alongside. Nothing: only traffic noise, and the man's hoarse breath.

'Right,' he said, after a strange moment of quiet. 'Fucking tell me where he is.'

Shit. Birch closed her eyes. This was *them.* This was one of the guys Charlie was hiding from.

'Who?'

The guy's hand was still over her mouth. He shifted it to her throat, so she could speak.

'Where *who* is?' Birch spluttered.

The man nudged the gun, pressing it harder against her skull. 'Dinnae fuck wi' me,' he said. 'Where's your fucking brother?'

Birch let herself relax in his grip. Just a little, nothing he'd notice. She shifted her feet so they were sprung, not flat.

'You've got the wrong person, arsehole.' She hoped to God she sounded sincere. 'I don't have a brother.'

He shook her. Birch used the movement to further shift her weight, inching the balance of their clinch to her advantage.

'I *said*,' he hissed, 'dinnae fuck wi' me. You think I dinnae ken who ye are?'

Birch swallowed. She felt her throat contract against the man's calloused palm. 'I'm Detective Inspector Helen Birch,' she said. 'And the only brother I've ever had is missing, presumed dead.'

The man moved his lips even closer to Birch's ear. 'You *sure* about that?'

Birch twisted her head round. In the chokehold he'd attempted, it hurt, but she was able to swivel far enough that she could eyeball him.

'*Fuck* you,' she said and then with all the force she could muster, she parted her lips and sank her teeth into his cheek.

The man started, twitching his head back and away from her. Birch knew she had one chance, but she'd prepared for it. She brought one hand up and closed it around the man's forearm, below the gun. She made her right hand into a fist, and drove it up hard under his chin. She felt his teeth clatter, and he spun out, letting go of her throat and reeling back. Now she could get both hands on the arm holding the gun. She dug her fingers in, planted her weight the way she'd been trained, bent her back and flipped him, hauling his weight over the top of her own and bringing him down hard on his back on the wet stone in front of her. She heard the back of his head crack off the concrete, and all the wind go out of his lungs at once: a sound like a mattress hitting wet ground. The gun fell from his grip and made a metallic skitter as it clattered away from them both. Unable to speak, the assailant stared up at her, his eyes wide and his mouth opening and closing like something beached.

Birch leaned down over him. 'Yeah,' she said. 'I'm *perfectly* sure.' Now she saw that her assessment had been right. The hoodie had fallen back in the tussle, and the man was indeed about fifty or so: his face hard-weathered, fight-scarred. A tattoo on his neck, in fancy gothic script: *Fenton*. 'What is it you *want*, scumbag?'

She was high on adrenalin, but knew it couldn't last. A lump was already growing in her throat, and she knew she could go into shock if she didn't ride the wave of the encounter.

The man spluttered.

'Speak up, there's a good lad.' Stop enjoying this, Helen, she thought. It's serious.

The man coughed, and the cough sounded thick as soup.

Remembering the gun, Birch glanced around her. It had disappeared into the darkness, and she didn't have time to hunt for it. But she'd *seen* it, and felt its snub nose against her skin.

'Assaulting a police officer, *and* possession of an illegal firearm? You're ambitious, I'll give you that.'

'It wasn't loaded.'

The man's voice was hoarse from coughing, and he was still short of breath, but he was also livid, Birch could tell. Beaten in an unfair fight, and by a *girl*. Perps always hated that.

'I'm no' fuckin' *stupid*,' he added.

Birch snorted, but she knew that time was short now: though still on his back, the man – Fenton – was recovering. For the first time, she realised that he might not be alone, and she needed to get down to the Grassmarket, along King's Stables Road and into the car without being followed, or attacked by any pals of his who might be hanging around. The adrenalin was ebbing and soon she'd be no good for anything.

'Really? Could've fooled me,' she said. *Time to go. Get out of here.*

'Now.' Birch leaned down over her assailant, and he flinched. 'I don't know who you are, and I don't know what you want, but you're going to leave me alone, do you understand?'

The man blinked at her.

'I've got evidence of all this,' she said, 'given the DNA you'll have left all over me – thanks, by the way, for being such a spitty talker. So I don't know what your deal is, but I'm frankly fucking sick and tired of you and your pal with the creepy phone calls and the blacked-out car and the flowers, okay? I thought I'd already warned you. *Leave. Me. Alone.*'

The man stared up at her. She could hear his breath still rattling in his lungs.

'Do you understand me?' She realised she sounded like a teacher, scolding a naughty schoolboy. She half expected him to reply, *yes, miss*.

Instead, the man nodded. It was a slight nod, and dismissive, but it was also her cue to leave.

'You'll be hearing from my colleagues,' Birch said. She straightened up, turned, and walked as slowly and as upright as she dared to the last turn of the close. When she got there, she made herself pause and look back, though the welcoming lights of the street were laid out below her, and she could see pedestrians crossing the bright opening at the close's foot. The man had rolled onto his side and propped himself on one elbow to watch her. Soon, he'd be able to stand, and then he could look for the gun. He could follow her. Birch plunged down the close steps as fast as she could, half fell out into the street, and ran.

I called Toad from the van. I was frantic, covered in Vyshnya's blood. Beside myself about Karen. The girls were loaded in the back, crying, freaking out. I drove as calmly as I could and prayed to God I wouldn't get pulled over and have to explain: three women in lingerie and dressing gowns carrying condoms and bondage gear and envelopes of tatty fivers. I'd brought the metal bar from behind the hatch and Hanna was clutching it. A couple of times, polis cars with the blues-and-twos going tore by, heading the opposite way. For the second time that night, I prayed.

I'd woken Toad, but he answered cheerily, thinking I was calling about the job.

'Fuck that,' I said. '*Skol'ko volka ni kormi, on vsyo v les smotrit.*'

This was a code Toad and I had worked out between us. The idiom meant, roughly, *a well-fed wolf still looks to the forest.* Between us, it meant *the shit has hit the fan and I need back-up.*

Toad didn't ask.

'You can get to my place?' he asked, in English.

'I've got the van,' I said.

'Then come.'

Toad calmed the girls down while I cleaned up. I remember peeling off my jeans in the shower, stamping on them as I scrubbed myself pink and raw, trying to get the water to run clear. Toad lent me a too-big outfit and said he'd dispose of everything for me. I was glad. The trainers I was wearing were brown and hardened with blood, the jeans ruined.

One by one, the girls went home, Toad calling cabs for them. We'd removed all the cash from the building and divided it between the four of us. I tried to give Toad part of my cut, but he refused. The girls stuffed the possessions they'd rescued into bin bags, told the cabbies they'd been at a pyjama party. Hanna went last. She hadn't looked at me since we'd been outside the stuck door in the sauna's corridor, calling Vyshnya's name. She'd sat on Toad's sofa in silence, her hands clasped together, palm to palm, and stuffed between her knees.

'I'll call you, babe,' I said, as she headed into the stair, the cab waiting outside in the dark.

'Yeah,' she said, 'whatever.'

I stayed at Toad's that night, and he made some calls. Yes, the ambulance had come and yes, the place had been raided, though I wasn't too worried. Our exit was more rushed than I'd have liked, but I'd been careful. The polis would have found no drugs, no money and no condoms. No information on johns, or on the girls. Only Karen was there to be found. I hoped, for her sake, that she was in police custody.

I reasoned that Vyshnya must be in one of the Glasgow hospitals, but I didn't dare try to find her. I didn't want to discuss it, even with Toad. I believed – still believe – that Solomon meant to kill her, or, at the very least, he didn't care if she died. I couldn't risk him discovering I'd looked for her, and I couldn't rule out the possibility that she might have a copper stationed at her bedside, waiting for known associates to appear. Worst of all: she could be in the morgue. That wasn't something I wanted to know for sure.

We got back into the sauna a week or two later: there wasn't much could be done about us without evidence, and this was back in the good old days when a degree of blind-eye turning went on. The girls made do in the meantime texting regulars for outcalls, and I kept my head down and listened for rumblings from Solomon. I'd already known to be scared of him *before* I'd seen how he went to work on Vyshnya, before I'd seen with my own eyes what he was capable of. I walked around like a man waiting for a piano to fall from the sky and obliterate him. But the blow never came. I'd saved the business, I supposed. The police saw what they thought was a sex worker beaten up by her john. They were looking for a punter, not Solomon. I was off the hook.

It was creepy, working there without Vyshnya. I had to become the mother hen as well as the muscle, and the girls were jumpy as fuck. News of the raid spread on the online punting forums, and business was slow to pick up for the first couple of months or so. There wasn't the good atmosphere there had been: we didn't joke around as much together, and it didn't take long for Hanna to tell me she didn't want to see me *like that* any more. She stood over me and made me delete all her nudes from my phone. After that it was all small talk: *good weekend? Yeah, you?* All that shit.

We all missed Karen and none of us talked about it. Or – I mean, I assume the girls talked about it when I wasn't around. No one knew where she'd gone. She didn't return anyone's texts and her phone just rang out, the voicemail message apparently wiped. I asked Izz – on his visits, Karen was the girl he'd always picked – but he was none the wiser. Toad could turn nothing up. I tried to tell myself she'd just skipped town: shaken up by the arrest, or maybe just sick of the work. I knew, somewhere at the bottom of my chest, that it wasn't true. Karen had helped Vyshnya, Karen had called the ambulance – only I knew different. Karen had got the place raided, and now, Karen was gone.

I thought time might help. It seemed to help the girls. It took us a couple of months, but we learned to do without Vyshnya. The girls shared some duties between them: running out for Red Bulls or wet wipes, making cuppas for everyone during the lulls. I took the sheets to the launderette, I unlocked the place and cleaned the loos and hoovered, and I locked up again after hours. We settled to it, and those couple of months became a year, and then three, and then five. The girls would talk about how Vyshnya was back in Ukraine: she'd gone home to recuperate and decided to stay. I thought it was a fairy tale they'd spun for each other so many times they believed it was true, but I kept quiet. Adultwork got big, and they helped each other tart up their profiles. It brought more punters in, and the girls would bitch about them after appointments, reading out the reviews the men left. The web reviews meant less aggro, too, and my role became even more mother hen, even less muscle. Hanna gave me all my CDs back, left one day and never came back. She only texted me once after that, when I got drunk and told her I missed her: *We're done, okay?* Then nothing. New girls came and went, and the dynamic changed. Time should have helped. We're talking about *years*, man. Time should have fixed it, but it didn't. It just made it worse.

Birch made it to the car, twitchy as hell all the way, and kicking herself. How could she have been in such a daydream that she'd had to cut down the close? How could she not have noticed that someone was following her? Had he been waiting for her all day? Had he followed her to her mother's house? And why didn't she arrest him, for fuck's sake? Because of what he might say to her colleagues? He'd have the power to unravel everything once and for all: Rab was already suspicious of her. But she was only thinking all this stuff now, too late. She'd been in such a dwam about Charlie that she couldn't think straight.

At the bottom of Granny's Green Steps she'd flinched at a couple, rattling too fast down towards the street, and shrieking. Halfway down King's Stables Road, a car engine started up right beside her, and she'd heard herself give a little yelp. Under the big road bridge, a busker had been playing saxophone: an eerie tune that sent echoes ringing through the multi-storey as she made her way to the car. The place was harshly lit, which made the night outside feel darker, and between cars and in the stairwells there were deep shadows Birch tried to avoid. She looked behind her every ten steps, but there was no one, or seemed to be no one. She got in the car, and locked herself in.

She drove along the Grassmarket slowly, retracing her steps to look for Fenton, but aware that she wasn't as attentive behind the wheel as she might be. No sign of her assailant: she'd just have to head for home. South Bridge was a snarl of double-deckers, cyclists weaving this way and that. Every movement in her rear-view spooked her. But as the adrenalin ebbed away, she tried to make sense of what had happened.

Where is he? the man had asked – meaning they didn't *know*, not yet. The skull-faced man had cased her house on Monday, and maybe again since, and seen nothing untoward. But they clearly suspected she'd hidden him, that she'd helped him, that she knew where he was. Birch felt grateful that, in the heat of the moment, she'd had the good sense to play clueless. But then, she thought, you are clueless. You have no idea where Charlie is now.

But they didn't either. Not yet.

Birch turned right up Waterloo Place to avoid the chaos of Leith Street roadworks. The buildings fell away and the cemetery arched its back in a dark, spiky mass beside her. Further on, the skyline stretched out to the south, and on the side of Salisbury Crags a little fire was burning. Something about seeing it made Birch shudder. How could she report the attack? The phone calls and flowers were one thing, but the assault of a police officer might trigger more scrutiny from her colleagues than she wanted. She'd have to pretend the man hadn't known who she was, hadn't asked her about Charlie. She knew she'd spent two days covering her own tracks, but an incomplete account of what the man had said would be *more* lying: this time, lying in an official police report. Birch almost laughed.

Not telling anyone about something is fine, she thought, but lying in the paperwork is just not cricket. She remembered how, when she was a child, her mother used to tell her and Charlie not to lie, because there was no such thing as just one. Each lie begat another, and then another, and then another. As a seven-year-old who thought she knew everything, little Helen Birch had scoffed at this. She'd learned from meeting scores of criminals that her mother was more correct than she could ever have known.

'What are you going to do, Helen?' she said aloud, then wished she hadn't. Even her own voice in the quiet bubble of the car made her uneasy.

Can I do nothing? she wondered. Her throat was sore where the man had clasped it, and the back of her neck had a twinge, like slight whiplash, from where he'd yanked her backward. She fancied she could taste the sweet-sour tang of blood, though she wasn't even sure she'd broken his skin. *Can I really pretend none of that ever happened?* It felt like the antithesis of everything she stood for. It might be the straw of *pretending nothing happened* that broke the camel's back of her own guilty silence. Plus, she'd be *letting him get away with it*, and the very idea made her skin itch.

The drive home fell away. As she approached Portobello High Street, Birch realised she'd switched to autopilot, too troubled by the dilemma, by the puzzle of what the attack meant, by the fear of what might come in its wake. A shadow of panic passed over her: *had she stopped for red lights?* Too late now. Another couple of blocks and she'd be home.

Instead of parking in the same place as last night, in well-heeled Elcho Terrace, Birch drove on past the road-end, past her own usual parking space near the China Express, and turned right. In low gear she crawled up the hill to Coillesdene Crescent, where long-time Portobello residents lived in extended bungalows on huge, grassy plots. Every other house had a Neighbourhood Watch sticker. Birch reverse-parked under a streetlight, gathered her courage to her, and got out of the car.

Walking down the hill towards her house, she hauled in a few lungfuls of good, cold air. It was quieter here, out of the city centre's scrum, and she could hear more clearly. There were no footsteps behind her, though that didn't stop her glancing back. Through the gaps in the houses, she caught glimpses of her own terrace, perhaps her own roof. Some of the skylights were lit, and she found their glow comforting. She thought of Charlie, and where he might be. If he hadn't found somewhere to stop then he was probably starving by now. Cold, hungry, alone. *Your fault.*

She made it to the main road, and the smell of the China Express mingled with the salt and seaweed stink of the beach. Mid-way out, the tide rocked and shushed itself. Birch scanned the parked cars as she crossed towards the prom. No dark-coloured Merc, no figures in the gloom. All quiet.

Her heart still pattered in her chest. She was getting sick of it, all this coil and nerve. She couldn't remember the last time she'd relaxed – she couldn't imagine ever relaxing again. As she slipped through the garden gate, her jaw seemed to set itself hard. The house was in darkness, and the front door appeared to be untouched.

Birch let herself in and, holding her breath, walked through the downstairs rooms on the balls of her feet. She didn't turn the lights on, just felt her way through, letting her eyes adjust and the contours of the furniture prickle into focus. The kitchen was half lit by the streetlamp out back, and beyond the still-locked back door the garden was its usual self. She stood listening for movement upstairs, checking that the smell and stillness of her house had not been disturbed. She believed it had not. There was no sign of a break-in.

She felt loath to turn her back on the front door, and climbed the stairs with her head part-turned, as though some new assailant might burst in at any time. Her encounter in the close had shaken her more than she could admit, right then: she could feel herself willing all thought of it away, except for its silver lining: they haven't found Charlie yet. Her bedroom was empty, and the spare room. She twitched the shower curtain aside in the bathroom: nothing. Her own face hung like a dim moon in the cabinet mirror, startling her. Again, she stood listening: nothing. Her house had never felt emptier. This was the part where, at work, she'd get on her police radio and say, *Clear*.

She realised she'd been doing a form of this listening for fourteen years, ever since Charlie had disappeared. Living in this house, she'd always hoped that one day the banging of the front gate wouldn't just be the sea wind, for once, but Charlie, her baby brother, finally coming home. She'd told herself he was dead, but of course some tiny sliver of her had refused to believe it. Now the listening was acute: it felt like the concentration you summon when your body is in pain and you need to get through to the other side of that pain. Birch found herself wondering, in that moment, if all this was the reason she'd stayed single for so much of her adult life. It wasn't just the long hours of the job, the independence, this house she loved and wasn't sure she wanted to share. Maybe she'd been saving space for something, all this time. She'd been waiting for Charlie's return.

When he'd left the night before, Birch hadn't dared open the door and go after him. She'd been frozen, at first, by his decisive exit, and then couldn't face running out through the garden and onto the prom to find that he really *had* gone, and he wasn't coming back. If she stood and waited, then it could still happen. She was doing it again now: standing at the top of the stairs, listening. Willing her little brother to come back to her, so she could try again and, this time, get things right.

And then – *oh God, Helen* – there did come the sound of the garden gate, and the heavy tread of a man outside on the path. Without waiting for the knock, Birch pounded down the stairs to open the door, ready to fling her arms around her brother and thank him for seeing sense and—

'Evening, lassie.'

Birch recoiled at the sight of Big Rab. She couldn't help it.

'You all right, darlin'?'

She tumbled backward into the hallway and sat down, hard, on the third step of the staircase. Big Rab manoeuvred himself into the small space and closed the door behind him.

'All right, now, hen. All right now,' he said. He crouched down on his haunches to put his head on the same level as hers. It looked difficult and undignified, for such a big man. Birch didn't care.

'Did I no' tell ye,' he said, 'to call me? If something went wrang?'

Birch had screwed her eyes closed. Go away, she thought, go away. What if Charlie comes back and you're here? Instead, she nodded.

'We're aw worried sick,' he went on. 'Your pal DC Kato's been beside herself.'

Birch blinked. 'Amy?'

'Aye,' Big Rab said. 'She's been ringing ye. No answer. Then she tells me and I try, and some bloke answers, not sounding too friendly.'

'A bloke?'

Rab nodded. 'De ye ken where your phone is, DI Birch?'

Birch realised she did not. She hadn't known since – when? She couldn't remember.

'Shit,' she said. You must have dropped it, she thought, when you flipped that guy. She couldn't remember it happening, but she knew, as soon as it occurred to her, that it was true. Just her luck. One of Solomon's goons has your phone now. That means that tomorrow morning, Solomon will have your phone.

'Shit,' she said again.

Big Rab straightened up. Birch heard his knees crack.

'Right,' he said, 'I'm away tae put the kettle on. You're going to come wi' me, and tell me what aw this is about, okay?'

Birch felt numb. Her mind was racing in two directions now: Charlie was gone, he was in the wind, with the worst kind of people looking for him. But also, those same people now had her phone, and it was full of work stuff, personal stuff, confidential information. The phone was locked, but she imagined it wouldn't take much for the likes of Solomon's guys to get past that. McLeod would kill her. There could be another disciplinary.

'Oh God,' she said, following Big Rab through the living room. 'Oh *shit*, Helen, you *idiot*.'

Rab calmed her down, sat her on the sofa, and shoved a cup of very milky tea into her hands. She shuffled, aware once again of the dent Charlie had left in her couch. Rab settled into the small chair where Birch usually sat. She tried to ignore the sound it made as he came to rest.

'Tell me,' he said.

Birch screwed her eyes closed, tight. Tell him *what*? Everything? Could she do that? If she told him about Charlie they could start a manhunt. They could find him and bring him in and he'd be safe, someone could maybe persuade him to testify . . . but no. She'd have to fess up to the fact he'd been here, and hiding. She'd have to fess up that she'd lied to Rab, jeopardised the investigation, lied upon lies, made mistakes upon mistakes. And Charlie might hate her for the rest of their lives, the thought of which she just could not bear. That was if they found him at all. If they found him *first* . . .

'I was attacked,' Birch heard herself say. 'Walking back to my car, from . . . in the city centre.'

She opened her eyes again, in time to see Rab grimace at her.

'I *telt* ye,' he said, 'to ring me, if—'

Birch spluttered. 'On what?' she said. 'The guy took my phone.'

'Where wis yer panic button?'

Birch waved a hand at the coffee table. The panic button sat in the middle of it.

Big Rab rolled his eyes, then looked around. 'Landline?'

'I don't have one,' Birch lied. There was an elderly phone with extra-large buttons plugged in upstairs in the bedroom. It had belonged to the old guy who'd lived in the house before. She never used it, no one ever called her, and it hadn't occurred to her that she might use it to phone Rab. She prayed to God that no one decided to place a cold call right then.

'I'm only just in, really,' she went on. Her voice came out high and stringy, making the statement sound like a lie, though it wasn't. 'I took it slow driving home, 'cause I'm shaken up, you know?'

That *you know* sounded just like Charlie.

Rab looked at her from under half-closed eyelids. 'All right,' he said.

She could see that same inkling of suspicion in his face, but she knew he wasn't going to say anything, or wouldn't yet, till he'd got more to go on.

'He attacked you how?'

Birch swallowed a sob. Keep it together, Helen. 'I ... went into town after work,' she said. 'I walked up Johnston Terrace but then ... needed to get down a level. I went down a close. It wasn't late. I thought I'd be fine. But he came up behind me, and ... well, we tussled.'

Rab smiled then. 'He came off worst?'

Birch nodded.

'You're no' going to get us sued, are ye, lassie?'

He was laughing. That was good.

'I'm more worried about the fact he's got my phone. I hadn't realised I'd lost it till now. I must have dropped it as ... you know, in the struggle.' Birch remembered the gun. 'I *did* hear something fall on the ground.' Well, she thought, that isn't a lie either. 'That's my work phone,' she went on. 'It's got all sorts on it.'

Rab shrugged. 'It's locked?'

'Yeah, but . . .'

He shook his head. 'If it's some wee nyaff of a mugger,' he said, 'he'll no' bother unlocking it. More likely it's away to Cash Converters already.'

Birch tried to keep her mouth in a line. It was difficult: it felt sore. Even if that were true, she thought, how would it help? It could end up in anyone's hands . . .

She knew Rab knew that. He was getting at something.

'Unless,' he said, 'he wis a bigger fish than that.'

He looked hard at her then. She hadn't noticed before, but his eyes were almost grey. In his pink face, they were piercing, when trained right at you. She could see how he'd break a perp under interrogation.

'I . . . have no idea who he was,' Birch managed. 'He was white, fifties, about five eleven, wearing a hoodie that might have been blue, or grey – I'm not sure, it was dark. West coast accent, Glaswegian I think. And he smelled . . . not too great.'

Rab smiled again. 'Well,' he said, 'that narrows it down.'

Birch tried to laugh. Her throat was full of water.

'Did he speak to ye?'

She swallowed, hard, like a cartoon gulp. She hoped he hadn't heard it. 'Nothing much,' she said. 'Told me not to fuck with him, called me a bitch. Etcetera.'

Rab raised an eyebrow. 'Didnae make demands?'

Birch tried to look wry. 'He didn't really have time,' she said, 'before I . . . neutralised things.'

She expected Rab to laugh, but he didn't. He did drop his gaze, though, and she felt herself slacken all over.

'You're going to tell me,' Rab said, 'what else he said to ye.'

It was a statement, not a question. Birch flinched.

'All of it,' Rab added.

Birch looked down into her tea cup, letting her thoughts race. Rab already knew about Charlie. He didn't know she'd hidden him. Telling the truth now didn't have to unravel the previous lie. She remembered her mother again: *one lie builds a tower.* May as well knock a little off the top.

'He asked where Charlie was,' she blurted. As she looked up at Rab, she saw the suspicion leave his face. He'd known that all along, he just wanted her to say it.

'It's aw connected, then,' he said, after a pause. His voice was grave.

'What?' she said.

He looked at her again. 'Now come oan, lassie. Yer skull-masked saloon-driving man? That flower delivery? This, now. My inform-ant on Citrine is yer wee brother. I thought you were the only person who knew that, but now we know that *they* know it, tae. And they either know that *you* know – which would mean you or I is bent, and talking to them. Or – more likely, given that I believe we're as pure as the driven – they've done the same as I did. They've assumed he'd run tae you.'

Birch nodded. She couldn't think what else to do. But his *pure as the driven* remark had made her cringe.

'That wid explain,' Rab was saying, 'why some gobshite in a mask has been peering in yer windaes.'

She tried to cast her mind back to the skull-masked man, and Monday. It felt like an age ago.

'I don't know, Rab,' she said. 'I don't know. I'm just tired.' She was telling the truth now. 'In fact,' she went on, 'I'm exhausted. I just want to jack it all in.' Is that true, Helen? she thought. Is that right?

'This might be another disciplinary.' She realised she was still speaking. 'Because my phone is in the wrong hands. If there's a leak of confidential information, I'm in big trouble. And yeah, you're right. I think Solomon's guys *have* got an interest in me and I'm scared, and I don't know what to do. And we can't do anything about Operation Citrine, and Solomon's going to walk free tomor-row, my little brother is out there somewhere, in the midst of it all . . . I just want to ditch out, Rab. I could hand in my notice to McLeod tomorrow.'

Silence hung between them. Birch felt shocked at herself.

'I dare say,' she added, 'he'd rather welcome it at this point.'

Rab frowned at her then. 'Believe that,' he said, 'and ye ken less about that man than ye think.'

She wanted to ask him what he meant, but didn't dare. The outburst seemed to have worked, though: the look of suspicion Rab had been wearing had fallen away.

'You've had a shock, lassie,' he said, gesturing to the tea. 'Another one. It's been a shite week for ye, no doubt about that.'

Birch took a sip of the hot liquid. It was loaded with sugar.

'We'll file a report on this,' he went on, 'this attack. But no' tomorrow. Christ knows I cannae deal wi' it tomorrow, seeing as I've to let a monster loose back intae the world. So just rest up. See what Monday brings.'

Birch was quiet. You don't want to report it right away, she thought, because you'd have to reveal who your informant is. We'd both have to name him. Her eyes widened. 'You still think we're going to be able to charge him, don't you?' she asked. 'You still think you might not have to own up to letting your informant run.'

Rab had stood, then, and straightened his limbs out in a series of clicks and groans. 'I think,' he said, 'that yer wee brother might still turn up at yer door, DI Birch. I ken it's a small hope now, but miracles do happen.'

Birch swallowed again. Feeling she ought to, she also stood.

'I'm glad you're okay, lassie,' he said. 'I'll let DC Kato know.'

He set off through the living room, back to the hallway. At the door, he turned, and gestured backward to the panic button. 'Put that by your bed, and get some sleep,' he said. 'I ken Solomon's boys, an' they won't do anything major without his say-so. I reckon you're all right tonight.'

Birch closed the door on Rab's retreating back, then turned to face the dim emptiness of her little house once again.

'Thanks a bunch,' she said.

Time passed, and all it did was make me hate him more.

I still dreamed about her – about Vyshnya. All the time. Sometimes it was a sort of twisted replay, where I walked into a room and she was lying there, like a pile of rags, and it was up to me to try to save her. Other times it was worse: it was me hurting her, working my way down her body, systematically trying to snap every bone I could find. And other times I was in a dark place and she was this ghoulish *thing* chasing me: this broken howling woman who somehow managed to run, on all fours, on her shattered limbs. I woke up from these dreams drenched, shaking. I would turn over and go back to sleep just to dream them all over again. I've been having them years now. Any night I don't dream is like *heaven*, a blessing.

For a while I drank. I thought it might help the dreams stop. It helped me fall asleep at night, sure, but the bad dreams still came and the alcohol just made me feel sicker, just made the room spin more. Fenton liked it when I was drinking: he was keen on a bevvy himself, and egged me on so he'd have a weeknight buddy to prop up the bar with. I liked it when he was there: we talked about stuff that wasn't the sauna, and sometimes, after the right number of beers, I could pretend we were just two guys with lousy day jobs out on the town after a bit of a long one. But eventually Fenton would be gone, and I'd have to be alone in my flat.

So I switched tactics. I'd get up, swing by HQ, go to work, pocket my cash, and go home. Sleep, try not to dream, and repeat. I made excuses to Fenton and quick enough he got the message and stopped asking.

I had to obsess over something, though. I had to find something else to fill the space. I guess the space was depression. But I never really thought about it that hard. What doctor would I go to? What therapist? I just found ways to survive instead.

I did three things: I worked out, I counted my money and I cultivated my hatred for Solomon. On a good night I'd walk out of the sauna with an envelope of cash in perfectly good, kosher notes. I'd train two hours minimum a day: weights, boxing. The punch-bag was Solomon, and I'd batter in the eye sockets of that sly, grinning face over and over in my mind. I'd go in even if I got sick, only taking a day off if I thought I was working up an injury. On days I didn't work out, I itched all over for movement, and the dreams were worse.

I knew it had become a fixation, the hatred, but I didn't care. I blamed Solomon for everything: pulling me out of my old life, turning me into a criminal so I couldn't go back without facing the jail. Without grassing. He'd made every option that wasn't *him* impossible. I worked for Solomon. I was one of Solomon's boys. I did bad things. That's it, the end. No choice.

And I hated what he'd done to Vyshnya. Yeah, I'd kicked the shit out of some guys, I'd followed people, I'd scared people on purpose because I could. I'd walked through the world swinging my dick and taking names and I'd enjoyed it. But I wouldn't do anything like *that*. I believed I couldn't, like that level of cruelty just wasn't in my bones. To hurt someone that badly, and to go on hurting them – to break them in every conceivable way – made Solomon inhuman, I decided. Literally not a person. And so I hated him with a fury that had no compassion. I knew it was based on my own fear. I was like a skinny dog in a corner, not chained but sticking around for its master's beatings. I hated what he'd done to Karen, too, which was make her disappear. I hated myself for making her my own personal cautionary tale, but she was.

The girls at work were different, too. After Hanna, the rest of the old crew fell away, moved on, disappeared one by one. When they were replaced, it was by girls who had baggage. They were addicts, and that changed the nature of the work. Solomon had got into the flakka business by then, and these new girls couldn't get enough. I couldn't stand the stuff, and I hated the way it made them, loopy and spaced out when they had it, jittery and violent when they didn't. I didn't want it on the premises and they'd try to sneak it in. They'd ask their regulars to bring them some. For the first time ever, I had to get heavy with them, impose the rules. No drugs was a Vyshnya rule, but it was a smart one: any drugs found during a raid and it was game over for everyone. These new girls didn't give a shit. They didn't listen to me. I was just *Schenok*, the beaten puppy.

At work, I sat behind the hatch and daydreamed about leaving. This was what I was counting the money for, I told myself: if I got out fast, I could use my Nick Smith passport one final time, get on a plane and disappear. I daydreamed about making it to Russia at last, finally making that teenage daydream come true. But I knew that Solomon had contacts everywhere in Russia. Even in Moscow, I'd stand out like a sore thumb: my self-taught Russian with Scots inflection, my unfamiliar tattoos. It was a big place, but even if I went to live in a shack in the Urals, I'd be looking over my shoulder for the rest of my life. I'd be forever waiting for the gunshot, the door kicked in, the poison seeping into my veins as I realised it was too late. And what would I do for work? The Solomon cash I'd acquired would only last so long. The criminal life came with its perks: swish flat all to myself, free gym, nice watch, whatever I wanted. I'd got used to that. I only drove Vic's van because a Maserati tends to draw attention when you're following some dude home. Did I *want* to go back to being a penniless translator? Of course I didn't. But the work was killing me: the work, the regrets, the dreams and the hatred. The thoughts were a circle, and the circle was endless.

Christmastime was the worst. I couldn't shut it out. From the windows of my flat I could see lit trees in every other window but mine. Vyshnya had always let the girls string tinsel in the sauna lounge: I stopped that. The punters, sitting waiting for their particular girls, would chat with me about it, like *doing much for Christmas, mate?*, and they'd tell me about their families. What they'd bought for their kids. Even Fenton had family he'd go to at Christmas, and Toad would disappear home to Russia and go to his old Orthodox church. The first few years I'd liked it, doing my own thing: I'd take myself out to some fancy hotel and get fed five courses then stagger home. When Hanna was around we'd even had a tree up. But these past few years, it was bed and a bottle of brandy on Christmas Eve and then trying to sleep it all away. I used to hope it would all just pass without me noticing. It never did.

Being an official Missing Person didn't help. I tried not to count the months, the years, but you do, you know? I couldn't help it. The ten-year anniversary was hard. Maw relaunched her appeal and my face was on lampposts again. Social media was more of a thing. I shaved my head that year, grew a beard, started dressing more like Fenton, copying the way he hid in his clothes. And of course all the press shit got dragged up about how Maw had supposedly got money she shouldn't have at the time I disappeared. Donations and that. And look, I'd never been found, they said. Look, I was probably dead. Where was that money? She ought to give it back. I wanted to go after every last one of them, especially that Lockley scumbag. I wanted to go home and see my maw and Nella and tell them I was okay and I was sorry and I dealt with Da and I've been fine this whole time and I'd missed them so much. But I couldn't. I couldn't risk blowing my own cover. And by now I'd done so many bad things that I wasn't sure if I could look my maw in the face. Nella might understand, but I felt like Maw would be so disappointed in me that it literally might have killed her. It was nearly killing me, sitting day after day with who I'd become. Worrying that not only had Charlie Birch fucked up, but Nick Smith had, too. It was bad enough the appeal waking up again, but I was also just waiting for the visit from Solomon, come to tell me I was too much of a risk. Come to make me disappear, like Karen and Vyshnya and Tsezar before me.

I was lonely for years, working a job that used to be bearable but turned to shit before my eyes. I saw one workmate get beaten to a bloody pulp, another one disappear without trace – I lived every day knowing that was my fate too if I put a toe out of line. I'd fallen out of my life, never to see my loved ones again. I'd watched them search for me, and I'd failed to reach out because I was too damn scared, too damn ashamed. I learned my maw had died from a column in the paper. I never even knew she had cancer. Why'd you decide to get out, Charlie? As if all of that wasn't enough.

Friday

After Rab had left, Birch sat on the couch, staring at nothing, feeling like all her edges had been dulled. Rab thought Charlie might come back, and although she knew better his conviction had planted its seed in her mind and she couldn't seem to shake it out again. He might come back. He might. You never know.

She'd decided to sleep on the couch, because she'd been asleep on the couch when Charlie first appeared, and she felt that repeating the same actions might summon him again, like the words of an incantation. She felt ridiculous, but did it nonetheless. It hadn't worked. All night she'd cramped and stretched under the pilled throw, the couch too short for her long frame – and her brother had not returned. She slept in short bursts, and woke from each one with a heavy thud of recollection: Charlie was here, but now he's gone. I might never see him again.

On Coillesdene Crescent the car gleamed under its streetlight. The sky was turning, but the streetlamps hadn't yet switched off, and Birch was glad of them. The tide was out: between buildings, she could see the dawn's gleam on the long stretch of beach it had left in its wake. Seagulls wheeled overhead, flinging their *hi, hi, hi* down at the world. The cries were ghostly in the grey streets. Birch climbed into the car, skipping the inspection. She figured, if the car blew up when she turned the key, she'd neither know nor care. And it didn't, of course. She drove to work with the radio on: Radio Scotland, so she could listen to the news. The fourth story in: *Solomon Carradice to be released without charge. Frustration for Police Scotland.*

'No kidding,' Birch said.

★   ★   ★

The station was in disarray. Even more than the previous day, she could feel that morale was low: it was in the air. It was 7.45 a.m. when she arrived: just over an hour until Solomon must be released. She'd seen Anjan's car in the car park. He always used the same space.

As she walked through the bullpen, a few of her fellow officers made eye contact, and she tried to smile for them. She just wanted to make it to the office, get inside, close the door, and regroup. Then, perhaps, coffee. Then she'd figure out how she was going to survive the day.

'Marm!'

Birch winced, and turned around. Amy clicked over to her on her high heels.

'I was looking for you yesterday evening, but Rab told me you were fine.' Her usual cheeriness seemed dampened: the low mood in the place was even getting to Amy.

'Thanks, Kato,' she said. 'Truth be told, I feel like crap today.' What the hell, she thought, may as well say it.

'He also told me,' Amy said, lowering her voice, 'about what happened last night. I'm so sorry.'

What happened last night, Birch thought. You don't know the half of it. Rab must have embroidered a little: it was probably a random mugging, as far as Amy knew.

'Are you okay?' Amy asked.

Birch shrugged. 'The other guy came off worse,' she said, making Amy grin.

'Kicking arse and taking names, marm?'

'Something like that.' Birch began to drift in the direction of her office door. 'Sorry, Amy, I've got to – things to catch up on, you know?'

It was a lie. With Solomon walking free any moment, and Rab asking her to hold off on reporting her attack until Monday, there was nothing for her to do, really, other than sit in her office and worry. But there was a part of her that wanted that: she wanted to be able to just sit and quietly unravel over her brother's where-abouts. She was well practised at it, after all.

'Sure thing,' Amy said. 'Got to get yourself set up with a new phone, for starters.'

'I guess I do,' Birch said. Oh Jesus. The phone. There was that to be anxious about, too.

'Have you heard anything,' Amy said, 'you know . . . last minute? About Solomon?'

Birch shook her head. 'I'm guessing, from the atmosphere,' she said, 'that the release is basically a done deal. But I reckon I know less than anyone.'

Amy nodded, and Birch waited for her to get the hint.

'Right,' Amy said. 'Well, okay.'

She felt bad, then. Sweet Amy, who always tried to paste a smile on, no matter what. She'd been hard done by on the Three Rivers case, for example, yet she'd stayed upbeat.

'Sorry,' Birch said. 'I know this makes no difference at all, but – this is policework. Can't win 'em all.'

Amy smiled again. There was that same grimness in her eyes. 'I know,' she said. 'I just sort of hoped we'd win *this* one, you know?'

See, Helen? You've fucked this up for absolutely everyone.

'Yeah,' Birch said, 'you and me both.'

She'd not been in the office long when someone knocked on the door. She was sitting behind her desk, spaced out, staring at a patch on the wall where there had once been a framed picture. The picture had fallen down, and now there was a nick in the plaster where the nail had been ripped out. It looked like a wound.

At the door, a second knock. Fuck off, Birch thought. 'Hello?' she said.

The door opened wide. It was Anjan. He stood in the doorway looking every bit as upright and spotless as usual. 'Hello,' he said. 'Do you mind if I come in?'

Birch tried not to let her various interactions with Anjan over the past week rush back to her, but rush back they did. It felt almost like relief: for a few seconds, at least, she wasn't worrying about Charlie.

'Sure,' she said. Her voice was very small.

Anjan closed the door behind him and approached the chair on the opposite side of the desk. Birch blushed as he gently lifted a small heap of items off the seat and placed them on the floor by the chair leg.

'Sorry,' she said, in that same small voice, gesturing around at the room. 'Sorry about all this.' She realised she didn't just mean her office, but everything. Herself. The mess she was in.

Anjan smiled at her as he sat, a warm smile. That surprised her. She wasn't sure how to feel about it.

'You act like I haven't been in here before,' he said. 'They ought to get you a PA.'

Birch snorted. 'They ought to get me a skip,' she said. She wanted to say more, but pressed her lips together, hard. She'd been short with him when he'd come over on Wednesday night and she'd been tempted to tell him a lie. She'd been cowardly, and run away, rather than face him. She mustn't do that again.

'So,' Anjan said. For perhaps the first time ever, he looked nervous. 'I didn't like how we parted ways last time we spoke. I feel I was insensitive. Provocative, even. And I want to apologise.'

Birch blinked. *He* was apologising to *her*? She felt, suddenly, like she wanted to cry. 'No, Anjan,' she said. 'It wasn't you. You didn't do anything. It was all me. I've been trying not to think about how I've been this week, not to replay it, but – I've been the one in the wrong, no question.' He looked as if he was going to argue, so she went on. 'I was just . . .' She was committed, now. 'I was disappointed, to be honest. We've had such a wonderful—' Relationship, Helen. Just say it. But she couldn't. 'We've had such a good *time together* lately. Like last weekend.'

Anjan nodded. 'Yes,' he said.

'And so . . . I was just disappointed, I guess. That all this – Operation Citrine, I mean – got in the way of that.' Birch saw him frown.

'It didn't have to,' he said. 'Doesn't have to. I want you to know that. In spite of – well, all that's been said. I'm still me. I don't see why it has to change anything.'

Birch was quiet for a moment, turning things over in her mind.

'Had my client been charged,' Anjan was saying, 'then we'd be in a trial situation, and that would be different. Any . . . well, any relationship not of a professional kind would present a conflict of interest. There would be problems.'

She felt as if she were hearing what he was saying after a slight delay, like the continuity on a live broadcast when things get out of sync. She watched his lips move, and then just a second later heard the words. And yet you came to my house, she thought. You invited me to the pub. But she let him go on.

'I couldn't have defended Solomon Carradice in court, and continued to . . . well, see you socially,' he went on. Then he smiled, and said, 'Why do you think I've been pushing so hard to make sure he's cleared?'

Birch felt her stomach fill, immediately, with dancing sparks. It was, by turns, the most romantic and the most fucked-up thing a man had ever said to her.

'Wait,' she said. 'Did you just say you pushed for a known scumbag to walk free . . . because of *me*?'

Anjan's smile faded. Something crackled between them. 'Forgive me,' he said. 'That was in poor taste.'

Birch pressed a hand to her forehead. 'It's a lot,' she said. Her palm part-covered her eyes. She could no longer see Anjan's face.

'I'm sorry,' he said. 'I just wanted to . . . make things right between us. If I could.'

Birch closed her eyes altogether. It made it easier to speak, somehow. 'I really wanted this man charged,' she said. 'We all did. But I have, in particular . . .' A vested interest, she thought. I have a brother whose life might just depend upon it.

'I know it's not my case,' she said, trying a different tack. 'But I just . . . it's personal. It *feels* personal. For all of us. Do you have any idea what I'm saying?' She squinted one eye open again.

Anjan was nodding. 'I do,' he said. 'This has been challenging for me, too.'

Challenging? She wanted to scream at him. You don't know the meaning of the word.

'I guess,' she said, inwardly urging herself to stay cool, 'I didn't expect it of you. That decision, to . . . well, to represent a man who's obviously very, very guilty.' She tried to look directly at Anjan. It was hard to do: he looked so sharp, so together. He was beautiful, in every sense of the word. Right now, she felt only half human: ill-slept, hungry, running entirely on worry. Anjan's presence amplified that feeling.

Birch waited for him to turn cold with her. Waited for the *it's my job* line. But he surprised her.

'I know,' he said. 'And I'm sorry.'

She felt her eyes widen.

'You surely didn't think,' he said, 'I took this case because I believed in Carradice? I'm so sorry. I tried to tell you.'

Birch blinked, once. Twice. 'Tell me what?'

'That it was the firm's decision. I was under some considerable pressure. We're growing our profile, and that means we get requests from defendants who are . . . well, let's just say they are *particularly keen* to be found innocent.'

Birch tried not to roll her eyes. 'Particularly keen,' she echoed, 'in the sense that they make it worth your while.'

Anjan nodded. 'Exactly,' he said. 'Though again, I stress, this isn't me. It is the firm. If we're willing to defend the guilty, and if we do it well, we can command a higher fee, and thus . . . well, the gyre spins wider.'

Birch nodded. 'Yeah,' she said. 'I know how it goes.'

Anjan looked rueful. 'You know,' he said. 'But I fear you don't understand. I fear you've decided I'm craven. The thought of that has been upsetting me all week.'

Birch gave her head a little shake. 'It has?'

'Yes.' Anjan shifted a little in his seat. 'That's why I've tried to see you. Why I asked if we could talk. I've been thinking of you. Often.'

She felt a pang of guilt, then. She wanted to say, *I've been thinking of you, too* – that was the romcom line, the line that just might seal the deal. But if she were to say it, it would be a lie. Whenever Anjan had ghosted into her thoughts, she'd tried to exorcise him.

She'd been completely immersed in the situation with Charlie these past few days – much good it had done her.

'I . . . really appreciate that,' she said. It sounded pathetic. She dug around for some truth. 'I wish none of this had ever happened.'

Anjan nodded. 'Isn't that so often the case,' he said, 'for all of us?'

Birch wasn't sure what else to say. Part of her brain screamed, Stay, Anjan, I like you so much. But another part hissed, Get out, Anjan. You've made everything worse. She opted to say nothing, and for a moment they simply looked at each other.

'I hope,' Anjan said at last, 'that you can forgive me. Maybe after a bit of time has passed.'

Still, Birch was dumbfounded. Say something, she thought. Anything would be good at this point. But now Anjan was on his feet.

'All right,' he said. 'I need to go and see to the final, grisly spectacle, I'm afraid.'

Birch nodded. 'Okay.' Her voice was hoarse. 'Thank you for coming to see me.'

'Of course. I'm glad we spoke.'

Anjan walked to the door, but then stopped and turned back to face her. 'You're always welcome to call me,' he said. 'I'll always be happy to hear from you.'

It was last November, late on in the month. I remember, because Toad was using the van that night and I'd had to get a bus. It was idling in traffic, right by George Square, and everything was held up by pedestrians in huge crowds milling around. It took me a minute to realise it was the official switching on of the Christmas lights. Then, right there, as the bus honked and inched along, the whole place lit up. The massive tree, the rows and rows of coloured lights. Seeing it, hearing the cheers go up, I got such a wave of nostalgia that I felt physically sick. I'd been down there, once. I'd been part of those crowds. I remembered being sat between the paws of one of the big white stone lions, my knees pulled up to my chest. Nella was between the paws of the other one, and she'd seemed so far away. We waved to each other, tried to throw sweetie wrappers across the divide. Maw had told us to stop it, to look up, it would happen any minute. And I remembered how the tree seemed to catch fire, it was covered with so many bulbs. I remembered jumping out from under the lion's jaws and running towards the lights. And I remembered that my maw was dead, and I hadn't seen her in fourteen whole years.

I got back to the flat and hit the drink: poured myself a triple Scotch and settled in to brood. My phone rang and I ignored it. Ignored it once, ignored it twice. The third time I looked to see who it was, and it was Toad. Fucksake, that guy really picked his moments.

'Schenok,' he said. I could hear he was somewhere loud, somewhere busy.

'Yeah, man,' I said. I'd already demolished most of the triple, and I could feel it prickling hot under my skin.

'I must,' he said, in English, 'ask a favour.'

Oh, here goes . . .

'Look, I'm sorry, pal, but we talked about this – I can't do these on-the-side jobs for you, I really—'

'This comes from Solomon,' he said.

My heart kicked. 'What does?'

I heard Toad sigh. This wasn't going to be good.

'He needs a body man,' he said. 'And driver. Temporary. Two weeks, maybe a month. He asked me.'

I blinked. 'What happened?'

I could hear Toad was moving. The noise around him ebbed.

'Abdul got beat up,' he said. 'Quite bad. He's in the hospital with . . . how do you say in English?' Toad rattled off some Russian.

'A punctured lung,' I said. 'Jesus.'

'Yes,' Toad said. 'Quite bad.'

'And he asked *you*?' I tried not to sound too surprised. Toad was a mountain of a man: huge, imposing, but also fucking ancient.

'A courtesy, I think,' Toad replied, 'or a test. But I am on my way to St Petersburg. Right now I am behind the security gates.'

An airport. That explained the noise.

Oh shit . . . 'Wait.' My brain was finally catching up with my ears. 'Are you saying you suggested *me*?'

'You have been working in that sauna too long, *Schenok*.'

I winced. That meant yes.

'Your skills are being wasted there. It is time you got more money. Time you got the good work.'

'Fucksake, Toad!' I was panicked then. He'd clearly just signed me up for the job. 'I don't *want* that sort of work! I don't want to be within a mile of that arsehole, you know that.'

There was a brief silence – or rather, Toad didn't speak, and I listened to the airport sounds as things happened around him.

'I have told you,' he said, 'it is not a good idea to speak of him this way. Not safe.'

Toad could be a renegade, but Solomon was *glavnyy*, the boss man. You could run your own jobs, you could do stupid shit like hire a random kid to translate your documents for you without running it by anyone; but speak ill of the boss? Apparently not okay.

I couldn't speak.

'It is important that you do this,' Toad said. 'We all work hard, it is necessary to. You have not been working hard. It is time for you to show loyalty. Not to Solomon, but to me. Time for you to trust me, when I say I need you to do this. And it is good money. Very good.'

I didn't doubt it.

'Toad . . .'

'I mean it.' I rarely heard him sound this stern. '*Schenok*, have I not saved you many times? Have I not spoken for you when no one else did? Do you not trust me?'

I closed my eyes. 'I do,' I said. It was true, after all.

'Then trust me now. There are reasons you must do this. They will become clear to you, and then you will thank me.'

I had no idea what he was on about. But I could hear the *you owe me one* in every syllable he uttered.

'But I don't have the van,' I spluttered at him. 'And who will take care of the girls? There's only me. I can't . . .'

These were shit excuses. I don't know why I thought they'd save me.

'No need for the van,' Toad said. 'But it is at the lock-up at my place. The key is hidden as always, you will find it. But you will be driving the car of Solomon. You can take a cab to his place. He will pay.'

I winced. I'd never been to Solomon's mansion, but I knew where it was. I'd Google Maps-ed it a few times, when I felt like making myself sick. It had a tennis court.

'But the sauna—'

I could practically hear Toad roll his eyes on the other end of the phone. He knew I was bullshitting him.

'I have spoken already with Izz,' he said. 'He knows the place well. He will take care of the girls while you are gone.'

Fuck. He had it all figured out.

'Do not exaggerate this, *Schenok*,' Toad was saying. 'It is two weeks. It is a month. The money is good. You can do this thing. You will do this thing, for me. For *zhaba*.'

His tone was peppy. He was giving me a *you go, girl*. I heard the buzz of a distant tannoy.

'My flight,' Toad said. 'You will go in the morning. When I land, I will text you more.'

My mind was racing. '*Zhaba*,' I said, '*puzhalsta . . .*'

'The thing is done, *Schenok*.'

The line went dead.

And then I was in the inner circle. In fact, I *was* the inner circle: Solomon went everywhere with four guys, four *body men*, who stood around him at all times. Abdul was also the chauffeur, so I took over that role, too. When I got there, I buzzed in at the electronic gates and then crunched up the drive on foot with my overnight bag – instructions from Toad's late-night text. Yew trees closed in on me on both sides, and overhead. I felt like I was walking into a horror movie.

But instead, Malkie met me outside the house. It was massive. Solomon had clearly had it built, because it looked newish, for all it had stone steps up to the front door and fancy columns. It looked like a cross between a Georgian mansion and a Barratt house, only . . . well, huge. But I didn't get much chance to stand and look at it: Malkie dumped my bag and then took me straight to the garage. Inside: Solomon's two identical Range Rovers. Both Autobiography models with V8 Supercharged engines, all matte black and muscle and chrome. Driven slowly, they'd be like cruise ships. Driven fast, they'd outrun any polis vehicle without even breaking a sweat. I whistled. I didn't want the job, but holy fuck was *this* a silver lining.

'Think you can handle one of these?' Malkie had his arms folded, smirking at me.

'D'you drive, pal?' I asked.

He shook his head.

'Then shut the fuck up, yeah?'

★   ★   ★

The body men were housed in a built-on wing at the side of the house. I took my bag into Abdul's room, and tried to get comfy. It felt weird. I felt like I was in *The Handmaid's Tale*. I sat on the bed and wondered what the chances were of me dying in this room, some time over the next two weeks, the next month. Abdul had postcards taped to the wall with lines from the Quran on them. *So verily with the hardship there is relief – verily with the hardship there is relief.* I wondered if Abdul felt relief now, free from Solomon for a short time, albeit in a hospital bed. But perhaps his hardship wasn't Solomon at all. Perhaps he liked this line of work. I realised how far I'd crawled into my own head, these past few years. I struggled to think how anyone else's reality could be different to my own.

Malkie went through my bag. 'These are fine,' he said, of my black jeans. 'But the shirts are no good.'

He went away, came back with a variety of black clothes: a crew neck, a button-down, a pullover. He carried them in in a pile, folded into squares. They were his, I assumed – he and I were roughly the same size, whereas Abdul was much bigger.

When I lifted the pile off Malkie's arms, I saw there was something else.

'This is yours,' he said, handing me the gun. 'Well, it's Abdul's, but you'll use it while he's gone.'

I nodded. I'd carried before, and I had a couple of handguns of my own: hand-me-downs from Toad. But at Vyshnya's request, there had never been a gun on the premises of the sauna, and I'd never actually done more than point mine at the odd guy who wouldn't toe the line. Fenton had taught me how to shoot, years back, but I'd never actually needed to. I thought myself lucky. I hoped that luck would hold out – just two weeks. Just a month.

'He doesn't need us all the time,' Malkie said. 'But when he needs us, you be ready.'

I nodded again. I felt like a wind-up toy.

'How will I know?' I asked.

'Don't worry. I'll come and get you.'

*   *   *

The first couple of days were uneventful. I'd arrived on a Friday, and Solomon observed the weekends, like normal people – this rather boggled my mind. He entertained a couple of business associates at home, took phone calls. My services weren't required. I met the other two guys: Fitz and Ez. We sat in the shared kitchen, the four of us, and drank some beers. I cracked a joke about all the 'z's in their names, thinking of Izz, too.

'I'm Turkish,' Ez said. 'If you tried to pronounce my full name, you'd choke on your tongue.' He rolled his eyes. 'You British,' he said.

The other guy was Scottish, through and through. He talked like Fenton. 'Clan Fitzgerald,' he said. 'It's no' my name, it was ma grannie's. It's a bonny tartan we've got, an' aw.'

I nodded. 'So what the hell's Izz, then?' I asked. 'What's that about?'

Malkie laughed. 'Years ago,' he said, 'we'd call him Scissors. All his fancy tailored suits, y'know? He liked it, thought it sounded gangster, started using it himself.'

Fitz cut in. 'Aye. But we couldnae be bothered wi' it, so it got shortened. Izz. Scissors. Ye ken?'

I couldn't get over it. These were just regular guys. I wanted to ask if they'd ever killed someone, wanted to say, *What's the worst thing Solomon has ever made you do?* But I couldn't. A part of me really didn't want to know.

'And you're just . . . Nick Smith?' Ez asked.

I rolled my eyes. 'I know, right?' I said. 'A bit obvious.'

Ez's brow wrinkled, but Malkie and Fitz laughed.

'But what's your other name?' Fitz asked.

'Oh. They call me *Schenok*. Toad started that one.' I screwed up my nose. 'It means . . . um, puppy. In Russian.'

Malkie laughed, but Fitz didn't.

'No,' he said. 'I mean your name. Your real name.'

Quiet fell between us like a ton of bricks.

'No one uses that name any more,' I said. 'Except my family, and I don't talk about my family. They're off limits.'

For a moment, all three of them watched me. I saw the little bit of trust I'd just built get folded away again, as their faces hardened.

'Okay,' Fitz said. 'I get it.'

What the fuck am I doing here? I texted to Toad.

You will find out, he wrote back. *You will have contact soon.*

Solomon needed us on Monday. I'd slept in, and woke to Malkie shaking my shoulder. I flinched: I'd no idea where I was. Then I remembered, and my heart seemed to hit the floor.

'Half an hour,' Malkie said. 'Then we're out front.'

I showered fast, got my hard-bastard uniform on, and grabbed my gun. Abdul's gun. Whatever. It bounced against my hip in its holster as I jogged down the stairs, and then I fell into formation with Fitz, Malkie and Ez.

Solomon waltzed out of the front door of the main house. It was the first time I'd seen him in person since the night with Vyshnya. I felt the blood rise in my temples: I could hear it sloshing somewhere between my ears.

Fuck that guy, I thought. My hands made fists, almost unbidden.

'Ah,' Solomon said, crunching towards me over the gravel. 'The new body man.'

He stepped up close, and I was surrounded by his smell. It took me right back to that terrible night in the sauna: Vyshnya in a bloodied heap, Karen balling up sheets to stem the blood. Me stuffing the girls' things into bin bags, chivvying them along while they flustered and cried. Telling the 999 dispatcher, *Never fucking mind who I am, just send the fucking ambulance.* Tearing off in Vic's van and leaving Karen to be picked up, disappeared. He smelled like all of that. I thought I might throw up.

'You look familiar,' he said.

I couldn't believe it. I could not fucking believe it. All this time – *years* – I had feared and hated this man. I had not passed a single day without thinking about him, without worrying that somehow I'd be found wanting, my number would be up, and he'd send the boys in to deal with me. This man was in my dreams, often: watching from the corner while I beat up Vyshnya on his orders, or stepping out to block my escape as her miserable bone-rattle and wail chased me down a corridor that never seemed to end. And yet, he'd forgotten me. With those three words, he blew up the last handful of years of my life. I was nothing to this man. Did he even remember Vyshnya? Did he remember that night at *all*?

'Toad recommended me,' I said. I gritted my teeth together and added, 'We have met once before.'

'Oh yes?'

I nodded. 'I'm *Schenok*,' I said.

Not a flicker of recognition passed over his face. His eyes were so impassive, they looked like they were made of glass.

'I'm . . . I run the Emerald for you,' I said. 'The sauna.'

His eyebrows twitched. The place, at least, he remembered. 'Ah yes,' he said. 'I know who you are.'

He reached for my hand, and I had to give it to him. His handshake was limp, wet-feeling, like touching rotten meat. But he held on to my hand, for a moment.

'Good to see you again,' he said.

I forced myself to hold his gaze.

After a moment, Malkie cleared his throat.

'Ah yes.' Solomon dropped my hand, but didn't break eye contact.

I didn't want to even blink. I wanted to *see* what was inside those eyes. I wanted to understand him, and then break him, and then break him some more. I could feel my nostrils flaring.

'You,' Solomon said, 'will be driving, I understand.'

He had me drive them all to Devonshire Gardens, the big fancy hotel there. I'd never driven anything quite like the Range Rover. Plodding through Glasgow's maddening grid, unable to use the power under my right foot, made me want to scream. The car made an absolute racket, the roar of its V8 echoing off the tenements, scattering pigeons.

'Just pull up,' Solomon said, as we approached. 'Someone will come out to take care of things.'

Sure enough, the throaty rev of the Range Rover brought out a suited man, who opened the passenger side doors for Ez – in the back – and Malkie, beside me in the front. He then walked round to my window, and I rolled it down, killing the engine. The man looked a little surprised: used to seeing Abdul, I guessed.

'You can leave the vehicle with me, sir,' he said. 'I'll ensure it's ready and waiting when you need it again.'

I glanced at Malkie, who nodded, so I climbed out, and handed over the fat, push-button key.

Ez and Fitz led the way, up the steps to the hotel's main door. They looked like thick-necked bridesmaids in black. Solomon walked queenly behind them in his slate-grey suit. For the first time, I noticed that he seemed to mince slightly, picking his feet up like a dressage horse. Malkie and I brought up the rear.

'There are signals.' Malkie had leaned towards me, and was whispering out of the corner of his mouth. 'Signals that he'll be ready to go in five minutes or so. Once you start seeing them, you have to go and get the car. Abdul knows, but you won't.'

'What are they?' I hissed back.

'Don't worry,' Malkie said, 'I'll give you the nod.'

Inside, the hotel was ideally temperate. In the lobby, piano music played at the perfect volume to ignore. Solomon breezed through, and I glanced around to see if any of the concierges looked afraid. Apparently not.

In the dining room, Solomon was met by an effusive maître d', who stepped between Ez and Fitz as though they simply weren't there.

'Welcome back, Mr Carradice,' the man simpered. 'We're so pleased you've come to join us again.'

Solomon gestured at Ez, and Ez made two fifty-pound notes appear. The maître d's attention seemed to sharpen.

'I'd like to be served only by you today,' Solomon said. 'This meeting is highly confidential.'

The maître d' practically folded himself in two as Ez handed him the hundred pounds. 'Absolutely, Mr Carradice,' he said. 'May I prepare your usual beverage?'

Solomon nodded.

And four tap waters, I thought – though of course, we four didn't get anything at all.

Solomon approached a table that had clearly been cordoned off at the far end of the dining room. The three tables around it all had *reserved* cards on them, which the maître d' began plucking up and taking away as we approached. Malkie gestured to me that I ought to sit down at the table nearest the door. I did, while Fitz and Malkie took the other two, and Ez stayed beside Solomon. Sitting at the cordoned-off table was a short, stocky man with the most Scottish-looking face I had ever seen. He was flushed, stuffed into a suit that looked dated. He stood, with some difficulty, as Solomon approached.

'James,' Solomon said, placing his slimy hand into the man's large, well-worn one. The dude looked afraid.

'Jimmy,' the man said. Solomon gave him a look of distaste, but said nothing. He gestured to the man's chair, and they both sat. Ez took his place beside Solomon, and folded his arms onto the table in front of him.

There were some pleasantries, some *how's business*, some *oh you know*, the bigger man clearly trying to move things on to the main event so he could get it over with and escape. The maître d' brought Solomon a short, amber drink with ice and a twist of orange. Jimmy/James had ordered a beer and flushed when the two drinks were put in front of them. I felt sorry for the guy. But I was also trying not to watch too closely: trying to emulate Malkie, who seemed able to stare into the middle distance, barely blinking, for an indefinite period of time.

I hated everything about Solomon. Now that I was in his presence but not the focus of his attention, I was able to observe him, and I couldn't help but detest his every move. His affected voice: the shadow of a Glaswegian accent painted over as though it were bad plaster. The salmon-coloured button-down he wore under his bespoke suit: though of obvious quality, the colour looked old-fashioned and old-mannish. The fact that the upholstery in the Range Rover had *SC* stitched through it. Solomon was loaded, without a doubt, and wanted the best; but in spite of his efforts he just came across as what Maw would have called *flash*. And most of all, of course, I hated that he didn't remember me.

In my pocket I felt my phone buzz: Toad, I guessed.

I zoned back in, aware that Solomon had lowered his voice.

'I must have your assurances,' he said, 'that the crew you're bringing in are all known to you, and are all completely trustworthy. The skippers especially. I will expect them to keep things on an even keel – if you'll pardon the pun – no one getting overexcited. Do you understand? Business as usual.'

'I do, sir.'

I had to stop myself from rolling my eyes. Had Jimmy been wearing a cap, he'd have doffed it: he was talking to Solomon as though he were some Dickensian lord of the manor. But then, of course, I reminded myself of that night in the sauna. I'd thought Solomon looked like someone's well-kept granda . . . but I quickly ended up on my knees. By comparison, Jimmy was doing pretty well.

'Excellent,' Solomon said. 'Forgive me. I do just like to be reassured.'

Jesus, Jimmy, I was thinking, run away as fast as you can. But Solomon was still speaking.

'My people will be on the dockside at Granton, to ensure a swift transfer into the vans,' he was saying. 'Many hands, as they say. As soon as every crate is accounted for, you and your crew will be compensated as agreed.'

Jimmy looked as though he wanted to say something.

'In cash,' Solomon added. 'Without strings. My man Toad has seen to it.'

Jimmy nodded. I could tell Solomon was irritated by him not talking.

Solomon eyeballed him. 'You look nervous, James,' he said. 'Do you have any concerns?'

Jimmy looked like a candidate who hadn't prepped for his interview and got the *do you have any questions for us?* bombshell.

'Well, um . . .' Jimmy's face got a little redder. 'My only worry is . . . ken, the Russians? If we cannae communicate, and there's any—'

Solomon held up a disdainful hand. 'Taken care of,' he said. 'I will have two men in attendance who can provide interpretation, where required. One of them is sitting at the next table, in fact.'

I froze, realising Solomon was looking at me.

'Smith, here,' he said, 'is a fluent Russian speaker.'

I wasn't sure what to do, but I didn't feel like I could pretend I hadn't heard. I turned my head slightly and nodded at Jimmy, then tried to readjust my gaze without meeting Solomon's cold eyes. He did remember me, then, and better than he'd suggested earlier. He was playing with me. A blood vessel in the side of my head began to twitch, and I hoped Solomon couldn't see it.

'Anyway.' He'd swept the conversation away from me again. 'It will be straightforward, and everyone will be well briefed, so there shouldn't be much need for chitchat. The salts will be loaded in Baltiysk, and each shipment will be accompanied by an employee of our Russian associate, in order to ensure safe passage.'

Solomon looked hard at Jimmy. 'By that I mean, no skimming off the top.'

Jimmy looked as though he'd been kicked. 'My boys widnae dae that.'

Solomon nodded. 'It is understood, James. But our Russian friend would prefer to have the safeguard.'

Jimmy lowered his eyes: a *whatever you say* gesture.

'Be not mistaken,' Solomon added. 'These salts are premium grade. Strong. We're all trusting you with a considerable asset.'

'It'll be safe wi' me,' Jimmy said, 'an' the boys.'

Solomon smiled his slippery smile then. 'And thereafter, it is all quite straightforward. You will follow the standard route, and then all boats will hold their agreed positions in the North Sea. It's vital that the skippers come in one by one, and the boat traffic on the approach to Granton does not look hurried or unusual.'

'We'll aw be on the radio channel,' Jimmy said. 'Each skipper'll come in when he's called.'

'Good,' Solomon said. 'The vans will be waiting. It will be an all-night job, but a fine start to what I hope can become a regular arrangement . . .'

My head flicked up then, and I stopped listening. Malkie was clicking his fingers. I looked over.

'Car,' he mouthed at me. Time to go.

I nodded, and tried to rise from the table as quietly as I could. I imagined Abdul – huge, clunky Abdul – trying to do the same. The information I'd just heard rattled about in my head. The fact that Solomon remembered me. The fact that I was about to get roped into something bigger than I'd ever even heard about. But I'm a small-time guy, I remember thinking – absurd, but I did. I just run a sauna. I'm not cut out for this sort of thing.

I wandered out into the lobby, and found the valet. I waited for him to bring the Range Rover round, my thoughts churning.

Have you had contact? Toad had texted me.

Contact with who? I wrote back.

No reply.

When Solomon emerged eight minutes later, the car was parked at the front door, and I was in the driver's seat, revving that V8 as much as I dared, and watching faces flick round to look all along the block.

The entire station gathered in the bullpen to watch the TV bolted to the wall above the coffee machine. They stood in rows, quiet but for a few consoling words whispered in pairs or threes. It felt like a funeral, or, rather, like the awkward fifteen minutes the funeral congregation spend milling around in the lobby of the crem, waiting for the previous set of mourners to file out. That collective sadness, collective frustration. The feeling of small comfort.

Birch hovered at the edge of the group. She didn't want to make her presence known to anyone: she couldn't stop the endless spiral of guilt. This gathering was her fault. Solomon walking free was her fault. A part of her hated the fact that she was getting away with it: the guilt might have been easier to handle were someone punishing her, yelling at her – were someone else, other than herself, pointing the finger and saying, *This was all your doing.* But no one knew of her lie, not even Rab. She'd got away with her crime, just as Solomon got away with his, and the very idea made her feel sick. So she hovered, making eye contact with no one, but – she realised – also looking for someone. Charlie: she was looking for Charlie in this, the last crowd on earth where he'd ever appear. She was still trying to spirit him up, produce him from somewhere the way a magician would produce their white rabbit in the nick of time. But the nick of time was gone. Instead her gaze lighted on Amy, stoic; on DS Scott, frowning; on Big Rab, hanging back the way she was at the opposite flank of the gathering, pink-faced and enraged, and yes, guilty-looking, too.

The familiar jingle came, and the small murmurs in the room fell quiet.

'This is STV daytime news,' the newsreader announced. 'I'm Geraldine Hazel. Today's headlines . . .'

Immediately, a shot of Solomon appeared on the screen. First, his mugshot, and then footage of him walking out of the front door of the very building they were all standing in, Anjan at his side.

'Alleged gangland boss Solomon Carradice is released today' – under Geraldine Hazel's voiceover, the picture switched to footage of McLeod, speaking at a podium, the sound muted – 'cleared of wrongdoing after four days in police custody in Edinburgh.'

A disgruntled rumble ran through the room. Geraldine Hazel skipped through the day's other headlines at full pelt. Birch's stomach churned.

'Our top story this morning,' the newsreader said, and the picture cut back to that same footage of Solomon walking out onto the steps of the station, a little over an hour ago. Paparazzi had formed a small gaggle outside, and the flashes of their cameras seemed to exaggerate Solomon's age. Birch imagined people watching at home, thinking to themselves, How could that sweet-looking old man possibly have done the things they're saying? Anjan walked slightly behind Solomon, his mouth a straight line, and his face impossible to read.

Solomon had, it seemed, done a short smile-and-wave session for the press before getting straight into a car – Birch noted with some annoyance that it was a black Range Rover, and not a Mercedes saloon – and being driven away. Cut to Anjan, standing at a temporary Police Scotland podium someone had thought to prop up on the steps.

'My client has been released,' Anjan said, 'following a period of ninety-six hours in police custody: the maximum amount of time that a person may be held without charge.'

He spoke as elegantly as ever, looking around at the assembled lenses, microphones, faces.

'Monday's raid,' he went on, 'which has been dubbed Operation Citrine, produced no hard evidence to implicate my client, and nor has any credible witness come forward.'

Charlie, Birch thought. Credible, credible Charlie.

'I am satisfied,' Anjan was saying, 'that this matter is resolved, and I am pleased at this result for my client and his family. Mr Carradice asks for privacy for him and his loved ones as he returns to his day-to-day activities.'

'Yeah,' said someone from across the bullpen, 'I fucking *bet* he does.'

The camera cut back to the news studio, and Geraldine Hazel in her nice Hobbs suit.

'Detective Chief Inspector James McLeod,' she said, 'also appeared at this morning's press conference, and gave this statement on behalf of Police Scotland.'

McLeod appeared on the screen, standing at that same podium. Over his left shoulder, DI Crosbie stood, gazing off at something above the camera. Both of them looked more flushed in the face than Birch thought she'd ever seen.

'In the early hours of Monday morning,' McLeod said, 'Police Scotland raided a convoy of branded vehicles and several fishing boats at Granton Harbour and in the surrounding area. We recovered over five hundred kilograms of the banned substance Alpha-PVP, more commonly known as flakka. We believe this illegal shipment originated in Russia. We are in contact with Russian authorities and have detained several individuals on charges relating to the transport and possession of this substance. It is our belief that this smuggling operation was masterminded by one high-profile individual or organised crime group, and our investigation *will* continue until the perpetrators behind these illegal shipments are brought to justice.' McLeod brought his hand down on the podium, which wobbled.

Birch remembered that cursed thing well: she'd stood at it herself several times over the course of the Three Rivers investigation.

'No questions,' McLeod said, and the camera cut away as he and Crosbie turned their backs on the press.

Geraldine Hazel appeared in the studio once again. 'We'll have more on that story,' she said, 'at six o'clock . . .'

Her words dropped out. Someone had switched the TV to mute. Birch looked round, and saw Big Rab on the other side of the room, holding the remote aloft.

'That's it then, lads,' he said to the assembled gathering. 'Don't let the bastards get ye down, and aw that. Back tae work, aye?'

There was a general rumble of agreement, and the group began to scatter. Birch took the opportunity to turn her eyes downward and march as purposefully as she dared in the direction of her office. Something was boiling inside her. She realised it was anger – at Charlie, as well as at herself – and it joined the erratic flutter of worry and guilt she'd been swimming in for . . . well, basically the entire week. You did this, Helen. You let this operation fail.

Birch closed the office door behind her and leaned back against it. The phone on her desk rang. She'd forgotten she didn't currently have a mobile, and she'd been out in the bullpen for a while now, uncontactable. Idiot, she thought again, as she sprang towards the sound. The little screen above the keypad showed it was a direct dial, not the switchboard – but beyond that, it displayed no number.

Birch fumbled to pick up the call.

'DI Birch?'

A sound on the other end, something like static. 'Charlie?'

She just said it. His name had been in her mouth all morning.

There was a long silence, and then Birch realised she could hear breathing.

Shit. Oh shit.

'No.' It was a man's voice that eventually spoke. A voice with a heavy accent. 'This is not your brother.'

Birch veered, and put out one hand to steady herself. It skidded over the desk, sending papers flying.

'But it's good to know you're reunited at last,' the voice said.

Birch tried to concentrate. The voice sounded familiar. Was this the same caller she'd spoken to, however briefly, after the flowers were delivered? Or was it one of the men whose interviews she'd sat in on, with DS Scott? It was only four days ago, but it felt like a lifetime.

'We know,' the voice said, 'that your brother Charlie Birch is the rat that you are hiding. We know you have him somewhere near you, now.'

Birch swallowed, tried to keep it together. 'Who is this?' she asked, then felt stupid. Like he was going to tell her.

'We are going to find him,' the man went on, as though she hadn't spoken. 'We are very good at finding people.'

Something clicked, then. Something about the inflection, the pattern. She remembered: *I speak good English.*

'Mr Toad,' she said. 'It's you, isn't it?'

There was a pause, and then the line went dead. That meant *yes*.

Birch closed her eyes for a moment, still leaning hard on the desk. She was afraid if she straightened up too fast she might fall over, as the blood rocketed back and forth between her heart and her head. She tried to picture the man who'd called himself Toad. They'd had to let him go on the grounds that he'd been arrested just hanging around, had nothing illegal about his person, and refused to comment in response to questioning. He'd been older than most of the suspects she'd seen: heavy-set, grey hair, imposing, but no prizefighter. Birch imagined she could take him.

'Scumbag,' Birch spat. She straightened her back slowly, found that she wasn't as dizzy as she'd anticipated. She skirted the desk, and fell into her chair.

She sat for a moment, thinking, her forehead screwed down into a kind of scowl. The call had rattled her, but the soup of worry inside her had simmered down a little. She'd fucked up, saying Charlie's name into the phone – she no longer had the plausible deniability she'd used when accosted by the Fenton guy. They knew now that she knew Charlie had come back: *great fucking job.* But they also thought that Charlie was still with her, that she was still hiding him. That meant that they hadn't yet found him. Wherever he was, he was still safe, and once again Birch felt just a little bit more able to breathe.

The longer she sat there, the longer she thought, Fine. Let them think he's with me. Let them follow me around to their heart's content. Let them stake me out. The longer they did that, the longer Charlie had to get as far away as he could. She really, really hoped he was doing that. If she couldn't have him back, if she couldn't protect him, then she at least hoped he'd been smart enough to start putting miles between himself and every single one of his contacts as soon as he'd stepped out of her door. The thought of it hurt . . . but Charlie was safe. For now. And if she did things right, she might be able to stall the bloodhounds on his trail.

There was a heavy knock at her office door. Birch snapped her spine up straight. Look normal, Helen, she thought. She had no idea what that might involve.

'Hello?'

The door opened, and Big Rab poked his round, red face through the gap. 'You all right, lassie?'

Birch slapped on a smile, and hoped it looked genuine. 'Just fine,' she said. 'Plodding along.'

Rab pushed the door open a little further, and came into the room. He hovered there, his hand still on the door knob, as though waiting for an invitation. Birch decided not to extend one.

'You're lookin' a wee bit pale,' he said.

Birch frowned. The impulse to tell him about the call was strong, but he was beginning to bother her. She felt under surveillance.

'Just tired, I think,' she said. Rab seemed to be waiting for her to say more. She didn't.

You're being dreadful, she thought. Rab meant well. He was struggling under the weight of his own indiscretion: one that, now Solomon was free, he'd have to confess to sooner or later. She was the only one who knew, and maybe it brought him a measure of comfort to talk to someone he wasn't hiding anything from. As the thought struck her, she felt a pang of jealousy.

'Well.' Rab seemed to sense the tension in the room. 'Jist wanted to check ye were all right after yer wee altercation. We'll no' get to the report on that till Monday, like I say. Will ye be okay over the weekend?'

Birch smiled again. 'Just fine,' she said. 'It almost feels like a fever dream now. Like it didn't really happen.'

She was telling the truth. Her encounter with Fenton had been so surreal, and the phone conversation with Toad seemed to place it in a different context, somehow. How selfish I've been, she thought, to worry about my own safety. Charlie was the precious one: if he couldn't be preserved to be put on the witness stand, he at least had to be able to get away clean. She'd been responsible for the collapse of Operation Citrine but she couldn't be responsible for Charlie's demise. She wouldn't be.

Rab was still looking at her.

'I'll be fine, Rab,' she said. 'I promise. I know I don't have my phone, but I've got the panic button. If I need help, I'll call the cavalry.'

His look was the same as it had been when she'd left the interview room, after he'd told her his informant was Charlie. He'd known then that something wasn't quite right, and he knew it now, too. Had the tables been turned, Birch would have given him the very same look. It made you suspicious, policework. Suspicious, jaded and, usually, right.

'I'm sorry,' she said, not giving him the chance to question her further, 'about Solomon.'

Rab shook his head. 'We just couldnae get it,' he said. 'Couldnae get an *in*.'

She watched him think of something, then shrug it off.

'My fault,' he said.

She dropped her gaze then, realising his internal monologue probably sounded much the same as hers. 'I'm sorry,' she said again, and realised she really meant it.

Quiet hung in the room, and then Rab seemed to sever the invisible wire that had been vibrating between them.

'Cannae be helped, lassie,' he said, beginning to back out of the door again. 'At least ye'll be rid o' me soon, an' the merry band o' Weegie bams I brought wi' me.'

Birch laughed. 'You'll be missed,' she said.

Rab eyed her then, halfway out into the corridor. 'DI Birch,' he said, 'you're a bad liar.'

★   ★   ★

Birch angsted the rest of the day away.

Five p.m. came and went. She had spent an hour or so tidying her office, a thing she couldn't quite believe. But it helped: she was standing up, moving around, pacing from desk to recycle bin to shredder to desk to filing cabinet. Movement turned the anxiety into fuel, prevented it from accumulating in the sloshing bottle of her body like so much lukewarm rain. She'd discovered all sorts of things in the clear-out: a nearly-year-old newspaper with a piece about the Three Rivers case, in which she was named. She'd found scissors, a stapler, and an unopened packet of Blu-Tack: all things she'd hunted for in a moment of need, and been unable to find. A photograph of her and her mum: hospital, tubes, forced smiles. A nurse had taken it. Seeing it again felt like a kick to the chest, but Birch slid it into a drawer. One day Charlie might come back, want to see it. The thought made her hate herself and want to cry, in equal measure.

Birch listened as the bullpen slowly emptied out. She heard the cries of *cheerio* and *have a good weekend*, and listened to her leaving colleagues' footsteps clop past her office door. At one point she caught a snippet of Amy's high, twinkly laugh, and she prayed that her friend wouldn't knock on the door to see if Birch was still there. But the door was closed, and Amy must have passed it by without thinking to knock, or assumed Birch had already gone. Once her heel-clicks had faded, Birch felt relief, and also a sadness she hadn't expected, and couldn't quite name.

Outside, it was pitch-dark. She could hear a cold wind starting up: it whistled through the elderly double-glazing out in the corridors, and the sound carried along the whole floor like the lonely call of some night-time bird. Seven p.m. came. Why am I still here? Birch mused. She knew why. When she got home, the house would be shut up. Charlie would not be there, no matter how much she wanted him to be. His ex-associates might be, though: the call had left her under no illusions. Birch doubted that the newly released Solomon would just let the sister of a supposed canary go about her business unscrutinised, especially after she'd blurted Charlie's name out to Toad. Visions of the skull-faced man returned; the smell of the stale tobacco on Fenton's hands. But for the first time, they inspired no terror. Let them come, she thought. Let them stake out my house for as long as they like. It was all buying time for Charlie, who wasn't there, and wouldn't come back now. She could pray and cry and worry all she liked. She'd fucked up from the start, and the only silver lining to be gleaned from the whole sorry mess was this: she could distract the bastards, and give her brother some time.

At 8 p.m., the cleaners arrived. In the bullpen, Birch heard a vacuum cleaner rev up and begin its droning back and forth. She'd worked this late before: the Three Rivers case had seen her kicked out by the cleaners a good few times. The hoover was her cue to go. She liked the cleaning folks well enough, but had no desire for idle chat or jokey admonishments at her timekeeping. Not tonight. It was time to go home, and face whatever music her brother's former friends had planned for her.

There were a lot of meetings like that one, over the ten days or so that I filled in for Abdul. A lot of the same sort of conversations. In between, I texted Toad: *Who's going to contact me? What's going on?* He wasn't replying. *Zhaba, you okay?* Nothing. I wondered if the previous text had been meant for someone else. I wondered if something bad had finally caught up with Toad.

That day, it was a meeting with some Russians: middle of the day, in a shitehole of a shut-up pub where the barman let us in then locked up the shutters behind us and bolted into the back room. The Russians were ex-cons, I could tell by their tattoos, and their idioms. I also learned that day the limited extent of Solomon's own Russian: at one point he faltered, threw up his hands and looked over at me. I finished his sentence for him, and then for the rest of the meeting acted as interpreter, letting Solomon speak English. Ez wasn't happy, I could tell. He was used to being the right-hand guy, the one that Solomon relied on most. You can fucking keep it, I thought, but I couldn't say anything.

It was dark outside by the time we got out of the pub. A few dickheads had started banging on the shutters, wanting to get in for their weeknight bevvy. They soon shuffled off once the doors opened and those *shpana* daundered out, followed by Ez, Fitz and Malkie. Solomon hung back till they'd gone, not wanting to be seen, I guess, or maybe just not wanting to mix with the hoi-polloi. I was behind him, and couldn't get out, so I just hovered there, too. I remember looking at the pale stripe of neck between the collar of his dreadful shirt – lilac, that day – and the neat bottom edge of his white hair. He'd been a fucking bam in his day: you could still see it. But now he was an old, old man. Of course I'd never broken anyone's neck before, but I had a fairly good idea of how it might be done, and there was no way he'd have been able to overpower me. In those few moments, while the Russians saw off the would-be pissheads outside, I let myself imagine it. The pleasure I would take at his shocked noise: the air punched out of his lungs, his whole body flung back against mine. The crack of his upper vertebrae as they crunched together. I let myself wonder if the spinal cord would make a discernible sound as it was crushed.

But he knew I wouldn't do it, and I knew he knew it. He stood with his back to me, after all – vulnerable to any manner of attack – but upright, calm. Fucking *smug*. The more I imagined twisting his head off, the smaller and more pathetic I felt. It was like he was daring me, saying, *Do it, you puppy. Do it*. He knew I wouldn't. He knew everything.

And then, of course, the moment passed. The Russians had gone, farewells already having been made. Malkie reappeared in the half-unshuttered doorway, silhouetted against the tang of streetlight behind. In my pocket, I felt my phone buzz: Toad had finally replied to me. But I didn't look. Solomon didn't like to see anyone's phone out during working hours.

'Good to go, boss,' Malkie said.

The drive back was tense. Malkie rode beside me as always, but Ez was over my left shoulder, and I could feel his eyes on me in the rear-view mirror the whole time. In my pocket, the persistent vibration of texts arriving: Toad catching up. Explaining, I hoped, though I couldn't check yet. I kept my eyes on the road. Solomon didn't talk, so neither did we. We were almost back at the mansion when he finally spoke.

'Malcolm.'

Malkie swivelled his head round so quickly I imagined he'd given himself whiplash.

'I believe we are expecting Abdul back shortly, am I correct?'

I stiffened.

'Yes, boss,' Malkie said. I felt him glance at me, but kept my eyes on the road. 'He's been out of the hospital two days, staying with family. He's still only good for driving just now, no heavy stuff. But he could be back tomorrow, if you want him.'

'I do.' Solomon barely missed a beat.

I felt heat spreading up my neck: all their eyes were on me. I should have felt relief. I'd be able to go back to my shite, boring life. Running the sauna. Going to the gym. Sleeping. Rinse and repeat. Yet I felt like I'd squandered something, wasted it. I hated Solomon more than I could say, yet there was a small part of me, I think, that wanted him to respect me. I think that small part of me had thought I might be kept on. I couldn't quite believe myself. I was feeling *rejected*. What the fuck, Charlie.

We got to the electronic gates, and Malkie pushed the remote to open them. I eased the Range Rover forward, out of the lit street and into the tree-lined darkness of Solomon's long drive. The gravel scattered under the tyres. Malkie pushed the button again, and in the rear-view, beyond the searching glare of Ez, I watched the gates whisper closed behind us.

Malkie and Solomon had begun talking again: Abdul would need to be briefed on the latest developments around what they were calling the Granton Job, and Malkie was agreeing that he would sit down with him, and they would—

But I wasn't listening. Up ahead, someone – or something – had run through the headlights' beam. Out of the dark, a flash of movement, maybe ten yards or so away. Then it was gone again.

'Did you guys see that?'

I spoke almost without thinking. Malkie's head whipped round again.

'See wh—'

A whir of white on my left-hand side. I flinched, jerking the steering wheel on the gravel and sending the whole vehicle into a skid. And then, *wham*. Her body hit the car, or the car hit her.

'Jesus *fuck*.'

She'd run at a diagonal, out of the darkness on the left-hand side, Malkie's side. She'd hurled herself at the car, seemingly at the back door, but the front passenger-side corner had clipped her in the skid, flung her backward. Now she must be down, but I didn't feel her under the wheels. She'd been thrown clear.

I stood on the brakes, and felt the whole car slide as the tyres skidded on the gravel. Before we'd even reached a standstill, Malkie had opened the passenger side door, and Fitz was already out, his feet scrabbling for balance. Ez stayed put, but I saw him put a protective arm across Solomon's chest. Through the open passenger-side doors, I could hear her howling, screaming, cursing.

No, no, no, no.

I squeezed my eyes closed, and tried to push down the vomit that was rising in my throat. Out of nowhere, I was pouring with sweat: the steering wheel was slippery in my grip, my knuckles whitened around it. My brain flooded like a fucked engine, flashbacks to every one of my God-awful trauma dreams, years of them playing out behind my eyelids at warp-speed, one after another. A woman, broken beyond repair, howling her pain and rage. Chasing me. Cursing the same curse words that streamed in through the Range Rover's open doors, here and now. She was on the ground, clearly hurt by the car's impact, pinned down by Malkie and Fitz, and screaming. Babbling what might have been nonsense, but was actually garbled Ukrainian.

'Vyshnya,' I said.

The vomit I'd been holding back spattered the inside of the windscreen.

Ez was out of the car, marching round to the driver's door, yelling at me in Turkish. I got it: I'd lost control of the car and now thrown up all over it. He felt someone else ought to drive. I assisted him by climbing over the centre console away from his waving arms and folding myself down into the passenger footwell, pressing my face into the upholstered seat. The car stank. I was aware that Malkie and Fitz were wrestling the screaming woman into the boot.

Vyshnya. Oh fuck, oh fuck.

I kept my head pressed down and tried to tell myself it was a bad dream, just another of my many bad Vyshnya-related fucked-up PTSD bullshit dreams, and if I just waited, I'd wake up. I heard the boot lid slam, and then I could hear the thrashing and thumping of an unrestrained body, flailing and shouting right behind the back seat where Solomon was still sitting. Malkie and Fitz got back in, on either side of Solomon, and I heard the doors shut. The engine was still running, and Ez eased the Range Rover into motion. It hurtled up the driveway and then Ez brought us to a sudden abortive stop. The body in the boot slammed into the back of Solomon's seat.

Again, there was the opening of doors, the slamming of doors. The battering in the boot stopped as the lid was opened and Vyshnya must have flung herself at Malkie and Fitz.

'*Bitch*,' I heard Malkie spit. 'Get her legs, man, get her fucking legs.' And all the while, those same wild screams, hoarser now, but loud enough to split open the night.

Ez cuffed me around the head, and I looked up. Solomon was sitting prissily in the middle of the back seat, looking at me. To my surprise, he looked amused.

'Move, idiot,' Ez growled, and the second time, I ducked his fist. I remember reaching behind me with a weird curl of the arm, and opening the passenger door. I let myself fall out onto the gravel below. I spat. I made myself stand before Ez had the chance to walk around the car and kick me: but of course, when I straightened up, I saw that he was ushering Solomon out of the back seat and guiding him towards the house, the way taxi drivers do for little old ladies.

The four of them had left the Range Rover pinging to itself: the lights still on, and every one of the doors open. The engine was still running. I shut the front passenger door, and then the back one. As I walked round the back to where the boot gaped open, I saw a trail of dark liquid – Vyshnya's blood – leading on to the pale pebbles of the driveway. There was a spatter, where she'd hit out at Fitz and Malkie, and then a smaller trail, up the steps and into the house.

I retched, but didn't throw up again. In the house above me, lights began to flick on in the windows. I heaved myself up and slammed the boot lid, then Malkie's door. Finally, I climbed back into the driver's seat. I thought for a brief moment about flooring the accelerator, racing back up the drive, and seeing if I could ram the Range Rover through the electronic gates and away. But then I'd have stolen Solomon's hundred-grand car, *on top* of everything else. If I wasn't a dead man now, I surely would be then. So instead, I turned off the ignition, got out, and locked the car.

I staggered into the house after the others. My head was swimming, and a big part of me was still hoping this was some heinously vivid nightmare from which I would eventually wake. Besides: where else could I have gone?

At first I didn't know where they were. I stood in the massive hallway – my first time inside the house itself – and gawped up at the hideous frescoed ceiling, the obnoxious chandelier. Solomon didn't have taste, he only had money. I couldn't believe I thought it in that moment, but I did. The voice in my head sounded like Maw.

But of course, there was the blood, and Solomon's carpets were pale-coloured and deep. Vyshnya's blood had smeared and spread: she'd clearly been half carried, half dragged, through a door to one side of the enormous staircase. I followed the trail, my gag reflex pulsing and pulsing. I didn't know what I would find. I knew it wouldn't be good. And I had to go, and be there, and try to pretend like I could still do my job. Try to save my own pathetic skin.

I found them in a basement kitchen: obviously not one Solomon used himself, the kind that was staffed. Stainless-steel everything and a tiled floor. I knew Solomon held parties at this house: Toad had once talked about how snubbed he felt now that he was no longer invited to them. Fucking Toad, I thought. This is all his fault. My whole fucking life is that cunt's fault. The walls were lined with kitchen utensils: steel kebab skewers, cleavers, long chef's knives that gleamed under the banks of white lights. I swallowed hard. They'd shoved a kitchen bench to one side, and tied Vyshnya to a chair in the middle of the open space. She was gagged with a tea towel. I could see that the blood trail I'd followed came from a gaping wound in her arm: a compound fracture, the pale drumstick of a bone peeking through the skin. So that's what happens, I thought, when you throw yourself into the path of a car.

She was still struggling against her restraints, and the chair's feet clattered against the tile floor as she jumped and twisted. I couldn't quite believe it was her, and that – with the exception of the split-open mess that was her arm – she was all one piece, a fully formed human being. Hadn't every bone in her body been shattered? Hadn't she been ripped open? It was true, then: she really had made it, gone home to Ukraine, and got better. The girls hadn't been lying. But now, like a fucking *idiot*, she'd come back. I wanted to scream at her, but I found I couldn't move, or make a sound. I could only stare.

Saturday

Birch woke to her pillow coated in saliva. She felt like she'd been dropped down a well: her hearing was muffled and a little buzzy, and her mouth tasted as though she'd been sucking on iron filings. Sitting painfully upright, she realised this was the reason for the drooling: the taste was so bad, she found she couldn't stop it. It was as though every filling in her mouth had decided to leak at once. In the half-light created by her blackout blind, Birch fumbled on the bedside table for a tissue, and spat. There was nothing in her mouth, and the taste didn't fade.

She looked at the clock: 15:02. She'd slept for over sixteen hours, and remembered none of it. It was as though she'd closed her eyes at ten thirtyish the night before, and then immediately reopened them. Somehow, it had become Saturday afternoon. Outside, she could hear the sounds of children laughing and squealing, the ringing of tiny bells on the handlebars of scooters or trikes. A dog barked. Though it was only early spring, she could hear the distant, twinkling tune of the ice-cream van.

The night before, she'd made a series of decisions that she now regretted. First, she'd decided to keep acting as she had been all week. She wanted to make it look, to anyone watching her, like Charlie was still in the house. Let them come, she'd thought in her office, and the thought had pulsed through her mind as she'd driven home. Let them stake me out, let them think he's here. The longer it took them to figure out he wasn't, the better.

So she'd parked the car on yet another side street, this time in the stretch of no-man's-land between Joppa and Musselburgh. She'd walked back, having forgotten how forbidding that stretch of the main road was. There were houses for a while – Seaview

Terrace, the street was called – but then the buildings fell away on her right-hand side, turning into a stretch of grassland that led down from the road to the sea wall. This wasn't a named park, and wasn't well lit: it was a place where locals let their dogs out for a run, and tourists sometimes stopped to photograph Kinghorn and Burntisland across the water. On a Friday night, it was deserted. Birch walked the thin strip of streetlit pavement, with the road on one side, and that enormous shoulder of dark on the other. Beyond the grassland, she could hear the sea, close by, and wished she couldn't. It created a kind of white noise that meant she was unable to fully sharpen her hearing, to listen for potential hazards. Had a light-footed man come up behind her, she might not have heard him until he was right on top of her. She glanced back repeatedly, and squinted out seaward for the slightest move-ment in the dark swim of the park.

She'd made it to the China Express, her pulse fast as a cricket's. On an impulse, she'd walked into the takeaway, glad of its warm light and friendly human presence. In the tiny waiting area, a man was reading a copy of the *Evening News*: on the front, a photo-graph of Solomon and Anjan, standing outside the front door of her station. From the angle it was taken, they could have been holding hands. Birch found it hurt to look at Anjan's face, so she'd turned away. She ordered her usual – vegetable spring rolls, tofu in black bean sauce – and paid with cash. She spent the ten minutes of food prep time peering out of the smeary glass door of the takeaway, looking for dark-coloured cars on the street, skull-masked figures in the dark.

She'd made it to the house, done her usual checks, and found nothing amiss. As before, she'd closed curtains and blinds, and turned on more lights than she might usually. She'd wolfed the food, sitting on the sofa, trying not to think about Charlie. Ten p.m. came around and she'd resisted the urge to watch the nightly news.

She'd been tired all week, the lack of sleep accumulating, making her eyes sting and her reflexes slow. Her limbs felt heavy, prickly, as though she were having to pull them through an invisible force field of static. As she'd driven home that night, she'd decided she needed a real meal, and some real sleep. What had happened after the takeaway was the primary bad decision.

Birch remembered the foil strip of tablets in the bathroom cabinet. She'd been prescribed them while her mother was ill. As the reality of her mother's protracted but impending death settled upon her, so did an anxiety so vicious that it kept her awake for nights at a time, her head buzzing with everything she could do, everything she couldn't and everything she'd *need* to in the weeks to come. The doctor had given her Zopiclone: not merely a sleeping tablet, but a tranquilliser so strong that it could probably have brought down an angry rhino. But she had discovered that the pills made her dozy, and she found it hard to wake in the early morning, like she needed to. At the time, she'd resorted to cutting them in half with a fruit knife, scattering grainy powder all over her worktop. Even a half-tablet would have her slightly woozy by the time she turned out the downstairs lights and climbed the stairs to bed. They worked like a charm: no matter how many intrusive thoughts she dreamed up, the Zopiclone put her out like a light.

That was over two years ago, and the remaining handful of tablets – which she'd come off after her mother died, finding grief an even more powerful sleeping aid – had expired. She hadn't thrown them out because . . . well, she just never had. And right then – on that jumpy, miserable Friday night without Charlie – the idea of simply switching herself off had a deep, visceral pull.

Let them sit out there, she'd thought, as at 10.30 p.m. she'd downed a full tablet and half a glass of lukewarm bathroom-sink water. I don't care any more. As the tablet had started to take effect, Birch had noticed the expiry date stamped on the blister pack's shiny foil. On the box was a laser-printed sticker that read: *Take ONE a day as directed. DO NOT EXCEED THE STATED DOSE.* But the tablets were old, and old things lose their efficacy.

'Oh, screw it,' Birch had said aloud, as she swallowed a second tablet and welcomed in the hazy, artificial tiredness that it brought her.

Now, she stood over the toilet and spat long strings of drool. Given the taste in her mouth, she expected it to come out the colour of mercury, but it was clear and thin. She knew a metallic taste in the mouth was one possible side effect of the pills, but she hadn't been prepared for this.

Eventually she clambered back upright, went to the sink, and brushed her teeth until her gums sang with pain. It helped lessen the taste a little. She looked at herself in the mirror: she was scarecrow-like and pale, but she realised that for the first time in over a week she felt fully rested.

She felt queasy from the pills, and still the Charlie anxiety buzzed in her bloodstream, making her wonder if it would ever leave. But otherwise, she cared about very little: wasted time, whether or not she was hungry. Everything felt flat, straightforward. She wondered if the tablets were responsible for that, too.

In the kitchen, she reached for the kettle, reasoning that a strong cup of coffee might put up a decent fight against the horrendous taste of pennies in her mouth. She shuffled back and forth between cupboards, finding a clean mug, teaspoon, sugar. She became aware of a repetitive sound – muffled, but nearby – a banging noise like someone hammering on wood. But more flimsy than that. Birch pulled open the kitchen blind.

Her back gate had been kicked in, and the banging she could hear was one ruined panel flapping against the wooden frame in the wall. She stepped back, and dropped the teaspoon. It hit her on the foot.

'Shit,' she said.

There was a pair of old flip-flops beside the waste bin: she'd been meaning to throw them out, but had ended up using them as shoes to take out the bins. She toed them on, unlocked the kitchen door and went outside.

It was chilly: she hugged her arms around herself as she stepped out. She was careful to close the back door behind her, struck by the absurd worry that some well-camouflaged person was lying in wait in the rangy grass, watching until her back was turned so they could tiptoe into the kitchen to stage an ambush. Sure enough, there *were* tracks of a sort, in that same thick, tangly grass, which she'd been meaning to cut and was now glad she hadn't. Someone had walked across it, perhaps in the early hours when it was dewy, and left a scuffed trail of bent stalks. The trail zigzagged: they'd gone to the shed, they'd gone as far as the little patio outside the back door. Presumably across it, too, to try the door or to attempt to peer in. Birch shivered. The gate had been locked with a deadbolt, and the force of the kick had detached the metal completely from the structure, sent it flying into the weeds on the far side of the little path. Birch fished the bolt out from where it lay. The screws that had held it in place were mangled.

She walked to the gate and examined the damage: splintered wood, the frame now not quite fitting its space in the high stone wall. She pulled the gate open and it swung a little too readily, feeling fragile, like it might come off its hinges in her hand. Her teeth chattered. Putting her head out of the gate, she could see nothing: the road behind the house was deserted, though she could hear distant traffic noise. She didn't know what she'd expected: a sentry, waiting to leap on her when she stepped out of the gate? Footprints? Another bouquet of stinking lilies?

There was nothing at all, and Birch shuddered. So they'd been here. They'd cased the house. Someone looking for Charlie, or looking for evidence of Charlie. They still thought he might be here.

Great, Birch tried to make herself think. This is what you wanted, isn't it? Her stomach churned. She had nothing she could use to fix the gate, so she took some of the bigger shards of broken wood and shoved them underneath it, wedging it closed. It would require only a shove from the outside to get back in again, but it stopped the banging, at least. Now her teeth were chattering in earnest: not just because of the chill outside, she knew. She went back into the kitchen, locked the door, then checked it was locked.

'Okay.' Birch leaned on the worktop and tried to slow down her breathing. 'Well . . . okay.'

She paced up and down as the coffee brewed, then carried it into the living room and sipped it. She'd been right: it did help with the iron filings taste. She found she couldn't stop fidgeting. Her feet tapped on the carpet. She drummed her fingernails against the side of her coffee mug, a little porcelain trill, over and over. She realised she'd bitten her bottom lip half to shreds.

Go somewhere, she thought. Go to a hotel. Hide out. She sat and considered the possibility. It was tempting: a nice, clean hotel room with a decent lock on the door and a twenty-four-hour reception desk. The idea of other humans only feet away, just the other side of stud walls, TVs buzzing softly, was comforting. But how long would she be gone for? A night, a week, a month? She'd have to come back eventually. And besides, she couldn't make it look like she was here if she wasn't, not now she knew the house was being watched. If they realised that she wasn't here – that no one was here – then she'd have led them one step closer to Charlie. They'd be able to eliminate the house as one possible place he might be hiding.

No, she had to stay. They weren't breaking in yet: Solomon wasn't stupid. Birch was a senior police officer, and he'd only just got out of Dodge. But they were getting bolder: the kicking-in of the gate proved that. No more sleeping pills: she'd learned her lesson. She was going to have to go back to being alert.

The resolve she felt now – that same *let them come* that had propelled her home in the car the previous night – seemed to battle with her worry, and her fear. There was no doubt that a part of her had been emboldened by her interactions with Fenton, in person, and then Toad, on the phone. She knew now that she could deal with Fenton, although if she came up against him again he'd be better prepared to deal with the strength he probably hadn't reckoned on her having. Toad was an older man, wheezy, past his prime. If those two turned up, she'd be just fine. She tried to ride this small high of bravado, and not think about the skull-masked man – who'd been younger, wirier, with big, frightening hands – or the many other hard-looking bastards she'd seen brought into the station the day of the raid. She tried not to think about being outnumbered, or caught unawares, or threatened with weaponry she couldn't match. Instead, she found the panic button, shoved it into her trouser pocket, and spent the rest of the day preparing the house as best she could for a potential break-in.

From the shed, Birch retrieved her glass-recycling box. It was collected fortnightly, and she'd missed a collection that week, having completely forgotten. She placed the plastic tub of bottles and jam-jars on the floor about six inches behind the back door. If anyone broke in that way, she'd hear them coming, and the box would hopefully send them flying in the process.

Also from the shed, she dug out a windchime her mother had once gifted her. Its metal piping was over a foot long. She'd never hung it up outside because it was loud, and she worried it would keep her and her neighbours awake at night. Now, she strung it up behind the locked front door: another early warning system. She found herself laughing: she felt like Macaulay Culkin in *Home Alone*, booby-trapping her house against the Wet Bandits.

'If only,' she said, and the sound of her own voice in the quiet hallway made her shudder.

Time scraped by. With the dark came a greater chill, and Birch lit the gas fire. She rummaged in the freezer and defrosted some weeks-old stew, ate it in slow, small bites, and felt each one drop into her churning stomach. She'd closed the curtains and blinds once again, and sat without turning on the TV, not even missing the bright glow of her still-unspoken-for mobile phone. She simply listened, feeling the little box of the panic button cutting into her hip. Every light in the house was switched on.

At around ten, Birch rose and turned off the kitchen light, and then the lights in the living room. The gas fire gave the room that same eerie, violet glow that Charlie had sat in four nights ago, sullen and afraid, when he'd first arrived.

They'll come tonight, Birch thought. I know they will. Hours sitting alone with the dark pressing in at every window had convinced her. They'd cased the house the night before. It made sense.

Should I call someone? she thought. But who? Amy was out of the question: she'd freak out. She'd send an armed response unit round without blinking; that, or she'd show up herself and pledge to fight off any and all bad guys, single-handed. Birch couldn't help but smile at the thought. How about Rab, then? Hadn't he always said to call him if she needed him? But no: she didn't know Rab well enough to know how he'd react. You have a panic button, she reminded herself. This is what a panic button is for.

She left the upstairs lights on for a while, then climbed the stairs and began to switch them off. Spare room first. She paused to pull the curtains aside and peer out over the little back garden. It was still blustery, and she could see the grass seething, blades catching the streetlight. No one out there, yet.

'Okay,' she said quietly. 'Good.'

In the bathroom she splashed cold water on her face, and brushed her teeth again. She gargled mouthwash, watched the green streak of it circle the plug. Then the bathroom light was out, too.

She left her bedroom light a little while longer. Let them wait, she thought. She imagined Solomon and his merry men out on the beach in the darkness, lined up with their faces upturned to watch her window, the square of curtained yellow light. She didn't pull down the blackout blind: let them know she was here. Birch sat on the end of the bed, staring at the laundry hamper. On the top of the pile was the cardigan of hers that Charlie had briefly worn. She realised now that she could smell him on it, and the smell made her eyes prickle. Her room smelled like *man*. Like her little brother, who might, by now, be thousands of miles away.

Don't be soft.

'If we make it through the night,' she told herself, 'you're washing that first thing in the morning.'

Eventually, she could wait no longer, and flicked off the bedroom light. The landing light was still on, but that wasn't unusual. The landing had no windows, and she imagined not much of the light would be visible from outside. As far as they knew, she'd turned in. Charlie, too, though he wasn't here. He hadn't been here now since Wednesday night. She tried to imagine him, where he might be sleeping – she hoped that he *was* sleeping. She hoped he was overseas by now, or on a plane, travelling at hundreds of miles an hour in the direction of safety. She let herself imagine him in one of those papery aeroplane sleep masks, trying to drop off in his rigid seat, dreaming of – well, who knew. She didn't know him now, not really. He'd become a stranger, a person who did bad things for money. She wished she'd asked him what he dreamed about, before he went.

'Snap out of it,' she hissed. She walked back out onto the landing, and took hold of the loft ladder. It took some doing to navigate it down the stairs without making a noise, but by taking every step with her breath held, then exhaling before the next, she managed it. She propped it up in the living room, and its long steel frame gleamed in the light of the gas fire.

The little red glowing digits of the clock on her TV told her it was 1.56 a.m. when the first blow hit the back door. With the second, she heard the lock make an unhealthy sound. With the fourth, it gave, and the house filled with the sound of bottles and jars scattering.

'Come on in, gentlemen!' Birch yelled from the living room. 'What took you so long?'

Malkie and Fitz were standing on either side of Vyshnya, just watching her as she struggled in the chair. I winced. Her arm looked bad. It was bleeding pretty hard. They hadn't done anything to strap it up, and the restraints they'd put her in were making things worse, pulling the flesh back so it kind of spilled out. I hoped that hadn't been deliberate on their part, but it gave me a real skin-crawling feeling. Solomon was some distance away, in Vyshnya's eyeline. He'd pulled off his tie, as though unwinding after a long day at work. He was leaning against one of the kitchen counters, and smiling at her. Ez was next to him. I wanted to fly at them both. I wanted to scratch that smile right off Solomon's face. But it was all I could do to stand upright, in that moment.

Solomon looked round at me.

'Smith!' he said, throwing out his arms and greeting me like I was an old friend he hadn't seen in years. '*Schenok!* Come and talk some sense into this woman, would you?'

I just looked at him. *This is a dream. Wake the fuck up, Charlie.*

'Well, come on!' Solomon said. 'She won't speak English and she won't speak sense. Come and calm her down.'

Yeah, fuckface, I wanted to say, *I wouldn't speak much sense if I was tied to a chair and bleeding heavily, either.* But I said nothing. I made myself walk forward, until I was standing directly in front of Vyshnya.

She stopped struggling, stopped puffing and swearing against her gag. Her eyes pleaded with me, though I didn't know what for. I was being watched from all sides. I felt like a Christian in the Roman ring with four very patient lions. Without asking for anyone's permission, I knelt down in front of the chair, and untied the tea towel from Vyshnya's face.

'Keep quiet, now,' I said in Russian. I hoped she and I would be able to communicate. We'd almost always used English in the sauna, and when we hadn't, I'd been unable to keep up with her fast Ukrainian.

'*Schenok.*' It was a whisper. Her voice sounded wet, and I realised she smelled strongly of alcohol.

'What are you *doing* here, Vyshnya?'

She closed her eyes for a short time, and swallowed. 'I came here to kill him,' she said.

I glanced at Solomon. He was watching, with that amused look on his face, but if he'd understood what she said, he didn't show it.

Vyshnya was still speaking. 'For revenge,' she said. 'He hurt me so badly. I didn't die, but he ended my life. I came to end his.'

I gawped at her. 'Honey,' I said. I thought of Nella then: she used to call me that, when she wanted to be tender. 'You shouldn't have come here. You should have stayed at home, in Ukraine. Stayed safe.'

Anger flashed across her face, and I thought she might start up her screaming again, but she didn't. The pool of blood from her ripped-open arm was spreading. I could feel it seeping into the knees of my jeans. Shit, I thought: there are arteries in your arms, aren't there? And she did seem to be weakening.

'I had no life there,' she said. 'I have no life. Not after . . .'

'I know,' I said. I didn't want her to describe the things that had happened in the sauna that night. I knew, only too well. Had dreamed them, over and over.

I took a risk, then, speaking fast, hoping that Vyshnya could understand me and Solomon could not.

'I know how you feel,' I said. 'I want to kill him, too. I've wanted to kill him ever since that night. I should have done it, before now, for you. I'm sorry I didn't.'

Vyshnya smiled, then. A small, grim smile, but a smile nevertheless. 'I would have hated you for it,' she said. 'I wanted it to be me. I know that Toad sent you here, but I wanted it to be me.'

I gawped. I suspected that even Solomon's Russian included *zhaba*, so I bit back the word.

'He knew I was coming,' Vyshnya said. 'He said he would make sure I had help. But I didn't want help.'

Have you had contact? Toad had texted me. It made sense now.

'You were supposed to call me,' I said.

'I was,' she said. 'But I never asked for his help. I wanted to do it.'

I took a moment to glance around: the knives on the walls. Two hefty wooden rolling pins in a tub on the counter. I still had Abdul's piece on me, and my hand itched to get hold of the gun. I allowed myself to wonder, for a brief moment, if, together, Vyshnya and I could overpower the four of them, make her dream come true. But I knew it was ridiculous. Malkie, Ez and Fitz were like tanks. They were all carrying guns, too. They were all likely far more adept at shooting than I was. And I was dispensable: they'd just take me out. Vyshnya was badly hurt. I could see in her eyes that she was unhinged, drunk, useless. There was no way.

'There's no way,' I said.

She smiled again. Her face was going very pale. 'I know,' she said.

I felt tears in my eyes. I reached up and put my hand on her face. Her cheek felt cold.

'It's nice to see you, *Schenok*,' she said.

I laughed a short sob of a laugh. 'I always thought you hated me,' I said.

She was still smiling, but the smile was fading. 'I thought you were an annoying little man-boy,' she said, making me laugh again, through my horror. 'But you were good to my girls. And you were good to me.'

My face was slick with tears. I couldn't help it.

'You are a good man, *Schenok*,' she said.

Her blood was everywhere.

'Right,' Solomon said. I turned and looked at him, and the amused expression was gone. His eyes were steely. 'I've had enough of this. Smith, I want you to dispense with this woman.'

I stood carefully, putting my palm down on the floor to steady myself, daubing it in the spreading sheet of blood.

'What?'

'I said *enough*.' Solomon showed his teeth. 'Put her out of her misery.'

I blinked. I knew what he was saying, but I didn't want to believe it. 'You want me to—?'

He took a step towards me, and I flinched.

'Show me you love me, *Schenok*,' he said. He spat the name out, like a bad taste in his mouth. 'Show me you love your*self*. If you want to leave this house alive, you will deal with this.'

I realised he couldn't say it. For all his gallusness, he couldn't actually say the words.

'You want me to kill her,' I said. My voice sounded like a dead thing.

Solomon threw me a theatrical eye-roll. 'At last,' he said, 'we are on the same page.'

Behind Solomon, Ez was smirking. I didn't dare turn to look at Fitz or Malkie. I knew they wouldn't help me.

'You are carrying a gun,' Solomon said slowly, as though speaking to a child. 'I believe you know how to use it.'

I looked down at Vyshnya. I thought her lips had a faint blue tinge, now.

'Please, *Schenok*,' she said in Ukrainian. 'It's okay. I'm ready.'

'I won't,' I replied in Russian, 'I can't.'

But she was nodding at me. I could see that her eyes were glassy, that she was mad and hurting. She'd thrown herself in front of a Range Rover. She'd gone about it all wrong.

'Yes,' she said. 'Look at me. I am bleeding. I'm dying. If you don't, he'll hurt me again. He'll do it anyway, and I don't want it to be him.'

I was crying, still. I saw a fat tear fall from my nose and land in the mess of blood on the floor.

'Do it, *Schenok*,' she said. 'Do what he says. End this.'

I took out Abdul's piece and balanced it on my palm. Now both my hands were smeared with blood.

'Smith,' Solomon said, 'we don't have all night.'

Out of the corner of my eye, I saw Malkie's hand go to his hip. Fitz copied. They were preparing to step in.

'Okay, okay,' I said, in English. I cocked the gun and took the safety off.

'Charlie,' Vyshnya whispered then, and I jumped. I didn't know she knew my real name: the only time I'd ever said it to her was in the room, that night, as she lay there broken and Karen and I fought to put her back together. She looked at me, her eyes big and wet, but her face calm. 'Do it right. Do it fast.'

I pressed the mouth of the gun to the centre of her forehead.

'Yes,' she said. 'Like that.'

I squeezed my eyes closed, so I wouldn't have to see.

'I'm sorry,' I whispered.

And I pulled the trigger.

The box of glass hadn't tripped them, but it had slowed them down. A stream of curses issued from the kitchen. Birch was already on her feet: had been at the sound of the first blow to the back door. She dipped one hand into her pocket and pushed the panic button, felt it vibrate in response: distress call received. Now all she needed to do was hold them until her colleagues arrived.

As the first man staggered over the shards of glass and into the living room, she toppled the loft ladder, catching him unawares. It struck him on one temple, and he reeled.

'Fucking *bitch*!'

The man swithered in the kitchen doorway, temporarily blocking the way for his two companions.

Three of them? Oh shit.

'Yeah?' Birch yelled. 'Then get the *fuck* out of my house!'

The first man lunged at her. It was still dark in the room, with only the gas fire lit, and she reached for the huge yellow LED torch she'd rescued from the loft earlier. It was the kind of torch the police used on search parties in dark countryside. Birch shone it directly into the first man's eyes. He swore, and threw up his arms. Birch saw he was wearing a bandanna tied around his nose and chin: the print of a glow-in-the-dark skull face on it.

'So,' she said, 'we meet again.'

The skull-faced man grabbed at her, but she'd dazzled him and was able to sidestep as he crashed past her. Still wielding the torch, she brought down on the back of his neck the weapon in her right hand: a silver-topped cane that had belonged to her mother. It was antique, heavy as lead. A supposed family heirloom. The skull-faced man went down, and she sent up a prayer of thanks to her mother.

But now she had her back to the other two, and one of them wrapped an arm around her throat. *Fenton.* She knew immediately by the smell of him.

'Jesus, ya fuckin daftie!' Fenton was hissing right into her ear, but speaking to the skull-faced man. 'Gies a hand wi' this bitch, will ye? She's a fuckin' radge all right!'

The third man had clambered over the sofa, past them, and she could now hear him tearing up the stairs. He was going to look for Charlie. She didn't have much time.

With as much force as she could, Birch brought the heavy torch up and swung it over her shoulder, at the place she thought Fenton's head was. It made contact, with a cracking sound.

'You little *cunt!*' he spat. With his free hand, he began trying to wrestle the torch from Birch's grip.

The skull-faced man had righted himself and staggered towards the two of them as they grappled, Fenton's chest pressed into Birch's back, and his arm round her neck tightening, trying to lift her feet off the floor so she couldn't flip him again, as she had in the alleyway. Though her lungs were empty and she was beginning to see patterns, Birch took the opportunity to lean into Fenton's pull and lift her feet up to kick the advancing skull-masked man square in the face. She heard his nose break, and he bent double, both hands thrown up over his eyes.

'Get out of my fucking *house!*' Birch yelled again, but her voice was weaker now due to Fenton's chokehold. He succeeded in wrenching the torch from her fingers, and he lobbed it across the room. It hit the gas fire, and the glass front shattered. The flames guttered out, and darkness fell. Immediately, Birch could smell gas.

The skull-faced man was whimpering.

'Jesus, Jones!' Fenton shouted at him. 'Find your fucking balls and *help me*, will ye?'

Birch twisted in Fenton's grip. Her vision was beginning to go in and out, but when Jones the masked man stood up, she saw even in the gloom that the outline of the white skull had disappeared, the bandanna soaked with blood.

'Get out!' she tried again. 'I'm a police officer!' She sounded like her own ghost.

'Get hold of her, will ye, Jones?'

Fenton made the mistake of loosening his grip, enough for Birch to haul in a lungful of air. It stung, but she felt a little of her strength return. The cane was still in her hand, and she lashed out again at Jones's face, hitting him in the eye.

'Bitch *bastard.*'

Fenton grabbed Birch's free left arm, tried to spin her around to twist it behind her back. He had to let her out of the chokehold, and she gulped down air. Anticipating Fenton's plan, she tried to run: she knew he wouldn't let go of her, but straightening her arm out and pulling away would make it harder for him to reel her in again. Jones looked afraid as she bolted towards him.

'Fuck*sake!*'

Fenton now had hold of both of her wrists, both of her arms outstretched behind her, like they were some sort of bizarre yoga duo. He was trying to get her back into a manageable hold, but she was strong, younger than he was, and they were equals in height. Birch took the opportunity to fill her lungs, and then screamed.

'Shut her the *fuck up*, Jones!'

The skull man finally found some initiative, and punched Birch square in the face. The blow landed right between her eyes.

Her vision fell out for a second, and when it came back, she could see a rainbow chimera over one eye. Her depth perception was broken. She tried to kick out at Jones once again, but she knew she wasn't anywhere near.

'*Fuck you,*' she hissed, and then screamed again. This time she was able to see the blow coming, but although she tried to duck, her weird vision meant she didn't go far enough, and he landed a glancing blow on the side of her head.

Fenton was dancing backward now, still holding her wrists: he was pulling her back with him, giving Jones more room to swing.

'Fuck her up, Jonesy,' Birch heard him say.

Jones made another punch that hit Birch in the jaw. At the back of her mouth, she felt something come loose. She gathered the blood and saliva in her mouth and spat it as hard as she could into Jones's face. As the wet missile left her mouth, she realised there was a tooth in it. At the same moment, Fenton took another step back: there was a metallic sound, and he let out a cry. He'd tangled his foot in the fallen loft ladder, and he went down like a tree, backward, pulling Birch with him. As she fell on top of him, she heard the air rush out of his lungs. He'd twisted one of her arms all wrong, and a bolt of white-hot pain shot through it. Birch's vision fluttered out again, just for a second or two. But in those two seconds, she heard windchimes.

Shit. There's another one, she thought. Someone was coming in the front door.

Birch struggled, trying to get her wrists out of Fenton's grip without letting him up off the floor. She was vulnerable like that, she knew: chest and stomach upturned, all the softest parts of her just ready to be punched or kicked by the skull man. But his attack never came. She could hear – *something*. Something going on where Jones had been standing. She heard him say, 'What the fuck, man?' and then there appeared to be a scuffle. She couldn't hear all that well, because her ears were ringing from the punches she'd taken, and underneath her weight, Fenton was roaring. The ladder was still hooked around his leg, and as he thrashed, it whined and clanked. All she could see was the ceiling, and the dark shapes of some of her furniture. The room stank of gas.

Fenton was yanking on her hurt arm, making her cry out in pain. Then he let go of that wrist, and manoeuvred one hand out from underneath her back. He clamped it over her mouth.

'Fucking *bitch*,' he spat, into her ear.

Birch opened her bloodied lips and bit down, as hard as she could, on Fenton's index finger. Fenton squealed: a sound like the yelp of a dog who's been whipped with a chain.

He'd had enough, she could tell. He seemed to summon a final burst of strength, arched his back, and rolled. Birch found herself face down on the floor, the ladder clattering between them, and Fenton's full weight on top of her. His hand was still over her mouth, but she realised that she had a small lump of his flesh, now detached, between her teeth. She gagged. Everything smelled and tasted like blood and gas and metal. She was down. This was it. She prayed for the sound of sirens.

'I'm going to enjoy this,' Fenton hissed into her ear. Birch braced for whatever impact might come, and indeed she felt a horrendous, bone-crushing blow. But no pain came, and the howl that went up was not from her own throat. The sound was Fenton's, a huge, guttural wail. His hands went limp, and he rolled off her, the ladder still caught round his foot, and rattling. He curled into a spiral on the floor beside her, clawing at his own skull.

'Nella.'

No. She must be hallucinating. It couldn't be—

She put her palms down and pushed herself to her knees, sending miserable lightning up and down her injured arm. A tattooed hand reached out and lifted her unhurt elbow, and hauled her to her feet. She reeled for a moment, her vision full of static. Then things righted a little and she turned round.

'Oh fuck, Nella. Oh fuck.'

Charlie was holding the silver-topped cane in his hand. Even in the dim light, blood gleamed on it.

Birch couldn't help it. She flung herself at her brother, pulling him in close to her. As his face made contact with her own, she felt her back bottom teeth sloshing in the gum. Jones had dislodged them. Everything hurt, but she didn't care. Charlie. Charlie had come back.

'All right, love,' he said, 'all right now.'

He put a hand on her shoulder and pushed her backward to arm's length. The expression on his face told Birch she looked really pretty bad.

'Let's finish this,' Charlie said, nodding at Fenton, still on the ground beside her, but beginning to gather himself. 'Then we can talk, yeah?'

Birch nodded. Charlie leaned over the crumpled form of the skull-masked man, and flicked on the overhead light. Birch blinked. Her depth perception had still not returned, and the light felt almost painfully bright, brighter than she knew it really was.

'You okay to help me with these cunts?'

'You bet,' Birch said. Her voice sounded thick and oily.

She'd tucked her handcuffs into the pocket of her jeans, and now she turned and stood over Fenton. He'd pulled himself into a sort of crouch, and was gingerly touching the open wound on his forehead. Birch gave thanks once again for the silver-topped cane.

'What's this scumbag's name?'

Charlie was standing over Jones, who was flat out on the carpet, whimpering. He smirked at her.

'Gordon,' he said.

Birch reached down and yanked Fenton's hand away from his wound. She clicked one cuff around his wrist.

'Gordon Fenton,' she said, 'I am arresting you for breaking and entering, and assaulting a police officer.'

Fenton tried to drag his hand away, pushing himself to his feet as he did so. He looked unsteady. Birch was ready: she did what he'd been trying to do to her, twirling him round as though they were dancing, and twisting the cuffed arm behind his back. His other hand flailed, trying to hit her.

'Oh,' Birch said, dodging the blow. 'Wanting to add *resisting arrest* to those charges, are we?'

'Fuck off,' Fenton said. But he dropped the flailing hand, and Birch slotted it into the other cuff.

'Good lad,' she said.

Fenton spat blood onto her carpet. 'Bitch,' he replied.

'You do not have to say anything,' Birch said, with some glee. 'But it may harm your defence if you do not mention when questioned something which you later rely on in court. Anything you do say may be given in evidence.'

'Yeah yeah, yadda yadda,' Fenton muttered.

Birch steered him round to the other side of the sofa, then gave him a good hard shove. He slumped into the cushions.

'Have a seat, why don't you?' she said. With her good hand, she patted Fenton down. In the pocket of his coat, her phone, its screen smashed and webbed with crazing. 'Thanks,' she said.

Her whole face hurt. She was going to have to do something about these injuries, soon. She was still listening for sirens, though she could tell her hearing wasn't functioning quite right. There was blood in her eyes, and she wiped it away with the back of her hand. For now, adrenalin was still spangling in her veins, keeping her going. And they weren't done.

She walked around the edge of the sofa, back to where Charlie was standing over Jones.

'What did you do?' she asked.

'Whacked him in the throat,' Charlie said. 'Then I just sort of . . . lost it.' He was still holding the cane.

'Holy shit, Charlie.'

Her brother snorted. On the floor, a bloodied Jones opened and closed his mouth like a guppy, trying to haul in small gulps of air.

'What?' he said. 'He was about to fucking *go* for you. I had to put him down.'

Birch nodded backward towards Fenton.

'Watch that one,' she said. Then she dropped to her knees beside Jones. 'Can you breathe?' she asked him.

He swivelled his eyes around to look at her, and made the face of a small child who's about to throw a tantrum.

'I'm asking,' Birch went on, 'because if you can't, I will need to give you a tracheotomy. That means I will need to cut your wind-pipe open.'

It was the adrenalin talking. For all the first-aid courses she'd been on, she'd have had no idea how to do this. But the bluff worked.

'I can breathe,' Jones coughed. He didn't sound healthy, but she didn't much care.

'Then you're not going to die,' she said. She stood, and inspected him for a moment, before walking to the kitchen and opening a drawer. Back in the living room, she could hear Fenton and her brother talking in low voices. It didn't sound friendly. She rummaged, and found a very old pair of handcuffs she'd managed to partially break a while ago. They would lock, but unlocking them was less straightforward: a suspect had struggled while being uncuffed, and managed to break off a tiny piece of the key in the keyhole.

'Get on your front,' she said to Jones, back in the living room. He stared up at her. She glanced over at Charlie, who was standing beside Fenton, glaring. Jones got the message.

'Okay, okay,' he said. With some apparent difficulty, he rolled over.

'Real name?' Birch asked, and to her surprise, it was Jones who answered, though she'd been addressing Charlie.

'Kristof,' he said.

'Kristof Jones, I'm—'

'No,' Jones said. 'Kristof Majewski.'

Birch snorted. 'Good lord,' she said. 'An honest thief.'

She read him his rights, then hauled him to his feet with Charlie's help, and deposited him on the sofa alongside Fenton.

'Well,' Charlie said, 'now what?'

Birch had entirely forgotten the third man, who'd gone upstairs. But now there was a clattering of feet, and a figure appeared in the unlit hallway.

'The *fuck*?'

Fenton twisted his head round. 'Get the fuck out, pal!' he yelled. 'Polis are on their way!'

The man's face was in shadow. Charlie began to advance towards him, the cane raised. Birch saw the man's hand twitch, near to his hip, and her heart kicked out. But then Fenton yelled again.

'Ye'd better be running, pal!'

Before Charlie could reach him, the third man wrenched open the front door, and was gone.

'Don't,' Birch called, and her brother turned. 'Don't go after him. I need you here.'

Charlie came back to stand next to her, and they looked down at Fenton and Jones – Gordon and Kristof – battered, sullen, hanging their heads. Out of nowhere, Charlie slid his hand into hers.

'Sorry, Nella,' he said. 'Sorry it took me so long.'

She looked at him. The adrenalin was starting to wear off now, and her whole head vibrated with pain. The arm Fenton had twisted hung useless at her side. At last, she could hear a siren on the road out back, then two, then three. Charlie, she thought, feeling the weight of brother's warm, wet hand in her own, this is Charlie. This is my little brother. There was no mistaking it now. Looking at his face then, she could see exactly what he was thinking.

'You ready for what's next?' she said.

He looked away for a moment, down at his feet. Then he lifted his head again. 'Yeah,' he said.

When I opened my eyes, Vyshnya was gone. The force of the bullet had thrown the chair over, and she was lying slumped on the ground. My face was spattered with blood. I looked down at my clothes: they were wet, sticky-looking. I was glad they were all black.

It turned out I didn't have anything left in my body to throw up, but I hawked bitter phlegm and spat it onto the swimmy red of the floor. I was able to look up at Malkie: my closest ally, I reckoned, in the room. One side of his face was flecked with flown blood. He looked amazed: I'd done it. I'd actually done it.

A hand hit my back and I flinched. It was Solomon, patting my shoulder blade.

'It's hard, isn't it?' he said in his forked voice. 'The first time.'

I couldn't look at him. My hands were shaking so much it scared me. I pulled the safety back into place on the gun.

'You've done well.' Solomon moved his hand to the back of my neck, and grasped it. 'You've walked through the fire, Smith. You've chosen your side. I'm pleased with you.'

Don't touch me, I wanted to scream. *Get your disgusting hands off me*. But I was mute. I felt sick, and I had the strong urge to lie down, right there in the gore on the hard tiles, and just sleep.

'You've proven yourself an excellent employee,' Solomon was saying. 'Which means you get to leave this house tomorrow, and go back to the Emerald.'

Still, I said nothing.

'Would you like that, Smith?'

Somehow, his words reached me.

'Yes,' I said. It was a child's voice, small and afraid.

'Good.' Out of the corner of my eye, I saw Solomon make a hand gesture at Malkie and Fitz. They walked over, stood behind him, alongside Ez. Outside my line of sight.

'There are a few things I need you to do before you go,' Solomon said. 'First, and most importantly: deal with this mess. I want this room and the car outside *forensically cleaned*, do you understand me? If a policeman were to walk in here in the morning, they would find nothing whatsoever amiss – am I correctly understood?'

I knew that would be impossible, and that he'd no doubt get some team of clean-up guys in after me. But I had no room to argue.

'Yes.'

'Second, I need this' – Solomon poked a wing-tipped toe in the direction of Vyshnya's body – 'cleanly disposed of. That needs to happen *tonight*. I assume I can entrust that task to you?'

'Yes.'

'And when I say cleanly disposed of, I mean without any link to this place, do you understand? It is in your interest to make that happen. I'm sure I don't need to tell you what would happen to you should this body be discovered.'

I glanced down at Vyshnya. I knew only too well the ways in which Solomon could hurt a person.

'Good. I expect you to have removed your personal items from Abdul's room by the morning. Malcolm here will contact your friend Mr Scissors, and let him know that you'll be back at the helm of the Emerald tomorrow night.'

I realised I was nodding, my head lolling loosely back and forth.

'You understand everything I have said.'

I looked round then, for the first time. Solomon was too close for my liking, and behind him, Malkie, Ez and Fitz rose up like a bank of storm cloud.

'I do,' I said. 'It'll all be done tonight.'

Solomon clapped me on the back again. It felt feeble.

'Good man, Smith,' he said. Malkie and Fitz were already headed towards the door. Solomon turned and followed them, letting Ez bring up the rear. Once Solomon's back was turned, Ez looked me up and down as though I were something poisoned, something rotten.

'If it was up to me?' he hissed. 'You'd be a dead man.'

I could say nothing. I dropped my gaze and looked at the pile of flesh and rags that had been Vyshnya. Ez stalked after Solomon, and I heard him close the door on me. End of discussion. Another box ticked.

I dealt with Vyshnya's body through a sort of haze. Her head was a detonated bomb, and I needed to gather all the pieces. It felt important to me that all those pieces be kept together: something about body and soul, something, something, something. I had no coherent thoughts. I untied the solid parts of her from the chair, and rolled her into one of the industrial black sacks I found under a sink. She was a smallish woman, but I had to fold her fast: the flesh was already stiffening, turning grey. She was lukewarm to the touch. Her hands had curled into tight fists, knots I couldn't undo.

I remember I swished chunks of her hair up from out of the ocean of spatter. I remember I used a dustpan to scrape up fragments of jelly and bone. I found her ear, intact, feet away, and wept over it.

Once all her solid parts – the body, and the many fragments made by the gunshot – were all wrapped in black plastic and put into the same big bag, I used up yards and yards of blue roll to mop up the blood. This soaked tissue went into the bag as well: I think now that I was working with the fucked-up delusion that if I got every single particle of her into the same place, she'd somehow coagulate, re-stitch, come back to me. Instead, of course, I had to tie up the bag and haul it out back. Solomon's garden was huge, and flat, and dark.

I left Vyshnya outside, swaddled in her plastic mourning gear, and returned to start the fiendish job of the clean. I was trying to do my allotted tasks in order of difficulty, from the very hardest, and working on down. With the blue roll and an antiseptic spray, I went around the kitchen inch by inch, foot by foot, mopping up any spatter, any droplet that I found. The stainless steel and the tiles all came clean, but anything fabric was forever soiled. There were oven gloves, spattered with a bright stripe of blood. Tea towels crusted with it. I dumped anything I couldn't clean into a sink, and ran the hot tap over it until steam cascaded up. No use.

With that same steaming hot water, I mopped every inch of the floor. It took over an hour. I mopped myself out of the back kitchen door, to where Vyshnya's black cocoon still lay between the back step and the decorative fencing that hid the bins from view. I reopened the black wrapping, unscrewed the soiled mop head, and threw it into the bag with Vyshnya.

'I'm sorry,' I said, and hoped she could hear me.

I sat outside on the step with her, waiting for the kitchen floor to dry so I could go back in and get the cloths, dispose of those, too. I was beyond shivering: my whole body radiated with the cold, pulsed with it. I didn't care.

I am alive, I thought. How dare I be alive? I wanted more than anything to throw up, but I'd tried, over and over. There was nothing left. My throat tasted like acid: I was filled with it. Acid ran in my veins, pumped through my heart.

Why aren't you dead, Charlie? I thought. You fucking well deserve it.

My phone told me it was after midnight. It also told me I had a dozen texts from Toad. He'd had to go quiet for a few days in Russia. He'd finally told me that Vyshnya was coming, that he hadn't heard from her, that she wasn't doing what he'd told her to do. I'd been standing in the darkness of the pub, watching the back of Solomon's neck, as those texts arrived. I had to be ready for her coming, Toad wrote. The texts were in Ukrainian, and translating them made my head ache. He'd told me I had to be ready to tell Solomon I knew nothing. *She has not followed the plan,* he'd written, *you will not be able to save her.* I could feel the anguish in his texts, the realisation that he'd fucked up. The last few were simply pleas for any sort of update: *What is happening?* Schenok, *are you safe?* I deleted the texts without replying.

Time seemed to have sped up and raced away. The cleaning had taken so long, and I had so much still to do. But eventually the floor was dry enough to cross, and I grabbed the soiled things from the sink, wrung them out as well as I could, and added them to the bag with Vyshnya. As I made to walk out of the kitchen for the last time, I saw Solomon's tie: it had slithered almost out of sight down the back of one of the cabinets. I heard Solomon's words in my head: *when I say cleanly disposed of, I mean without any link to this place.* Putting the tie into the bag with Vyshnya felt particularly cruel, but I had to do it. It was an insurance policy, or something. I was still struggling to think straight.

'I'm so sorry,' I kept saying. I felt like a cuckoo clock. *Sorry. Sorry. Sorry.*

I left her there, by the step, and walked round the side of the house to get the car. I stood, psyching myself up to get in, and looked back at the house. One light was on in the centre of the top floor. I imagined Solomon reclining in bed, alone, reading perhaps, or watching TV. I imagined stealing up the stairs and breaking in, strangling him with a pillowcase or just blowing his face off, the way he'd made me do to Vyshnya. But as much as I hated him, the fight in me was mostly gone. I'd killed a person, and I was pretty sure I couldn't do it again.

I got into the car, started the engine as gingerly as I could, and eased it round to the back. It seemed to purr.

I wandered back and forth between the car and the back kitchen door for a while, fetching more black bags to line the boot with, then scooping up the terrible bundle that had once been Vyshnya, and carrying it over the gravel. In spite of Solomon's efforts to cut himself off from the world, I could still hear the distant hum of the M8, and every so often a plane passed overhead, flashing red and green like a Christmas toy and pulling a dim blue vapour trail behind it. There was a half-moon, sliced through with a perfectly straight line.

I drove until the city was a dim red glow in the rear-view mirror. I found a narrow, straight road that said 'access only', and must have led to a farm. The hedges were high: I tucked the Range Rover into a field gate, got out and hopped the fence. There was a copse at one corner of the big empty square of ploughed earth, a black, noisy mass I headed towards. The trees were big there: I liked the sound they made. In the wind, a fat oak bent and creaked. There were birches: I knew them from their glowy white trunks. I'd always liked being named after a tree, and Maw used to tell me they were magic. They had no leaves yet, but the night moved through their bristly twigs. I didn't think I'd ever feel happy again, but I felt a little less wretched, standing under them.

The digging was the hardest physical work I had ever done. I'd found a shovel in the broom cupboard in the kitchen, the same place where I found the mop. One shovel, and me: shaking, sweating, fucked-up Charlie Birch. I must have spent years of my life in the gym but that night I couldn't feel it. About two feet down, I cursed myself for picking that spot with the trees: the soil was lousy with roots, and they wept sap and water as I hacked into them. The ground was hard. I sweated and spat. I took off my sweater and worked topless in the freezing night, seeing my own arms wet and gleaming and still burning up with the effort of it.

But this is for Vyshnya, Charlie, I told myself. This is for her.

By the time I was done, the sky had started to lighten. In the trees all around me, the dawn chorus had begun.

'Sorry,' I whispered, to the trees whose roots I'd hacked at, to the birds who mocked me with their sweet voices. *Sorry. Sorry. Sorry.*

I dragged myself back across the field and knocked the head of the shovel against the back wheel of the car, leaving a little spray of soil. My arms were shaking, every tendon hot and loose, every nerve exhausted.

But somehow I found the strength to heft Vyshnya onto my shoulder, and stagger back down the field to the crap grave. The effort made my feet go numb. When I got Vyshnya to the lip of the hole, I tried not to drop her in too hard, but there wasn't much could be done. The black wrapping fell into the dark pit, and the early grey light gleamed on it.

I lowered myself down to the edge of the grave, and sat there, my legs swinging into the gap. If I stretched down, I could brush the top of the plastic wrapping with my wet, numbed toes. I felt dizzy and unhinged, my heart beating faster than I thought was possible.

I knew I ought to do something, say something. What happens at funerals? I found myself humming a tune that Maw used to sing around the house – what was that? I droned away at it, until a few words came back to me, and I sang.

'And we'll all go together – to pluck wild mountain thyme all among the blooming heather . . .'

A Scottish song. Vyshnya probably wouldn't have known it. I felt stupid. I remember wishing I knew some prayers, some right things to say when you bury someone. All I could remember was the Lord's Prayer from school: after all these years, I could recite it without thinking, like the alphabet, or my own phone number. I said it, spluttering tears on 'forgive us our trespasses'. Could I be forgiven for Vyshnya's death? *Dear God: I have done what is unforgivable.*

There was proper light now, though the sun wasn't quite up: the world was no longer shades of grey. The traffic noise was louder, the planes more frequent. No cars had passed down the little access road yet, but I knew farmers got up early. And I still had tasks to do.

It was easier to fill the grave than it had been to dig it. I'd left the shovel leaning against the car, so initially I just got on my knees beside the pile of soil, and used my arms and body to shove it back into the hole in huge mounds. I went back to the Range Rover only when it was nearly filled, to retrieve the spade and finish things off. I caught a glimpse of myself in the dark glass of the car window as I approached. Still shirtless, I was clothed in mud, twigs, the old bones of leaves. I realised too late that I'd thrown my sweater on to the pile as I'd done the digging. It was now buried along with Vyshnya.

I tidied the gravesite. The soil was obviously disturbed, but I made it flat. I stamped it down, and then swept it over with the ends of a fallen branch. I found as much in the way of twigs and leaf litter as I could. I scattered the packed earth, and hoped that some grass would grow.

'Goodbye, Vyshnya,' I said, and once again, because no amount would ever be enough, I added, 'I'm sorry.'

B irch had heard three sirens, and three panda cars had come. It was 2.45 a.m., and she could only imagine the stir that blue flashing lights and sirens on the Portobello prom at such an hour would cause.

The doors and windows were all open now, to clear the gas: she'd had Charlie find the switch by the meter and disable it. Then Charlie had gone out into the back garden, not wanting to stay in the room with Jones – whose face was beginning to turn purple, making Birch wonder what her own was doing – and Fenton, who seemed unable to prevent himself from snarling insults.

'I fuckin' helped you, kid,' he'd said. 'I fuckin' nearly ended yer da.'

Birch had looked over at Charlie then, and the alarm must have shown on her face, because Charlie blushed.

'Sorry, Nella,' he'd said. 'It's a long story.'

From the living room, Birch watched her brother.

'It's okay,' he'd called back, as he picked his way over the littered bottles by the door, 'I won't run away again.'

She believed him.

Now he stood, framed by the doorway, on her weedy little patio. He'd turned the kitchen light on, and its glow illuminated a long stripe of flagstones, grass, the foot of the shed. His shadow hung in that stripe, like something spilled.

'Marm?'

A female uniform poked her head around the front door, and, seeing Birch in the living room, stepped inside.

'She's here, boys,' she said, over her shoulder.

It was PC Park. Birch had worked with her a few times. She was a petite, compact woman with a core of steel, Birch had learned. Nothing fazed her.

'Oh my God,' Park said, as she moved into the living room.

Birch could feel that her face was swollen: below one eye, she could see an indistinct mound of cheek, where a blow had been landed and the flesh had risen and purpled. Her nose had bled, she was fairly sure, and her teeth felt swimmy and loose. She was cradling her hurt, left arm with her good one, as it eased the pain a little. She hadn't yet looked in a mirror.

'Well, Park,' Birch said, 'am I glad to see you.'

Park's partner, a very tall, thin male officer, followed her in. For a fleeting second, Birch imagined the two of them on patrol together, how funny they must look walking side by side. Then the other two pairs appeared: four male constables, all of whom seemed impossibly young to Birch. They were pale from what she assumed was the tail-end of their night-shift rotation.

'Jesus.' One of the men whistled as he approached Birch.

'Well, quite,' she said. 'All the handiwork of these two.'

She nodded towards Fenton and Jones, who were staring intently at the wrecked gas fire, apparently refusing to acknowledge that the room was suddenly very, very full of policemen.

'I've read them their rights already,' Birch said.

Park was looking at Jones. 'Ambulance is on its way,' she said. 'You, er – really gave as good as you got, didn't you?'

Birch flushed. 'Most of that,' she said, 'wasn't me. My brother was here, thank goodness. That's his doing.'

As if on cue, Charlie turned and paced back into the living room.

'Folks,' Birch said, gesturing awkwardly, 'this is my brother, Charlie Birch.'

She saw the name ring a bell with Park's partner, who she guessed was the oldest of the six constables.

'He'll be coming in with you too.' Birch's voice shook as she said it.

'As . . . a witness?' Park asked. One of her eyebrows was raised.

I suppose I did just shop him for assault, Birch thought.

'Yes and no,' Birch said. 'I'm going to follow you all, and things will become clear at the station.'

One of the male constables found some initiative. 'Right,' he said. He stepped round the side of the sofa and nudged Jones on the arm. 'Can you get up, son?'

Jones said nothing, but stuck his elbow out to be helped. Two of the constables hauled him upright.

'No station for you,' the officer went on, 'till we get you cleaned up. Ambulance is just round the corner. I reckon you could use some fresh air.'

Jones shrugged. The two policemen flanked him, and began to march him slowly, wincing, out into the hallway.

Park was eyeing Fenton's head injury: the one Charlie had inflicted with the silver-topped cane. The top of his bald head was smeared with dried-on blood, but to Birch's eye, the wound didn't look like it needed to be stitched.

'Does this one need a medic, too, do you reckon, marm?'

Fenton looked up at Park for the first time, and curled his lip. 'Fuck off, you ching-chong bitch.'

Birch took a sharp inward breath, but before she had a chance to react further, Park's tall, gangly partner had crossed the room and was dragging Fenton up off the sofa.

'I don't think so, mate,' he said, bringing Fenton upright. Fenton slid his eyes over to Park again.

'Hey!' the male officer barked, snapping Fenton's gaze back to him. 'We'd have absolutely no problem lining you up for a racial hatred charge as well, pal, so don't even try it.'

Fenton shrugged one shoulder out of the man's hands. 'Dinnae touch me,' he said. 'Pig scum.'

Birch saw Park roll her eyes.

'I'll take that as a *no thanks* to the medic, then,' she said. 'Lads, let's get him in the car.'

Park's partner led Fenton out, still gripping his left shoulder. One of the other officers followed. Birch noticed Fenton wasn't walking all that well: the ladder had twisted his ankle. Good. He wouldn't try to make a run for it, then.

'Are you all right?' Birch asked, but Park just shrugged.

'Happens a lot,' she said. 'It sucks, but you get past it.'

Birch nodded. 'I'm sorry,' she said.

Park only shrugged again. 'Thanks,' she said. 'But it's all good. I've got Amy. She gets it.'

One male uniform remained in the room. He was looking at Charlie: his bloodied hands and clothes, his tattoos.

'Marm, your – brother?'

'Oh yes,' Birch said. 'I haven't done the necessary there, yet, have I, Charlie? But I will.'

Another set of blue flashing lights joined the panda cars outside: the room's weird discotheque intensified. Park's partner stuck his head back in through the front door.

'That's the ambulance here,' he said. 'Paramedic motorcycle, too.' He disappeared again.

'You really ought to get checked,' Park said. 'Is that arm broken?'

Birch glanced down: she looked as though she were carrying an invisible baby. Pain pulsed through at regular intervals. 'I guess it might be,' she said, 'yeah.'

Park lifted her hand, gesturing to her remaining male colleague.

'No, it's okay,' Birch cut in. 'I'll get all this seen to shortly. I just . . .' She glanced at Charlie. 'Will you both give us a minute?'

The male officer turned, and headed out into the hallway almost as Birch spoke. Park, meanwhile, hung back, looking at Charlie. Birch remembered: her brother looked like a radge these days.

'You'll be okay?'

Birch tried to smile. Her jaw hurt. 'Just fine,' she said. 'We'll be out in two shakes, promise.'

Park nodded, and walked to the hallway, eyeing Charlie all the way. Birch saw her take up a sort of sentry position outside the open front door.

Suddenly overtaken by exhaustion, Birch sank onto the couch. The adrenalin was gone now: everything hurt, and her throat felt as though it had been sandblasted from the inside. Blood congealed on her lips. She found herself wishing for a Zopiclone tablet, right then: that just-turn-it-all-off feeling.

'Come and sit with me,' she said. Charlie flopped down on the couch. They were quiet for a moment.

'This is it, then,' Birch said.

Beside her, Charlie seemed to have deflated. He looked flat, beaten.

'You were right,' he said, after a moment.

'About what?'

'When we fought, the other night, before I went. You said you thought I'd killed people.'

'Charlie, I—'

'You were right. I have. Well . . . not *people*. But a person.'

Birch blinked. She shouldn't be shocked: you predicted this, Helen. But she was.

'Who?'

'A woman I knew. Just a few weeks ago. It was what made me turn informant on Solomon, after all these years. I couldn't carry on. Fucked me up, to be honest – I hadn't caught a single decent night of sleep in those few weeks, hadn't laughed, even, since it happened. Not till I got here.'

Birch watched Charlie. His forehead had creased into a deep frown.

'I didn't feel safe here,' he said, 'because I knew they'd come eventually. But . . . it felt like such a relief. To see you again. To feel like maybe I could start to be okay again. To come *home*, you know?'

Birch nodded. 'I know, honey,' she said. She didn't have any idea, but it was the right thing to say.

'I was so fucking naïve,' he went on. 'About everything. I should have run from the start. Fourteen years ago, I could have walked into any polis station that first night, told them I was in trouble, and it might all have been fine. I didn't. Then I had chances, over and over again, to get out, and I never took them. I know that, now. I know I had chances. You were right, I did. I was too much of a fucking coward. Even when I finally did it – when I finally talked to that Glasgow polis – I was too much of a selfish bastard to just *do* it. I still thought I could get immunity. I thought it was like in the movies. Like I could just walk away after.' He turned to look at Birch, and his face was wet.

'I've been so selfish,' he said. 'I've been such a total fucking brat about everything. I put you in danger – look at you, I got you properly beat up – because I was still clinging to the idea that I could be absolved. Like I deserve to be! I've done so many bad things. I've watched other people do so many bad things. I let Vyshnya get beat up by Solomon, let her get raped, and then I killed her.'

His whole body was heaving beside her.

'I felt like he made me,' he said, 'but he didn't. I could have turned the gun on him and ended it all. I could have killed him in front of her and then she'd have got her wish. The others would have killed her anyway, and me too, but at least I would have dealt with him. With Solomon. At least he wouldn't be walking around now, enjoying *his* fucking life. Vyshnya deserved that. And I was too fucking scared.'

Birch's head swam. Only about a third of what Charlie was saying really made any sense. Carefully, she laid her bad left arm down on her lap, and put the good one around his shoulders.

'Charlie,' she said. But there was nothing else. Words failed her.

'Send the boys in, to his house.' Charlie had sucked in a long breath and now seemed more alert, as though he'd surfaced from the deep water of his memories. 'Get a warrant, or whatever. He's got this kitchen in the basement. That's where I killed her. I cleaned up, but you've got . . . I dunno, *forensics*. You'll find something.'

He was gasping, as though he wanted to cry but wasn't letting himself.

'There's a field,' he went on, 'it's a way out of town towards – fuck, I don't know, but I could find it again for you. At the bottom corner there's a wood, and there are birch trees at the edge. Silver birch trees, with the white trunks. The ground is all disturbed there. That's where I buried her. Deep as I could, but you'll find her. She's wrapped in bin bags. The cause of death is a bullet to the head, but she'd broken her arm as well. She'd lost a lot of blood.'

Charlie's eyes had gone distant again, remembering.

'The bone was sticking up out of the skin,' he said. 'I buried my sweater with her, too, by accident. And some cloths from the kitchen. Towels and stuff. Her blood was on them, and . . .' He faded out, as though he'd run low on breath.

'And a tie,' he said quietly. 'A tie that belonged to Solomon. He was wearing it that night. You'll find that there, too.'

Birch squeezed his shoulder, pulling him in a little closer.

'That's good, honey,' she said. 'That's hard evidence. If we can find her, that'll give us a good enough reason to arrest Solomon again. We can hold him while you talk to my colleagues. We'll interview him again. If you give all that information again, as a proper statement, we'll be able to put him back in a cell. And if you tell us *everything* you know, and you stand up and say it in court, we'll be able to leave him there. Hopefully for the rest of his life.'

Charlie nodded.

'I have to tell you,' she said, 'you're facing time inside. I think you know that.'

Charlie was still nodding.

'But,' she added, 'I know a really, *really* good lawyer . . . and I sense he's about to ditch out of his current case.'

She couldn't help but smile. Charlie noticed and, to her surprise, smiled back.

'Sounds good,' he said.

'Marm?'

Park had stuck her head back into the living room.

Birch turned her head. 'Okay,' she said, 'almost with you.'

Park nodded, and ducked out again. Charlie was still looking at Birch, though his smile had faded. His mouth had become a hard, serious line.

'I'm ready,' he said.

Birch nodded, blinked back tears, and gave his shoulder a final squeeze. Then she slung her good arm onto the back of the sofa, and used it to steady herself as she stood.

'Charlie Birch,' she said, 'I am arresting you for participating in the criminal activities of an organised crime group. You do not have to say anything, but it may harm your defence if you do not mention when questioned something which you later rely on in court. Anything you do say may be given in evidence.'

I walked down Solomon's driveway that morning, and I thought about Abdul's room. I thought about his Quran verses, the way those cards might leave a dark square on the paint if they were ever taken down. I thought about his gun, the one I had used to kill Vyshnya, now cleaned up and lying on the bedside table, harmless-looking in the early morning sun. Lighter, by one round. I felt light myself, walking down that drive: light-headed from the deed I'd done and the work that followed it, empty, sick, as though I might float away. There was nothing to stop me disappearing. No one to miss me if I did.

I passed the spot where Vyshnya had thrown herself at the car. On the gravel, there was a spill of blood, and two thick, twisty marks where the wheels had skidded through to the dirt below the stones. As I walked, I texted Toad back at last.

The plan was blown, I wrote. *I am okay, but Vyshnya is dead.*

I thought for a moment, and then added, *I'm sorry.*

The walk to the road seemed endless, and I waited to be picked off: Ez with a sniper rifle, somewhere in the trees. But when I rounded the final bend, I saw the electronic gates standing open. I waited for them to slam closed in my face – they'd let me believe I'd got away before they struck – but no. I walked through. I stood on the side of the road, my overnight bag in my hand. Cars passed: cars filled with ordinary people who had ordinary lives. It was just after 9 a.m.: these folk might be on their way to work, or heading home having dropped their kids at the school gates. These people, I felt, were *good*: they were nurses and postmen and physiotherapists, people who lived clean, moral lives. I felt like they could see that I was drenched in someone else's blood: that when they looked at me, they saw a degenerate, a thug, a man who'd been okay with beating his own father, murdering his so-called friend. I'd been surrounded by others like me for too long, and the compass that spun inside me was fucked. Abdul had seemed like a *good guy*. Izz had, too. And Toad. I didn't even want to think about Toad's inherent good-or-bad-ness: my surrogate father, my mentor-in-crime. I felt like I'd woken up from a fourteen-year nightmare, and the reality I'd entered was suddenly, somehow, worse. My head buzzed with it. Who was I? Who the fuck had I become? I needed to *do* something. I'd have to think about what. But I had to get out, and I had the thought, *even if it kills me*. It made me shiver, but yes, it was time. In fact, it was long, long overdue.

I waited to see if the gates would close behind me, to see if someone was watching me on the in-built CCTV. If they were, they did nothing. I turned my back on the driveway and walked. At the bus stop, I texted Izz, and then made my way back into town, to the Emerald, which would be – I knew – just the way I had left it.

Sunday

B irch had not been able to follow the panda cars to the station as she'd hoped. Fenton had broken the radius in her lower left arm, the paramedics informed her. She really needed to get to A&E – they'd given her quite the stern telling-off – and she absolutely could not drive. The rather schoolmarmish motorcycle medic cleaned and patched up Birch's face: daubing stinging fluid onto the wounds as she tried to sit very still on her couch, and not flinch.

'You'll get yourself to a dentist at the earliest possible opportunity,' the woman said. It was very much a command. 'And I don't think it's broken, but this jaw could do with an x-ray, too, just in case.'

Yeah, yeah, Birch thought, I'll add it to the to-do list.

'Sure,' she said, the medic's face very close to her own. 'Of course. Yes.'

They took Kristof/Jones away in the back of the ambulance, then. Birch knew his nose was broken, though she kept quiet about the fact that she'd administered the blow. Charlie, it turned out, had bruised his ribs, and the man was pretty well bloodied all over. But the medics' cursory check – Birch's neighbours out on the prom in dressing gowns, Jones sitting gawped-at in the half-open back of the ambulance – found no life-threatening injuries. The motorcycle paramedic and one of the panda cars followed behind as the ambulance set off, flinging its blue neon out across the beach. The other two police cars had already gone: Birch had watched from the doorstep as Park had ushered Charlie into the back seat of her car.

'I'll be right behind you,' she'd called out to him, though it was Park who looked up at her and nodded, as though the remark belonged to her. As the young officer closed the door on his tear-stained face, Charlie attempted to press one palm against the inside of the car window. He was cuffed, and Birch could see it was a struggle. She gulped down the lump in her throat.

'See you soon,' she'd mouthed, as the panda car rolled away.

He and Fenton would be at the station by now, most likely. She imagined Charlie in the custody suite, a place he'd avoided for fourteen years. The medic's face floated across Birch's vision.

'Call a taxi,' the medic advised, 'go and get yourself checked out.' But no, A&E could take a flying jump. Birch needed to be *there*. She needed to be wherever her brother was.

As the ambulance and its motorcycle escort crawled off up the pedestrian-only prom, Birch felt like waving: they were relatives who'd overstayed their welcome, and were finally leaving her alone. It was nearing four in the morning, and for the first time Birch's house felt peaceful again – safe, even. She sat down on the couch and dialled Big Rab's number, her fingers prickling on the broken screen of the phone. She no longer needed the scribbled business card: she remembered the number off by heart.

'Sorry to wake you, Rab.' She didn't even give him a chance to say hello. 'But I need to get to Fettes Avenue, *now*, and my arm is broken so I can't drive.'

On the other end, she heard him make a spluttering noise.

'Oh,' she said, 'it's Birch. I can brief you on the way in.'

They'd reached the Leith Street roundabout by the time Birch finally paused, and drew breath. She'd been waiting for him on the street beside the China Express when he arrived, her handbag slung over her still-good shoulder, her breath fogging the black air. Rab stopped in the middle of the road, yanked his handbrake on and got out, leaving the driver's door open, the dashboard pinging to tell him his lights were still on. Birch noted that his was an Insignia, the model above her car, and newer. But before she could turn up her nose, Rab was on the pavement next to her, his hands outstretched towards her wrecked face.

'Oh Jesus Mary Mother of God,' he said. She saw his cheeks whiten, even under the streetlights. He was dressed, but still wearing his slippers. 'What in the name of Christ *happened* to ye?'

As they drove, Birch reeled off the edited version she'd been mentally rehearsing. It helped that Rab already knew about Fenton, about Thursday's assault in the close. She wasn't going to tell him – or anyone – that Charlie had shown up four nights earlier, but by the time they reached Leith Street, he knew Charlie had turned up, which was all that really mattered. He'd skipped out the night before the Operation Citrine raid and showed up at her place only hours ago. Where was he in the intervening days?

'I don't know,' Birch had said. 'Hiding out, I guess. Running.'

She talked at a fast clip, her edited version of the last few days' timeline falling out of her into the still air of the car. She was worried that if she kept quiet for any length of time, Big Rab would do what the paramedics had: tell her she needed to be going to A&E, not to work. He might offer to handle things for her, taking away the last chance she might have to see her brother, or hear him speak. She also didn't want him asking too many questions, knowing Charlie as he did, and perhaps still suspecting her of something. But when she finally fell quiet, Rab said nothing. She looked over at him, surprised, and saw he was chewing over her story, almost literally: his mouth was making silent words in the air.

'The night you got attacked,' he said eventually, 'doon the close.'

'Yes?'

'That wis Thursday night.'

'Yes.'

'And the guy asked where yer wee brother was.'

'He did.'

'And did ye *know*?'

Birch frowned. 'Sorry?'

'Did ye *know*, on Thursday night, where your brother was?'

No, Birch thought. By that time he'd left me again. 'No,' she said. 'Like I said, at that point I had no idea.'

It wasn't a lie, but still, being questioned on the timeline of the last week made her want to close her eyes, screw up her face. The reply felt like a sour taste in her mouth. Look normal, she told herself. You're going to have to do this again, a lot of times.

'He jist showed up?' Big Rab asked.

'Yeah.'

'Tonight?'

Birch nodded, as emphatically as she dared. 'Yeah.'

Rab made a sort of snort noise in his throat. 'Fuck me,' he said, a smile beginning to occur to his face, 'if that isnae some bloody magical timing.'

Birch waited a moment, then smiled too, though Rab wasn't looking at her. He'd either bought it, or decided to buy it – decided to let her off. The smile said, *Okay, I'm with you.* He was helping her. He'd been helping her all along.

That seemed to put an end to the conversation. She could see from the movement in his jaw that Rab was still chewing things over. Every so often he took an inward breath that was a little deeper, as though he might be about to say something. But the words never followed. She had, after all, made his own problem – the lost informant, and the hunch that never came good – disappear. Besides, her jaw rang with pain, and she'd talked enough as it was. She'd be fine with making the rest of the journey in silence.

But as they approached Comely Bank, Birch realised Rab had relaxed his face and broken into a broad smile. Apparently he'd done his thinking, and was satisfied with whatever conclusion he'd reached.

'Remember how I said I wis careful about who I bought drinks for?' Rab was steering with one hand, and wagging a finger at her with the other. 'In Kay's Bar, Monday night, ken how I said that?'

Birch raised an eyebrow. 'I do.'

Rab stabbed the finger of his pointing hand at her once more, as though drawing a full-stop in the air. 'I wis right,' he said.

Birch couldn't help it. She smiled, too.

As the car slowed to turn into the car park, she remembered what she'd said to Charlie: *I know a really, really good lawyer.* She fumbled her shattered phone unlocked and thumbed out a text to Anjan.

It might be a good idea, she wrote, *if you head along to Fettes Avenue, asap. Major new breakthrough re Solomon Carradice. Feel you ought to be in the loop. H x*

'Who're ye texting?' Big Rab had pulled into the staff car park, and now leaned over her, trying to read.

'A friend,' Birch said. 'But I was thinking I'd text DCI McLeod, too.'

Rab let out a hoot of laughter. '*Text* him? Jesus, lassie!'

Birch smiled. 'What, you think I ought not to?'

Rab opened the driver's door, and began rearranging himself in order to climb out.

'Jesus, no,' he said, trying to sound serious in spite of his obvious mirth. 'We'll phone him! *I'm* awake. No fucking reason he shouldn't be, too.'

Charlie had been put into the custody suite, in a cell at the opposite end to Fenton. They'd led Charlie in first, and advised him to keep quiet. Fenton had no idea he was there. When Birch walked in, with Big Rab beside her and DCI McLeod bringing up the rear, it was clear that Fenton thought they were there for him.

'Come to let me out, have ye?'

He pressed his face against the little gap in the cell door. Someone must have examined the wound on his head – there was a large, comically orange-coloured plaster on it – and he'd been allowed to wash his face. But Birch could smell the stale odour of him even with a steel door between them.

DCI McLeod stopped at Fenton's little window. Birch watched him rise to his full height and peer down at Fenton's boxed-in rodent face.

'Who,' McLeod said, in the voice he usually reserved for brand-new police constables who'd made a fuck-up, 'is *this*?'

Birch tried not to smile. McLeod was dressed in plain clothes, looking more dishevelled than she'd ever seen him, but he was still a *presence*. She imagined Fenton's knees shaking under him.

'Wan o' the lads involved in the attack, sir,' Rab said.

Birch was glad that Fenton couldn't see Rab's slippered feet.

McLeod looked down at Fenton as though he were something that had crawled up from a drain. 'A frenzied attack on a senior police officer?' he said.

Fenton smirked, rolled his eyes at Birch.

'I am ad*dress*ing you.'

McLeod's raised voice echoed off the concrete walls. Birch saw Fenton jump, hitting his forehead on the little sill that ran around the opening. No one spoke until the echoes had subsided. Inside the gloom of the cell, Fenton seemed to shrink.

'Come to let you out?' McLeod went on at last. 'I think not. Rather, I suggest you make yourself at home.'

He reached up and slammed the little window, blocking out Fenton's face as he opened his mouth to reply.

'Thanks, boss,' Birch said.

McLeod sniffed. 'You do look dreadful, Helen,' he said. 'We really must get you to the hospital, soon.'

Birch bit her tongue. Guess a 'you're welcome' was out of the question, then ...

They walked on down the suite, and stopped outside the furthermost cell, where the custody sergeant was already waiting, a fistful of various keys and fobs in his hand. McLeod nodded at Birch.

'Five minutes,' he said.

She felt her eyes widen.

'Yes,' McLeod said, 'I mean it. But literally: five.'

The custody sergeant swung the cell door open.

'Thanks, boss,' Birch said again, then she was inside, and the heavy steel door had swung closed at her back.

She felt tears, again, for about the thousandth time that week, come burning up the back of her throat, threatening to spill over. Charlie was curled up on a bench, hugging his knees. She'd been in the cells before of course, plenty of times, but they'd never seemed as grim as this one did, right now, with her baby brother inside it. It was cold. The smell of disinfectant made the air feel thick. Birch walked the two steps over to her brother, and he unfolded himself to make space for her to sit down.

'Well,' he said, stitching together a false, watery smile, 'it's not the Balmoral.'

'Sorry,' Birch said. She'd meant it to sound jokey, but it didn't.

Charlie shrugged. 'I had this girlfriend for a while,' he said, 'Hanna. She was Russian. Like, five foot tall, tiny feet, white-blonde hair. Really sweet girl. She was an amazing cook.'

Birch was able to smile at this, for real. She'd always imagined Charlie alone, the whole time he'd been gone, and this gave her a weird kind of cheer, to know he had been loved, for some of the time, by someone.

'She believed in all sorts of folklore and stuff,' Charlie was saying. 'She was into her old sayings and her superstitions and all that. Used to tell me children's stories she'd grown up with. Anyway, she had this thing she'd say: that there was really only one curse – or one spell – that could ever be put on you. And whether it was a curse or a spell depended on who you were and what you were like.'

Birch frowned. 'What was it?'

Charlie looked at her for a second. His eyes were just the same as they'd always been: the same freckles and quirks in all the same places.

'*May you get what you pay for,*' he said. 'Makes so much fucking sense, doesn't it?'

Both of them sat for a moment, in the weird silence those words left behind.

'What happened to Hanna?' Birch asked.

Charlie shrugged. 'Fucked up, didn't I? Like always.'

Birch saw him register her frown, the alarm in it.

'Oh,' he said, 'I didn't do anything to her, Nella, I just mean I let her down. I disappointed her. She left me. It was for the best.'

Birch nodded. 'I'm sorry.'

'It's okay,' Charlie replied. 'She was right, wasn't she? Got what I paid for. I always have, really. Stupid of me to think I could outrun it.'

Birch gave her head a small shake. She couldn't believe how sanguine he seemed now, how resigned.

'Charlie,' she said. 'You were so determined, on Wednesday night. You were so determined to run.'

He looked shamefaced. 'Yeah.'

'So . . . what made you come back?'

Charlie blinked at her. 'Oh jeez,' he said. 'Of course, you don't know! I've got to feeling like you know everything – that's the way I used to feel as a kid. I thought you could see what was in my head, and I could see what was in yours.'

Birch smiled. 'Felt that way sometimes, right?'

Charlie smiled back. Birch could see her mother in him, then.

'So yeah,' he said. 'After I left your place, I took a risk. I went to a phone box, and I called a guy I know. One of Solomon's guys. Turns out you've met him, in fact—'

'Wait . . . Mr Toad?'

'Yeah, that's the one. I know you'll think he's a scumbag, but he's been the closest thing to a da that I've ever had. I swear he's saved my life, more than once.' Charlie's voice faded.

'He tried to save Vyshnya's, too. He had this deference to Solomon, I think because he'd been in prison in Russia, years ago. Hierarchy is huge in that world. But he also has this weird moral code: to Toad, there are some lines you just don't cross. Turned out, Vyshnya was his second cousin. Solomon was the boss man, but even the boss man doesn't come before family.'

Charlie hung his head. 'It's a lesson I ought to have learned from him, I know. He had his priorities right, in the end.'

Birch smiled. 'A nice gangster.'

Charlie nudged her, though not hard. 'Whatever. Anyway, Toad came through to Edinburgh and met me, bought me a drink, and we talked. He told me about Vyshnya. So much stuff made sense: the guy Toad got rid of, the murder I witnessed the night I disappeared? He was Vyshnya's boyfriend. A really nasty piece of work. It turned out Toad put me in the sauna to keep an eye on her. He trusted me.'

Charlie's eyes had gone glassy. Birch didn't follow everything he was saying, but she could see the revelation was significant, and he was processing it slowly, turning it over in his mind.

'Then what?' she asked. McLeod's five minutes were ticking away.

'Oh,' Charlie said. 'He didn't stay long. Left me with some cash. Got me a cheap shite phone, too.'

Birch nodded. When she'd arrived, she and Rab had looked at the list of items the custody sergeant had confiscated from Charlie. It wasn't much: a wedge of cash, in twenties. A wristwatch. A mobile phone.

He was still talking. 'Anyway, last night he texted that phone. Said he felt like I'd been a son to him, and they were coming to storm your place at 2 a.m., and if I ever let anyone know he'd told me then he'd rip my throat out before anyone else had a chance.'

Birch laughed. 'Yeah, *what* a nice guy.'

Charlie dropped his gaze, but he was smiling, too. 'That's Toady for you,' he said.

Birch tried to recall the huge, tattooed man she'd attempted to interview alongside DS Scott. It had only been a week ago, but it felt like a lifetime. She couldn't square this tip-off to Charlie – this act of altruism on Toad's part – with that smug, gap-toothed perp, nor with the snarled phone call he'd made to her office on Friday afternoon.

'He didn't seem nice at all, when I tangled with him,' she said.

Charlie shrugged. 'He's complicated, I guess. We all are.'

Birch could think of no reply. She sat and looked down at her feet on the painted concrete floor, her brother's feet next to them. They'd had the same shoe size since Charlie was seventeen, and used to share Doc Martens, slippers, flip-flops. She'd forgotten all about that, until right now.

'I do have a confession to make,' Charlie said.

Birch snorted. 'Honey,' she said, 'you have a whole *load* of confessions to make.'

Her brother laughed then, properly. The sound bounced off the cell walls.

'No,' he said, still grinning, 'I mean . . . okay, so, they said I got a phone call.'

'To inform someone that you are in custody,' Birch said, 'yes. The custody sergeant mentioned that, when we came in. He said whoever you called, you didn't speak English.'

'Yeah,' Charlie said. 'I . . . *may* have called Toad, and let him know he might want to leave town.'

Again, she saw Charlie register her alarmed expression.

'Don't worry,' he said. 'Toad won't tell Solomon. I promise you. I know you don't believe me, but I *promise*. He's smart. I mean . . . actually, he's decidedly *not* smart, but that's kind of part of it. He was never in Solomon's thrall, not really. Not like the rest of us. He grew up in Russia. The guy's *seen* some shit. I don't think he was ever really all that frightened of Solomon. He'll just disappear, I absolutely promise you. And . . . I owed him. If he hadn't told me they were coming to your place last night, Fenton might have killed you before the polis arrived. We owe him one.'

Birch spluttered. *A tip-off for a tip-off.* She could see the logic, but . . .

'Charlie Birch, if you have blown this operation *again* . . .'

Charlie sat up straight, smacking one palm down over his heart. 'I swear. I absolutely swear. If I know Toad he'll be on a flight already. He might even be in Russia already. He won't have breathed a word to anyone. He'll know how to disappear. And I know you won't understand this, but he deserves a second chance. I figured that if I get one, so does he.'

Birch was quiet for a moment, but then began to nod. She had no choice but to trust him.

'You and your *Russian*,' she said, at last. 'To think, Mum was always so bloody proud of you for doing that degree.'

Charlie shrugged. He was grinning again. '*Mne zhal*,' he said.

'Yeah,' Birch replied, 'you bloody will be.'

Once again, she slung her uninjured arm around her brother's shoulders. This time, he wrapped both of his own arms around her, and pulled her into a hug.

On the other side of the door, McLeod knocked, and then the metal hatch clanged open.

'That's five minutes, Helen.'

Birch looked back, and nodded at her boss. Then she unhooked herself from his grasp, and let her brother go.

Anjan was sitting in her office. It was still before seven in the morning, yet he looked as well groomed and together as he ever did. His long, caramel-coloured coat was hung over the back of the chair: there were water droplets on it, and Birch realised it was raining outside. He didn't turn when she walked in: he was sitting in the chair facing her desk, his briefcase laid across his knees.

'Good morning,' he said, as she walked into his eyeline.

Birch flushed a little. It was like she always forgot quite how handsome he was, and only remembered when he turned his dark brown eyes on her.

'Thanks for coming.'

She settled into her own chair, placing her tablet on the desk in front of her, and made herself look across at him.

'Good grief,' Anjan said.

Birch remembered her bruised and swollen face, the arm strapped up across her chest.

'Helen . . . what happened? Are you all right? No – what a stupid question, you're obviously not all right. Have you—'

Birch held up her good hand to stop him.

'Anjan,' she said, 'I'm fine. I'm functioning. You'll find out soon enough what happened, but right now I don't really want to get into it. In fact, in just a minute I'm going to the hospital to be properly sorted out. But I wanted to do this first. To talk to you.'

Anjan looked unsettled, unsatisfied with her answer. But she watched as he made himself calm back down, and return to the matter at hand.

'So,' he said, 'what's the development, with my client's case?'

Birch took a deep breath. 'We are in receipt of new evidence,' she said, 'that we felt you ought to be aware of.'

Anjan blinked, but said nothing. He was waiting for her to show her hand.

'This morning,' she went on, 'I've been in touch with my colleagues over in Glasgow. We're in the process of obtaining a warrant to search Solomon's main residence, and a stretch of farmland about twelve miles away from his house.'

Anjan started in his seat. 'On what grounds?'

'On the grounds of our new evidence,' Birch said, 'which suggests that there is the body of a woman buried' – she passed her open tablet across the desk to him. On the screen was a Google map, with a pin at the place that Charlie had indicated – 'there, in a shallow grave, under those trees. We believe that when we exhume her remains, we will find clothing with DNA evidence linking her death to Solomon Carradice.'

Anjan looked down at the map for a moment. 'Where is this new evidence coming from?'

Birch set her teeth. He was going to try and argue with her. 'Our informant,' she said, 'on Operation Citrine.'

Anjan threw up one dismissive hand. 'That informant's evidence proved faulty at best over this past week,' he said. 'You were unable to charge my client based on that informant's testimony.'

Birch shook her head. 'No. We were unable to charge Solomon because we didn't have the informant's *full* testimony.'

Anjan cut in. 'And suddenly the informant talks about a body? This seems highly—'

'*The reason*,' Birch went on, 'we didn't have that testimony was because the informant was in the wind.'

It wasn't Anjan's style to interrupt, ordinarily. She'd got him worried.

'But he's now in our custody suite,' she added. 'And he's talking.'

Anjan's expression didn't change, but Birch saw him go pale. 'Who is he?'

She smiled. Good, this was working. 'Obviously,' she said, 'I can't divulge his identity at this stage. But I will tell you that he's been witness to key meetings that Solomon has taken in recent times. We believe he can provide evidence to show your client's involvement in criminal activity – both on these shores and over-seas – dating back over fourteen years. And now he's telling us about this woman's body. If we find it, we expect to see injuries and find a cause of death consistent with his testimony. We believe we can prove that' – Birch swallowed hard – 'that she was murdered, on Solomon's orders, just weeks ago.'

Anjan said nothing. His hands were now sitting on top of the briefcase in his lap, and after a moment his gaze flicked away from Birch's, and he looked down at those long, neat hands.

'This informant—'

Birch shook her head. 'I can't tell you any more about him,' she said. 'Except that I believe that he is a good person, in spite of his criminal actions. We believe his testimony is credible.'

Anjan was still looking down. 'And he's willing to bring this testimony to court?'

'He is,' Birch replied. Her heart swelled: she could say that, and it was true. 'Which means he is also looking for a decent lawyer.'

She looked hard at Anjan, until he tipped his head back up and met her gaze. Then she held it, watching his eyes.

'I'm going to have to back off this case,' Birch went on, 'in about five minutes, for reasons that will soon become clear to you. But right now as a friend . . .' She paused. 'Hell, as more than a friend, I hope . . . I'm asking you, Anjan. Do the right thing.'

He was quiet again, but the pause this time was shorter.

'I'll wait to hear more,' he said, 'but if there is anything to this, I'll make the call. To the firm. Let them know that I am no longer willing to represent Solomon Carradice.'

Birch smiled, wider than she had in over a week. 'Thank you,' she said.

'As for your informant,' he added, 'we shall see.'

Birch stood, and Anjan copied her. He reached behind him, and shook out the length of the camel-hair coat.

'I hope,' he said, 'that once this wretched business is straightened out, we can . . .' He trailed off.

Wow, she thought, have I just seen Anjan Chaudhry look bashful?

Birch was still smiling. 'It's going to be complicated,' she said. 'But yes, I hope so too.'

DI Crosbie wasn't a morning person, Charlie could tell. DI Robson didn't look all that chipper either, but Charlie had learned he always looked like that. Weather-beaten. Perhaps a little partial to the drink.

They'd brought in coffee; that had surprised him. Biscuits, too. He wasn't sure what he'd expected – water and gruel? He was just happy to be out of that cell, albeit in another too-bright room with plain walls. But coffee. And biscuits. And a seat with padding on it. Just don't think about the cell – that one, or any one in the future. It hasn't happened yet. Okay, it's happened, but . . . just don't think about it, Charlie.

DI Crosbie chucked a Dictaphone onto the table. Charlie marvelled at how small it was. Again, he'd expected something different. Cop dramas always showed those big, clunky reel-to-reel tape recorder things. Mind you, it'd been years since he'd watched one. Perhaps *Morse* was all high-tech now. If it was even on TV any more . . .

Focus, *Schenok*. Crosbie was saying the date, the time, his name, DI Robson's name.

'State your full name and date of birth for the record, please.'

'Charles Arthur Birch, 20 January 1982.'

'Thank you,' Crosbie said. He didn't sound the least bit grateful. He threw a look at DI Robson that said, *Right, I've done my bit, it's your go.*

DI Robson folded his arms and put them on the table, then leaned forward. The table creaked.

'Charlie,' he said. 'Ye prefer tae be Charlie, right?'

'Yeah. Well, I mean – I'm only ever Charles when I'm in trouble. But I guess I'm in some trouble now, so . . .'

Crosbie rolled his eyes, but DI Robson laughed. A pity laugh, maybe, but he laughed.

'We'll see, son,' he said.

Charlie took a sip of the coffee. It wasn't great, but it would do. He was fucking knackered. His hands hurt, from where he'd punched Jones. His eyes stung from crying. He very much hoped that Nella was in the hospital now – she'd promised him she'd go, right after she'd talked to the lawyer. She looked like shit, though he'd tried not to say that. She needed fixing up.

'This might be a long auld slog, Charlie,' Robson was saying. 'Are ye ready fer that?'

'Ready as I'll ever be.'

Robson nodded. 'Okay,' he said. 'We've a lot to get through, son, so . . . I tell ye what. Why don't ye tell us what ye remember. Everything, right from the start.'

Charlie raised an eyebrow. 'The *very* start?'

Robson unfolded his arms and sat back in the chair, getting comfy. 'Aye, sure,' he said. 'Why not? Tell us what ye remember, Charlie.'

Charlie Birch knocked back his coffee, and pushed the cup to one side. What *did* he remember? First, before anything else? *Ah yes. That.*

He opened his mouth, and began to speak.

Acknowledgements

I have been lucky enough to work with a team of absolute power-house women over the past year, and I am incredibly grateful for all their help and support. Cathryn Summerhayes is the best agent a girl could ask for, and Ruth Tross is the best editor. Thank you to Louise Swannell for helping me to reach readers in so many places, and thank you to Hannah Bond, Myrto Kalavrezou, Irene Magrelli, Lydia Seleska and Morag Lyall for supporting all of this and more.

Thank you to Lewis Csizmazia for the truly stunning hardback cover design: Edinburgh looks gorgeous in it.

I'm forever grateful to Scottish Book Trust for all the opportunities and encouragement they provide, and to my colleagues at the University of Edinburgh and Edinburgh International Book Festival for their support. The first third of this book was written during a residency at the Curfew Tower in Cushendall, Northern Ireland: thank you to Neu! Reekie! for making it happen, and special thanks to Zippy Kearney, keeper of the Tower keys.

Huge thanks to Bella Hramova for assistance with the Russian words and idioms. Thank you to all those folks on Twitter who've answered my weird and wonderful research queries over the past year, and especially to Jenni Fagan for the word 'rooked'! Any errors are, of course, mine.

To all the friends I've stood up or flaked out on over the past year: thank you for your endless patience and encouragement. Alice Tarbuck, Stella Birrell, Leon Crosby, Sasha de Buyl, Jane Bradley, Kerry Ryan, Natalie Fergie, Colin McGuire, Dean Rhetoric. I love you all. Special mentions for Julie Danskin, who is not only a great friend but the greatest bookseller in the known world; and to Debz Butler, the strongest woman I know.

Love and gratitude to Team Askew, who always have my back no matter how harebrained my schemes. And to Dom – maker of tea, deliverer of pep talks – I love you. Thank you.